Praise for Lesley Kelly

'Written with brio, *A Fine House in Trinity* is fast, edgy and funny, a sure-fire hit with the tartan noir set. A standout debut, if there is justice in the world this book will find its audience.' **Michael J. Malone**

'Kelly's tartan noir debut… [has] a hero well worthy of the starring role.' *Kirkus Reviews*

'The storyline is strong, the characters believable and the tempo fast-moving.' *Scots Magazine*

'This is a romp of a novel which is both entertaining and amusing. The violent/funny combination brings to mind Keith Nixon's Konstanin series and is reminiscent of Alison Taft and Dougie Brimson. It's certainly the funniest crime novel I've read since Fidelis Morgan's *The Murder Quadrille* and a first class debut.' *Crime Fiction Lover*

'Joseph Staines is one of the most realistic lead characters I have encountered for ages. He is flawed, cowardly in the face of danger and generally not as well liked as he may like to believe. He is also strangely endearing, frequently amusing and has a really well developed back story which makes *A Fine House in Trinity* a really fun read.' *Grab This Book*

'This is the author's debut novel and it is one heck of a book. The ending leaves the way open for a series and I sincerely hope that this will be the case, as I can't wait to see what Joseph Staines gets up to next.'

Best Crime Books and More

'If you want a twist on the crime novel with a large helping of Scottish humour, this is the book for you. A very entertaining fast-paced debut novel. I'm looking forward to reading more by Lesley Kelly and rather hope that Stainsey might feature again!'

Portobello Book Blog

'Razor sharp Scottish wit is suffused throughout and this makes *A Fine House in Trinity* a very sweet shot of noir crime fiction. This cleverly constructed romp around Leith will have readers grinning from ear to ear and some of the turns of phrase deserve a standing ovation in themselves.'

The Reading Corner

'A welcome addition to the Tartan Noir scene, providing as it does a more light-hearted approach to solving a crime. Lesley Kelly is a fine writer, entertaining us throughout. The near-300 pages are deceptive, as this is a book perfect for romping through in one sitting.'

Crime Worm

'A compelling mystery brimming over with sharp wit, keen observation and peppered throughout with fascinating titbits of Leith history.'

Lothian Life

Lesley Kelly has worked in the public and voluntary sectors for the past twenty years, dabbling in poetry and stand-up comedy along the way. She has won a number of writing competitions, including the Scotsman's Short Story award in 2008. Her first novel, *A Fine House in Trinity* was long-listed for the McIlvanney Prize.

By the same author

A Fine House in Trinity

THE HEALTH
OF
STRANGERS

LESLEY KELLY

SANDSTONEPRESS
HIGHLAND | SCOTLAND

First published in Great Britain by
Sandstone Press Ltd
Dochcarty Road
Dingwall
Ross-shire
IV15 9UG
Scotland

www.sandstonepress.com

The publisher acknowledges subsidy from
Creative Scotland towards publication of this volume.

ISBN: 978-1-910985-66-3
ISBNe: 978-1-910985-67-0

Cover design by Blacksheep, London
Typeset by Iolaire Typography Ltd, Newtonmore
Printed and bound by Totem, Poland

To Phemie, Jimmy and Keith

CONTENTS

MONDAY

SHALLOW BREATHING

I

'He's dead all right.'

Mona stepped back, and ran her eye over the corpse. She'd seen worse than this, much worse in fact, but not in the last few months. Funny how quickly you forgot the sights and smells of death. Maybe you had to forget, maybe the amnesia was some kind of defensive mechanism; if you remembered what it was like you'd spend every night downing a bottle of wine while surfing jobs websites for less traumatising employment. She glanced over her shoulder to where her partner, Bernard, was standing, and quickly stifled a laugh at the expression on his face. From past experience she recognised the signs that he was channelling all his energy into keeping his breakfast safely lodged in its rightful place. He ran his hands over his short hair a couple of times, tugged at the collar of his polo shirt, and, despite his distress, managed to choke out a few words.

'The Virus?'

'Hard to say, with him being so decomposed.' She took a further step away from the armchair. 'I mean, when the skin's turned black like this, and the teeth and hair have started to fall out there's not much to go on. And look at this – there's some kind of larvae on his cheek here.' She waved him closer. 'Come and see.'

He bolted out the door, and Mona gave in to a grin.

You either had the nerve for these kinds of things, or you didn't. That being said, the smell of the room wasn't doing her stomach any good either. She gave a quick look over to the door to check Bernard wasn't about to reappear, then negotiated her way between the heavy wooden furniture toward the window, stopping only to pull a handkerchief out of her pocket and clamp it over her nose.

The curtains were a seventies relic, a lurid orange-and-brown mess of swirls and curlicues. She pulled at them one-handed, and after a couple of tugs they opened, filling the room with weak April sunshine. Yellowed netting covered the length of the pane; she reached behind it and found the catch. She fiddled with it for a minute, succeeding only in cutting herself on the rusting paintwork. She cursed and pulled her hand back. The rust had dyed her fingertips brown, and a small cut was sending a river of red down her index finger. Wiping her hand on her jeans, she made a mental note to dig out the Savlon when she got back to the office. There were enough ways to die at the moment, without succumbing to good old-fashioned tetanus. She gave the catch another try, and to her relief, it opened. She hauled the window up a couple of inches and crouched on the floor next to the fresh air.

Mona pulled her notes out of her bag and gave herself a quick refresher on the facts. Their visit had been triggered by the non-appearance of one Reginald Dwyer at his monthly Virus Prevention Health Check. According to her notes Reginald was in his seventies, Caucasian, 5'6" tall, with grey hair and blue eyes. She poked her head and handkerchief back round the curtain and eyed up the corpse. The nylon trousers and woolly cardigan

4

combination suggested a senior citizen's wardrobe, but the other facts were lost to the indignities of decomposition.

Now it was a judgement call – phone the Health Enforcement Team first or the Police? Alerting the Police to a potentially suspicious death made it their problem. Phoning it in to the office as a Health Check Violation Due to Fatality left it resting firmly in her in tray, with a tonne of attached paperwork. She walked back into the middle of the room, and looked round in search of anything that could justify her phoning her former colleagues in Police Scotland.

A little wooden side table next to the corpse had a newspaper resting on it, open at the TV listings. She picked it up, trying her hardest not to disturb the deceased. The last thing she wanted was a shower of teeth, hair, or worse, falling off the late Mr Dwyer. The date on the paper was the 21st February, just over a month ago. Probably the length of time he'd been lying here, which fitted in well with her gut feeling about how long he'd been dead.

'Bernard?' She removed the hanky from her face.

'Yes?' Her partner's voiced echoed feebly down the hall.

'Can you check with the neighbours when they last saw him? Or when they first noticed the smell?' She put her makeshift face mask back on.

'I tried. No-one's in, apart from a woman in the ground floor flat who doesn't speak English.'

No surprise there. Getting the average Edinburgh tenement dweller to answer their doors to a stranger had always been a struggle, but these days a warm welcome would have been some kind of miracle. She didn't blame people for their caution. After you'd spent a fortune germ-proofing your home, why take the risk of opening

5

up to find someone coughing and spluttering on your doorstep?

Bernard's face appeared in the doorway, wan as a waxing moon. 'I peered through the letterbox of the flat across the hall and I don't think it's occupied.' He paused and grimaced. 'Can we get out of here now?'

'Just a sec.'

There were two doors leading off the living room. She threw open the nearest one, which revealed a bedroom, the divan resplendent with an orange candlewick cover. She took a couple of strides and pushed open what she assumed was the door to the kitchen.

'Bernard – look at this.'

He appeared at her side, and gaped, as she had done, at the tinned goods that were stacked from floor to ceiling all across the room.

'He didn't pay much attention to our advice about not hoarding food, did he?' Bernard took a step back. 'Ironic really, given how he ended up.'

Mona smiled. 'Poor sod.'

'Can we go?'

She took a last look around the room, and sighed. 'Yup. Just let me phone it in.' She dug out her mobile and selected the North Edinburgh HET office from her contacts list as she walked toward the stairwell. 'Maitland, it's me, Mona.' She pulled the door of Reginald Dwyer (deceased) firmly closed. 'We've got a stiff.'

'So – did you puke?'

Bernard ignored the question and walked purposefully in the direction of his desk. Undeterred, Maitland rolled his chair across the office and ground to a halt an inch from his side, trapping Bernard's little toe under a castor. Bernard pulled his trainer loose, booted Maitland back toward his desk, and was gratified to hear a tiny squeak of pain from him as he collided with a sharp edge. Unfortunately, the injury was not enough to silence him.

'But did you?' Maitland was beaming from ear to ear, every inch of his six foot three frame bouncing up and down with pleasure at Bernard's discomfort. He sat back, knitted his fingers together, and rested them on his dark hair. 'C'mon, Bern, did you spew when you found the body?'

'No, Maitland, I did not spew, as you put it.' Bernard reached the safety of his own workspace, and lowered himself into his seat. OK, so he had left Mona to deal with it and stood outside trying to overcome his nausea. But he wasn't going to give his colleague the satisfaction of admitting it. 'I've seen dead bodies before, as you are well aware.'

'Aye,' Maitland grinned and dived toward Bernard's desk, 'but those were in a medical setting, where everything is nice and clean and neat.' He rested his elbows on the back of Bernard's chair, and lowered his voice. 'This time, we're not talking hospital corners and disinfectant. We're talking weeks-old corpse, maggots, bluebottles burying their eggs in the decaying flesh ...'

Bernard's stomach heaved, and he leaned on his desk with his hand over his mouth. After a moment, he pushed Maitland's arm off the back of his chair, and his tormentor turned away, laughing.

'Mona, so did he puke or what?'

She dismissed Maitland's question with a wave of her hand. Her hair hid her face and Bernard wondered if she too was mocking him under the blonde bob. It was impossible to tell. He thought about going over to see if

7

she *was* actually laughing, but worried he would seem overanxious. Mona had made it plain over the past few months that she did not like needy men.

Maitland wandered back to his side of the office, still chuckling.

Bernard sighed, and started looking for the piece of paper that would let him know just how bad the rest of his day was going to be.

It wasn't in his tray, or on top of the neat pile of previous cases he'd left sitting prominently in the centre of the desk, in the hope that someone would file them. It wasn't caught up in his personal papers, and, when he picked up his copy of the *Guardian* and shook it, it didn't fall out from within its pages.

Bernard leaned back in his chair, sighing again. There was definitely no Defaulter List on his desk. 'Mona – have you got our DL?'

Across the room his partner was still engrossed in paperwork. She looked up, shook her head, and shrugged.

In the four months he'd been working for the Health Enforcement Team this had never happened before. As surely as night followed day, by 9am every morning a memo appeared on each of their desks outlining who had defaulted on their Health Checks that week. The idea was that this notification arrived the day after someone had defaulted. The demise of Reg Dwyer was testament to how well this system worked. Bernard looked round the office for someone else to ask. Maitland's desk was now empty, although his coat was thrown over the back of his chair.

He looked over at Carole Brooks's desk. In amongst the pictures of her kids, and a range of handmade and, probably, fair trade clutter, Carole was on her mobile. Bernard overheard snippets of her conversation.

'So, how much is his temperature up by?'

Bernard winced, and feeling suddenly breathless, sat down at his desk. This was what grief felt like, the poleaxing power of a stray comment, or a TV show, or, like this, an overheard conversation to knock him sideways. Six months now since his son had died, too young and weak to fight off the Virus. And when the memory hit him, it wasn't just of the boy's death; it was of the paralysis, the helplessness, the overwhelming impotency he had felt in the face of the illness. He'd not told his colleagues about his loss; how to describe it to these people he barely knew?

Carole ended the conversation but sat staring at her desk. She pulled out the band that was holding her hair up, and let it fall loose. She ran her hands through it, then after a second she gathered up the strands and tucked them away.

He decided not to bother her and reluctantly looked in the direction of his boss's office. Once upon a time, the building that the HET occupied had been a grand Georgian house on the Southside of Edinburgh. It had remained intact until the owner had racked up gambling debts so astronomical that the only method of staving off creditors was the sale of the family home to the newly formed South Eastern Regional Hospital Board. Lothian Health Board had taken the premises over in 1972, and had knocked through rooms, boarded up chimneys, and bricked up doors with a cheerful disregard for the intricacy of the cornicing, or the delicate tiling on the Adam fireplaces. In a final mortification, when the HET moved in, a corner of the room had been partitioned off with MDF to create an internal office for the head of the team. Bernard knew that deep within this temporary structure

9

sat Team Leader Paterson, drinking tea, regretting the day he left the Police, and thinking of new ways to make Bernard's life miserable.

Bernard caught Paterson's eye through the office's window, and within seconds his boss threw open the door. He stood in the doorway, his greying crew cut scraping the top of the door frame. Paterson was a very big man, in a very small office.

He pointed a large finger at Mona, then Bernard. 'You two – in here now.'

They exchanged glances and got to their feet.

'You were right, Guv, the No Show was dead. Looked like he'd been lying there for weeks. Seems that he'd ...'

Mona broke off as she walked into Paterson's office. Bernard peered round her side and saw there was someone else in the room. This was interesting; Paterson was not in the habit of entertaining visitors. A stranger in the boss's office, hot on the heels of the missing Defaulter List, meant that today was veering off the fairly repetitive course that Bernard had experienced since his arrival at the HET.

The man was tall, with neat blonde hair and square, brown-rimmed glasses. A raincoat was folded across his knees, and at his side was a brown leather briefcase. He radiated an air of controlled competency not often found nestling in the chaos of the HET office. The new arrival had been given the only comfortable seat in the office and was sitting behind Paterson's desk.

The Team Leader leaned his considerable bulk against his desk, and gestured a thumb in the stranger's direction.

'This is Doctor Toller.'

The three of them shook hands, which involved a fair bit of manoeuvring, given the limited dimensions of the office. Mona sat on the plastic chair that Paterson had swiped from the canteen some months ago. Bernard looked round for somewhere to sit, and in the absence of options, stayed standing.

'Toller here works for the German Government and is investigating a Missing Person. Heidi Weber, eighteen years old, exchange student at Edinburgh University. Showing up on our Defaulter List for the first time today.' He passed a case file across the desk which Mona grabbed and started reading. 'I want you to give Doctor Toller every assistance in locating this young lady.' Paterson pointed his finger at each of them to emphasise the point. 'Every assistance.'

Mona spoke without looking up from the file. 'Can I ask why she is of interest to you, Sir?'

The Doctor smiled. 'She is not, of herself, of particular interest.' His English was good, but tinged with a German accent. 'We are concerned about the Health Status of all our nationals who are living abroad. As you know our infected population is much lower than yours, which is twenty-eight per cent, I believe?'

'Twenty-eight per cent average, lower for older people and children, higher for young adults.'

Paterson coughed. Bernard ignored the hint and carried on.

'But the infection rate is falling year-on-year. We're anticipating an eight per cent infection rate next year.'

A thin blonde eyebrow was raised by the German. 'Yet you still have mortality of 2.5 per cent?'

'2.4 per cent, to be precise.'

'Bernard ...' Paterson had a familiar tone of warning in his voice. He wasn't a big fan of Bernard's ability to remember facts and figures relating to the Virus. Bernard was torn between avoiding his boss's wrath and defending

11

his country's public health record. Patriotism won.

'And twenty per cent of the population is already immune.' He finished the sentence as quickly as he could.

'In Germany we have mortality of less than two per cent.' The Doctor smiled and folded his arms. 'You can see why we are concerned about any health risk that our citizens may be encountering.'

Before Bernard could open his mouth to pursue the point, Mona spoke up. 'She hasn't been reported missing by her parents.' She waved the case file in the air. 'Although they have expressed concern that they hadn't heard from her?'

Paterson jumped to his feet. 'Doctor, I think my colleagues have enough to go on. I need to brief them about a couple of things, then the three of you can make a start on locating young Heidi.' He yanked opened the door, causing the walls of the office to vibrate.

The Doctor stayed seated for a moment staring at Paterson, then slowly stood up. 'I wish to use the lavatory before we leave. I will meet you in the main entrance.' He stopped and turned to address Mona and Bernard. 'I am not overly concerned about this young woman. We made a check of her room, and all her documents were there, including her passport.'

Paterson smiled expansively at his guest and extended an arm in the direction of the exit. He waited until the door shut behind the German. 'Dickhead,' he said, making only a slight attempt to lower his voice.

Bernard wondered about the sound insulation properties of MDF, but Doctor Toller didn't look back.

'So, what was all that about, Guv?' Mona had joined the HET from Edinburgh CID, and had brought both Police jargon and respect for hierarchy with her. 'Something

12

about this isn't right. Her parents are concerned about her but haven't reported her missing? She's not been seen for the best part of a week. The Police should be dealing with this as a Missing Person.'

There was strict protocol on this point: the Police dealt, or chose not to deal, with people who had been reported missing. The HET dealt only with people who had not turned up for their Health Check, but were not listed as missing persons. In Mona's experience, there was usually a reason that nobody had missed a Health Defaulter.

Paterson cut through her protests. 'Ignore all the bollocks about health concerns. Heidi's the daughter of a member of the – crap, what did he call it? The Brundiesdag?'

'Bundestag?' suggested Bernard.

'What?' Paterson squeezed past Bernard to get to the kettle, managing to hit him on the head with his mug on the way past.

Bernard rubbed his temple. 'The German Parliament?'

'Yeah, that's the thing. He's like an MP, only German. So his lassie, well, she's probably shacked up with some boyfriend or other, but it's a major embarrassment for Herr Weber if his daughter's found to have skipped a Health Status test, especially after the German Chancellor made a big deal about the UK having such high infection rates.'

'And she *has* missed a Health Check?' asked Mona.

'Yup.' Paterson smiled. 'Missed her Health Check on Friday, and a week later it lands on our desk. And if you are about to ask me why it took a week to get here, don't, because I don't know the answer.'

'Can we talk to Herr Weber?' asked Bernard.

13

'Yes. Herr Weber and his wife are staying at The George Hotel and Toller's waiting to take you there. They've already passed Heidi's laptop on to us, so check with IT what they've found on it.'

'Anything else, Guv?' Mona was already on her feet.

'Yeah – pull your fingers out and get this lassie found. One morning of Doctor Tosser has been more than enough for me.'

He followed Mona back to their desks. She was reading the files as she walked.

'Do you suppose Doctor Toller's driving, or do you think he's expecting us to provide transport?' His colleague shrugged on her waterproof and reached for her bag. 'Should we sign out a pool car?'

'Hmm.' Lending half an ear to her, Bernard logged into his computer.

'Bernard! Are you listening?'

'Yep. Pool car. Good idea. Just give me two minutes.' Ignoring the look of impatience on Mona's face, Bernard called up a search engine. He typed 'German Chancellor' into Google. The computer failed to react.

'Hurry up, Bernard!'

'Hold on,' he jabbed the Enter key several times, 'it's not my fault we're still on Windows 7. Would it have killed them to splash out on an upgrade?'

He hit Enter a couple more times, and, finally, he was reading the German Chancellor's much-publicised attack on the Scottish response to the Virus.

'Mona – listen to this. "The lax response by the Scottish Government to the Virus has put the whole of the European Union at risk. The reliance on a monthly health check-up, compared to weekly or fortnightly across most of Europe, has led to high levels of infection. Inadequate

14

policing of Health Defaulters means a hardcore of resisters with no known Health Status which endangers the wider population . . ."'

Mona snorted. 'Bullshit. We'd never get away with the kind of regime they've got on the Continent. Remember all the outcry when the idea of Health Checks was first suggested?'

'Yup.' Bernard had watched the demos on TV, fascinated by the mixture of protest banners – Amnesty and Socialist Worker, of course, but all the new groups as well. Teenagers Against Health Checks had been all over the news, partly because of the photogenic nature of the girls involved. 'But you can see why Toller's worried. I mean, what's his boss going to say when they find out his daughter's a "hardcore resister"?'

Mona grinned. 'Let's find the Doctor and ask him.'

As she turned to leave, she almost crashed into Carole Brooks, and dropped her car keys.

'Sorry.'

Their colleague didn't move.

'Are you OK?' Bernard thought back to the conversation he'd overheard earlier.

'They're sending my son home from school. His temperature's up.'

'What to?'

'38 degrees.' She stared at Bernard.

'Kids get temperatures all the time. It's probably nothing.'

'He's coughing a lot.'

'Could just be a cold. Kids still get colds, even in this day and age.'

'Mm.' She didn't sound convinced. 'Can you make sure Maitland lets Mr Paterson know I've gone?'

15

Bernard patted Carole's arm. 'Yeah, don't worry about that. We'll see he gets the message.'

They watched her disappear through the office door.

'I take it her boy isn't immune then?' Mona asked. 'I just assumed her whole family would all have had it.'

'Nah, I heard she got the Virus on a hen week with her sister. Ended up quarantined in Ayia Napa.'

'Oh dear. How old is her lad?'

'Fifteen or sixteen.' Bernard thought for a moment. 'I'm not sure exactly.'

Mona stooped to pick up her keys. 'Still, at least you reassured her.'

Something in her tone betrayed a certain insincerity.

'Well, I tried.' His tone was defensive, but he could guess what Mona was thinking. He'd done his best, but Carole was an ex-nurse, and Bernard knew he hadn't had any reassurance to give.

Mona elbowed him and pointed in the direction of the door. 'C'mon. We've got somewhere to be.'

The three of them had been in the car for fourteen minutes, according to Bernard's watch, and no-one had yet spoken.

He stared through the windscreen, willing the traffic on the Mound to move faster. The number 23 bus in front of them indicated that it was pulling into the bus stop opposite the National Galleries. A couple of schoolgirls wearing brightly coloured mouth masks dived across the road in front of them, bumping the bonnet in a doomed attempt to catch the bus. Mona cursed under her breath, and the car ground to a halt. Bernard couldn't stand it any longer and turned round to Doctor Toller with the intention of making small talk. This wasn't made any easier by the soundproofed Perspex window separating them. Bernard's finger hovered over the intercom, but, as on the previous two or three times he had considered speaking, the Doctor was staring out of the window in a manner that suggested he was not open to pleasantries. Bernard resigned himself to the atmosphere.

The bus moved and the car inched forward again, only to stop when the traffic lights turned red. His mind wandered. He wondered what his wife was doing; she'd still been in bed when he left the house that morning. Not, he suspected, actually asleep, but hermetically sealed within her duvet and ignoring all conversational attempts. People, it seemed to Bernard, went to great lengths to avoid speaking to him. There was a hammering on the Perspex, causing him to jump. He turned to see Toller pointing out of the window. He reached forward and pressed the communication button. 'Your public health information is out of date,' said the German.

'Sorry – what?'

Toller extended a long, elegant finger in the direction of a laminated sign attached to a lamp post. 'Remember to cover your mouth when you cough. Throw away your tissues immediately. Wash your hands frequently . . .'

'Oh, that.' Bernard laughed. 'Those were all supposed to have been removed ages ago. A legacy of our Duck-and-Cover days.'

The German stared at him, puzzled. 'Duck-and-Cover?'

'You know – once upon a time we thought we could deal with a nuclear attack by hiding under the table.' Bernard did a little mime, sheltering under his hands. He pointed at the poster. 'This was about as effective in stopping the Virus spreading.'

17

Toller's thin lips pulled into a smile. 'I see. Very droll.'

Bernard smiled. He started to turn back in his seat when the doctor spoke again.

'You are not very popular, I think.'

'Me?' Bernard's tone betrayed his slight feeling of panic. What had Toller heard? Had Paterson said something about him?

The German gave his narrow smile again. 'You misunderstand me. I mean the HET is not very popular.'

'I'm not sure I would say that...'

Mona snorted, and Bernard gave up attempting to defend his organisation's reputation.

'I have noticed that many of your public health billboards have been defaced,' Toller stared at him, 'likening your Health Enforcement Team to, of all things...'

Bernard closed his eyes, aware what was coming.

'Nazis.'

The lights changed, and Bernard swivelled gratefully back toward the front. Mona drove up Hanover Street, turned right round the statue of George IV, and into the street that bore his name. She bumped the car up on the pavement outside The George Hotel, ignoring the double yellow lines.

Bernard looked at her in horror. 'You're not going to leave it parked here?'

'Why not?' She slid the gears into neutral and opened her door. She tapped the HET sticker on her windscreen. 'It's not like they are going to fine us. We are the Police after all.'

'Except we're not. We're the Health Enforcement Team,' said Bernard, to Mona's back.

'Whatever.' She rapped on the internal window. 'Can you show us to the Webers' room, Doctor Toller?'

18

'Yes, of course.' He slid out of the car and walked briskly in the direction of the hotel, leaving Bernard to worry about the parking arrangements.

Herr Weber was in his fifties, thin, and wearing what Bernard thought looked like a very expensive suit. He shook each of their hands in turn.

'It is very good of you to come and see us.' Unlike Toller, his English bore almost no trace of a German accent, but had a slight American twang. 'Please, sit.'

The Webers were staying in one of The George's finer suites, with a separate lounge and bedroom. The room was tastefully decorated with muted shades of green, its gleaming oak furniture a testament to intensive levels of housekeeping. It was quite unlike any of the hotel rooms Bernard had ever stayed in, most of which had been located near motorway intersections. In one corner of the living area there was a meeting space already set up for them. They settled themselves at the table, while Toller lolled in one of the armchairs, hiding himself behind the room's complimentary copy of *The Telegraph*. Bernard read the headlines. *Industry Chiefs Call for an End to Virus Restrictions*. It was a familiar theme. Almost as soon as the Virus infection rates had started to fall, business leaders had begun agitating for relaxations on Green Cards, group meeting restrictions and Health Checks. It wasn't an easy time to be running a business, unless you were an online provider of home entertainment. He leaned forward a little to read Professor Bircham-Fowler's case for the defence. *The evidence indicates that regular Health Checks reduce the infectivity potential of Virus-infected individuals by half* ... Perhaps the HET was useful, after all.

'Can I get you a coffee, or perhaps a cup of tea?' Herr Weber hovered anxiously by the kettle. With polite murmurs they declined the offer.

'Shall we make a start, Sir?' asked Mona.

'One moment, please.' Herr Weber walked to the bedroom door and knocked gently on it. 'My wife will be joining us.' He lowered his voice. 'She is extremely upset.'

'Understandably, Sir,' said Mona.

Frau Weber was around the same age as her husband, but considerably larger. She had obviously made recent efforts to put on make-up, which, unfortunately, was not responding well to her distress. Mascara was cascading down her cheeks, like two black railway sleepers.

Herr Weber took her by the hand. 'My wife does not speak much English, I'm afraid, but she was very keen to meet with you.'

Bernard and Mona smiled at her. She gave them a little wave, then returned to dabbing at her eyes with a handkerchief.

Bernard opened his mouth to speak, but before he could say anything Frau Weber began to talk.

'She says that her daughter has never done this before.' The Doctor put down his newspaper, and translated from his armchair. 'She says Heidi always rings her on a Sunday evening, every week without fail. She says she tried to call her but the phone went straight to voicemail.'

Mona smiled sympathetically in Frau Weber's direction, then asked Toller, 'Have we found her mobile?'

'No,' Herr Weber responded to Mona's question. 'We searched her room and found her passport and her diary, but no phone. I assume you will want to look for yourself?'

'Yes. So, to clarify, she didn't phone on Sunday, and

20

then missed her Health Check on Monday. Does her diary give any idea of her movements?'

'Yes and no,' Herr Weber replied. 'We're having it translated for you at the moment. She seemed to frequent a couple of pubs in Edinburgh – Morley's and the Railway Tavern. Her last entry mentions plans to meet friends at Morley's. Are you familiar with these establishments?'

Mona nodded. 'I'm certainly familiar with Morley's. Useful leads, Sir.' She turned to Doctor Toller. 'Could you please tell Frau Weber that it is very unlikely that anything has happened to her daughter, and that she will probably turn up unharmed?'

Herr Weber answered. 'I hope for all our sakes that you are right.'

'Mona.'

Paterson appeared out of his office the second they walked into the room, red-faced and purposeful, like an overheated shark. He strode toward them, and Mona noticed Bernard take a half-step behind her.

'You're a woman.'

'Very nearly,' piped up Maitland, cheerfully.

They all turned and glared at him. He smirked and ducked down behind his computer.

'Shut up, Maitland.' Paterson returned to his theme. 'You are a woman, and good at all that touchy-feely crap.'

Mona stared at her boss, and wondered if in the past six months he had learned anything about her at all. 'I wouldn't really say those were my particular strengths, Guv. Perhaps Bernard would be a better choice for whatever you've got in mind?'

'He *is* practically a woman.' Maitland's voice came from behind his PC.

'Shut up, Maitland,' said Bernard, and blushed.

Paterson ignored the interruptions. 'Carole Brooks phoned to say she's at the hospital with her kid.'

'Poor Carole.'

'Is her son all right?' asked Bernard.

'We don't know.' Paterson turned to Mona. 'I need you to get up there and check she's OK.'

She looked at her boss in surprise. 'That's very thoughtful of you.'

'Yeah, and while you're there find out how long she's going to be off. If it's going to be more than a couple of days we're in trouble.' He turned on his heel. 'But be tactful. I don't want another of those harassment-bullying tribunal thingies.'

Mona decided not to wonder about the Guv's past HR record. She picked up her bag. 'OK, Guv. What's the rush to get Carole back, though? We can cover for a few days at least.'

He handed her a sheet of paper. 'Here's why. Our glorious leader has woken up to the fact that people have either not heard of the HET, or if they have heard of us they consider us a bunch of health fascists...'

'Which isn't exactly fair, Guv,' said Maitland. 'There is an epidemic going on.'

'You don't have to convince me. Everyone's 100 per cent in favour of us enforcing the Health Checks, right up until the minute they forget to tell us they are going on holiday, and come back to a full-scale HET investigation. Then it's all articles in the *Daily Mail* about our heavy-handed response, blah, blah, blah.'

'Basically, people want us to enforce Health Checks for everyone except them,' said Mona.

'Exactly! Anyway, in an attempt to win hearts and

22

minds, the Powers That Be now want us to ...' he gestured at the memo Mona was holding.

She looked down. 'Tour local high schools promoting the work of the HET? You've got to be kidding.'

'Yes, it appears that the million pounds Health Communications has spent on adverts in the middle of *Coronation Street* still hasn't raised our profile sufficiently for people to see us as the fluffy bunnies we really are, so now someone has to go and speak to school assemblies across Edinburgh.'

Maitland's head appeared above his computer. 'Carole is definitely your man on that one, Guv.'

The car park at the Edinburgh Royal Infirmary was full. Mona circled round half a dozen times before spying a woman walking toward a Ford Focus. She tailed her at a discreet distance, then sat drumming her fingers on the steering wheel while the woman hunted for her keys, got in, and slowly reversed out. Mona gave a polite wave to the disappearing tail lights, and swung sharply into the vacated space, narrowly missing the wing mirror of the neighbouring car.

The ERI loomed in the distance, a low modern building with rounded turrets at each end. Its white squatness always reminded Mona of the bottom tier of a wedding cake. She reached into her pocket for her Green Card as she approached the security gate between the car park and the hospital grounds. A man coming in the other direction held the gate open and winked at her as she passed through. She smiled politely and wondered exactly how many plaques outlining the dangers of letting people through the barriers the NHS would have to pin up before people actually took notice.

She walked at a smart pace into the foyer, ignored the queue of non-immune visitors waiting to plead their case with the Admissions Officer, and pressed her Green Card against the security turnstile. The light turned from Stop to Go, and she entered, nearly bumping into a woman who stepped forward and thrust a leaflet at her. She glared at her assailant, then noticed the Hospital Volunteer badge on her lapel and quickly morphed her features into a polite smile. The helper nodded at her, and let her pass. She looked down at the leaflet, and saw it was a Health Communications publication about Virus precautions.

The influenza virus is spread by close personal contact ...

She scanned down to a box at the bottom. The author had gone overboard on the use of exclamation marks.

Remember: A single sneeze can spread the Virus up to 6 feet away!
Remember: A person has the Virus for up to four days before showing symptoms – just because someone looks healthy doesn't mean they are Virus-free!
Remember: You are infectious from the day before your symptoms show until up to seven days after you become ill – if you don't feel well STAY AT HOME!

Remember: punctuation overuse can kill!

She shoved the leaflet in her pocket, walking past the café and bookshops until she found a board listing the different wards. There were an apparently endless number of possibilities. Would Carole and her son be in Virus Immediate Quarantine, Children's Virus Ward, or Young People's Virus Ward? At what age did a child become a young person? They'd discussed her family when she'd joined the HET, in the usual getting to know your colleagues way. Carole had obviously sussed that children weren't her thing though, as Mona couldn't remember ever discussing her kid again – or was it kids? And Christ – what was his name?

She pulled out her mobile. 'Carole, hi, it's Mona.'

'Mona, how are you?' Her colleague's voice was quiet.

'I'm in the foyer of the ERI but I don't know what ward you're on.'

'You're here?' She sounded surprised. 'Did Mr Paterson send you to check up on me?'

'He's concerned about you. In his own way.'

There was a brief pause. 'Ward Four. It's marked Young People.'

Carole and her son were in a small side room, with a sign marked 'Caution: Virus Assessment' on its door. It had taken a bit of manoeuvring on Mona's part to get this far; the double whammy of child protection and Virus control concerns meant that a letter from God himself was required to get on to a ward. Mona had the next best thing – an HET ID card. The nurse on duty had looked a bit doubtful, but a few veiled threats about the power of the Health Enforcement Team had given her enough leverage to get shown to the correct place.

Mona hovered in the doorway. Carole was sitting by the bed, holding her son's hand. Her eyes were closed and her head bent slightly forward, as if she was praying. Was she a Christian? Mona didn't know. Maybe everyone in this position appealed to a higher power. When her father had had his heart attack she remembered a long night of bargaining with a deity she wasn't sure she believed in. Much good it had done.

A bank of monitoring equipment stood in position at the top end of the room, its light flashing rhythmically red then green. The covers of the bed had been thrown back, and the long limbs of the teenager were shifting restlessly. The pinkness of the boy's cheeks stood out against the sea of hospital white. He looked like a textbook example of a Virus case. He could have appeared on a Virus protection ad with the PHeDA logo underneath: *Phone Help. Don't Approach.*

Indecision gripped her. Was it really worth bothering her colleague right now? It was pretty obvious Carole wasn't going to be rushing back to work anytime soon, despite the Guv's school assembly emergency. She was just coming down on the side of lying to her boss, when Carole opened her eyes and caught sight of her.

'Hello, Mona.' She attempted a not very convincing smile.

To Mona's relief, the boy's details were written in pen on a white board above his head. Michael Brooks. He was only fifteen.

'How is Michael?'

'Not so good. The doctor ...'

The machine that was monitoring Michael's heart rate gave out a loud buzzing sound. The flashing light changed to a persistent red.

Carole leapt in alarm, dropped the magazine, and pushed past her to the door. Mona followed her into the corridor, scanning up and down the whitewashed walls for a sign of assistance. Carole stood in the middle of the hallway, and spun round in an anxious pirouette.

'Where are they?'

'I'm sure they'll be ...' She stopped when the blue-clad form of a Virus nurse appeared at the end of the hall and ran in their direction. They followed her back into the room.

'Don't worry,' she said, pressing a button. 'This machine does that from time to time.'

The buzzing ceased. Relieved, the pair of them exchanged a look.

'Are you OK?' asked Mona, then realised how stupid the question was. 'I mean, of course you are not OK, but are you ...'

'Coping?' Carole walked round the bed and collapsed back into her seat. 'I've been living on my nerves ever since the school phoned this morning.'

Mona spied a chair in the corridor and nabbed it. She edged past the nurse, who was now taking Michael's pulse, and settled down next to Michael's feet.

'Did they send him home?'

'No, I went to the school to get him. I took one look at him when I got there and jumped straight into a taxi. He started coughing up blood on the way. The driver was immune – thank God – and helped me carry him in.'

'It's Carole Brooks, isn't it?'

Surprised, they both turned in the direction of the nurse. Mona looked at her properly for the first time. She put her at about thirty, with brown hair pulled back in a bun. She was round-faced, with slightly buck teeth, which, combined with her air of eagerness, made her resemble an enthusiastic hamster. Carole looked as if she vaguely recognised her, but couldn't put a name to her. The nurse helped her out.

'Amy Wilson, Phillips as was. I was a student nurse on your ward about ten years ago?'

'Sorry,' said Carole, reprising the barely-there smile that Mona had seen earlier. 'Long time ago.'

'Yeah, you left to set up your ...' her face screwed up as she thought, 'shop, was it?'

'A herbalist shop, yeah.'

The herbalist shop was a source of much amusement in the HET office. Maitland had visited it and reported back on the range of crystals, herbs, and other 'wacko shit' that it purveyed. Even Bernard had been heard to comment on the dangers of homeopathic remedies in the current climate. Amy Wilson didn't seem to find it funny, her hamster cheeks working overtime as she nodded.

'Yes, of course it was. Is that still going strong?'

'Business has never been better, actually.' Carole gave a bitter little laugh. 'Everyone's desperate for a cure.'

They all looked at Michael.

'I just wish I had one.'

Amy Wilson, Phillips as was, smiled and smoothed the sheets back over Michael's legs. 'How's Jimmy? Will he be in?'

'No. He's not immune, nor is my other son, so sadly it's just me.'

'That's a shame. So, you've left him minding the shop?'

'Actually he's been running the business since I started working for the Health Enforcement Team.'

Amy's eyes widened. 'You're with the HET now? How did you end up there?'

Carole turned her face away, and shrugged. 'Oh, you know,' she looked at Michael, 'there were all those adverts for nurses who'd left the profession ...'

Mona could see her colleague's attention was drifting back to her son's bed.

28

' … and, what was I saying? Sorry, my head's not in the best place right now.'

Michael shifted uneasily on the bed.

'It's all right, sweetheart.' She stroked his hand. 'Mum's here.'

Amy moved toward the door, and as she did so a man in blue scrubs appeared in the doorway.

'Just press the red buzzer if you need anything.' She smiled at them both. 'Good to see you again.'

Carole muttered something, but Mona could see that all of her attention was now focused on the doctor.

The doctor was young, with blonde hair in a perfect Marcel Wave. He looked like a 1920s Hollywood starlet, albeit a star who had just worked a twelve-hour shift saving the lives of fever-stricken minors.

'Which one of you ladies is Michael's mum?'

Carole let go of her son's hand. 'I am.'

'I'm Doctor McMenamie.' He stuck out a hand to shake hers.

Mona stood up to leave, 'I'll head off now.'

The medic picked up Michael's notes from the end of the bed.

'Could you stay, Mona, just until the doctor's gone?'

There was a tone in Carole's voice that Mona hadn't heard before, and the hint of a plea was playing around her eyes. She reluctantly sat back down. 'Sure.'

The doctor looked at them both.

'As you know, the blood tests confirmed that Michael is suffering from H1N1-variant influenza, or as we usually call it, the Virus.'

Carole nodded.

'So, I just wanted to run through with you what we will be doing with Michael's treatment.'

Mona stood up and motioned to the doctor to sit down in her place.

'Thanks.' He took a deep breath. 'The Virus, as you may be aware, is particularly dangerous for young people.'

Mona waited for Carole to admit to being a nurse, but she didn't enlighten him. Mona wondered why; Carole had been out of nursing for around ten years – perhaps she was unsure of the latest responses to the Virus? Maybe she just wanted to hear it all again as a refresher? Mona looked over at Carole and got her answer – Carole was trying so hard not to cry she couldn't speak.

'This is due to a phenomenon called a cytokine storm, which basically means that your body's immune system completely overreacts to the Virus.'

Carole dug a hanky out of her pocket and wiped her eyes. 'I've heard the term.'

The doctor smiled. 'It's amazing the terminology everyone has become familiar with over the past couple of years. So, this overreaction is bad in adults, but in young people like your son, it's particularly powerful as they have the strongest immune system.'

'Oh God.'

'But you got him to us really quickly.' He held up a reassuring hand. 'He stands a very good chance of recovery. Our main concern is making sure that this doesn't develop into bacterial pneumonia, and to that end we'll be monitoring him throughout the day.' He stood up. 'Any questions, just ask.'

Carole covered her face with her hands.

Mona reached over and patted her shoulder. 'Thanks, Doctor.'

He gave a nod of acknowledgement and disappeared out of the door.

Carole laid her head face down on the bed, next to Michael's hand. 'Sorry, Mona,' she said, her voice muffled by the bed sheet.

'Don't apologise, it's totally understandable.' What did it feel like to have your son go through this? The idea of having a child was quite difficult enough for Mona to imagine, without factoring in life-threatening illnesses. 'I could stay for a while.'

'No.' Carole sat back upright, wiping her eyes. 'No, get back to work. Try and save some other poor bugger from going through this.'

Mona backed slowly out of the room. 'Take care, Carole.'

As soon as she was out of sight she started to run, and didn't stop until she was back at her car.

2

Bernard stared at his screen saver, willing the shoals of brightly coloured fish to spring into life and tell him what it was that he should be doing right now. Usually Mona took the lead in their investigations, bringing her decade of experience in law enforcement to their work, as she prodded and patronised him in the right direction. He should probably go and talk to Heidi's flatmate, but he'd like a second opinion that this was the best course of action. There were two people currently in the office who could assist him with this dilemma. One of them was his extremely scary boss, and Bernard immediately ruled out this option as he didn't fancy being told, as he had been on previous occasions, that he was an idiotic waste of space and lacking in the common-sense department. Unfortunately, the only person this left was Maitland.

He turned round and stared at his teammate, who was unusually focused on his computer. Bernard moved slightly to see what he was looking at, and had an uninterrupted view of what appeared to be an online rundown of America's Top Ten Sexiest Babes. This probably wasn't the best time to disturb him. Bernard turned back to his virtual fish tank, only to see Paterson moving stealthily across the office, with a finger pressed to his lips, forbidding him from warning his colleague of his approach. Bernard cringed and waited for the explosion.

'Is that official work business?'

Maitland turned to see Paterson watching the video over his shoulders. He grabbed the mouse to turn it off, but only succeeded in freezing the screen with a picture of Christina Aguilera in a bikini. Bernard silently rejoiced at this gift provided by the HET's elderly hardware.

'Eh . . .' Maitland looked up at his boss's outraged face. 'I was just doing some research?'

'Is that what you call it?' Paterson snorted. 'Anyway, my room, now. You too, Brains.'

Maitland got to his feet, flicked a surreptitious V-sign at Bernard, and ambled along behind Paterson. Bernard followed them into the office, where their boss had already squeezed himself into his chair. Maitland threw himself into the other available place to sit. As Bernard wasn't invited to make himself comfortable, he leaned against the wall, which moved slightly under his weight.

'Right, I've got a No Show needs chasing up by you. Eighteen-year-old girl, name of Colette Greenwood. Her parents last spoke to her on Sunday, who suggested we talk to these people.' Paterson waved a sheet of A4 in Maitland's direction.

'Thing is, Guv, we're not supposed to chase up No Shows single-handed and Carole's not here, so . . .'

Paterson threw the memo in Maitland's direction. It fluttered gently and landed at his feet.

'I'm well aware of the health and safety implications of you flying solo, Maitland, hence Bernard's presence in this discussion. Although, to be honest, in this instance I think I can guarantee you are not about to get your head kicked in.'

33

Bernard picked up the paper. 'The Church of the Lord Arisen?'

'Yeah, it's on Persevere Street.' Paterson smiled. 'You may remember it from the TV coverage.'

Maitland snatched the memo from Bernard's hand, folded it in four, and shoved it into the back pocket of his jeans. Bernard tried to remember what the story was with the Church. He vaguely remembered there being a scandal – was it drugs?

'Can't blame the Press, I suppose. Three God-fearing teenagers trying to kill themselves in the space of a week is always going to be news. But you never know what you're getting with these Evangelical types, so tread lightly, OK? Don't want their lawyers on the phone.' Paterson's hand made a sweeping movement in the direction of the door.

Bernard started walking. His colleague didn't move.

Paterson made a further shooing motion with his hand. 'Goodbye, Maitland, don't let the door hit your pasty arse on the way out.'

Bernard waited for his colleague to follow him. Maitland was stepping from foot to foot, as if some burning hot coals had been placed beneath him. Bernard wasn't sure what was causing his discomfort, but he was definitely enjoying watching it.

'Thing is, Guv, I'm not sure I'm the best person to be dealing with this ...?'

Paterson picked a file off the top of his in tray, and shook the contents out onto his desk. 'Neither am I, Maitland, particularly in light of your Internet habits, but you and Genius here are all I've got.'

The reluctant HET officer still didn't move.

'What?' said Paterson, flicking through the papers in

front of him. 'Are you scared of clergymen or something? Were you felt up by a naughty vicar when you were a kid?'

Maitland gave up. 'We're on our way, Guv.'

Bernard looked at the memo and back at the door. It was a perfectly serviceable office door, the last in a row of similar entrances on a 1930s block on the fringes of Leith. Therein lay Bernard's concern. There was nothing on it that identified the building as a church; in fact there was nothing that identified it as anything. But it did have a large 2 and 9 screwed to the woodwork, and this was Persevere Street, so unless the memo was wrong this was where they were supposed to be.

Bernard wandered back up the street, and peered in the window of number 27. From what he could see through the dusty panes, it appeared to be empty. He walked in the other direction, and stared back at the side of the building. A billboard advised people of the importance of hand-washing. True to form, someone had spray-painted 'health fascists' across it in silver. Nowhere did it mention the Almighty.

'For God's sake, Bernard, this must be it,' Maitland shouted over to him.

He took one last look round, hoping to see someone local who could advise them. It was, he knew, unlikely. There was no such thing as an amenable passer-by these days, no old men or young mums who were happy to stop and chat. You got up in the morning, you went to work, went home, and at every stage of the day, you kept interactions with strangers to an absolute minimum.

'Right, I'm knocking.' Maitland took matters into his own hands. He hammered loudly on the door, and cursed when there was no immediate answer.

35

'Word-of-mouth must be working well for the Church of the Lord Arisen,' said Bernard.

'What?' snapped Maitland.

'Because they certainly aren't feeling the need to advertise.' He gestured to the nameplate-free entrance.

His colleague grunted. 'I don't think this is their church. It's probably just an office.'

Bernard couldn't resist doing a bit of digging. 'So, what is your problem about coming here?'

Maitland sighed. 'I don't have an issue about this job, other than being partnered by a midget who never shuts up.'

'Five foot seven does not make me a midget, and yes, you do – I saw the way you were carrying on in Paterson's office.' Bernard did an impersonation of his teammate hopping from foot to foot. 'You were all over the place trying to get out of this.'

'OK, OK.' Maitland hammered on the door again. 'My girlfriend goes to this church, the minister's a twat, I've met him a couple of times, I hope he doesn't remember me, end of story. Happy now?'

For Bernard, this statement raised more questions than it answered. 'So your girlfriend's religious. Are you ...?'

'No, I am not. And neither was she until she started freaking out about being non-immune. In my opinion, places like this just prey on ...'

'Yes?'

The door had opened, and in its frame stood a man in his late twenties, wearing jeans and a hoodie. His hair was long and loose, the dark tresses reaching down to his shoulders. He had the air of an indie musician, the kind of anonymous guitar player that backed up a good-looking female singer. However, he also looked exactly like the picture in the Defaulter File, which had been cut out of one of the recent newspaper articles about the church, so Bernard assumed he was in the right place.

'I thought I heard something,' said the man. 'Can I help you?'

Bernard held his ID up. 'Pastor Mackenzie, we need to talk to you about one of your members.'

The clergyman glanced at the card, then looked him up and down. 'You don't look like an agent of law enforcement.'

You don't look like a minister, thought Bernard. He preferred his clergymen elderly, dressed in black, and with hair, if they had any, that was cut in a nice short-back-and-sides. He forced a smile. 'We're Health Enforcement, not law enforcement. I'm from the *Health* Enforcement Team.'

The Pastor surveyed him again, and smiled politely. 'You'd better come in then, Mr eh ...?'

'Bernard. Just Bernard, I mean, not Mr. And this is Maitland Stevenson.'

Pastor Mackenzie glanced in Maitland's direction, then turned back into the building. 'If you and your colleague would like to follow me?'

Bernard looked up at his teammate, who shrugged. If the clergyman recognised Maitland, he certainly hadn't shown it.

'You can ...' the minister pointed at a dispenser of alcohol gel attached to the wall. 'If you want.'

'Oh, right.' Bernard plunged some of the liquid onto his hands, and made a show of rubbing them thoroughly. One of the best things about being immune was no longer feeling the need to wash his hands twenty times a day. When the Virus had been building to its second peak he'd

37

almost taken the skin off them. Now, the gel was more a matter of politeness, an outward show of consideration.

They followed the cleric along a narrow corridor and down a flight of stairs.

'I wasn't sure if I was at the right place,' he said. 'It doesn't look like a church.'

The Pastor laughed. 'It's our head office, I suppose you would call it. We don't actually hold our services here. We use a hall on Great Junction Street.' He pushed open a door and ushered them into his office. Bernard's eyes flitted over the desk and the walls. There was nothing he could see that indicated that this was the office of a cleric – not a cross or a Church magazine in sight. There was, however, a red electric guitar propped up against one wall. Bernard gave an inward groan at the thought of hymns played in a rock-and-roll style, then immediately felt bad. Just because his Church of Scotland upbringing had left him nostalgic for the swirling bass of the organ didn't mean it was for everyone. And it was probably good at attracting in a younger congregation . . .

'Pastor Mackenzie . . .' His colleague was taking charge.

The minister laid a hand on Maitland's arm. 'We don't hold with these kinds of formalities here. Malcolm will do nicely.'

Bernard stifled a smile watching his teammate fight the urge to shake the Pastor's hand off his sleeve. His colleague opted instead to step back and lower himself onto an ancient sofa that took up most of one of the walls. Bernard joined him. The Pastor walked slowly to the other side of the desk, sat, and laid both his arms on the desktop, with his hands clasped together.

Maitland carried on. 'We're trying to trace a young woman who has missed her Health Check.'

The Pastor looked surprised. 'Are missing people not the remit of the Police anymore?'

Bernard sighed inwardly. Despite the near-constant adverts on TV, still nobody understood what the HET did.

'Yes, absolutely,' said Maitland. 'But if someone has defaulted on a Health Check without being registered as missing, we step in.'

The Pastor raised a quizzical eyebrow. 'Because of your specialist abilities?'

'Because if someone has been reported missing by their loved ones, there's usually a variety of reasons why they've gone AWOL. But if someone has defaulted on a Health Check without anyone missing them, nine times out of ten it's because they are suffering from the Virus.' Maitland reached into his pocket and passed a crumpled information leaflet over the desk. 'The Health Enforcement Team are all immune. Your average Bobby isn't.'

The Pastor placed the leaflet in a drawer, unread. 'Forgive my nosiness. I wasn't sure how it all worked. But roles and responsibilities aside, I'm not sure how my church can help?'

Maitland sat forward on the sofa. 'One of the last verified sightings of the woman in question was at your church, at the Sunday evening service. We'd value any information that you could give us about the missing woman.'

The minister stared at him. 'I'm sorry, Mr Maitland, but it's the policy of our church not to discuss any of our congregation with third parties.'

Pastor Mackenzie got to his feet. The HET team didn't.

'You may not be aware of this, Sir,' said Maitland,

'but the Health Enforcement Team have powers of arrest similar to the Police, and can require anyone suspected of hindering our recovery of a Defaulter to immediately accompany them to the nearest Police Station for further investigation.'

The Pastor's lips formed a tight, thin, line. 'Amazing how at the first sign of crisis civil liberties go out of the window.'

'Amazing how at the first sign of crisis church attendance goes through the roof.' Maitland paused for a moment. 'Sir.'

The two men stared at each other, the Pastor still poised at his desk and Maitland balanced on the edge of his chair. It reminded Bernard of every stand-off he'd ever seen in the playground at school, the rising tension before one participant snapped and lashed out at the other. Although, if he was honest, playground violence was exactly the kind of thing he'd spent thirteen years of education avoiding. He had no useful skills to bring to conflict resolution and before inspiration could hit him, Maitland spoke again.

'You haven't even asked the identity of the Health Defaulter. Not very caring for a clergyman.'

The Pastor opened his mouth to speak then closed it again. He sighed, and sat down at his desk. 'Of course I am concerned. I'm just a little sensitive since the Police involvement following our recent troubles.'

Maitland snorted. 'How outrageous of the Police to investigate the church after a mere three of your young, female, parishioners overdose on antidepressants. How many of them died? Two, was it?'

'There's no need for sarcasm.' For the first time in the meeting the cleric looked annoyed. He picked an elastic

40

band off his desk and used it to tie his hair back in a ponytail. Bernard found it an oddly intimate gesture, like a woman shaking loose her hair, but in reverse. Perhaps the Pastor was trying to reinstate the formality he'd been so eager to lose before. 'As you are aware, two of our parishioners did commit suicide, a very unfortunate sign of the times we live in. Your colleagues in the Police made a thorough investigation into that incident, and nothing was found to link the overdoses to the church.' He folded his arms. 'Please tell me who you are looking for.'

Bernard jumped in. 'Colette Greenwood.'

The Pastor nodded. 'I know her. Nice girl. A regular attender.'

'Last heard of heading out to your Sunday night service. Any idea where she would have gone after church?'

'How would I know?' The Pastor sighed. 'I see the young people for a couple of hours a week, more if they want to come and talk to me. I assume, like any other woman of her age, she had a social life and went on to a pub? Clubbing?'

'Rather unlikely, seeing as she is not immune.' Maitland's tone wasn't any friendlier.

'OK, then. Perhaps she went round to a boyfriend's house? Maybe she caught a train and went to visit her parents?'

'Possibly,' said Maitland. 'Or maybe she bought some antidepressants and is lying dead somewhere?'

'Maybe.' The Pastor got to his feet, again. 'But she didn't buy them at this church. As your Police colleagues will tell you, one of the poor girls who died had a prescription for the drugs.'

Bernard leaned forward, anticipating that the interview

41

was over, when he realised that his colleague hadn't moved.

'When did you last speak to Colette?'

The clergyman's eyes flicked toward the door. After a second's internal debate he seemed to realise his visitors weren't going anywhere. 'A few weeks ago, I think?'

'And how was she?'

Pastor Mackenzie sighed. 'She seemed all right, I suppose. I don't remember anything out of the ordinary.'

'Did Colette come to church on her own, or with friends?'

'Usually with a couple of other girls – Kate, and another girl, Louise I think her name is.'

'Boyfriends?'

'None that I am aware of. I think we are done here.' He walked to the door, opened it, and stood waiting for them to leave.

'For the moment, perhaps,' said Maitland. 'We may need to talk to you again. And I must warn you that under the Health Enforcement and Recovery of Defaulters Act you are not allowed to inform anyone else that we are seeking Colette.'

The Pastor shook his head, in a small pantomime of disbelief.

Bernard was about to explain to the clergyman that this had actually been a strong concession on civil liberties within the Act, when he caught his colleague's eye.

'C'mon.' Maitland walked through the door, and headed in the direction of the stairs.

'How's your girlfriend, Mr Stevenson?'

His colleague stopped in his tracks.

Bernard was impressed; Pastor Mackenzie could play

poker with a bunch of Texan cowboys without giving his hand away. He would have sworn that the cleric hadn't recognised his teammate.

'Will you be accompanying Emma to any future services?'

Maitland reached for the banister. As he climbed the stairs he said, 'I think that's unlikely.'

The Pastor turned back to Bernard. 'I trust that's all you need from me?'

Bernard thought it safest to echo his colleague. 'For the moment.' He stuck out his hand. After a slight delay the Pastor shook it.

'Thanks for your help, eh, Malcolm.'

'Planning to change gear anytime soon?'

'Planning to get out and walk anytime soon?' Chauffeuring Maitland was not fun, particularly in his current temper. Bernard wasn't sure how he'd ended up driving; he suspected that it fitted into the list of dogsbody tasks that Maitland thought he was fit for. He slipped the car into fourth. 'Stop taking your bad mood out on me.'

Maitland stared out of the window. 'You drive like a girl.'

'Mackenzie will probably complain, you know, about the way that you spoke to him.'

His colleague didn't respond.

'Maitland?'

There was no answer, so Bernard gave up and switched on the radio. They made their way back to the HET office to the sound of a heated phone-in on whether home-schooling was an appropriate parental response to Virus fears.

43

Bernard parked the car in one of the HET's designated spaces, and hurried into the office, in the hope that Mona would be there and he could offload a range of emotions relating to Maitland onto her, before Maitland told her his side of the story. He was delighted to see her standing by her desk.

'Mona,' he began, then stopped as she reached for her coat. 'You're going out?'

'Yup.'

Maitland appeared in the doorway. 'Mona – are you going out somewhere?'

'Yes! Yes, everyone, I am going out.'

Bernard sighed. An afternoon alone in the office with Maitland might result in one or other of them being fired, or possibly murdered.

Mona dropped her mobile into her bag, and slung it over her shoulder. 'Bernard – I need backup.' Bernard felt a sudden pain in his shoulder as Maitland elbowed him out of the way. 'If you need muscle you'd be better off with me.'

'If I need a constant stream of innuendo, bad jokes and borderline sexual harassment I'd be better off with you. C'mon, Bernard.'

Bernard smiled smugly and waved to Maitland as he followed Mona out of the office.

Maitland responded with a gesture that Mona probably wouldn't have liked.

3

'This is it.'

Mona pointed at the tenement. In common with many Edinburgh buildings it was set back from the pavement. Pedestrians were prevented from plunging into the basement yard by a spiked iron fence, and the gap between pavement and front door was bridged by a small set of steps.

Her partner frowned. 'It looks more like a laundrette.'

'Not the Spinderella – there.' Mona sighed and refined her gesturing by moving her finger along and down.

Bernard adjusted his gaze ground-wards and finally noticed the flight of metal stairs. 'A basement bar?'

'Yes!'

Bernard gave her one of his patented long-suffering glances. 'Everything I say today seems to provoke an exasperated hiss. It's like being on reconnaissance with a grumpy and slightly asthmatic snake.'

'Ssssshut up.'

They walked over to the stairs, which led down to a small concreted area, running the length of the laundrette. There was a black painted door, and a window with a matching shutter.

'Are you sure this is it?' Her partner still looked sceptical, and she could feel little prickles of irritation rising on her skin.

'I mean,' Bernard continued, 'I can't see anything that indicates this is a pub, never mind a sign saying Morley's.'

'Believe me, before I joined CID I was called here often enough on a Saturday night.'

'Oh.' Her partner looked concerned. 'Bit rough is it?'

'Yep, but I've got your back.'

She gave him a gentle push, and he lost his footing and grabbed at the metal handrail. Balance restored, he turned and glared at her. 'Thanks, Mona. Good to know.'

Bernard walked slowly and carefully down the remaining steps, and she resisted, with some difficulty, the urge to push him again. The sign on Morley's door said it was closed, so Bernard tapped gently on the wood.

'Oh, for God's sake.' She turned the handle and pushed the door open.

Morley's was large, low-ceilinged, and dark. Mona took a second to adjust to the lack of light, then gave the room a once-over. On the left there was a bar that curved along two walls, and on the right were a selection of mismatched chairs, benches, and whisky barrels masquerading as tables. There were other rooms leading off the central area, but it was too dark to see them properly. What she could see, however, was a young man behind the bar washing glasses.

'Hi.'

The man stopped his cleaning momentarily and looked up in surprise.

'We're not op—'

'I know.' Mona pushed past Bernard, and flashed her ID card over the counter. 'We're from the Health Enforcement Team.'

The barman grimaced. 'Green Cards, please.'

They dutifully held up their Health Status Cards which he glanced at, without stopping his work.

'Immune? Lucky you.'

'Is the manager in?' she asked.

'The manager no, the owner yes. You want a word?'

'Yes, please.'

'He's through the back.'

The barman reached behind him and flicked a switch. The lights came on and the alcoves and doorways leading off the room lit up. He flicked a further switch, and the room they were in was flooded with light, illuminating the badly stained paintwork and carpet. She saw a look of horror on her colleague's face, and wondered if he was personally or professionally disgusted. She found it hard to picture Bernard in a pub for pleasure; a wine bar maybe, at a push. She caught the barman's eye. He appeared to be amused by Bernard's distaste.

'It's a paradise, isn't it?'

Bernard smiled weakly, and Mona pushed him in the direction of the back room.

Victor Thompson was a well-kent face on the Edinburgh pub and club scene. He was a dapper fifty-something, with a nice line in expensive suits and cashmere coats, and he sported a hair colour that didn't entirely fit with the lines on his face. He recognised Mona, and looked puzzled.

'I thought you worked for CID?'

'I've been seconded to Health Enforcement.'

'Congratulations.'

She nodded her thanks without smiling.

'Take the weight off.' Victor pointed to the small sofa next to him, and swept the papers he had spread out on

47

the table in front of him into a neat pile. She had a discreet look at the room they were in. It was a small function suite, of a size that could comfortably hold around fifty people, assuming they had no objection to partying in a room with only one entrance, no windows, and a floor that your shoes stuck to.

Victor continued. 'I don't know what brings you here though. I'm doing everything by the book. Every bastard that sets foot through that door gets carded by the bouncers.'

'I don't doubt that, Mr Thompson, but we're here on a different matter. We're looking for this woman.' Mona unfolded a photograph of Heidi. 'We believe she was a regular here before she went missing.'

The entrepreneur gave the picture a cursory glance. 'Can't say I recognise her. But then I'm not here that much. You'd be better off talking to the staff.'

'Can we leave this with your manager, ask him to get in touch if any of the bar staff recognise her?'

Victor picked up the photo. 'The number of punters I get in here these days, if she was here they'd know it.'

'Business is bad?' asked Bernard.

'Bad?' Victor leaned back in his seat and stared at her partner. 'Let me see, I've got you lot telling me I've got to card everyone that walks through that door. I've got a restaurant that I'm not allowed more than twenty people in – have you ever tried to make a profit out of twenty covers? I had to dish out the best part of ten grand to install contact-free toilet flushing systems, because the Government decided the general public can't be relied upon to wash their hands, even though your mob has adverts on the TV every ten minutes telling us to soap-and-go. And,' his voice rose an octave, 'to cap it all, I've

48

got a nightclub sitting empty because you folk won't let me open.'

'But the Virus spreads most easily in hot, crowded environments . . .'

'Thanks for your time, Sir.' Mona cut across her colleague, and turned on her heel, leaving Bernard to follow behind her, nodding his goodbyes to Victor and the barman.

'Why did you start explaining how the Virus spreads?' Mona didn't try to hide her irritation. She pressed the doorbell to Heidi's tenement flat for the second time, and this time kept leaning on the buzzer.

Bernard pointed at her finger, and she glared at him. Some days everything about her new partner annoyed her. She hated his endless ability to remain reasonable, even when members of the public were being completely ridiculous. She hated his ability to remember every fact and figure he'd ever heard relating to the Virus. But most of all, she hated the fact that he wasn't Police.

When her boss had said he was nominating her to the HET she'd been flattered. DCI Rodgers had called her into his office.

'Thing is, Mona, loath as I am to let you go . . .'

'Go?'

She stared at his round, florid face. He seemed to be finding it difficult to meet her eye, and she started to panic. Was this payback for the nastiness earlier in the year? She knew that Rodgers and Bill Hamilton were friends from their Police college days, but she'd thought he wasn't taking sides.

'It's orders from on high, really, what with you being immune. We're under a lot of pressure to recommend decent people to the HETs.'

49

'The HETs?'

'Health Enforcement Teams – they're elite squads, sort of, made up of Police and health care workers – all immune, of course.'

Mona frowned. 'And doing what?'

'Tracking down Health Defaulters. The hardcore ones, I mean, not just folk that are a day late back from holiday.'

She relaxed a little. 'And what do we do with them when we track them down?'

'Frogmarch them to the nearest Health Check Centre.'

'And if they refuse?'

'A night in a clean-cell, then a visit to the doctor, or for repeat offenders, a short prison sentence and fine.'

Mona liked the sound of being part of a crack team. Had to be a step up from CID, which wasn't all it was made out to be.

She uncrossed her legs and sat forward in her chair. 'So, would this be a sideways move then, Guv?'

'Well, on paper.' Rodgers pointed at her with a biro. 'But, in reality it's got to be seen as a promotion, hasn't it? I mean, the Virus is where everything is at these days, isn't it? The work there is cutting edge, and of course, desperately needed.'

If her country needed her to fight the Virus, she wasn't going to say no. Especially if it was going to look good on her CV as well.

'And things here aren't as busy as they were.'

This was true. Some staff could be spared; the absence of nightclubs and the increased regulation of pubs meant less public disorder on Friday and Saturday nights. CID had fewer drink-fuelled stabbings to investigate. People went out less, which meant fewer empty houses to be burgled.

'So, you'll do it then?'

'Of course, Guv.'

Rodgers looked relieved. He stood up, reached over his desk and gave her a playful punch on the shoulder. 'We'll miss you, of course, Mona.'

'Well, I'll probably be back in a month or two.' She stood up. 'There's bound to be a cure any day now.'

Rodgers stuck his hand out and shook Mona's. 'Bound to be. Bound to be.'

He shook her hand for slightly longer than felt comfortable.

Mona's enthusiasm for the HET lasted right up until meeting the other team members, particularly Bernard, who, in Paterson's words, had a degree in health-whatsit and was some kind of ex-athlete thingy. Health conscious and sporty her new partner may be. A top-notch crime fighter he was not.

'What did you say, Mona?' said Bernard. 'And I think you can stop ringing now. If there's anyone in they'll have heard you.'

'I said, why did you go into all that shit about how the Virus spreads with Vic Thompson? We're Enforcement Officers. We can *make* people do things, we don't have to talk them into it.'

Bernard had a look on his face that she'd come to hate over the past few months. It conveyed disbelief that she didn't share his point of view, with an undercurrent of bitter disappointment in her.

'Maybe some of us prefer people to comply because they understand *why* we're doing something, rather than doing it because they're scared of us?'

She decided not to engage with the lefty bullshit. 'I get it, Bernard. We're not the Police.'

Mona pressed the bell again, and gave it three short blasts. If it hadn't been for Bernard, if she'd been teamed with a half-decent Police colleague, she'd have been quite enjoying today. Over the six months she'd spent at the HET the work had settled into a certain pattern, week after week of chasing individuals whose erratic lifestyles prevented them embracing the routine of a Health Check. She'd dragged addicts out of crack dens and into doctor's surgeries, chased up truants spending schooldays in arcades, tracked down drinkers who slept through their appointment times on piss-stained memorial benches. And she was sick of it, bored stiff by the monotony of chaos.

But this case, this Heidi woman, was different. For one thing, their usual Health Defaulters didn't live in Marchmont. The area was green and leafy, bordering on to the city centre park called the Meadows, and filled with flats shared by affluent Edinburgh University students. She looked at the well-polished nameplates at the side of the door to Heidi's tenement, and thought it was unlikely she'd be stepping on any discarded syringes in her hallway.

Her colleague's phone rang, and even from three feet away she could hear the loud tones of Marcus from IT.

'Bernard? Marcus here. We've finished with that German lassie's laptop. Some interesting stuff on it – can you pop over?'

Bernard put his hand over the mouthpiece. 'We might as well – there's obviously no-one in.'

Mona stepped back into the road to get a better look at the second-floor windows. Her partner was right, unfortunately. There was no sign of life.

'Is the lovely Mona coming with you?'

Mona rolled her eyes. She could do without an hour of the HET's leading geek trying to impress her. She communicated this to Bernard with a shake of her head. Bernard stifled a smile.

'Eh, think it'll just be me. See you soon.'

They walked back in the direction of the car. They passed a bus stop emblazoned with a full-length purple and green PHeDA poster, which Bernard ducked into to check the timetable. She took pity on him.

'I'll drop you off.'

'Thanks, that'd be great.'

He looked unnecessarily grateful, and Mona felt a twinge of guilt. She should be nicer to him, really. He was harmless, if annoying. They reached the car and she stepped out into the road.

'What are you going to do while I'm with IT?' asked Bernard, over the Audi's roof.

It was a good question. 'Back to the office.' She pulled open the door. 'Review the case notes and look for more potential leads.'

A decent outcome to the search would look good for her; show she'd still got her detective wits about her. Maybe she could even wangle a return to CID on the back of it. Let Bernard bugger about with the IT section – she was going to crack this case if it killed her. She had one foot in the car when her phone rang.

'Mona.'

It was Maitland.

'What do you want?'

'I need to interview a vulnerable teenage girl, and for some reason Paterson won't let me go on my own.'

'Oh, Christ. Where do I need to be?'

'Milne's Court Hall of Residence on the High Street. And Mona?'

'What?'

'Do you think they'll be having a pillow fight in their underwear when we get there?'

She hung up, cursing her bad luck.

She turned to face her partner, who was putting on his seat belt.

'Sorry, Bernard, change of plan. You're on the bus.'

4

Maitland, Mona and the girl sat in silence. She was late teens, slim, with long brown hair that was pulled back at one side with a red hairgrip. She perched on the end of the bed, avoiding eye contact, and nervously twisting the corner of the quilt in her hand.

Mona hadn't visited a Hall of Residence in years. She'd been in Milne's Court once before, years before the Virus, when a night out in Edinburgh had resulted in a one-night stand with a student. The room had been similar to this, with two beds – God, where had the room-mate gone for the night! – but not identical. She suspected that no two rooms in the place were the same, not with the age of it. It must be three, maybe four hundred years old?

'This has got to be a great place to live,' she said. 'I mean you're only metres from the castle. Couldn't be much more central.'

'Yes,' said the girl, still tugging at the quilt.

'And it's like living inside a piece of history, isn't it?'

'I suppose.'

She could have an English accent, but she'd said so little it was hard to tell. Her room didn't give too much away about her either. There was a clip frame hanging over her bed, full of what looked like family pictures, and a framed prayer asking for protection from the Virus on her cabinet. At a guess Mona'd say she had two parents, a young brother, a dog, a lack of Immunity, and an active Christian faith. With those kinds of leads, the case would be solved by teatime.

Maitland and Mona looked at each other, and she pointedly looked at her watch.

Maitland was awkwardly balancing a cup of tea he had been given, for which the girl had not had any milk. He blew into the cup and took a sip. 'So, your friend will be . . .'

'She'll be here any minute.'

The interview wasn't going well. On their arrival at her door, the girl had panicked. She'd refused to give as much as her name until her friend arrived as moral support. Mona looked at her watch again, and considered leaning a little more heavily on the teenager. She was all in favour of softly-softly, but she wanted back to the office, and back to her own case. She reached out a foot and gave Maitland a discreet kick.

He glared at her but before he could respond there was a knock, the door flew open and a girl bounded into the room. She had long, curly hair which spiralled down to a mature pair of breasts. Mona's eyes lingered on them for a moment, then she turned to look at Maitland. As she had anticipated, his tongue was all but hanging out. The girl smiled at him.

'I'm Kate, what did I miss?'

'Absolutely nothing,' said Maitland, and stood up to shake her hand. 'Believe me.'

She stared at him for a second, with her head on one side. 'You look familiar – have we met before?'

'I don't think so.'

Maitland looked slightly flustered, and Mona was intrigued. Where would her colleague have met a teenage Christian?

The girl looked in her direction, and Mona smiled back. 'We're trying to speak to your friend here, but she's a little tongue-tied.'

Kate laughed, and bounced on to the bed. The two girls sat holding hands.

'So,' said Mona, 'now that your pal is here, are you happy to confirm that you are Louise Jones, room-mate of Colette Greenwood?'

She looked at her friend before answering. 'Yes.'

Mona felt a stab of irritation. If Louise needed backup to confirm her own name it was going to be a very frustrating interview. She ploughed on.

'And, are you aware that she missed her Health Check last week?'

'Did she?' Kate didn't appear concerned. 'I didn't know.' She smiled. 'But I suppose everyone misses one at some point.'

'No,' said Mona, 'because not turning up to your Health Check is a criminal offence. Most people try very, very hard not to miss their Health Check.'

Kate was contemplating her fingernails.

'When was the last time you saw Colette?'

The girl shrugged. 'Two, three weeks ago, perhaps? She's not been around for a while.'

'Not been around?' Maitland jumped in. 'Louise, did you report her missing?'

Kate answered. 'We think she's at her parents'. She leaned forward on the bed and said in a stage whisper, 'Boy trouble.' She sat back with a smile.

Mona looked at the two of them. They were both twenty, if that, and a teenager going home to her mother after splitting up with a boyfriend didn't seem unlikely. And yet, there was something in the pat way that Kate had

57

said it that didn't ring true. Also, Louise was shaking a lot for a girl who wasn't lying. She wondered if Maitland was thinking the same. She caught his eye, and he winked at her.

'Boy trouble? What, had she been sleeping around?'

For the first time since she arrived, Kate appeared annoyed. 'We're Christians, Mr Stevenson. We don't believe in sex before marriage.'

Maitland drained his mug and put it at his feet. 'I thought Christians didn't believe in telling lies either, yet the pair of you are sitting there fibbing your little hearts out.'

Mona half-expected some further denials from Kate, but it seemed that she'd run out of bravado. The girls sat staring at the floor.

'So, Louise, what do you say you start telling me the truth, or do we relocate this interview to a Police Station, minus your pal here?'

'No! I ...' She turned to her friend, with a look of terror on her face. This was not a reaction that Mona usually encountered in her HET work. Indifference often, defiance from time to time, but the actual provoking of fear was pretty rare.

Kate put a protective arm round her friend's shoulders. 'Relax, he can't do that.'

'Guess again,' said Mona. 'We have all the powers that the Police do, plus a few more.' She stood up. 'OK, Louise, on your feet. We'll continue this discussion at our HQ.'

The girl didn't move, and burst into tears.

'OK, OK, OK.' Kate motioned for her to sit back down. 'She's not at her parents'.'

'Just tell us where she is and we'll be out of here.'

The girls exchanged a glance.

'We don't know,' said Louise.

58

'And that's the truth,' added Kate, hastily. 'But we know she's OK.'

Louise reached into her bag and pulled out her mobile phone. She fiddled with it then passed it to Maitland. 'Look at Colette's text messages.'

Maitland scrolled through the texts.

'*Taking some time out to think about stuff. Cover 4 me at uni.*' He read the message out loud for Mona's benefit. 'What stuff?'

'Boy trouble!' said Kate. 'We already told you that, although you don't seem to believe us.'

'And you have no idea, none whatsoever, who she is staying with?'

The girls both shook their heads.

'OK, let's go back. When was the last time you saw Colette face-to-face?'

'About three weeks ago, at the Sunday evening service.'

'OK. And did you go anywhere after the service?'

They nodded.

'Where did you go?'

Kate said 'A pub' and Louise said 'Morley's' at the same time.

A look of annoyance fleeted across Kate's face. She caught Mona's eye, and quickly looked away.

Morley's. This had to be more than a coincidence. She leaned forward. 'Morley's? Is that not a bit of a dive? Why would nice girls like you hang out there?'

Neither of them answered.

Maitland took up the baton. 'Looking to buy something?'

Kate's glare shifted to Maitland. 'I know what you're getting at. We don't take drugs. We're not regulars there or anything.'

'OK, OK.' Mona tried to defuse the situation. 'So you are at Morley's. What next?'

'We had an argument with Colette,' said Louise.

Kate glowered at her again. Mona cursed herself for not pushing Louise before her friend showed up. Five minutes alone with the nervous teen and she'd have had the full story. In fact, she might suggest to Maitland that they call back later.

'What did you argue about, Louise?'

'You wouldn't understand,' said Kate.

Maitland leaned forward in his chair. 'Try us. My colleague is smart, and even I'm not as stupid as I look.' He shot Kate a grin, and in spite of herself, she showed a hint of a smile in return.

'We, I mean, Louise and I,' she gestured in her friend's direction, 'have different views from Colette on some religious issues.'

'You were arguing about God?' Mona raised an eyebrow.

If Kate noticed her scepticism, she didn't acknowledge it. 'Well, it was more a heated discussion than a real argument. About the best way to spread His Word.'

'Uh-huh. So, after your "heated discussion", what next?'

'We left.'

'All of you?'

'Just Louise and me.'

'You left Colette in Morley's?'

'Yes.'

'Not the best of places for a young girl to be hanging around on her own,' said Mona. 'Not sure I'd have left one of my pals there solo.'

Louise sniffed loudly. Again, Kate shot her a look of

annoyance, which Mona noted. Whatever was going on here, Kate was definitely the one in charge.

'We didn't leave her on her own, she was waiting for a friend of hers.'

Mona pulled out her notepad. 'OK, give me her name.'

'*His* name. Donny,' said Kate. 'Louise, what's his surname?'

She shrugged.

'So, this Donny, is he Colette's boyfriend?'

'I don't think so.'

Louise spoke. 'He's just a friend. Definitely just a friend.'

'And you don't know his surname, or address or anything like that?'

'Sorry.'

Mona looked over at Maitland.

'OK,' she said, 'let's leave it for now. Here's our card if you find out Donny's address, or if you hear from Colette again.'

She could see the girls begin to relax. Louise let go of Kate's hand for the first time since she'd arrived.

Maitland stooped back down to pick up his empty mug and handed it to Louise. 'By the way, did you know the girls from your church who overdosed?'

There was a brief silence, then Louise burst into tears again. Kate put an arm around her shoulder. 'They were friends of ours.'

Mona and Maitland walked back along the High Street, each of them deep in their own thoughts.

'What did you make of all that?' she asked.

'Load of bullshit. Even the nerdiest teenager on the planet wouldn't spend an evening debating theology in Morley's.' He kicked a stone down the street. 'And definitely not a good-looking girl like Kate.'

'So, why did they tell us that's what they were doing?'

'To look good.' He chased after the stone again, and fired it, in a cup-winning fashion, in the direction of a nearby bin. 'That's what Christianity is all about – it's all style over substance. Let's tell the HET we were discussing God, when really we were knocking back vodka and cokes.'

'That's a pretty negative view of religion.'

'Yup, unfortunately, that's been my experience.'

'You know a lot of Christians, do you?' Mona laughed, but to her surprise, Maitland didn't.

'I do these days,' he said, morosely. 'My girlfriend thinks God's going to save her from the Virus. She's never away from the Church.'

'Oh.' Mona struggled for something to say. 'I suppose when you're immune it's easy to ...'

'Act like a rational human being?'

She smiled. 'You want a lift back to the office?'

'No thanks,' said Maitland, and started to walk off. 'Bit of business to attend to.'

'But ...' Mona watched him disappear, annoyed that she'd been robbed of the chance of discussing the Morley's connection further. Irritating as Maitland was, he was also sharp as a tack, and she wanted to hear what he thought. She slammed the car door shut and set off in the direction of the HET's home.

The office was deserted, which suited her just fine. However, before Mona even reached her desk the door to Paterson's room flew open.

'How's Carole?'

She thought back to her visit. 'As well as can be expected.

Her son's on a Virus Ward and they're monitoring him.'

'All they can do really.' Paterson wandered through to the office. 'Any sign of her coming back to work?'

'I wouldn't say it was imminent, Guv.'

'Pity. Pity.' He looked round the deserted office. 'And where is everyone else?'

'Bernard's with IT, and Maitland,' she glanced at his empty desk, 'well, he's probably off shagging some bird or other on work time.'

Paterson looked at her for a second, then laughed. 'In here.'

They settled into chairs on either side of Paterson's desk. Mona noticed a pile of old Police Journals next to her seat.

'Tea?' Paterson waved an ancient mug with a Lothian and Borders Police crest at her.

'No, thanks.' Mona thought that perhaps her boss hadn't entirely embraced his late career change.

'So, this missing German lassie – what are your thoughts?'

'It's an interesting one, Guv. But given her age it's probably a boyfriend thing and she'll turn up safe and well in a couple of days.'

'My thoughts exactly. But it's sensitive, as you know. So let's give it the best possible investigation.' Paterson reached into his desk drawer and passed Mona a package. 'The delightful Doctor Toller dropped this off for you.'

Mona reached into the envelope, and pulled out a fluffy, pink, A5 book. 'Heidi's diary, at a guess?'

'I can see why you made CID, Mona.' Paterson picked up the envelope and shook out several pages of typewritten notes. 'Freshly translated by the German Consulate.'

She sat forward in her chair, and bumped the stack of Police Journals, which slid slowly across the floor. 'The Consulate?'

'Oh aye. Toller's got us all running round after this lassie.' Paterson stood up and flicked the kettle's on switch. 'Like I said, sensitive. So don't let your idiot partner mess anything up.'

Mona reached down to tidy up the Journals. 'Bernard's not that bad. He's just a bit . . .' She searched half-heartedly for a word to defend him.

'Clueless?'

She laughed. 'Maybe a little.'

There was a brief silence. Mona got to her feet then spoke again. 'Guv?'

'What?'

'This German girl, right, her registered address is in Marchmont. The dead guy from this morning, registered in Newington. We're the North Edinburgh Team, but neither of these are what I would call in the North of the City. Why are we picking them up?'

Paterson rolled his chair far enough back from the desk that he could rest his feet on it. He picked up his empty Lothian and Borders mug and began rolling it back and forth in his hands. 'You noticed that then?'

'Noticed it a while back, to be honest. What's going on?'

Paterson sighed, then abruptly brought his feet back down off the desk. He pointed to the seat that Mona had recently vacated.

'Sit. We live and work in an era of almost total media intrusion, wouldn't you say, Mona?'

'True, Guv.'

'And if you were keen to keep the Press's noses out of something, you might think that the best way to do that would be to name a specialist team something completely bland.'

Mona stared at him. 'We've got a specialist remit?' This was news to her. As far as she was aware they weren't doing anything different from the Teams in the South, West and East of the City.

'It's not our remit that's different, it's the nature of the cases that we take on.'

'What's unusual about our cases?'

Her boss waved his mug in her direction. 'I've got a question for you. What are the three things you are not supposed to talk about at dinner parties?'

Mona considered the puzzle for a moment. 'Politics, obviously, and religion.' She thought for a longer period. 'And I suppose it depends on the dinner party, but probably not sex either.'

Paterson laughed. 'Congratulations, Ms Whyte, your company would be welcomed at any dining table throughout the land. Sex, religion and politics. Any case relating to these three topics wings its way to us, wherever the Defaulter is registered.'

She stared thoughtfully at Paterson.

'You have a question, Mona?'

'Well, it's just that, Guv, shouldn't these kinds of cases be being dealt with by specialists, instead of ...' She left the sentence hanging.

Paterson raised an eyebrow. 'Instead of what, Mona? Instead of my crack team, present company excepted of course, consisting of Maitland, who might be all right once he's had a bit of experience, Carole Brooks who gave up being a nurse to retrain as an aromatherapist, for Christ's sake ...'

'And Bernard ...'

'Who isn't even a nurse. He's got a degree in health promotion and a year's experience of taking old ladies' blood pressure. And you know the worst thing, Mona?'

'No.'

'We are cutting edge compared to the other three Teams. South?' He counted off the Teams on his fingers. 'Run by a drunk. East? Had to get some superannuated bugger back off retirement to head it up. West? Doesn't even have a Team Leader. Someone's been acting up since they were established.'

Mona asked a question that had been on her mind for some time, ever since she left CID in fact. 'Why don't the HETs have better-quality staff?'

'Because nobody good wants to work in Health Enforcement!' Paterson shouted his reply, then started laughing. 'This is the best we could do with the available pool of immune workers. For the Police recruits it's not much of a job because either a vaccine is found for the Virus, and you've spent years of your career developing skills nobody wants, or they don't find a cure, and eventually we're all either dead or immune anyway. The only Police that volunteered were young bucks like Maitland who wanted a bit of variety for their CV.'

This conversation was beginning to hurt, but she felt compelled to pick the scab a little bit further. 'But the Police can just compel people to do different jobs.'

'True, but the Powers That Be were reluctant to lose their best staff to this and just seconded second-raters they could spare.'

Mona glared at him. Paterson realised his mistake. 'Of course, I fought to get you.'

She'd been kidding herself. The whole Bill Hamilton

thing hadn't been forgotten, not by anyone, and now she was paying for it. Her penance was to be bored to death hunting down junkies and alcoholics. This Heidi case was as interesting as it was ever going to get.

'Yeah, well. Thanks, Guv.' She stood up. 'But you forgot one other option.'

'How do you mean?' Paterson looked surprised.

'Either they find a cure, or we're all immune or dead, or,' she sighed, 'the Virus mutates just enough for us to no longer have Immunity to it.'

'That's a cheery thought.' Paterson winced. 'One minute you've won life's lottery, then the next you're back being one of the hoi polloi.' He thought for a minute. 'And the HET's business model would be completely ruined.'

Mona laughed. 'Anyway, now I'm off to read the innermost thoughts of an eighteen-year-old girl.'

'Enjoy. Any word on Carole Brooks's son? He will be OK, won't he?'

'I think so. They got him to hospital quickly, and they're monitoring him.' She turned to leave again, then stopped. 'Guv?'

'Uh-huh?'

'Well, Bernard and I are investigating a German MP's daughter, and Maitland's poking around a church. So, we've covered politics and religion.' She smiled. 'But where's the sex?'

'Mona, Mona, Mona.' Paterson pushed himself back from the desk and put his feet up on it again. 'When will you learn? Every case we deal with is really all about sex.'

5

The Edinburgh Health Enforcement Team IT Section operated out of Police Headquarters at Fettes. It wasn't a large team; when Bernard had a brief placement there as part of his induction he'd increased team membership to three. In keeping with the rest of the HET, Personnel had maintained a strict 50/50 balance in recruitment between law enforcement and health professionals. Marcus was tall, extremely thin, and sported little round specs and a ponytail. He had been recruited from the Central Scotland E-crime Unit, while Bryce (shorter and fatter) had been liberated from the bowels of the Edinburgh Royal Infirmary IT Section. Bernard had yet to hear Bryce speak, although his partner made up for it. They were the Penn and Teller of information technology.

'Bernard!' Marcus waved a cheery welcome across the open-plan office. 'Good to see you. Bryce and I were just enjoying the latest conspiracy theories circulating on the forums of the-virus.com.'

'Anything I haven't heard before?' asked Bernard, looking round for a spare chair. He found one with wheels, and had a moment's enjoyment rolling across the carpet to Marcus's desk.

'Nah, the Government is still widely considered to

blame, unless you are of the shaven headed, Doctor Marten-wearing persuasion, in which case you are holding al-Qaida responsible.'

'And God?'

'The Virus being a smiting by the Almighty remains popular in the US, and, I'd say is gaining in popularity over here too. What do you think, Bryce?'

His colleague nodded agreement, without looking up from the computer screen.

'Work is just non-stop entertainment for you guys, isn't it?'

Marcus laughed. 'If you think the conspiracy theories are fun, you should check out the herbal remedies discussion forum.'

'Any good ideas?'

'There seems to be a strong reliance on massive doses of zinc and Vitamin C. The average subscriber to the-virus.com must have pure orange juice running through their veins.'

Bernard wondered what Carole Brooks would think of the conversation. He suspected she sold a lot of Vitamin C in her shop.

'Anyway ...'

'Anyway, back to work ...take a look at this.' Marcus pointed to a picture on his screen of a pretty, dark-haired young woman. 'Not typically German colouring, but something in the cheekbones screams out Teuton.'

'Heidi?'

'Heidi Kristina Weber, indeed. Or Heidi-Hi as her G-mail address has it.'

Bernard smiled. He hadn't expected Heidi to be familiar with 1980s sitcoms. 'Did you find anything useful?'

'That's for you to say, me being merely a humble IT

technician, but I don't think you'll be disappointed.' Marcus leaned back on his chair. 'Have you heard of a group called "The Children of Camus"?'

'Camus? As in the writer?'

'Yep. Very popular with your typical angst-ridden undergraduate looking to pull. Read him myself as a fresher. Did you?'

'I studied Sport Science.'

'My condolences.' He leaned back in his chair and stared at Bernard for a minute. 'Sport Science? Really? I wouldn't have had you down as a meathead jock.'

'I wasn't typical. The other students called me "Prof".'

'Ah – a sensitive and literate soul in an army of philistines. How your life has changed.'

Bernard smiled. 'Anyway . . .'

'Anyway, Camus – as in the writer of "The Plague."'

'Nice. Very topical. Very literary.'

'I thought so. Well, Heidi appears to be a signed-up member of this particular bunch of nutters.'

Bernard spun round on his seat. It was immensely pleasurable. 'What do they believe in?'

Marcus laughed. 'From what I can make out from the ramblings on their website, their main gripes are that the Government did not act quickly enough to tackle the Virus, that pharmaceutical companies know how to cure the Virus but are sitting on it so they can make an even bigger profit out of it, and that the Virus is the result of global warming. I have to hand it to them – they cover a lot of ground in the conspiracy field. Hold on – I'll get it on screen.'

The two of them stared at the site in silence.

Bernard spoke. 'Does it say anywhere what their plan of action is?'

This provoked a shaking of the head. 'Not explicitly, but in my humble role ...'

'As a lowly IT backroom boy ...'

'Exactly. I would draw your attention to a couple of their gripes. Whinge Number One: the Man don't want us kids meeting up in groups of more than twenty – I'm paraphrasing here – cos the Man don't want no opposition to their policies.'

'You think they're organising illegal meet-ups?'

'In my humble opinion. Little bit silly, but they're not the only ones doing that by a long way. Whinge Number Two worries me a lot more. Read this.'

'"Fact: everyone knows that there are a number of combinations of drugs that have been shown to work, but the Government has helped the pharmaceutical industry to suppress that information, to allow them to maximise future profits. Scientific research has demonstrated that a combination of the antidepressant Luprophen and antibiotic Hyrdosol, when taken with high dose Vitamin C has proved an effective prophylactic."' He looked at Marcus. 'Bonkers, but so what? People have been taking this kind of stuff preventatively ever since the Virus started.'

'True,' said Marcus, peering over the top of his specs. 'But what makes Heidi a little bit special is the scale on which she's operating. Check out this e-mail.'

Bernard read the correspondence in Heidi's inbox. 'She's been buying Luprophen and Hyrdosol over the Internet?'

'In massive quantities, at a cost of several thousand pounds.'

Bernard gave a low whistle while he took this in. 'Where's she getting the drugs from?'

'Me-hi-co. And when that little Tijuana surprise arrives, young Heidi-Hi is going to have enough pharmaceuticals to kill herself, and all the other Children of Camus too.'

6

Mona made herself a cup of tea, read her e-mails, tidied her desk, and then, when she really couldn't put it off any longer, opened the diary. Some of the pink fluff from the cover caught under her nail. She pushed the diary to one side of her desk, and opened the envelope she'd received from the German Consulate. She sorted through the pages until she had them in the correct order, and laid them next to the diary.

The first page of the journal was covered in hand-drawn hearts. This confirmed Mona's suspicions about the content of the diaries. She prepared herself for an onslaught of hormonal angst, anticipating an outpouring of concerns about boys, exams, the Virus, perhaps even rants about the world. She turned the page.

The first page of the diary had the date written in the top left-hand corner, and a single line of text.

Morley's. Alle waren da. Eine gute Zeit hatten alle. Gott segne K!!!

She flicked across to the translated pages.

Morley's. Everyone was there. Good night had by all. God bless K!!!

She thought back to her visit to the pub earlier that day. Was Morley's really where students went for a good time these days? When she was in uniform, a student would have been taking their life in their hands drinking there. She read on.

Railway Tavern. Eine tolle Nacht. Dr Beeching wäre stolz gewesen. K rocks!

Railway Tavern. The kind of night Dr Beeching would be proud of. K rocks!

Mona went into her drawer and pulled out a Yellow Pages. She leafed through it, then checked her suspicions on the Internet. Nowhere could she find any evidence that there was a pub in Edinburgh called the Railway Tavern. She searched further afield, and found Railway Taverns in Prestonpans, Lochgelly and Bathgate. She noted these down, but again, doubted that these would be regular haunts for students.

She worked methodically through the diary noting dates, but it appeared that the only places Heidi socialised were these two pubs. None of the entries was longer than two sentences, and there was little mention of friends or family. It was like reading a code. And who was K?

She closed the diary and sat staring at it. A thought occurred to her. She opened the first page of the diary and slipped her finger under the pink fluffy cover. With a bit of manoeuvring the cover came off. As she suspected, there was something written there.

So Wise So Young, They Say Do Never Live Long

Song lyrics? she wondered. Poetry?

'All right if I . . .?'

Mona jumped at the sound of the voice. It was one of the cleaners, who was standing in the doorway brandishing a vacuum cleaner.

Mona looked at her watch. 6.05pm. 'Sorry, I didn't realise the time.'

'I could do next door and then come back, if you like.'

'Thanks.'

Bernard still hadn't returned to the office. She grabbed her phone and speed-dialled his number.

'Where are you?'

It was noisy. 'On the bus.'

'Going where?'

There was a brief pause and in the background Mona could hear someone asking to get past Bernard.

'Home. It was after five when I got through with IT.'

'After five?' Mona almost dropped the phone in frustration. 'For God's sake, Bernard, we've got a Health Defaulter here, you can't just clock off at teatime.'

There was a long silence at the other end of the phone. She sat on her rage and asked a question. 'So, what did you find out at IT?'

Mona listened in silence while Bernard updated her about The Children of Camus. 'That sounds important, Bernard. If she is messing about with drugs it does make it more likely that she is in some kind of trouble.' Mona was beginning to reconsider her earlier flippancy about the case. 'I really think you need to come back to the office.'

There was another long pause before Bernard spoke. 'I'll see you tomorrow, Mona.'

Mona slammed the phone down and looked round for someone to complain to. She stared over at Paterson's room. She didn't want to drop Bernard in it but, Jesus, you couldn't just clock off at five like you were working at Tesco or something. People's lives depended on their work. She walked over and knocked on Paterson's door. Without waiting for an invite she went in.

It was deserted. The L & B mug was washed and draining neatly by the kettle, and Paterson's coat was gone.

'Does anyone give a shit about this apart from me?' she said to the empty room. In reply, her phone rang.

'Mona.' Paterson's voice. 'I need you and Bernard at HQ now. You-Know-Who wants to talk to us about this German lassie.'

'Bernard's gone for the day.'

'What? At . . .'

She could picture the Guv looking at his watch.

'Ten past six?'

'Mm,' she said, trying not to get her partner into any further trouble.

'Though,' the Guv sounded thoughtful, 'possibly for the best. I can do without a Bernard indiscretion in front of our glorious leader. How quickly can you get here?'

'Quarter of an hour?'

Paterson hung up, which she took to mean satisfaction with her proposed timescale. She picked up her coat and walked out the door, pausing only to turn out the light. She poked her head into the neighbouring office. 'It's all yours.'

The cleaner gave a wave of acknowledgement.

Paterson looked furious.

'Fifty-five minutes I've been sitting here, and all he's done is stick his head out and say, "I thought you'd have the HET officers with you". He could have asked me to bring you when he phoned. Bloody mind games, this is. Arseho—'

'John! Always a pleasure.'

The Chief Executive of the Scottish Health Enforcement

Partnership appeared in the doorway of the room, and gave a smile of such insincerity that she could see the Guv fighting the urge to give his superior a swift right hook. Instead he smiled back and extended his hand in greeting.

'Cameron. This is Mona Whyte, the HET officer working on the case.'

The SHEP boss looked at her for a minute. 'Rab Whyte's daughter, is that right?'

'Yes.'

'And your partner?'

'Unfortunately he's been detained, Sir.'

'Perhaps for the best. Easier to speak freely amongst ourselves.'

Cameron was also a Police secondee. Despite the Government trumpeting the benefits of the fully integrated Police/Health interface of the HET, in reality most staff had brought their previous mindsets with them. Mona and Paterson had shared many raised eyebrows at the naïvety of their health colleagues, while she'd frequently seen Carole and Bernard huddled together moaning, usually about something politically incorrect Paterson had said. Small wonder, then, that the SHEP chief thought there would be a freer exchange without any health do-gooders involved.

Cameron held open the large oak door leading to his room.

'Nice offices you've got here,' said Paterson.

The SHEP boss looked round the wooden panelling of his office, as if he was seeing it for the first time. 'Not bad, is it? We're very grateful to the City Council for accommodating us.' He motioned to them to sit, and walked over to the window and looked out. 'I'm told it's a bugger during the Festival though, after all, we're right on the High Street here.'

'My heart bleeds for you, truly it does.'

Cameron laughed and returned to his desk. Mona settled herself into a supremely comfortable wood and leather chair, and wondered what her chances were of smuggling it out of the building and back to the office.

'So, John, this German lassie. When and where will she be turning up?'

Paterson leaned his head back and contemplated the ornate wooden ceiling. '2pm Wednesday on the top of Arthur's Seat.' He looked straight at Cameron. 'How do I know?'

Cameron gave an icy smile. 'I remember your penchant for sarcasm from the days when I used to work for you.'

'And now you've leapfrogged over my head to the dizzy heights of Chief Executive of SHEP you don't need to listen to it anymore.'

'Certainly be harder to hear it if you get moved on to traffic duty.'

Paterson snorted. 'Oh, don't threaten me with being pensioned off. I'm already at the arse-end of policing in the HET. Traffic duty would be a step up from managing the team you landed me with.' He smiled at Mona. 'Present company excluded.' Cameron laughed. 'Who've you got?'

'Aside from the undoubted talents of Ms Whyte here, I've got two health freaks, and a PC with eighteen months' experience.'

There was a knock on the door, and a secretary entered carrying a tray with three cups of tea, and a plate of biscuits. She shot them both a cheery smile and left without saying a word.

'China cups, Cameron. Nothing but the best.'

'Well, I knew you were coming, John, so I requested them specially.' Cameron poured tea into all the cups. 'So, the German lassie?'

'Now to answer the question you should have asked me, we're not yet sure if this German lassie has run off with a boyfriend or is lying in a coma somewhere, but we're working on it.'

'But you are on top of it?'

Paterson leaned forward, and the leather chair creaked under his weight. 'What's the deal here? I thought you lot didn't get involved in individual cases?'

'We don't. We're not getting involved now, in fact. Just keeping an eye on the politics of the case.'

'Granted the father's a politician, but I'm not even sure that anyone in Berlin's heard of him.'

Cameron laughed. 'A little bird tells me that may be about to change, and I don't want the Press over here making something out of it.'

'Any chance you could share this tiny sparrow's input with me?'

'Nothing to tell, John, just backroom gossip. But just in case, get your staff focused on this, get her found, and get her into a Health Check before this turns into a diplomatic incident.'

'Wouldn't want to interfere with you getting your knighthood, Cam.' He put his cup back on the table. 'Why us?'

'What do you mean, "why us?" She's a Health Defaulter – it's your territory.'

'Granted. But a sensitive case like this could be dealt with directly by yourselves, or the Police. I mean, the HET's just . . .' He tailed off.

'Just for show?' finished Cameron, with a smile on his face. 'Just there to reassure voters that Health Defaulters are actually being tracked down? Just there as a nice piece of window dressing on the real work undertaken by the Health Service?'

Mona could see Paterson was gripping the side of his chair very tightly.

'We provide a lot of reassurance for the public,' said Paterson.

Mona wondered if he really thought that. She didn't.

Cameron smirked. 'I'm sure we all sleep easier at night, knowing that you're around.' His gaze fell on Mona. 'Not the most exciting of career moves for you, Ms Whyte, I wouldn't have thought?'

Damn right, thought Mona, but the Guv's barely contained rage made her think better of agreeing.

'I wouldn't say that, Sir,' she settled for.

'Very diplomatic. We could use the talents of someone like you after all this Virus stuff blows over. Certainly would be good to get your perspective on how things are going at the HET, from time to time?'

'We're going.' The Guv stood up. 'That's if you're quite finished trying to get my staff to spy on me?'

Cameron waved in the direction of the door. 'Be my guest.' He smiled at Mona. 'Don't let your boss steal the china on the way out.'

7

Bernard put his keys into the door of his flat, and, quiet as the night, pushed the door open. He stood for a second, letting his eye bounce round the hallway, from the table to the floor, to the open door of their tiny kitchen. This was his nightly routine, surveying his room for clues, looking for anything that would give him a warning about his wife's state of mind. He could hear the television playing in the lounge; this was good. She was out of bed, at the very least. There had been too many evenings when he'd come home from the HET only to find the house in darkness, and an inert figure under a duvet.

An object lying on the table caught his eye, its black plastic weighing down a small pile of unopened mail. A hairdryer! This was a positive sign. Doctor Sutherland had said that taking an interest in her appearance was a definite sign of recovery. Bernard leaned down, switched off the socket, and unplugged the device. He was glad his wife had started to blow dry her hair again, but he didn't want to die in a hairdressing-related inferno.

Time to brave the living room. He had a final look at himself in the hall mirror, and practised a smile. A nervous-looking man, slightly balding at the temples, and holding a large bunch of yellow roses, smiled warily back. He reached for the door, and stepped through into the living room of their flat.

'Happy Birthday, Carrie.'

Bernard's wife didn't look round from her seat in the middle of their stripy sofa. She seemed to be concentrating all her efforts on watching a celebrity chef produce a meal for four from a list of preordained ingredients. He shook his head. If Carrie had spent as much time cooking or eating over the last year as she had watching cookery shows she wouldn't be such a bag of bones.

He hugged the flowers to his chest, and tried to guess her mood from looking at the back of her head. She didn't appear to be crying, but he'd been caught out before. He took a step forward to get a better look and check that she wasn't still wearing pyjamas. He could see a jean-encased leg and furry-socked foot resting on the coffee table. He tiptoed up behind her and held the blooms in front of her face.

She sat up in surprise, then laughed.

'I didn't hear you come in. These are lovely.' She took the offering from him and sniffed the petals, then reached over and hugged him. 'And to think I didn't believe you when you said you'd be home at six.'

'Don't feel bad – I nearly had to go back to the office.' He shivered at the thought of his partner's fury on the phone. 'But I told them your birthday definitely comes first.'

Carrie stood up and kissed him. There was the slightest smell of alcohol on her breath. Bernard flinched, and his mind flew back to his last meeting with Dr Sutherland, in his airless, book-filled office at the back of the Sick Kids. While Carrie had been with the nurse, Dr Sutherland had warned him about the possibility of relapse, then yawned. He'd been full of apologies, which Bernard had shrugged away, while yawning himself. It was a late-night appointment, and he'd guessed the doctor had been working since 9am, in a futile attempt to see every bereaved parent who required counselling. He'd wondered idly to Carrie what Dr Sutherland would do when they found a cure for the Virus. She'd shrugged.

'He'll go back to traffic accidents and meningitis, I suppose.'

Bernard's mind came back to the present and he pulled away. His wife didn't notice, and got to her feet. She stumbled a little as she stepped past him, and he put out a hand to steady her. She took his hand, put it to her lips and kissed it, then walked on through to the kitchen. He followed, hovering in the doorway while she rooted around in the cupboards until she found a vase. Carrie arranged the flowers to her satisfaction, and placed them on the window ledge.

'So, how was work?' she asked.

'Oh, same as always. Eight hours spent in the company of people who hate me.' He hesitated. 'And you ...what did you do with your day?'

Carrie shrugged. 'Not much. Met Mum for lunch,' she turned back to the sink, 'then went to the cemetery.'

Bernard looked at her back. It was her birthday, maybe he should let it go. He grappled with his conscience for a minute and decided he couldn't. 'I thought we'd agreed ...'

'Agreed what?'

She spun round, and he was subjected to his second lot of female wrath of the day.

'That I wouldn't go there because it upsets me too much? Well, tough. It's my birthday and if I want to spend it with my dead son I think that's up to me.'

'OK, OK.' Bernard put his hands up in surrender and did his best to change the subject. 'So, are we eating out tonight? What do you fancy? Mexican?'

It was too late, and Carrie's tears were already in full flow.

'We could eat in?'

'Oh, forget the food. Thirty-eight, Bernard, I'm thirty-eight years old.'

He stared at his feet. They'd had this discussion so many times it wasn't even an argument now, it was a ritual.

Carrie stood in front of him and put her hands on his chest. 'I want us to have another baby, and we're running out of time.'

He took her hands in his, and kissed them. 'We talked about this . . .'

She pulled her hands away. 'No – you talked. The only thing that could make this whole situation bearable is the thought of another child.' She sobbed. 'It's the only thing that could make things better.'

'Better?' Bernard felt an uncontrollable wave of anger rising from his chest, anger that he knew should be directed at anyone other than his wife. He took a deep breath and lowered his voice. 'You want us to bring a tiny, helpless creature into this world to take its chances with the Virus? And what if this baby dies?'

His wife stood crying, her shoulders shaking with the vast unrestrained sorrow of a child, or a drunk. Once her weeping would have destroyed him, but these days it just seemed to make him angrier.

'Carrie, remember what we went through when Jamie died?' His own memories of the time were blurred, a montage of hospitals, and cemeteries, and support groups full of other bereaved parents. His tone was gentler. 'I'm scared what would happen if we had another child.'

He went to touch her but she pushed him away, and ran from the room. He followed her into the hall, and was horrified to see her putting on her coat.

'Carrie, don't go out.' He put a hand on her shoulder. 'Stay. We can talk about this, as much as you want.'

She shook his hand off. 'What's the point? You've made your mind up.'

He noticed she had her car keys in her hand. 'Carrie, you can't drive. You've been drinking.'

'No, I haven't.'

'Give them to me, Carrie.' He made a grab for the keys and they fell to the floor. Carrie lifted her hand and slapped him as hard as she could, then clasped her hand to her mouth, her eyes wide with horror.

The two of them stared at each other for a moment, then Carrie wrenched open the door and fled.

Bernard picked up the keys and put them in his pocket. He stood still for a moment, grateful for the silence. Dr Sutherland had told them that anger was good, that anger was a sign of moving on, of healing. It didn't feel like that from where Bernard was standing. He touched his cheek. This felt like war. This felt like fighting a battle day after day with the one person he should be caring for. Was it like this for the traffic accident parents, or the meningitis-bereaved? Or was this hell just for those robbed by the Virus? Or worse still, was it just for them?

Bernard kicked off his shoes, and placed them neatly under the hall table. The first time Carrie had hit him, he'd been devastated; the second time, he'd been furious. Now he just felt numb. He wandered slowly through to the kitchen. He contemplated looking in the fridge, then changed his mind and reached for a takeaway menu.

Her mother was looking old.

She seemed to have lost even more weight in the past couple of weeks. The skin across her nose was stretched tight, and her cheekbones jutted out, overshadowing her cheeks. Mona thought how easy it was, when your whole life revolved around the Virus, to forget the millions of other diseases there were out there, mutating, and replicating, and seeking out weakness. She wondered if her mother was getting the correct care. Had she seen the oncologist again? With the Virus consuming hospital resources, you needed to fight for treatment for any other illness.

'Come through.'

Her mother waved her past and she wandered down the narrow hall into the living room. It looked the same as always; the cream sofa was immaculate and everything was hoovered and dusted to perfection. The room felt cold, though, and Mona wondered if her mother was economising.

'I've not heard from you for a while.'

Mona heard the accusation under the mild tone. 'It's only been a couple of weeks, Mum.' She wondered how often other people visited their mothers – *was* two weeks a long time? Bernard, she knew from his endless chatter, spoke to his mother two or three times a week on the phone. Maitland – Christ, Maitland was probably round his mother's every night looking for a free meal and his washing done.

'I'm just saying.' Her mother hovered by the living room door. 'Shall I stick the kettle on?'

'No, don't bother. I actually popped round to have a look at some of my old stuff.'

Her mother nodded, knowingly. That explains it, her expression read. It's not like my daughter to drop in just to chat.

Feeling guilty, Mona was about to change her mind on the offer of tea, but her mother had vanished into the dark of the kitchen.

'Well, you know where your room is.'

Mona sat on the floor of her old room and reached under the bed. She pulled out a suitcase, and noted the lack of dust on top of it. Her mother's cleaning reached everywhere. The case was locked with a numerical padlock. After a minute or two's contemplation she put the correct combination in. 2-8-0-6. Her father's birthday. She smiled. How predictable.

Two years and three months since her father had passed away. She wondered what he would make of her work at the HET; the Virus had barely been an issue when he died. There'd been discussion of a new strain of influenza. European flu they'd called it at first in the UK papers, due to the ongoing inability of Fleet Street to recognise that Britain was, in fact, located in Europe. There had been the usual talk of epidemics, and pictures of teenagers in Barcelona wearing facemasks, but no-one had really thought much of it, desensitised by the threats of Avian flu and SARS epidemics that never materialised. She was glad her dad had been spared the panics of the past few years.

She lifted the lid of the suitcase and stared at the ephemera of her teenage years: a bundle of letters, a couple of Valentine cards, and six hardback notebooks with varied covers. Her diaries. She picked one up at random and started to read.

Dance practice. Good rehearsal for end of term show. Hockey. League game against St Christy's. Scored two goals but still lost 6-3.

Terse. Limited. As if written by a girl with a secret.

TUESDAY

FINDING RELIGION

I

'You're in early.'

Mona looked up to see Bernard standing in the office doorway. She gave him a wave and tried to force her features into some shape that didn't reveal her deep irritation. She'd been relying on some quiet time in the office to have another attempt at Heidi's journal. It was her own fault, she supposed, for bawling him out last night. He'd suddenly developed a work ethic.

'I don't think my wife is speaking to me.'

He wandered toward her, sighed loudly, and loitered by her chair, playing idly with the pink fluff of the diary. She was wrong. He wasn't here because he was worried about the case; he was just avoiding his other half. And was that a black eye? She'd enquire later, once she'd got these diaries cracked.

Her partner continued to hover around her desk, raising the awful possibility in Mona's mind that he wanted to have a heart-to-heart with her about his marital troubles. Really, Bernard? I'm the best you can do? Lived alone since I left my parents, not even a cat; I'm your surest bet? *Poor bastard.*

She edged the diary away from his fingers. 'Oh well, I'm sure she'll get over it.'

Bernard didn't move. She resigned herself to a conversation but decided to move it on to safer ground.

'What have you got there?' She pointed to the Waterstones bag he had under his arm.

'I thought this might be useful.' He delved into the carrier and produced a book.

'*The Plague* by Camus,' she read. The cover was illustrated with the picture of a scythe. It looked a cheery read.

'I thought it might give us an insight into what The Children of Camus were up to.'

'Good idea. Best get on and start reading it.'

Bernard was still failing to take the hint when Maitland appeared and sat on her desk.

'Morning, all.'

She elbowed him in the back. 'Hoi, get your fat arse off my desk!'

'Sorry,' he grinned, but stayed put. 'Didn't mean to intrude on your discussion about literature, but I just wanted to tell you I heard from Carole.'

'Oh, God – how is Michael?' She hadn't thought about her colleague since she left the hospital. A tiny tremor of guilt ran down her spine.

'Apparently they had a big scare about 3am when his temperature spiked – you know, lights flashing, doctors appearing from nowhere. Michael got whisked off to intensive care, with Carole left sitting there on her own.'

'Poor woman,' said Bernard. 'How is Michael now?'

'Out of danger.' Maitland rested his foot on the edge of Mona's chair, who immediately slapped it back off. 'Although the hospital will be keeping him in for a few days.'

'Well, that's good.' Mona wondered how long she had to wait before turning the subject back to work. 'Anyway . . .'

'Do you think we should send her some flowers?' asked Maitland.

'Flowers?' Mona was always amazed at how well Maitland and his partner got on. She seemed to find him considerably less annoying than the rest of the office did. Mona put it down to Carole consuming one too many of the herbal relaxation tablets her shop sold. Nobody could spend all day with Maitland and actually like him.

'Not flowers,' said Bernard. 'They don't let you take them into hospital these days.'

'Anyway, about Morley's . . .'

Bernard continued as though she hadn't spoken. 'Though I suppose we could pop out and visit her later?'

'Can I get a word in edgeways?'

The two of them stopped talking and turned toward her, two sets of eyebrows raised in surprise. She felt a little foolish.

'I just wanted to draw your attention to the fact that Morley's features in both the Heidi Weber and the Colette Greenwood investigations.'

'Really?' said Maitland. 'How come?' He rested his trainer back on Mona's chair.

'Seriously, put your foot there again and I'll chop it off.'

He smirked but moved his lanky frame onto his own chair.

'So, to recap, Colette Greenwood, student, missed her Health Check last week. Last known sightings were church on Sunday night followed by a night out with her Christian pals in Morley's. Would you have Morley's down as the kind of place three God-fearing girlies would go?'

'No.'

'Though Maitland's better placed than us to know,' said Bernard, smiling, 'seeing as he is a regular at Pastor Mackenzie's church.'

'No, I'm not.' Maitland glared at Bernard. 'Are you having a go, shortass?'

Mona tried to work out if Bernard was joking. She guessed from Maitland's irritation there was something of substance in her partner's remark. 'Really? I know you said your girlfriend was a churchgoer but I didn't know you were.'

'No, I just went a couple of times with Emma to keep her company.'

'He thinks the Pastor's an arsehole though.'

'Shut up, Bernard.' Maitland's annoyance manifested itself in a half-hearted kick in Bernard's direction.

Mona grinned. 'Anyway, at the same time, Heidi Weber, also a student, with a German MP for a dad, is missing. According to her diary, she is also a regular at Morley's. Would you have Morley's down as the kind of place the daughter of a politician would hang out?'

'I wouldn't really have Morley's down as the kind of place anyone would go if they weren't actively looking for drugs, or a good rammy.' Maitland's bad mood appeared to be ebbing, being replaced by something more reflective. 'Especially in this day and age. I can't imagine anywhere you'd be more likely to catch something.'

Mona looked from Bernard to Maitland, and back. 'Coincidence?'

'What are you lot jabbering about?' Paterson walked into the room, opened his office door, and threw his briefcase in the direction of his desk.

Mona turned round in her seat. 'We're discussing the Edinburgh institution that is Morley's.'

'Morley's?' Paterson walked over to them. 'Victor Thompson's gaff?'

'Yup.'

'It's a hole!' said Paterson. 'What's our interest in it?'

'Both our No Shows were regulars there,' said Mona. 'Neither of them what I'd call the usual clientele.'

'Interesting.' Paterson looked thoughtful. 'Anyone paying him another visit?'

Mona raised a hand. 'I was thinking about it.'

Paterson let out a long whistle. 'Tough place, Morley's.' He folded his arms. 'You know the only way to get in and out safely?'

Mona waited for the punchline.

'Don't eat a thing while you are in there. I had the shits for about two days after one of their bar lunches.'

Mona smiled. 'Thanks.'

'So, let's prioritise this Morley's thing. Mona, you and Bernard head over there now, see if you can speak to Vic again.'

'I can't, Guv,' she checked her watch, 'I'm due at the University for 9.30, to see Heidi Weber's Religious Studies tutor.'

'Professor Withington?' asked Maitland.

'Yes.' She frowned. 'How did ...?'

'He's on my list of people to speak to about Colette Greenwood.' Maitland drummed his fingers on the desk. 'Another connection between these cases. Can I tag along?'

'Oh, God. I suppose so. Would be good to follow up the Morley's angle soon, though.' She shot a doubtful look at her partner. 'I suppose Bernard could still go, Guv.'

'Not keen for Brains here to venture into Morley's solo.' He thought for a moment. 'Tell you what – I'll go with him.'

95

'Really, Mr Paterson?' There was an edge of panic to Bernard's voice.

'Yeah. It'll be educational.'

'Who for?' asked Mona, picking up her bag, and smiled.

The University of Edinburgh Faculty of Divinity was a near neighbour of the castle. Mona and Maitland stood staring at its twin-towered grandeur.

'Is this the right place?' Maitland peered suspiciously at their destination.

'Yes,' said Mona, irritably. 'I told you before that it was the building at the top of the Mound where lots of shit happened during the Festival, and here it is. Just picture it with a huge Fringe banner hanging on it.'

'Hmm, actually that does kind of ring a bell. I think I saw some bloke doing stand-up there last year.' Persuaded that they were in the right place, he began to walk.

'Was he good?'

'Nah. I think I heckled him.'

Of course you did, thought Mona.

Maitland nudged her. 'It's a masterpiece of Gothic architecture, you know.'

She looked at him in surprise. 'Did Bernard tell you that?'

'Yup. And did you realise that the piece of ground under John Knox's statue actually belongs to the Church of Scotland?'

'Fantastic. Now I've got Maitland and Bernard all rolled into one, and twice as annoying.'

Maitland grinned and walked up to the courtyard gates. He held his card against the Health Card barrier, which gave a satisfied beep and let him through. When

96

Mona caught up with Maitland he was pointing at something over her shoulder.

'Say hi to John Knox.'

She turned to look at the statue of the preacher, one arm aloft and the Good Book tucked firmly under the other. She spun back to see Maitland bounding on ahead, up the wide stone stairs and into the building. She ran after him, muttering.

'I don't see any directions.' Maitland frowned.

'Let's start walking. There's sure to be a sign.'

They wandered the corridors of the Faculty looking for the correct office. The number of young women they passed surprised her. She'd expected the place to be full of serious young chaps with beards.

'Shall we ask someone?'

A girl with dreadlocks and a floor-length skirt was reading a noticeboard. Maitland went up to her and asked where they could find the Professor. The student said nothing, just pointed over her shoulder at the door directly behind her. Professor Withington.

He smiled his thanks and Mona knocked on the tutor's door.

'Come.'

'Professor Withington?'

The don didn't look up when they walked in, just carried on reading. His appearance – male, bearded, sixty-something – fitted closely Mona's idea of what a divinity prof should look like. She gazed at the room's book-lined walls for a few seconds then coughed. The tutor raised his head and took off his glasses.

'Are you my students?'

'No.' Maitland stepped forward and offered his ID card. 'We're from the Health Enforcement Team.'

The Professor put his specs back on and examined it closely.

'I'm sorry,' he said, passing Maitland his card back, and gesturing them to sit down all in the one smooth motion. 'What is that?'

Mona sat down in a cracked leather chair. 'We're the agency that traces people who have missed a Health Check – you know, your monthly ...'

'Yes, yes,' said the tutor, with a wave of his hand. 'An annoyance, but a necessary evil in these times. Sorry, I was aware such an agency existed, I just didn't realise that was your name.'

'Absolutely, Sir. If you've never missed a Health Check you wouldn't have encountered us.'

A light appeared to go on in the don's eyes. 'Is this about Heidi Weber? The memo I sent to Student Health Services?'

'The memo?'

'Yes, Heidi missed a tutorial yesterday, so I fired off an e-mail to Student Health Services – we have all kinds of protocols for these things now.'

'We're currently looking for two of your students who have missed Health Checks, Heidi Weber and another girl called Colette Greenwood. Although I must warn you that under the terms of the Health Enforcement and Defaulter Recovery Act you are not allowed to tell anyone else that we are seeking them.'

'Of course.' He frowned. 'I know both the students, but I wasn't aware they were friends.'

'We don't think they are together, but there are a number of similarities in their background that lead us to believe that their disappearance might be related. Has Colette missed any tutorials?'

'I'll have to check my records.' He reached behind him for a folder. 'Colette is such a reticent girl, doesn't speak up much in class. I can't remember off the top of my head . . . ah, here we are. If I can read my own handwriting correctly, it says "C Greenwood absent but friend said she is sick with stomach upset."'

Cover 4 me at uni.

'And is Heidi equally shy?'

He laughed, a surprisingly deep and warm sound. 'Oh, goodness me, no. Heidi is a very opinionated young woman. A real pleasure to teach.'

'So,' said Mona. 'Any thoughts at all where either girl might be?'

'Parents?'

'Our first port of call.' Maitland joined in. 'Both sets haven't heard from their girls, and obviously, are now very worried, but they couldn't think where the girls would be. Or why they'd run off, for that matter. It appears to be out of character in both cases. What kind of information do you hold about your students?'

'Not much, to be honest,' said Professor Withington. He started tapping at his computer. 'Really just name, address, grades, and of course in this day and age, their Health Status. Let me pull up Colette's record.' He swivelled the screen round to face them. 'Is that her?'

Mona looked at the on-screen picture of a teenage girl. She had long, straight, blonde hair, high cheekbones and blue eyes.

'Wow,' said Maitland, leaning in for a closer look. 'Her Health Check photograph really didn't do her justice.'

'Yes, she's a pretty one.' His face clouded. 'You don't think anything has happened to her? Or to Heidi?'

'No,' said Mona. 'Colette's friends seem to think it is

"boy trouble". We're not so sure about Heidi, but it will probably turn out to be nothing.'

Withington looked unconvinced. 'But a lot of the people you look for must be in serious trouble. I mean, a number of the people you are seeking must have missed their checks because they have contracted the Virus?' He doodled thoughtfully on the edge of one of his papers. 'Could Colette or Heidi be,' he paused, 'dead?'

'Unlikely, Sir,' said Mona. 'In the six months I've been with the HET, we've had five, maybe six, deaths. A few of the people we've found do have the Virus, but by and large they are people with chaotic lives – junkies or whatever – who just can't get themselves together enough to attend their Health Check.'

The tutor's eyes widened. 'You don't think drugs could be an issue here, do you?'

A few weeks ago, she would have discounted the idea, but now she wasn't so sure.

They left the Faculty, and stood at the traffic lights at the top of the Mound. The green man came on and Mona stepped out into the road, then realised that Maitland wasn't following.

'Come on! I want to go and follow up Heidi's flatmate.'

Maitland didn't move. 'I'm going to head over to the Students' Union on Potterrow and check out the posters. Maybe someone is advertising events at Morley's.'

'That's a shit idea.'

'Yeah,' said Maitland, starting to walk. 'Well, that's what I'm planning to do and unless you've got a better idea I suggest you join me.'

'I've got plenty of suggestions, like we follow up my

100

Defaulter, the one we are supposed to be throwing all our resources at?'

Her colleague seemed indifferent to the logic of this argument as his pace quickened, and he disappeared round the corner.

Mona tutted, but started to run. 'Ten minutes, Maitland, then we're going.'

'Told you this was a crap idea.'

In amongst all the posters for Happy Hours, 2-4-1 offers, and Intimate Gatherings for Non-Immunes, she couldn't find a single mention of Morley's.

'There must be something here.' Maitland was unwilling to admit defeat. 'I'm going to check the other wall.'

He strode across the concourse, dodging around the tables, students, and pot plants.

'Suit yourself,' she shouted after him. 'I'm going to get a drink, then we're heading to Marchmont.'

She strode toward the coffee shop, buoyed up by having being proved right. The weather had picked up, and the spring sunshine was streaming through the transparent dome that served as a roof to the building. She ordered an Americano from the impossibly young assistant, debated about ordering a muffin, then decided against it. As she emerged from the café she saw a familiar, curly-haired figure bounding across the floor of Potterrow, in the general direction of Maitland. Kate.

Mona walked slowly in the direction of her colleague, wondering whether to announce her presence. Maybe her colleague would be better handling this one-to-one, turning on the charm that everyone seemed so certain he had.

'Hello,' said Kate, to Maitland's back.

He turned round, his face registering surprise as he saw who it was. Kate was waving a piece of paper at him. 'This saves me a phone call – I've got an address for Donny.'

He took the offered information, looked at it, then folded it up and stuck it in his inside pocket. 'Thanks.'

She stood staring at him, her head on one side and hand on her hip. 'Fancy a drink?'

'I can't consume alcohol when I'm working.'

Idiot, thought Mona. Get her into a pub, have a lemonade, get her talking about what's going on with her friend.

Kate laughed. 'That wasn't what I meant. I don't drink. I was more thinking coffee at Teviot.'

Maitland was smiling that annoying little grin of his. 'In a Students' Union? I'm not sure they'd let me in.'

'Oh, come on, I'm sure you just flash that pass of yours and you get in anywhere.'

Was Kate flirting with Maitland? His appeal to women definitely eluded Mona. Maybe it was a pheromone thing. She wondered what to do. She didn't fancy waiting around for him, and debated with herself whether to follow up Heidi's flatmate solo, or head back to the office.

She watched them walk toward the door of Potterrow.

'So, Kate, you don't have sex, you don't drink …' her colleague's voice drifted across to her ' … isn't student life wasted on you?'

She cringed, and decided Maitland couldn't be trusted not to cock this up. She put her coffee on the table, and ran after them.

'Hoi!'

The two of them turned round. Kate looked surprised,

and Maitland smirked over the top of the student's head.

'Can I join you?'

The three of them walked through the arched doorway of the Teviot Row House Students' Union.

'This is nice,' said Maitland, looking round at the polished wood walls. 'Very olde worlde.'

'It's the oldest purpose-built Students' Union in the world.'

'Really?' Maitland elbowed Mona. 'We'll have to remember that one to tell Bernard.'

They showed their health cards to the doorman, who made a point of reading each one in turn. Kate led the way, and they followed her up the broad stone steps in silence. Mona read the posters on the wall as she climbed: an obligatory *Phone Help Don't Approach* advert, two posters advising people to cover their mouths and keep their distance, and, just for variety, a warning about AIDS. Did students still have casual sex? If they did, they were the only ones. Promiscuity in the Virus age was definitely out of fashion; it was up there with nightclubs, cinemas and public transport as things best avoided if possible.

The cafeteria was quiet; it was still too early for the lunchtime rush. Kate walked swiftly up to a table, dumping her bag on one chair and herself on another, her curly hair bouncing as she sat.

'Mine's a coffee, milk no sugar.'

'So I'm buying, am I?'

Maitland looked irritated, and Mona felt a surge of alarm. Kate being here was a gift to their investigation, and her colleague was going to blow it because he was too tight to spring for a couple of coffees. Fortunately,

Kate didn't appear to have noticed his annoyance, and sat curling her hair round her finger.

'I'm a poor student.' She folded her arms and looked up at him, a smile of expectation on her face.

Maitland tutted, and stomped off toward the tills.

Mona smiled a silent apology. 'I'll give him a hand.'

Her colleague was clattering cups onto a tray.

'What was all that about?' she asked.

'These students have such a bloody sense of entitlement. She lied to us, and now she expects me to run round after her.'

'She's a good-looking girl – and she is just a girl – of course she's used to men running after her.' Mona put a third cup and saucer onto the tray. 'And we want information from her.'

Maitland looked back over at Kate. 'She is a bit of all right, isn't she?'

Mona glared at him. 'That's not exactly professional, is it?'

'OK, sorry, I've just had an excess of wood-panelling today. Look,' he picked up three cakes and put them on the tray, 'peace offerings all round.'

In spite of herself, Mona smiled. She headed back toward the table, and over her shoulder said, 'You're still paying, though.'

Kate returned her smile, a little uncertainly, as she sat down.

Maitland appeared, placed the spoils on the table, and settled himself onto a chair. 'So, Morley's.'

'What about it?'

'I just think it's an odd choice of night out.'

She shrugged, but Mona thought she seemed slightly uncomfortable.

104

'And did Colette often suggest that you go to pubs frequented by bikers? Did she enjoy a good bar brawl?'

'Don't be silly.' Kate smiled at Maitland. 'It was just somewhere to go.'

'And you spent the night arguing about religion?'

Kate giggled. 'We are Divinity students.'

'And what were the finer points of your discussion? In words a heathen like me might understand?' Maitland winked. Mona had to work to stop herself rolling her eyes.

'We were discussing the active and reactive approaches to Mission.'

'That sounds fascinating.'

'I understand that religion is not your thing, Mr Stevenson.' Kate sighed. 'Can we talk about something else?'

There was a brief silence. 'OK, what do you think of Pastor Mackenzie?'

Kate's face went through a number of contortions, all of them denoting surprise. She put down the remains of her cake and smiled. 'You know Malcolm?'

'I spoke to him about Colette, and I'd value your opinion about him.'

'I think he's completely inspirational.'

Mona stood on Maitland's foot to warn him not to express an opinion. 'In what way?'

Kate thought for a minute. 'Well, with all this Virus stuff. He's been fantastic at helping people cope with all the uncertainty.'

'And people are grateful for that?'

The colour was rising in Kate's cheeks. 'It's just a shame some of the things that people say about him.'

Maitland pulled his foot out from under Mona's and spoke. 'Like what?'

'Like total nonsense. Malcolm has been magnificent at supporting people through the Virus, but some people are just ...'

'Just what?' asked Mona.

Kate looked at her watch. 'I've got a lecture to go to.' She got to her feet, leaving her cake unfinished. 'Good luck finding Donny.'

Maitland watched her hurry out the door.

'You know what, Mona?'

'What?'

'That girl has got a really fine arse.'

2

'Well, Bernard, this is fun, isn't it?'

Paterson smiled at him. He slouched further down in his seat, arms folded, watching the streets flash by the car window. He had a sneaking suspicion that his discomfort made Paterson feel more cheerful. If his boss wanted to make him miserable, let him. He couldn't make him feel worse than his wife already had. She had returned to their flat in the early hours of the morning, and they hadn't yet spoken.

'So, the way I see it, Bern, we go down there, throw a few chairs about until Vic Thompson tells us what the hell is going on.'

'Throw some chairs about?' He attempted to sit upright, but was trapped by the seat belt. 'Is that, strictly speaking, legal, Mr Paterson?'

'Metaphorical chairs, Bernie, metaphorical chairs.' Paterson grinned. 'Can't bloody touch people's property these days. I remember once, when I'd just started in the Force . . .'

'I think that's us here.' Bernard pointed to the railings outside Morley's, glad of the excuse to stop his boss's reminiscences of violence past. Paterson slammed on the brakes and looked round for a place to park. He reversed back a couple of car lengths into an available space. Bernard got out and stared pointedly at the double yellow lines under the back wheels of the car.

'Something to say, Bernie?'

He opened his mouth, then thought better of it.

'OK, let's roll.' Paterson jogged down the stairs, and paused with a hand on the door. 'And let me do the talking.'

There was a familiar barman polishing glasses.

'I'm pretty sure they've relocated the bar from one side of the room to the other,' Paterson scanned round the room, 'but the ambience remains the same.'

'Can I help you?'

'Is Vic in?' Paterson asked.

'Cards,' said the barman. He recognised Bernard. 'You again.'

'Hi,' said Bernard and gave the barman a wave, which he regretted when Paterson raised his eyes to the ceiling. Bernard wondered what an acceptable way to greet a potential Defaulter witness would be in Paterson's eyes. He suspected it involved overturned furniture and swearing.

Paterson turned to the barman. 'Get your boss. Now.'

He tutted, but disappeared into the back. A minute later Victor Thompson appeared, with a smirk on his face.

'No offence, Mr Paterson, but I prefer it when you send the pretty lady round to ruin my day instead of doing it in person.'

'Yeah, but she said she didn't want that old pervert Thompson staring at her tits again, so I said I'd call round myself.'

Vic Thomson smiled. 'From what I hear Ms Whyte's got no objections to older men.'

108

Bernard felt his mouth shape itself into a perfect o of horror.

Vic looked at his face and laughed. 'Well, that's the pleasantries out of the way.'

'Shall we go through the back?' said Paterson, gesturing at the empty room. 'I wouldn't want to disturb any of your customers.'

Ignoring the jibe, Vic opened the door to the back room and waved them through. Bernard sat down at the same table as the previous day. Paterson threw himself onto the chair that had obviously just been vacated by Vic, who leaned across and grabbed the papers that were now lying in front of the HET boss.

'So, what is it today, Mr Paterson? I told your colleague here that I didn't recognise the young woman you were looking for.'

Bernard spoke. 'You said we could leave the picture for your bar staff to look at – did anyone else know her?'

'No, I'm afraid not,' said Vic. 'No-one recognised her at all. Sorry you've had another wasted trip.'

He looked at Paterson as if he was expecting him to leave. Paterson settled down further in the chair. 'Thing is, Mr Thompson, we've now got a second No Show who was known to frequent here.'

'So what?' Vic pulled up a chair and joined them at the table. 'Lots of people come here. You looking for two of my clientele is what I'd call a coincidence.'

'I'd agree with that, if the two people in question were hairy-arsed bikers with tattoos and drug habits. But these are two young, middle-class students we're talking about. Since when was this place the hang-out of choice for your ivory tower types?'

'Times have changed, Mr Paterson. Since this Virus

109

came along lots of youngsters are seizing the day, in case they don't see another one.'

Paterson looked ostentatiously round the room. 'How many times have I been in your gaff?'

'Do I get to say "too many"?'

'Don't remember this being the set-up last time I was in?'

'Aye, well, that would be a while back, before you got pensioned off into chasing missing students.'

Paterson smiled. 'So, what prompted the change of layout?'

'What do you think? All the restrictions you lot have placed on who I can and can't have in here means I've got rooms lying empty.'

'Thought so. And what are you using them for? Illicit parties? Uncarded meet-ups?' Paterson leapt to his feet and walked round the room. 'Used to be a door round about here, if I'm not mistaken.'

'Sit down,' said Vic. 'You're embarrassing yourself.'

Paterson pulled back a curtain to reveal a door.

Bernard thought he saw a slight look of concern fleet across Vic's face, before it resumed its usual look of mild amusement.

'What you got in there? Drugs, is it? Stash of illegal arms?'

'You know me, Mr Paterson, I'm a keen hunter, but I can assure you that I have a licence for every firearm I possess.' He smirked.

'Hunter, my arse.' Paterson knocked on the door. 'Care to open up?'

This provoked a snort of derision. 'Not without a search warrant.'

'We could get one, you know. But we've got powers

110

of immediate access to anywhere that we think a Health Defaulter is hiding – or being hidden.'

The two of them stared at each other

Vic sat back. 'So what?'

'Bernard, can you hear a woman's voice calling for help?'

He wasn't sure what his boss was up to, but he was fairly certain it was about to involve him in an illegal activity. 'Eh, no?'

'Well, I can.' He turned the handle of the door, and looked surprised that it opened.

Bernard got to his feet and walked over to his boss. Turning his back on Vic he spoke as quietly as he could. 'Mr Paterson, are you sure you should be doing this?' He looked over his shoulder at the businessman, who winked at him.

Paterson ignored him. 'Well, well, Victor. What are we going to find? Secret party room? Stash of PMA tablets for selling to unsuspecting...what is this?'

Bernard stuck his head round the door. The room was set up with row after row of chairs, pointing toward a dais. Over the platform, pinned to the wall, was a wooden cross.

'Looks like some kind of church, Mr Paterson.'

The two of them turned round and stared at Vic.

'An illegal place of worship? How many uncarded Christians are you letting in here?'

Vic Thomson put his hands up. 'It's all strictly legit. Check it out for yourself, the room is registered to ...'

'The Church of the Lord Arisen?' Bernard spoke up. Paterson glared at him, and he wished he'd kept quiet.

Vic looked surprised. 'You've heard of it?'

'Everyone's heard of it after all that bother with the

111

drug overdoses,' said Paterson, 'although suddenly that particular affair seems a little clearer.'

'Oh, no, that was nothing to do with Morley's. I don't tolerate that kind of thing on my premises.'

'Bullshit. So, what's in it for you?'

A look of theatrical innocence adorned Vic's face. 'Nothing. The Virus – it's just made me think about life. Made me want to do something good for the community.'

Paterson pretended to gag. 'Come on, Bernard, let's get out of here before this place makes me lose my lunch again.' He pointed at Vic. 'And when I figure out what your angle is, I'll be back.'

They were halfway out the door when Vic shouted to them, 'God bless!'

3

Mona pressed the intercom buzzer to Heidi's flat.

Maitland was sulking against the door. 'Is this going to take long? I want to follow up this address for Donny.'

'I have a Defaulter to find too, Maitland. One we're supposed to be prioritising.'

'Give it another buzz, then let's get out of here.'

She pressed again, and kept her finger there until an irate voice on the other end answered.

'Who is it?'

The Dream Team, she thought. *Your Lucky Day. Or maybe your Worst Nightmare.* She sighed and said, 'The Health Enforcement Team.'

'The what?'

She leaned her head against the top of the intercom. 'The people that come to visit you if you've missed a health check-up.'

The intercom was silent. 'But I've not missed ...oh. Heidi.'

The door buzzed and Maitland pushed it open.

As Mona had suspected, Heidi's tenement had a very nice stair. Not as ornate as some – there was no mosaic tiling or anything like that – but it was clean and in good repair. A couple of the doors had plants and ornaments outside them. She suspected that there weren't too many students living here.

The woman who answered the door was tiny. Spiky brown hair and a pair of sleepy hazel eyes poked out of the top of a duvet she was using as a makeshift dressing gown. Bare legs were sticking out of the bottom of the quilt. Mona wondered if there was anything covering the in-between. She hoped Maitland wasn't staring too intently.

The woman stepped back so they could enter the flat. Mona squeezed past, trying hard not to bump into her, and fixed her eyes firmly on the ceiling. The entrance hall was narrow but high-roofed, with no furniture in it apart from a small bookcase, which was topped with a selection of tiny china ornaments. A naked lightbulb was shining not-enough light down on them. There were five wooden doors leading off the hallway, all of which were closed. Mona was reminded of something from *Alice in Wonderland* – or was it *Through the Looking Glass*?

'Sorry – did we get you up?' said Mona, flashing her HET card.

'Yeah.' The woman held Mona's ID for a moment and had a good look at it. She handed it back, ran a hand over her hair and yawned, then noticed Mona looking discreetly at her watch. 'I work at an old folks' home and I had a night shift last night. You're looking for Heidi?'

'Yes.' Mona pointed at the duvet. 'Do you want to get dressed first?'

She nodded and disappeared through a door, but left it partly open behind her. It was a welcome source of extra light. Maitland crouched down and looked at the books on the bookshelf.

'Keep talking.' The woman's voice floated back into the hallway. 'I can still hear you.'

'Oh,' said Mona, listening to the sound of drawers

114

opening and closing. 'OK. Heidi missed her last Health Status Check. As you're probably aware we're obliged to chase up all No Shows. Can I ask your name?'

'Amanda Harris.'

She had an English accent. *Northern*, thought Mona. *Leeds, or maybe York?*

'And you share the flat with Heidi?'

'Yes.'

'Just the two of you?' asked Maitland.

'Yup.'

'No boyfriends?'

'Nope.'

'So, when was the last time you saw Heidi?'

'Saturday evening.' There was the sound of bed springs creaking. 'She was getting ready to go out.'

Mona walked toward the door, and stopped short when she realised she could see the dressing table mirror in Amanda's room. Amanda's reflection was sitting on the bed dressed only in her bra and pants. Mona looked round at Maitland, who was busy leafing through a book. She closed her eyes. 'Any idea where she was going?'

'She said she was meeting some friends in town?'

The bed springs creaked again. Mona opened one eye and watched Amanda zip up a pair of jeans. 'Do you know who these friends were?'

Amanda's reflection pulled a stripy T-shirt on. 'Sorry, I've no idea. We just share a flat – we don't really socialise.'

'Really, you never met any of them? She didn't ever mention someone called K? Or perhaps had a friend whose name began with K?'

'Sorry, really don't know.'

'OK,' Mona cut her losses. 'So, has she been back to the flat since Saturday night?'

'I don't know.' The bedroom door opened and Amanda stood there holding a pair of socks. 'I don't think so but we might just have missed each other.'

They stared at each other for a moment.

'We need to search Heidi's room.' Maitland stood up.

'Why?' Amanda leaned against the door jamb and pulled on a sock. 'The German guy already searched it.'

'I know, I've spoken to him. We'd just like to check it again.'

Amanda lowered her socked foot to the ground. 'Suit yourself. It's that door there.'

Mona pushed open the door and looked in. The room was a mess. The bed was unmade and clothes were draped across all of the available surfaces.

Maitland appeared at her shoulder. 'Tidy sort, your friend.'

'Flatmate,' corrected Amanda. She turned and opened another of the doors. Mona peered back at her. The kitchen.

Maitland pointed to the wardrobe. She nodded her agreement, and while he set to work on Heidi's clothes, she worked methodically round the room. Starting with the chest of drawers, she opened each drawer in turn, pulling them out far enough that she could check the underside as well. The search yielded nothing beyond a selection of underwear and socks.

She threw back the duvet cover, checked under the pillow, but found only a hanky.

'Maitland.'

She pointed toward the bed, and he helped her to lift up the mattress. There was no secret stash of drugs or Children of Camus literature hidden there.

She borrowed a magazine from the dressing table,

opened it up and emptied the contents of Heidi's bin onto it. Using a pen, she moved it around but there was nothing of interest in amongst the used cotton buds.

She looked over at Maitland, who was checking the pockets of a pink checked waterproof jacket. 'Anything?'

'Not yet.'

'Keep looking in here,' she said in a low voice, and pointed toward the door.

Mona slipped out into the hall. Another of the doors had been opened. She could see Amanda sitting on a sofa eating a bowl of cornflakes, in what Mona took to be the living room. She took the opportunity to quietly push open the door to Amanda's room and peered in.

The room was as tidy as Heidi's was messy. There were no clothes to be seen, and the surfaces were clear. In fact the only sign that anyone actually lived there was the fact that the duvet had been dumped untidily on the bed, the duvet that had recently been wrapped round Heidi's flatmate.

'She's not in there.' Amanda appeared at her side.

'Sorry to invade your privacy. Just worried about your friend.'

'Flatmate.' Amanda went back to the living room. Mona followed her through, and was surprised at how large and airy the room was.

'Not bad for student accommodation, this.' Maitland appeared in the doorway.

Amanda sat down on the leather sofa. 'I'm not a student.'

'You're not?'

She pulled her legs up and sat cross-legged. 'I told you – I work at an old folks' home.'

'Sorry, I just assumed you were working there part-time while studying.'

'Nah.' She spread her arms along the back of the sofa. 'Do you want a cup of tea or something?'

'No, no thanks. We'll probably be back to speak to you again if Heidi doesn't show up soon.'

'No problem.' She hopped off the sofa and scrabbled around on the table until she found a pen. She scribbled her number on the side of a magazine and ripped it off. 'Give me a ring if you need me.'

Mona pocketed the scrap of paper. 'Thanks.' She stepped backwards into the hall. 'We'll see ourselves out.'

She pulled the flat door firmly closed behind them, and set off down the stairs, with Maitland a step behind her.

'What did you think of that for a student flat?' He fell into step beside her. 'Living off daddy's money?'

'Maybe.' She jumped down the last two steps. 'Heidi, certainly, but Amanda didn't strike me as the type. Why would she be working in an old folks' home if her dad was bankrolling her?'

'Fair point.' He pulled open the tenement door, and held it for Mona to walk through. 'Did you see she was starkers under that duvet when we arrived?'

'You can't know that, you didn't see anything.'

'I did! Not much, mind – just a snatch.' He winked at her.

Her mind flew back to the reflection she had seen earlier, and she blushed. 'Shut up, Maitland.'

They were halfway down Leith Walk when Maitland's phone rang. He'd insisted on following up Donny's address, although Mona was still itching to get back to the office.

Maitland stopped and dug into his pocket. After thirty seconds' fumbling he got the phone to his ear. Mona held her arm out in front of him and tapped her watch.

118

'Carole!' Maitland pointed to the phone.

He ducked into a doorway, and Mona followed. He pressed the speaker icon, and she strained to hear Carole over the traffic noise.

'How's the boy?'

'Better, we think.' They could hear Carole taking a deep breath. 'His temperature is under control now. It's just a case of keeping an eye on him and praying he doesn't develop pneumonia.'

'Thank God for that,' said Maitland. 'So, what are you doing phoning me?'

'I'm back in the office ...'

'Really? What about Michael?'

'Oh, they kick visitors out as soon as the patient is out of immediate danger. I thought I'd come back to the office because I was feeling bad at deserting you.'

'Don't feel bad, I've got Mona for company.' He smirked at her.

She ignored him. 'Hi, Carole.'

'Hi, Mona. I'm back in the office but nobody's here! Who are you chasing today?'

Mona leaned into the phone. 'A beautiful student, who is a member of the Church of the Lord Arisen, but also goes drinking in a biker bar.'

'She sounds interesting.' There was a pause. 'The Church of the Lord Arisen? I remember the stuff in the paper. Drugs, wasn't it?'

Maitland moved his phone slightly away from her and continued speaking. 'Yeah, but none of the kids I've met so far strike me as the drug-taking types. Gullible though; they are members of an organisation called The Children of Camus who believe that the Government could cure the Virus if they only chose to.'

'Oh, good grief.' There was a brief pause. 'Camus, as in the author?'

'Yeah, are these kids nuts or what?'

'Well, you've got to feel sorry for ...'

They heard a voice in the background.

'I've got to go,' said Carole quickly. 'That's Mr Paterson just come in.'

'Cheers. You take care.'

Maitland shoved his phone back into his pocket, and grunted.

'What?'

He shrugged. 'Just missing Carole. She's a laugh.'

Mona got the point. Maitland didn't enjoy her company, and didn't hide it. Maitland and Carole had joined the HET at the same time, some six weeks or so after her. On his arrival Maitland had made it clear he wasn't happy to be partnered with Carole. He'd complained about having to work with 'a dumpy mum with crystal earrings and weird wristbands' and had made a fairly embarrassing attempt to get partnered with her, Mona, instead. She was pretty sure he was thanking his lucky stars that that hadn't happened.

Maitland set off again. Annoyingly, he wouldn't tell her the address that Kate had given him, so she was forced to follow his lead. She kept a sulky couple of metres behind him, and planned how she would get her revenge.

At the Boundary bar they turned off Leith Walk onto Albert Street. A couple of minutes later Maitland stopped outside a tenement door.

'This is it, if my sources are to be believed.'

The intercom was giving out a low buzz. Mona jabbed it a couple of time, fruitlessly. She tried pushing the door open, but it didn't move.

'Stand back.' Maitland put a shoulder to the door, and after a couple of thrusts the door flew open.

Mona looked round, but no-one was within view to witness the forced entry. Damage to property might be pushing the HET's powers to its limits.

She stepped inside and within seconds she wished she was back on the street. The stair light was broken, and someone had dumped a couple of black bin bags of rubbish at the end of the hall. Just inside the door a bag of chips had been dropped, the smell of vinegar almost, but not quite, covering the smell of piss coming from the stair.

Nice address, she thought.

Watching carefully where she put her feet, she followed her colleague up the stairs until Maitland came to a halt outside flat 2f2. Maitland went to knock on the door, but she grabbed his hand before it made contact. She always liked to listen for signs of life before announcing her presence. Better to know, if possible, who you were going to be dealing with. HET officers appearing on the doorstep provoked all kinds of reactions, most of them bad. She could hear a TV or radio playing, but she wasn't sure which flat the noise was coming from. Maitland pointed at the door, impatient to get started. She nodded, and he hammered on the wood. There was no answer, so he knocked again. After a brief pause an Australian voice sounded from inside.

'All right, mate, I'm coming.'

The door was flung open by a young man dressed in jeans, and a faded T-shirt featuring a monkey hanging from a noose. Primates had come in for a lot of stick in the early days of the Virus, wrongly accused of being the originator of the disease.

'Sorry to disturb you.'

The man grinned and looked at them both in turn. 'No worries. What do you want?'

'Are you Donny?'

'Nah.' The Australian folded his arms round him, and rocked back and forth in an attempt to keep warm.

'Is he in?'

'I don't know.' He turned back into the property, leaving the door open. Maitland and Mona took this as a signal to follow him.

The flat was an improvement on the outside, but not by much. The hall was missing most of its carpet, and someone had abandoned an attempt to paint the hallway eggshell blue with the paint reaching only to hip level. There was a faint smell of marijuana, which she had to admit at least smelled better than the stair.

'Donny?' The Australian battered on a door. 'You in there?'

There was no reply. He tried the handle, and threw open the door to reveal a mattress on the floor with a duvet on it. Clothes and books were spread across the carpet, but there was no occupant.

'He's not in,' said Donny's flatmate, unnecessarily. 'His bike's gone. You a friend of his, mate?'

'We're actually friends of his girlfriend.' Mona waited for a reaction.

'His girlfriend?' He looked surprised. 'Donny's got a woman?'

'Yeah. Colette – long blonde hair? Gorgeous?'

The Australian looked puzzled, then decided it was all beyond him. 'Can't say I've met her, mate, but good on him. Do you want me to tell him you were looking for him?'

'No. Any idea where I could find him?'

He thought for a minute. 'You could try his work?'

'Where's that?'

'Bike Central, on Broughton Street.'

'Cheers,' said Maitland.

The Australian waved them a cheery goodbye, as they ran back down the stairs and negotiated the hallway, out into the fresh Leith air.

'So,' said Maitland, clapping his hands together, 'Bike Central?'

'No!' Mona walked off. 'We do have another case we're supposed to be focusing on, remember?'

After a few steps she realised Maitland wasn't following her.

'Are you coming?'

He shook his head. 'I'm going to get some lunch. See you back there.'

She tutted, and headed in the direction of the office.

4

'So what does that actually mean?'

The Guv seemed to be annoyed with Bernard about something. Mona hovered in the doorway and watched as her boss jabbed a stubby finger at Bernard's computer screen. Bernard leaned rapidly back in his chair to avoid being bumped by his elbow.

'It means, Mr Paterson, that Victor Thompson was telling the truth. See,' Bernard tapped the computer screen, 'Church of the Lord Arisen, registered sites April 2014, 34 Persevere Street and 501 Great Junction Street. Then, an additional registration earlier this year of 2 Industry Terrace, which is the address of Morley's. Licence for twenty non-immune gatherees at any given time, plus unlimited immune gatherees, up to the limit of fire regulations.'

The Guv swivelled round on his chair, and Bernard nearly toppled over in an attempt not to get hit. Mona couldn't help feeling that her boss would have been quite happy if he had.

'But why didn't he tell me straight off that was what was there?'

Bernard wheeled his chair away. 'Maybe he was embarrassed?'

Paterson snorted. 'Vic Thompson has a brass neck. He's not going to bother about my opinion.'

'Maybe he's genuine.' Bernard looked thoughtful. 'He's worried about the Virus and he's found religion? He wouldn't be the first person to react to extreme circumstances by finding solace in the Church.'

'Finding solace? Speak English, for Christ's sake. And while you're at it, get a grip, Bernard.' Paterson was now pacing up and down the office. 'This is a dyed-in-the-wool criminal here, not some teenage lassie looking to find God.'

Bernard threw his hands up in exasperation and turned back to his computer.

'I thought you were supposed to be at SHEP, Guv?' Mona announced her arrival.

'Change of plans. Mona, glad you are here – I need someone with an iota of common sense.' Paterson stopped walking. 'Vic Thompson has got an outpost of the Church of the Lord Arisen in his back room.'

She laughed in surprise. 'For real? Is it illegal?'

'No, legit, but he was pretty cagey about admitting to it. What's his game?'

She thought for a moment. 'Well, it's footfall isn't it, twenty Christians at a time plus any immunes.'

'Yeah, and each of them ordering half a lager shandy.' Paterson slapped his hand on Bernard's desk, making him jump. 'Nah, there's more to it than that.'

'Drugs is the obvious one,' said Mona, 'what with Morley's reputation. And the Church's reputation for that matter.'

Paterson started walking toward his office. 'I'm going to make some calls about Mr Thompson's sudden conversion.' Over his shoulder he asked, 'Any further forward with the German lassie, Mona?'

'Nowhere fast, Guv.' Mona picked up her bag. 'Diaries aren't giving much away, except they keep referring to someone called "K".' She slid into her own chair, and turned on her computer.

'Well, keep at it. We need a result there.'

An e-mail from Marcus pinged into her inbox, entitled 'Heidi Weber Social Media.'

Hey Mona, Had a trawl through the usual sites and thought you might like to see Heidi's Facebook page. Working on cracking the password to the private area, but the public bit's pretty full . . .get in touch if you need anything else . . .happy to chat over a drink sometime? M

In your dreams, thought Mona, and clicked on the link. Once in the site, she went straight to the photo gallery. After a couple of minutes' searching she leapt to her feet and grabbed her bag.

Bernard looked up. 'Where are you going?'

'To see Amanda again.'

'I'll come too,' he said, getting to his feet.

'No need.' The last thing she wanted was more time with Bernard. And anyway, she'd like a shot questioning Amanda on her own.

'It's OK, I want to come.'

'Whatever. But I'm going now.'

She set off down the stairs as fast as she could in the hope that Bernard would take the hint, and cursed as she saw the short, stocky figure of the chattiest Admin assistant coming the other way.

'Hi, Marguerite.'

She tried to squeeze past, flattening herself against the wall. Marguerite was obviously in the mood to talk and remained firmly in the middle of the stair, smiling and immovable.

'How's the big man?'

'The Guv? Oh, he's fine.' Mona tried unsuccessfully to keep moving. 'Hasn't eaten any babies or anything today.'

Marguerite laughed, a full-bodied snort. 'I've got his post. Gets here later every day.'

'Well, that's the post for you,' said Mona, finally succeeding in manoeuvring past. 'Sorry, in a bit of a rush.'

She legged it out of the building, then stopped. She knew that she shouldn't be investigating solo. In the earliest days of the HET, there had been a couple of near misses with unaccompanied HET officers being threatened with violence. This had resulted in an immediate diktat that all investigations were undertaken in pairs, regardless of the potential risk. This had halved their manpower at a stroke, and meant that Mona spent far more time in Bernard's company than was good for either of them. She should take him with her to Amanda's, but just for once she wanted to carry out an inquiry without him there, popping his tuppence worth in.

She heard the sound of feet behind her.

'Mona, why are we going back to see Ms Harris again?'

A vision of Heidi's flatmate's naked arms struggling to hold her duvet in place crossed Mona's mind.

'Marcus sent me through a link to her Facebook page, which is full of pictures of Amanda, out on the town with Heidi, the flatmate she claimed to never socialise with.'

'She lied?'

'Looks like it.'

'I wonder why?' Bernard's footsteps stopped as they passed the entrance to the car park. 'Are we not taking the car?'

'I thought I'd walk.'

127

'Oh, OK.' Bernard caught up with her. 'Nice day for some fresh air.'

They walked in silence for a minute or two.

'I saw Marguerite on the way down.'

Mona grunted.

'Have you noticed she's the only one from Admin who ever visits our office? None of the rest of them come near us.'

'Marguerite is the only one of the Admin staff the Guv hasn't managed to offend totally. I think her dad was in the Police, or Army or something, so she's used to the sense of humour.'

'What did Mr Paterson say to them?'

'He made some joke about them all wetting their knickers over Maitland. They said they were offended by the language, but I think they were really pissed off because he'd hit the nail on the head.'

'What? The entire Admin team fancies Maitland?' Bernard stopped. 'Why?'

'Because he's tall, and dark, and chats them all up, so none of them have actually noticed he's got a face like a bag of spanners.'

Bernard walked on in silence for a minute. 'Do you think he's attractive?'

'No,' said Mona, crossing the road. 'I think he's Maitland.'

Mona gave the bell a short and authoritative push.

After a brief pause, a 'hello?' emanated from the intercom.

'Hi Amanda, it's the Health Enforcement Team again.'

There was a brief pause. 'OK.' The intercom buzzed as she let them in.

Mona walked briskly up the stairs with Bernard

128

following her. She looked up to see Amanda watching them over the banister. The girl's brown eyes followed them as they climbed the steps. Mona tripped on the top landing and Bernard took her arm, which she shrugged off.

'This is my partner, Bernard.'

'Is he, like, your boyfriend?' Amanda looked over the top of the handrail at them. Mona felt a ridiculous blush spreading across her face.

'No, I mean my partner HET officer.'

'Oh, OK, I see.' Amanda gave a small exhalation of breath, which could have been a laugh.

'Can we come in?' asked Mona, pointing to the flat door.

Amanda retreated into the flat, with the two of them following.

'Do you want a cup of tea, or something?' she asked over her shoulder.

Mona put a hand on Bernard's arm to stop him refusing. 'Yes, that would be lovely.'

'Come and have a seat.'

Amanda went into the kitchen and Bernard and Mona settled themselves at the table. Mona had a discreet look at their surroundings. It was a good-sized room, with SMEG appliances and granite worktops. The table they were sitting round was oak. She could understand Heidi, the daughter of a rich MP being able to afford the accommodation, but Amanda? On a care worker's wage?

'We hope you're not worrying too much about Heidi,' said Bernard.

Amanda shrugged without turning round. 'I'm sure she'll turn up when she's ready.'

Ready? thought Mona. An interesting choice of words.

'Do you think there's a reason Heidi has gone away?'

Amanda put three cups of black tea on the table. 'I don't know. But there must be something.' She opened the fridge door. 'Milk?'

'Please.'

Mona waited for Amanda to ask why they were there, but she sat in silence. Was she playing it cool, or was she intimidated by their presence? Lots of people were a little bit overawed when the HET arrived, and generally couldn't wait to get rid of them. But maybe Amanda wasn't like that; there was something almost otherworldly about her.

'I've been reading Heidi's diaries.'

'Really? I didn't know she kept a diary.'

'She did, and it's given us quite an insight into how she spent her time. Morley's, the Railway Tavern – did you ever go there with her?'

Amanda took her time answering. 'We didn't really socialise.'

'How come you ended up sharing a flat?' asked Bernard. 'As you're not really friends, I mean.'

'I answered her ad.'

'Her ad?' asked Mona.

'Yup. I moved to Edinburgh and was looking for somewhere to live. She seemed a nice, quiet sort so I took the room.'

'And is she?' asked Mona.

'Is she what?'

'A nice, quiet sort?'

Amanda thought for a minute. 'I guess so. Kept the flat clean, which was what I was mainly bothered about. We didn't really socialise. I told you that before.' Amanda sighed. 'I didn't realise that missing your Health Check was such a big deal. That people would come looking for you.'

Bernard's mouth opened, and Mona knew he was about to launch into a long and detailed explanation of exactly what happened when someone missed a Health Check. Before he could speak, however, there was a sound of ringing.

'Is that your phone?'

Amanda stood up. 'It's in the living room. I'd better get it.'

Mona and Bernard looked at each other.

'She's sticking to her story about not knowing Heidi too well,' said Bernard. 'Why is she lying?'

'I'm going to find out.' Mona got to her feet. 'See if you can find any mail or anything lying about.'

She walked along the narrow hall and pushed open the door. Amanda hung up as she entered.

'They were trying to sell me solar panels.'

Mona smiled. 'Bit of a long shot when you live in a flat.'

She looked round the living room. The sofa was pristine leather, and the sideboard looked mahogany or some other quality wood. The polished floor was covered by a woollen rug with an intricate pattern that didn't look like it had come cheap, and the ceiling-to-floor drapes in the bay window alone must have cost a fortune.

'This really is a very nice flat.'

'You said that before.'

'Splitting the rent 50/50, are you?'

'Maybe. I don't know.' Amanda sighed, exasperated. 'It's Heidi's flat, she deals with all that.'

'Heidi, who you hardly know.'

Amanda shrugged.

131

'Except we've been on Heidi's Facebook page, this flat-mate of yours, the one you hardly know, and you seem to feature a lot. Care to explain?'

Amanda turned her back on Mona, and stood staring out of the window. 'I don't know where she is. If I did I would tell you.'

Mona joined her at the window. As she did so she noticed that placed neatly behind the curtain was a holdall.

'Who does that belong to?'

Amanda looked alarmed as Mona bent down to open it up.

'That's not your – don't you need a warrant or something before you go raking through people's stuff?'

Mona rummaged through the bag, unearthing amongst its contents a selection of men's clothing, a towel, and a washbag.

'What's going on?' Bernard appeared in the doorway.

Mona stood up holding a pair of boxer shorts in each hand. 'I don't think Amanda's been quite open with us. Care to tell us who your visitor is?'

There was silence.

'I appreciate that you don't want to talk to us, Amanda, but I'm afraid you are going to have to.'

'I know.' Amanda shifted uncomfortably. She sighed. 'They're Kevin's.'

'Kevin?' Mona and Bernard looked at each other. Bernard silently mouthed the letter K to her over the top of Amanda's head.

'And Kevin would be?'

'Look, I really don't want to say any more, it's none of my business.'

'Heidi is missing. Heidi, whose Facebook page has

132

numerous pictures of you. Heidi, who I'm willing to bet is actually a very good friend of yours.'

'I'm sorry.' Amanda started putting the clothes back into the holdall. She put it behind the curtain and threw herself onto one of the large leather sofas. 'I know.'

'Amanda, if you, or Heidi, are in some kind of trouble we can help. We just need you to be honest. Maybe you could start by explaining why you've been lying to us?'

Amanda let out a deep sigh, and wiped her eyes with the corner of her T-shirt.

'Because I promised her I wouldn't tell anyone.'

'Tell anyone what?'

'About her and Kevin.'

'Kevin's her boyfriend?' asked Bernard.

'Yeah.' Amanda gave her eyes another wipe. 'Her parents are really strict so she made me promise I wouldn't tell anyone about him living here.'

'What's Kevin's surname?'

'Calman.'

'Is he registered here?'

She shrugged. 'I don't know – either here or the Pollock Halls.'

'Is he a friend of yours too?' asked Mona.

'Nope.'

'You're not a fan of your pal's boyfriend?'

Amanda sat on the sofa, legs curled under. 'None of my business.'

Mona and Bernard walked slowly through the tree-lined walk that bisected the Meadows, reflecting on their visit.

'Well,' said Mona, 'an explanation of sorts. Are you convinced?'

'Maybe,' said Bernard, stepping out of the way of a cyclist.

Mona shivered. The spring sunshine that had warmed the day had faded. It was too chilly to be dawdling, but neither of them felt inclined to go back to the office. She looked out across the expanse of green and tried to focus the thoughts that were in her head.

'Anything else strike you as odd there, Bernard?'

He looked at her, eyebrows raised. 'Like what?'

'Like she desperately doesn't want us to know about Kevin, but she makes a pretty half-arsed attempt to hide his stuff.'

'Didn't make much of an effort to hide her dislike of him.' Bernard pulled out his phone, and sidetracked toward a bench, throwing himself down onto the seat.

'Let's check his Health Status. Nothing for Marchmont, so let's try Pollock Halls.' His fingers flicked over the screen.

Mona sat down next to him and peered over his shoulder.

'Turned up for his last check OK, which was...twenty-eight days ago.' Bernard turned his phone toward her.

'So, Kevin should be at the Pollock Halls Health Status Clinic at 8.45am Thursday morning.' Mona smiled. 'Do you think we should meet him there?'

'I certainly do.' Bernard shoved his phone into his pocket. 'And in the meantime?'

She got to her feet, stamping them to keep warm. 'I need to check on Maitland.'

5

Maitland was waiting on the corner of the street where he'd told her to meet him.

'I don't need babysitting.' He started speaking before she'd even reached him. 'I could have done this on my own.'

'I know.' Mona was glad she'd tracked Maitland down. If Donny was here she was keen to speak to him. 'Where are we going?'

He pointed across the road to a shop that sold bikes and offered cycle repairs.

'You look in need of some exercise. Ever thought of taking to the road on two wheels?'

'Ha, ha.'

The shop smelled of oil and sweat. Mona didn't understand the appeal of cycling. Give her a sports car every time. She idly turned over a price ticket hanging from a bike and blanched at the price. A sports car wouldn't be that much dearer. She stepped away from the display, and watched a man with dreadlocks and long shorts crouch down on all fours in order to squirt liquid into the wheel of an upturned bike.

Maitland pushed past her and spoke to the much-pierced man who was sitting behind the counter, reading.

'Is Donny in?' He flashed his HET card at him.

The assistant lowered his cycling magazine and looked at the card.

'What does HET stand for, mate?' The bike man's stretched vowels revealing him to be another Australian.

'Health Enforcement Team,' said Maitland. Mona could hear the impatience in his tone. 'Does Donny work here?'

'Past tense, mate' said the bike man, rolling up his magazine. 'He's not worked here for,' he turned to the other assistant, 'how long would you say?'

The other assistant shrugged, without turning round.

'Maybe two months since he went?' The bike man let go of the magazine which unfurled itself and plopped onto the desk. Mona wondered which of the Australians was giving them the runaround.

'Why did he leave?' she asked.

The bike man put the magazine back on display. 'Said he'd got a better job.'

Mona stared at him. He didn't look like he was lying. 'Do you know where he's working now?'

'Sorry, mate.' He gave a firm shake of his head. 'No idea.'

Maitland looked round the shop. 'You realise that it's a criminal offence to hinder a Health Enforcement Officer in the search for a Defaulter?'

The bike man pulled a face. 'You managed to prosecute anyone under that legislation?'

The answer to that question was no. The legislation had been rushed through so fast, and was so riddled with holes it was widely agreed that a prosecution would be nigh on impossible. Mona wondered if the bike man was more on the ball than she'd thought.

'You could be the first. Or,' she had an idea, 'I could ask my colleagues at Revenue and Customs to pop round, make sure that everyone here is properly on the payroll, got the appropriate visa, your National Insurance payments are all up to date, that kind of thing.'

The bike man glared at her, and reached under the counter. He picked out a box file, and raked around in it until he found what he was looking for, and slammed it down on the counter top.

'Donald Mathieson's P45 – check the date he left here.'

Maitland and Mona looked over the document. It showed Donny as having left a couple of months earlier.

'Somebody's yanking your chain, mate.'

'Looks like it.'

Mona pulled open the door to leave. 'Thanks for your time.'

The bike man didn't return her smile.

Bernard sat staring at the phone, wondering what he should be doing.

'Hello.'

He looked up to see Carole standing in the doorway.

'Carole! How's the young 'un?'

'On the mend, thank God.'

'That's great news.' He looked at the files she was carrying. 'You're not back at work, are you?'

'Yeah, they kicked me out this morning, so I came in at lunchtime. Mr Paterson immediately sent me off to meet with an Education Officer at the Council about ...'

'Oh, God, the visit to schools thing.'

'Yeah.' She laughed. 'Bernard, can I ask you something?'

'OK. Probably be better to ask Maitland or Mona but ...'

'I spoke to Maitland earlier about the girl they were chasing, and something he said reminded me about a weird thing that happened at the hospital, and it's probably nothing but ...'

'What?'

'Well, with Michael stabilised, the nurses told me to go and have a shower, and something to eat.'

'Good advice.'

'Yeah,' she gave out a breath, 'anyway, on the way there I decided to stop at the Sanctuary – you know what that is?'

'Yes.' It would have been called the hospital chapel in less secular times.

'So, I was sitting there when this woman came in. Anyway, she bursts into tears—'

'Not surprising really, the Virus,' he swallowed, 'is devastating.' He tried to stay focused on what Carole was saying, and not on his own memories.

'That's what I said to her, more or less, and here's the thing. She said it wasn't the Virus, but her daughter, I think she said her name was Kirsty, was in a coma after overdosing.'

'OK, but ...' Bernard didn't want to jump to any conclusions on this.

'Wait, there's more. She starts going on about how her daughter was never like that, top of her class, played hockey, never missed church.'

Bernard sat upright. 'Never missed church?'

'Yep, and started hanging around with a new crowd that were all into French authors and stuff.'

'Like Camus, for instance?'

'Am I making too much of this, Bernard?'

He didn't know.

Mona walked into the office.

'Carole – good to see you.'

138

She sat down at her desk and started bashing away at her computer. Bernard felt relief that she was back, and embarrassment at his inability to deal with this on his own. He exchanged a glance with Carole over the top of Mona's head.

'Carole befriended a woman at the hospital whose daughter's in a coma.'

Mona carried on typing.

'Mona, are you listening?'

'Coma, yeah, whatever.'

'And this woman's God-fearing daughter overdosed on drugs, after taking an interest in French authors.'

Mona stopped typing and swivelled round to face Carole.

'Children of Camus?'

'I don't know. I hadn't heard of them until I spoke to Maitland this morning.' She shrugged. 'Possibly.'

Mona looked thoughtful. 'Maybe you should see if you can find her again.'

'I'm heading back to the hospital now, actually.' Carole looked at her watch. 'I don't want to be late for visiting time.'

Mona stood up. 'I'll walk you out.'

'Oh, you're going out again?' Bernard felt a childish sense of disappointment. 'Should I come?'

'I thought I'd try and catch up with some of my old CID colleagues, see if anyone recognises the "Railway Tavern". I was thinking it might be an old name for a pub – you know, like everyone calls the Athletic Arms, Diggers.'

'Why?'

'Because that's what it used to be called.' She shot him an impatient look. 'After the gravediggers that drank

139

there. Anyway, maybe one of the older CID guys would remember it.'

'OK, while you're gone I was wondering if I could have a look at Heidi's diaries?'

'What, a quick half-hour's read of them before you rush off early, Bernard?'

'No, I—' He stopped himself. It was none of her business why he'd refused to stay on last night. He didn't feel inclined to share the finer details of his wife's mental health with Mona. She didn't strike him as overly sympathetic to relationship problems.

She smiled, and picked up her bag. Bernard wondered, not for the first time, why Mona always stayed late at the office. She'd never mentioned a boyfriend, though, of course, he hadn't asked.

When he'd first joined the HET, back when Maitland was still bothering to talk to him, he had told him a story about Mona having an affair with a married colleague. At least he thought that was what his colleague was saying; some of his more colourful language slightly mystified him. He told Maitland that he didn't like to gossip about colleagues, at which point his teammate had rolled his eyes and told him to stop being such a 'bloody nancy boy.' They hadn't shared any secrets since.

'So, it's OK if I have the diary?'

Mona gave him a look that he couldn't quite work out.

'OK.' She opened her desk drawer and put the diary on her desk. 'Though I've been through it pretty thoroughly. I'm not sure what you're hoping to find.'

Her tone clarified the look. 'I'm not saying you've missed anything. I just thought fresh pair of eyes and all that ...'

140

Mona slipped on her jacket, and threw the notebook onto his desk. 'Knock yourself out.'

Silence reclaimed the office. In the early days of the HET's establishment there'd been talk of a 24-hour service, a Health Defaulter response that never slept. This notion had been swiftly axed as part of ongoing resource issues, along with any budget that had existed for over-time. The HET was a crisis response team that operated strictly nine to five, if you didn't count all the additional hours put in by members of staff who were dedicated to the job, looking for an early promotion, or desperately trying to avoid going home.

Tokenism, thought Bernard. I'm a token.

He shuffled the papers on his desk. Where was Heidi? And why had she gone?

He read the translations through from beginning to end. Like Mona, he was struck by how terse they were. The diaries covered the short period of time Heidi had been in the country and he wondered if she had kept a diary before that. It would have been good to compare the tone.

He laid the translated pages out side by side on his desk, and read across them, looking for patterns.

Morley's. Morley's. Morley's. Good night. Soirée. Party.

No direct mention of drugs, but the occasional French word could be a reference to The Children of Camus.

Railway Tavern. Dr Beeching.

A railway theme, but more specifically a British railway theme. How would a German teenager know about Dr Beeching, the man responsible for reshaping the rail system in Britain? Someone was obviously feeding her information. Was it a code? And if 'Dr Beeching' *was* code, who was to say that the non-existent pub wasn't a code for something too?

A thought occurred to Bernard. He leapt up and started rooting around in Mona's desk drawer. He found what he was looking for, went back to his desk and spread Mona's Ordnance Survey map of Edinburgh out across the top. He traced a finger across it, and nodded to himself.

He might just have it.

His phone rang, and Maitland's name flashed up. He looked at his watch. It was nearly six o'clock, and he wondered if he could get away with ignoring him. His conscience got the better of him and he answered.

'Bernard. I need some backup.'

'And you thought of me?' He didn't know whether he should be flattered or worried.

'Mona's already told me to get lost.'

He sighed, but even assisting Maitland beat going home. 'OK, where do I need to be?'

6

Maitland was sitting on the steps of Leith Library, with a face that betrayed a very bad mood. Bernard eyed the cigarette his colleague was smoking.

'I didn't realise that you ...'

'Oh, shut up. I don't need a lecture about the public health dangers caused by fags.'

He walked off, and Bernard stood staring after him with his mouth open.

'Hi, Bernard, thanks for agreeing to come to Morley's with me,' he shouted after his colleague's retreating figure.

Maitland stopped, and looked round. He caught up with him.

'Sorry, Bern.' Maitland dropped his cigarette butt and stepped on it. 'Had a fight with Emma and I'm still a bit tense.'

Bernard grunted his acceptance of the apology, and the two of them began walking.

'What were you fighting about?'

'Oh, the usual.' Maitland sighed. 'You know, the fact that she's a religious nutter these days.'

'She not immune, is she?'

'No, she's not, and I understand what you are getting at.' Maitland's voice was growing louder, the earlier aggression creeping back in.

Bernard decided not to bother replying to this. To his surprise, Maitland continued anyway.

'I mean, I know it must be scary, the thought that you could get a life-threatening illness at any point, but you know, the NHS is on top of it now, isn't it? It's not like in the Second Wave when people were dropping like flies. Hardly anyone dies these days.'

'Well, I wouldn't say "hardly anyone" ...' His contribution was ignored.

'And what is religion going to do about it, anyway? It's not like God can keep you safe.'

'But a lot of people are looking for some kind of certainty about the future. I mean, my wife ...'

His colleague appeared to be speeding up. Bernard ran to keep up with him.

'Maitland, are you sure this is official HET business?'

'Yes. Of course it is.'

'And it's not some kind of vendetta that you have against Pastor Mackenzie, just because your girlfriend has found religion?'

Maitland ground to a halt. 'It's not a vendetta. But I knew he was dodgy the first time I met him, then I find out about his links to Morley's.' He started walking again, at a slower pace than before. 'I want him, and his bloody church, out of Emma's life, and the sooner we find out what he's up to, the better.'

'But we are still looking for Colette?'

'Of course we are. Anyway, we're here.' Maitland gestured at Morley's. 'Let's get inside and mingle.'

The entrance to the pub's back rooms was being guarded by what could only be described as a bouncer. A Christian, God-fearing bouncer, no doubt, but not somebody that even Maitland was going to push his way past without a fight.

144

'We're here for the service.'

The doorman put up a hand. 'It's not public worship. You want the Great Junction Street service.'

Maitland got out his HET ID card and showed it to him. 'I don't think I do. I want to talk to Pastor Mackenzie.'

The bouncer looked at Maitland's card, trying to establish if this was someone he had to bother with. 'I'll see if he's available.'

One of the bar staff walked out of the back room pulling his coat on. Bernard stood aside to let him past.

'Night, Donny,' shouted the barman.

'Don't bother,' said Maitland to the bouncer, and took off after the barman disappearing rapidly up Morley's stairs.

Bernard stared after his colleague in confusion, then started to run.

7

'Mona Whyte! You're the last person I expected to see at Reception.'

Mona had only been in the CID office five minutes, but she was already regretting her decision to drop in unannounced. The only person in the office was Jane Fairgrieve, who wasn't a great fan of hers. Mona wasn't sure if it was personal, or if she just preferred the idea of being the lone female on the team. Well, she'd certainly got her way on that one.

'Railway Tavern?' Her ex-colleague shook her head. 'Never heard of it. Where did you say it was?'

'We don't know – that's the point.'

'Looking for imaginary pubs?' Jane smirked, and made a great show of moving the papers around her desk. 'The fun just never stops on the Health Enforcement Team, does it?'

Mona ignored the jibe. 'If one of the older guys calls in just run it past them will you? See if they can remember a pub being called that years back?'

Jane went back to her paperwork. Mona turned to leave.

'So how's your love life these days, Mona?'

Mind your own business, bitch.

'Fine, thanks.'

And as she left, Mona wondered if she was always

going to be remembered as the woman who tried to wreck Bill Hamilton's marriage.

Bill Hamilton. The affair that didn't happen.

Bill Hamilton. The family man, doting father of a girl only a couple of years older than her.

Bill Hamilton. Liar.

The situation had arisen largely from grief. If Mona's father hadn't died a couple of months before she joined CID, and if her new colleagues hadn't seemed so utterly indifferent to her suffering, then Bill's support wouldn't have been quite so seductive. If she'd understood the banter better, or been invited to the pub more often by her peers, then maybe, just maybe, Bill's hand on her shoulder would have been easier to shrug off. Yet, despite her initial misgivings, Bill never overstepped the mark. His avuncular interest in her never became anything more. She reminded him, he said, of his daughter, Catriona, who had recently graduated in law, and was working in a women's refuge in Hackney, while deciding what to do with her life.

'Call me Cat.'

Having decided in advance to hate her, Mona was surprised, on her first meeting with the daughter, to find her both funny, and, well, attractive. Like Bill in looks, only so much more Mona's type. Cat, having undertaken a module in Women's Studies while completing her degree, placed Mona's previously unacknowledged desires in such a firm social, political, and cultural context over a glass of wine in their local pub, that it would have seemed rude to not to kiss her back, or brush away the hand that strayed up toward her breast. Catriona Hamilton was confident, liberated, and still entirely in the closet where her parents were concerned.

Mona opted to overlook this minor flaw, and placed Ms Hamilton firmly on a pedestal marked 'Woman I Want to Be'. After a couple of weekends spent with Cat and her friends in London, she started fantasising about things she had never thought possible – coming out, visiting a gay bar. She started doing things she never thought possible – including writing poetry, a move which led, inadvertently, to the end of both her first proper relationship, and her only friendship at work. A cringingly bad, in retrospect, erotic poem about Mona's yearnings was left lying by Cat (deliberately? by mistake?) on a visit to the family home, and was discovered by her mother who assumed (deliberately? by mistake?) that the intended recipient was her husband. Mrs Hamilton made her feelings clear in a loud and public visit to the Station, placing Mona squarely in the role of homewrecker.

Bill did not clarify the situation with his colleagues.

Cat never got back in touch.

And Mona never, ever, wrote poetry again.

Mona sat on a bench in the Meadows. The trip to CID had been so annoying she didn't want to go home to her flat and brood on it. She might as well sulk here. A young man on roller skates nearly ran over her feet. She jumped up and shouted after him, but he didn't stop. Tugging back her sleeve, she checked her watch, debating whether to go home. It wasn't getting any warmer, and she wasn't achieving anything here. A small growl from her stomach reminded her that she hadn't yet eaten. *Food. A good idea.* She shouldered her bag, and headed off in the direction of sustenance.

8

By the time Bernard had reached the top of Morley's stairs, the man Maitland had been chasing had disappeared. Bernard found it hard to believe he could have vanished so quickly. Maitland appeared to think the same, as he stepped out into the road to make sure their quarry wasn't hiding behind a car. Scanning the pavement, Bernard suddenly spotted him coming out of an alleyway.

'Are you Donny?'

Maitland came bounding over and put a hand on his shoulder to stop him.

'Health Status card, please.'

'What?'

Without letting go of the man Maitland pulled his ID card and flashed it at him. 'Under the Health Enforcement Act we have the right to stop and ascertain the Health Status of any individual. Health Status card, please.'

The man shook Maitland's hand off his arm. Some punters walked past, heading for Morley's and when Bernard stood to one side to let them by, he bumped into Maitland, who dropped his ID card. Their captive saw his opportunity and took to his heels.

'Nice one, Bernard.'

Maitland set off in pursuit. Bernard picked up Maitland's ID and stood watching for a minute, before realising that he should probably be assisting.

Donny was fast but from what Bernard could see Maitland seemed to be keeping up with him. He expected Donny to duck down an alley, or at least dodge through a few back streets, but instead he stayed on a relentlessly straight line.

Bernard picked up his pace as he saw Maitland dis appearing into Leith Links. Alarm bells were going in his head. Donny hadn't tried to shake them off. Perhaps this was a trap, and they were being lured into the gloom of the Links for a good kicking. Bernard hesitated for a second at the edge of the grass, then went in.

He walked slowly through the trees, keeping an eye out on all sides, and nearly ran straight into Maitland. His teammate silently raised a finger and pointed. Bernard followed his gaze, and was surprised to see their target sitting on a park bench. Donny saw them but didn't move. It crossed Bernard's mind that the barman might have a gun or knife on him. As if he had read his mind, Donny raised both his hands in a gesture of surrender.

'Sorry, guys, I just didn't want to talk to you at work.'

'Bullshit.'

'No, really. I guessed you'd find me sooner or later.' Donny looked up. 'I expect you want to see Colette.'

Maitland and Bernard sat down next to him, one on either side. Bernard was happy to note he was considerably less out of breath than his colleague. 'We certainly do. So, care to tell us why Colette missed her Health Check?' asked Maitland.

'Not really my place, is it?' Donny pulled out a packet of fags. He offered Bernard one, was refused, and lit up himself without offering Maitland one.

'Maybe not,' Maitland said, 'but you'll be helping both of you, seeing as she's committing a criminal offence by missing her Health Check, and you're committing a criminal offence by harbouring a Health Defaulter.'

Donny blew out a long puff of smoke, but didn't answer. Maitland sighed, his impatience barely contained. 'Is Colette your girlfriend?'

Donny snorted. 'I wish!'

Bernard had thought Colette was out of Donny's league, and felt something almost like pleasure that he was right, swiftly followed by guilt. Just because his love life was falling apart didn't mean he should be taking pleasure in Donny's unrequited love.

Maitland didn't appear to share Bernard's concern for Donny's feelings. 'Yeah, she's way too good-looking for you.'

'How did you meet her?' Bernard asked.

Donny stubbed his cigarette out on the side of his shoe. 'She started coming into the bar when Vic opened up the back room to that prick of a minister a couple of months back.'

'Pastor Mackenzie.' Maitland snorted.

Bernard smiled to himself. It appeared that Donny and Maitland were in agreement about something.

'Yeah, that's him. So Colette and I got talking and I hung out a bit with her and her pals.'

'So, she was a regular attender at the services?'

'Oh, yeah, I don't think she ever missed one.'

'Is Colette in some kind of trouble?'

Donny said something so quietly that Bernard couldn't hear.

'What did you say?'

'She's worried she might be pregnant.'

'Yours?' Maitland leaned forward.

Donny snorted but didn't answer.

151

'I thought her and her pals don't do sex before marriage,' Maitland said.

'She doesn't. She didn't ...' Donny pulled out another fag. He lit up and took a long drag. 'It wasn't consensual.' There was a silence while the two of them took this information in.

'She was raped?' asked Bernard, quietly.

'Yeah.'

'Who ...?'

'Who do you think? That back room's been full of pretty girls since the Church opened. Good-looking, naïve lassies.'

Bernard and Maitland exchanged a glance.

'Pastor Mackenzie raped Colette?'

'Donny?'

He gave the slightest of nods.

'Right, on your feet.' Maitland stood up. 'Time to go see Colette.'

Donny stayed seated, but got to his feet sharpish when Maitland grabbed his arm. The three of them walked back to the side of the Links.

'So, where is she?' Maitland stuck his hand out and hailed a passing taxi, which pulled in in front of them.

Donny didn't reply, but climbed into the cab. 'Albert Street, pal.' He tapped on the driver's window then threw himself into the back seat.

Maitland nabbed the other window seat. 'Your flat? That's your secret hideaway?'

Bernard debated whether to squeeze in between them, then opted for the pull-down chair.

'Was she there when we called round this morning?' Maitland asked. 'No wonder your flatmate was so keen to send us off on a wild goose chase.'

152

The taxi pulled away, and Bernard nearly fell off his perch. He grabbed the hand rail. 'Does your flatmate know that he committed an offence this morning by lying about Colette?'

Donny turned back to face them. 'Give me a break. I'm helping now, aren't I?'

'Why didn't you help in the first place?'

He shrugged. 'Colette needed a bit of time to decide what to do, if she is up the duff.'

'Colette could still have attended her Health Check even though she was expecting, you know.'

'No way, man,' said Donny. 'Everyone knows what you lot do to pregnant lassies if they get the Virus.'

Bernard was appalled. 'We give them the best possible hospital care.'

'Yeah, right.' Donny looked at him. 'You'd make her abort it. Fact.'

The taxi turned across Leith Walk and into Albert Street.

'This do you?' The taxi driver double-parked, and turned round to face them.

'Cheers.' Maitland offered a twenty pound note through the hole in the glass. 'Want to make the receipt out for ten?'

'Right you are.'

Donny reached for the door. Instinctively, Bernard grabbed his arm to stop him climbing out, then released his grip when the barman glared at him.

'Easy there, pal.'

Maitland pushed past them both, and they followed Donny into the tenement with the broken door. The smell in the stair made Bernard gag, and he did his best not to draw breath.

Donny bounded up the stairs, and unlocked the door to the flat. They followed him into the half-painted hallway.

'Colette? Are you awake?'

The question hung in the air, without a response.

'Colette?'

Donny pushed open the door to reveal his unlit room. He flicked the light switch on and went in, with the HET officers trailing in his wake. Bernard looked around. It was tidier than before, with the books that had been littered across the floor stacked neatly, and the clothes tidied up into a pile. Someone had also taken the time to make the bed, and lying slap on the middle of the duvet was an envelope.

Donny snatched it up, and read the letter while they watched.

'What does it say?' asked Maitland.

'Read it for yourself.'

Bernard scanned the letter.

'Sorry I've been so much trouble, Donny. I've taken the test and it is bad news. I know I can't stay here any longer so I've gone somewhere I feel safe. Thank you so much for everything. Love, Colette.'

'So, she is pregnant.' Donny sank down onto the mattress. 'Crap.'

9

Mona stood in the relative shelter of the trees that surrounded the Meadows and stared up at Amanda's flat. She'd had a decent feed in a vegetarian restaurant in the heart of student land. The meal had warmed her, but the temperature was dropping now, and she wasn't really dressed for surveillance.

A man walking past caught sight of her, his curiosity aroused by a woman loitering in the woodland. His eyes dropped toward her feet, obviously expecting to see a dog being walked. She moved purposefully along, and the man kept walking. A dog would have been great cover. Maybe she should suggest that to the Guv – the HET should have a part-share in some kind of animal that would give them the opportunity to loiter in parks without drawing attention to themselves. But that would involve some complicated conversations with her boss about why she was on a solo, unauthorised stake-out. Why was she here? What was she expecting to see? Heidi sneaking back into her own home? Kevin coming round to pick up his stuff? Or, was it just a pathetic attempt to fool herself that she wasn't really here just on the off-chance that she had another reason to go and visit Amanda?

The lights were on in the living room, and every so often Mona caught sight of a figure moving about. Could she go up and see her? Sure, it was late for HET business, but she was convinced Amanda knew something, either consciously or unconsciously, that would help to trace Heidi. But arriving unannounced at this hour would look pretty heavy-handed.

She stamped her feet to keep warm, then decided it was time to go home. She bent down to pick up her rucksack, and stood back up just in time to see the curtains in the flat being pulled shut. She only had a brief glance of the figure doing the drawing, more an impression than a real look, but she was pretty sure it wasn't Amanda. In fact, she was certain the figure she saw was male.

WEDNESDAY

WELCOME
TO THE
RAILWAY TAVERN

The pink fluffy book sat where he'd left it on Mona's desk the previous night. Bernard stopped next to her workspace and dropped his bag to the floor. He placed his cup down on a clear patch between two collections of files while he leafed through the journal again. Some of the coffee splashed onto a document; he rubbed at it absent-mindedly with his coat cuff as he worked his way through the entries, looking for evidence to support his theory.

'Have you been here all night?'

'Mona, hi.'

She stared back, unsmiling.

'I just got here.' He got quickly to his feet. 'Sorry, thought I'd have another look.'

'Be my guest.' Mona shrugged her coat off and hung it over the back of her chair. He took this as a hint to return to his own desk.

'Anyway, Bernard, last night I drove past Amanda's, just to see if there was any sign of life, and I'm pretty sure I saw some bloke in her living room.'

'Kevin?'

'Don't know. Maybe, anyway, I need caffeine inside me before I do any thinking.'

Bernard picked up his bag, and stood for a second with it hanging from his fingers.

'Mona?'

'Uh-huh?' She was rifling through her bag and didn't look up.

'I've got a theory about some of the stuff in the diaries.' Finally locating her purse, she straightened up. 'Well, save that thought, and tell me when I get back from the canteen.'

'But...'

'Seriously, Bernard, I can't take anything in until I've got a coffee inside me.'

Bernard settled into his chair, and after a minute's deliberation, picked up his copy of *The Plague* and started reading. Most of the first chapter revolved around dying rats, which made Bernard feel slightly nauseous. He was on his third page of dead rodents when Paterson swept into the office.

'Team meeting, five minutes' time.' He stopped in front of him. 'Bernard, do your reading on your own time. We've got a Missing Person Inquiry here.'

He waved the book at his boss's retreating figure. 'It's research.'

Paterson ignored him, and Bernard followed him into his office. 'And have we, though?'

The Team Leader stopped ladling coffee into his Lothian and Borders mug and looked up in irritation. '"Have we though" what?'

'Have we got a Missing Person Inquiry?' He could feel himself wilting under Paterson's gaze, but he kept going. 'Heidi's not a Missing Person, is she? She's a Health Check No Show. If she was a Missing Person the Police...'

'Would be investigating.'

His boss poured boiling water into his mug, grabbing a piece of paper from his desk to mop up the overflow.

Bernard caught sight of the words 'Parliamentary Committee' and hoped Paterson wasn't using an important document as a dishrag.

'It would just be nice, Brains, to have one meeting where we didn't end up debating, what's the word ...?'

'Semantics?'

'What am I missing?' Maitland appeared in the doorway, followed by Mona.

'Nothing, just Bernard nipping my head as usual.' He shooed them back into the outer office and pulled up a seat facing their desks.

Bernard went on standing in the doorway. 'It's just that I'm not sure that the Police shouldn't actually be investigating ...'

'Bernard, shove that book up your arse and shut up. Now what do we know?'

Bernard opened his mouth to argue but caught Mona's eye. She gave a tiny shake of her head, so he admitted defeat and resumed his place.

'Mona, what have we got?'

She consulted the handwritten notes she had balanced on her knees. 'OK, Guv, interview with the parents didn't turn up much. Spoke to her flatmate – very nice flat, by the way – who gave us the runaround, said she didn't know much about Heidi, then changed her story and said they were pals.'

'Interesting,' said Paterson.

'Yeah, and it gets better. Heidi's got a boyfriend who's been staying there, parents don't know about him ...'

'Well, there you go,' Paterson chipped in. 'She's off somewhere with the bloke.'

Mona looked unconvinced. 'Possibly. But Heidi's been buying Luprophen and Hyrdosol over the Internet.'

'Why?' Paterson frowned.

'A conspiracy theory, Guv. They think these drugs can ward off the Virus.'

'Idiots. So, where are they selling the stuff?'

'Her diary identified that she frequented Morley's ...'

Paterson snorted. 'That figures.'

'Which we've checked out, and the Railway Tavern which, bizarrely, doesn't appear to exist.'

Bernard raised his hand. 'I've been thinking about that.'

Mona and Paterson both looked at him with vexed expressions.

'What are you thinking?' said Paterson, with barely disguised impatience.

'Well, remember that TV programme about the policeman who goes back in time and ends up in the 1970s, and there's a huge culture clash, which is in no way relevant here ...'

Maitland snorted with laughter, then shut up quickly when he saw Paterson's face.

'Anyway, in the programme there's a pub called the Railway Arms, which isn't real but is actually a representation of Heaven ...'

'Bernard, I swear to God if you do not stop talking ...'

He held his hand up again, both in an attempt to placate his boss and also to get to the end of his sentence. 'Just let me finish – which made me think, what if the Railway Tavern isn't an actual place but is really a symbol? And then there are references in the diary to Dr Beeching ...'

Maitland leaned forward. 'Is he the virologist that's always on the telly?'

'No, he was Chairman of British Rail in the 1960s.'

Paterson was turning purple. 'Bernard ...'

It was time to speed up. 'He was responsible for closing down lots of branch lines, and I think it might be a satirical reference in the diary, and if I was an eighteen-year-old looking for somewhere out of the way to hold an illegal meet-up I might choose ...'

'The old railway lines under the city!' Mona broke in, and he nodded vehemently in agreement. 'So, if Bernard is correct in his thinking,' she went on, 'these particular idiots are holding raves in the disused railway tunnels. Perfect, really, for a late-night meet-up. No-one in their right mind is going to be hanging around there after dark.'

'Hmm.' Paterson's eyes flicked from Mona to Bernard, his expression exhibiting a degree of scepticism. 'OK, let's reread the diaries and see if Bernard's outrageous suggestion has any merit. Mona, I take it you'll be having another go at the flatmate today?'

'Soon as I can, Guv, but you and I have that Parliament thing this morning.'

'As if I could possibly forget. Maitland, you're working on this case too now.'

Maitland's mouth fell open. Bernard savoured the look of intense annoyance on his colleague's face.

'What about my Defaulter?'

'What's the deal with your case?'

'Pregnant lassie. Friend of the barman in Morley's.'

'Interesting. Morley's angle to both these Defaulters that we need to follow up.'

'That's what I'm saying, Guv.'

'But we need to find the German lassie first.'

'Guv – things are at a pretty crucial stage with my Defaulter.'

163

'Out of my hands. Orders from above. Mona, get Shagger here doing something useful on your case.' He stood up. 'OK, anything else?'

'Yeah,' said Maitland, sulkily. 'Where's Carole?'

'Out doing sterling work touring Edinburgh's secondary education establishments.'

Bernard left the meeting, with an unaccustomed feeling that he couldn't quite place. Something that resembled, but wasn't quite, satisfaction.

2

Maitland was behaving oddly. Mona had watched him pick up the phone three times, only to put it down again when the Guv loomed into view. Surmising that he was up to something, she settled back and waited. For the fourth time, he picked up the phone, checked that the Guv was safely contained in his office, and dialled.

'Donny, it's me, Maitland. Any word from Colette yet?'

So, her colleague was still working on his old case.

'Did you ring round her friends?'

There was a brief pause, and Maitland's face registered disbelief. 'Really?' Paterson's figure appeared in the doorway of his office. Her teammate ducked down slightly in his chair. 'Nobody? None of her friends? Not Kate, not Louise, not anyone?'

Another pause.

Maitland crouched down even lower. 'You know what the mortality is for pregnant women that get the Virus?' he hissed.

He clocked Mona watching him, turned his back on her and lowered his voice further.

'Without getting them into hospital where they can get the correct prenatal care, Colette stands an eighty per cent chance of dying or losing her baby, if she gets the Virus. Eighty per cent, for Christ's sake. We're not talking a slight chance of something going wrong here, we're talking odds-on catastrophe. You want that on your conscience, Donny?'

There was a brief silence, then Maitland swore. Mona guessed Donny had just hung up.

Maitland shrugged on his coat and went over to her desk.

'I need to tie something up on my Defaulter. Cover for me.'

'Are you insane?' She swung back on her chair. 'Paterson's going to freak if he finds out you're not looking for Heidi.'

'The cases are connected, we all know that.'

Mona was unconvinced this would cut much ice with Paterson. 'Yeah, but ...'

'The least streetwise twenty-year-old in the world is pregnant and on the run from us.'

'Yeah, you said. The barman from Morley's knocked her up.'

'No, he didn't,' Maitland noticed Bernard looking over, and lowered his voice. 'It looks like she was raped, by the Minister at the Church of the Lord Arisen.'

'Christ!'

Bernard looked over. 'What's going on?'

They ignored him.

'I said ...' Bernard's phone rang before he could pester them any further.

'How do you know this happened?' asked Mona.

Maitland looked a little defensive. 'The barman from Morley's told us.'

Mona laughed in disbelief. 'He doesn't entirely sound like a reliable source.'

'Well, maybe not, but I still want to know that Colette is OK.'

Mona absent-mindedly doodled a row of question marks on the edge of her paper while she thought. 'She might have gone to a refuge or something?'

'Maybe,' said Maitland. 'In fact, probably. And I think her friend knows where she is. Cover for me – an hour tops?'

She sighed.

'Come on, Mona, if this was the Police we wouldn't be pissing about after some rich German lassie who's probably off with her boyfriend somewhere. We'd be looking for the vulnerable rape victim.'

A large part of her agreed with Maitland. She looked over at her boss's office. Paterson was standing by his desk, frowning at the document he had in his hand.

'OK. The Guv's going to be out all morning at some Parliamentary thing he wants me to carry his bags at. He'll probably not even notice you've gone. But Maitland . . .'

'What?'

'Take Bernard with you.'

His mouth fell open. 'You are kidding, aren't you?'

'No. This is serious stuff you're talking about. You need a witness for any conversation you have.'

Maitland looked irritated, but the logic of what Mona was saying got to him, and he nodded.

'And make this the last thing you do on this case until Heidi is found.'

'Are you ready?' Paterson stuck his head out of his office.

'Coming, Guv.' Mona got to her feet and shot Maitland a smile. 'Later.'

She followed her boss, who was charging down the stairs muttering to himself. He held the fire door open to let Mona through.

167

'I hate the Parliamentary Virus Coordination Committee.'

'Understandable, Guv.'

Now they were out of the building, Paterson's pace had slowed to a crawl.

'I mean,' said Mona, 'I totally get that you hate having to stand up and justify the HET's work in front of the likes of Carlotta Carmichael . . .'

'Bitch.'

'Obviously, Guv, but I just don't understand why you need me there.'

'Because, Mona,' Paterson ground to a complete halt. 'I turned up to my first Coordination Committee meeting, six, or was it seven, months back on my own, only to find Cameron Stuttle waiting for me with some twelve-year-old desk-hugger laden down with his papers. Turns out all the politicians bowl up with flunkies and researchers, and all manner of Bright Young Things. So the HET can't go in there without a bag-carrier each. We'll be shown up.'

'Yeah, I see but why . . .?'

Paterson stuck out his hand and hailed a cab. 'Why you? Because last time, when I took Marguerite from the Admin team, they were filming proceedings. She caught a brief glimpse of herself on the Scottish teatime news, and talked of nothing else for a week.'

Mona laughed, and climbed in after her boss. 'I suppose it is quite exciting, isn't it? Watching all those decisions being made about the Virus.'

Paterson snorted. 'I can assure you, Mona, that nobody ever made an actual decision at this Committee.' He stared out of the window. 'Every single decision that is made about the Virus is done behind closed doors, by

168

people who actually know what they are talking about.'

'So, why do they bother holding them?'

'Because they're politicians!'

The taxi braked sharply at a mini-roundabout, narrowly avoiding a car that was turning right. Paterson regained his balance and continued.

'They need a platform where they can grandstand about everything they are doing, and give a kicking to people like me who are doing their best to sort out the mess the MSPs have made of this all.'

Mona smiled, trying not to laugh at her boss's cynicism. 'So, are you all prepared for this, Guv?'

He grunted. 'Well, I missed the briefing meeting yesterday due to that fiasco with Vic Thompson, and I should probably have spent a bit longer reading the papers. I'm sure I can wing it, though.'

The cab turned into Holyrood Park, and the two of them sat in silence until they pulled up outside the Parliament building. Cameron Stuttle was waiting for them, as predicted, with a young man holding a stack of papers.

'Cutting it a bit fine, John,' muttered Cameron. He set off at a brisk walk. 'Prepared for this, I hope?'

'Yes,' Paterson snapped back. 'But I don't see why it's always up to me to represent the HETs.'

'Which of your colleagues do you suggest I send? The drunk, the over-promoted one, or the one who doesn't exist?'

'Maybe you could throw the net a bit wider than just Edinburgh? Maybe . . .'

Paterson broke off as a placard appeared in front of his face.

'No vaccine testing on animals!'

169

The protester was small, green-haired, and female. Mona watched in amusement as her boss tried to work out how to continue on his way without pushing her. He opted for a wide sidestep, and she followed him, refusing the leaflet that the animal rights protester thrust at her.

'I wouldn't mind if there was actually a vaccine,' Paterson muttered. He caught up with his superior. 'Will we hear anything about that today?'

'It's all commercially sensitive, John. You know that.' Stuttle pulled open the door to the Parliament building. 'We'll hear as soon as one of the pharmaceutical companies has something to sell to us, believe me.'

'And exactly when will that be?'

'As soon as the bastard Virus stops mutating, I assume. I'm not a bloody scientist.' He held the door open and gestured them through. 'Hurry up.'

Mona and Paterson exchanged a glance. They showed their Green Cards to the security guard, and surrendered their bags and coats for scanning. As Paterson went through the metal detector the machine beeped, and he was pulled to one side by a guard who frisked him. Cameron pointedly tapped his watch.

In the Chamber Mona slid into a row of seats behind Cameron Stuttle, with her boss following her. The seating arrangements struck Mona as gladiatorial. The politicians sat in a row at the front looking out to the massed rows of workers involved in fighting the Virus. Behind the assembled staff, in a small gallery, sat the Press.

The MSPs were already in place. There were a couple that she recognised from previous meetings, both of them non-entities from minor parties. The Labour member was well known for his opposition to the Virus

170

policies, and had built a fairly successful media career on the back of it. Her eye went past him to the Chair, Carlotta Carmichael. She had her back to them and was deep in conversation with one of the civil servants responsible for organising the Committee. From the expression on the bureaucrat's face, it wasn't a pleasant conversation.

She turned to look at the journalists who were filling up the back row. The Committee still got a reasonable turnout from the Press, with both national and local papers sending reps, as well as the broadcast media. Paterson followed her gaze.

'Don't know what they get out of these meetings,' he said to her, in a low voice, 'nobody says anything interesting.'

She saw a face she recognised from CID Press briefings and waved to him. She kept scanning along until she caught sight of Jonathon Carmichael, Carlotta's husband.

'Guv,' she said quietly. 'Jonathon Carmichael's here.'

Paterson sighed, and she smiled sympathetically. He had arrested Carlotta's other half on suspicion of drink-driving several years back. Despite Paterson's best attempts, it hadn't gone to court.

'Has he forgiven you?'

'No,' said Paterson, slumping in his seat, 'and neither has his missus.'

On cue, Carlotta walked to her seat and motioned to everyone to quieten down. A hush spread quickly across the auditorium. The men on the Committee took up their places on either side of her. 'OK, everyone, let's make a start.'

Carlotta nodded to a man in the audience, who took his

171

cue, stood up, and introduced himself as the Enterprise rep. His report was depressing listening: Scotland remained in recession for the fourth consecutive quarter, High Streets were 'facing a fundamental challenge to pre-existing business models' as people refused to go out or spend money, absenteeism was at an all-time high ... Mona drifted off, her attention returning only when a young woman in the row in front of her stood up. She announced herself as the Health Communications rep, in a slightly quavering tone, her papers shaking in her hand. Mona winced. She suspected Carlotta didn't have much truck with nerves.

'The H1N1-variant is a zoonotic virus originating in chickens...'

'Stop!' Carlotta glared over the top of her glasses at the speaker. 'Stop right there. Please tell me you are not going to rehash the whole history of the Virus for a room full of people who have been involved in Viral policy for the past two years? Please focus on the public health response, not the cause.'

The back of the beleaguered health rep's neck was bright red. She stumbled, extremely quickly, through an update of the success of the PHeDA adverts, the difficulties of effectively communicating Health Check information to the 18-24 demographic, and noted that the stocks of antiviral drugs, antibiotics and bacterial vaccines were now back at the levels they were prior to the Second Wave of the Virus.

'Any questions?' asked Carlotta of her fellow MSPs, before continuing almost in the same breath, 'No? OK, local authority rep, please.'

The woman sank gratefully back into her seat, and Mona turned to look at her boss. He looked a little pale.

'You OK, Guv?' she whispered.

He leaned toward her. 'She's saving her energy for the next bit, when she lays into me.'

Stuttle turned and glared at them, and held a finger up to his lips.

'And is the Health Enforcement Team representative here?' She made a show of scanning the benches. Mona doubted very much that she didn't recognise Paterson, and hadn't already seen him. Even if she didn't recognise him from his last two appearances before the Committee, the length of time she'd spent trying to get him sacked for arresting her husband should have made his face stick in her memory.

Paterson pressed the button that turned his microphone on. 'John Paterson, Head of North Edinburgh HET.'

'Well, Mr Paterson, perhaps you could tell us what the HET has been up to?'

'I refer the Committee to Item 16 on the agenda, the report on ...'

'I am well aware of your report, Mr Paterson.' She looked at him over the top of her tortoiseshell glasses. 'I was rather hoping you could explain why the HET is now in the business of searching for international missing persons?'

Mona saw Stuttle stiffen in his seat. He leaned forward and engaged his microphone. 'The HET doesn't deal with missing persons, Chair, that would be the responsibility ...'

'I was asking Mr Paterson!' Carlotta cut him off. 'I do believe he is the operational HET representative.'

Stuttle and Mona looked at each other. Neither of them had any faith that Paterson could answer this question without sparking a diplomatic incident.

'We're waiting, Mr Paterson.'

The silence was painful. Mona had an idea, and kicked her boss under the table. She put her hands onto her desk, one finger on her left hand extended, and four on her right.

Paterson looked at her hands with a look of slightly panicked confusion on his face. She spread all ten digits out, balled her fingers, then extended four. This time her boss got the point, and again pressed the button to make his mike live.

'As my colleague has pointed out to the Committee, we do not chase missing persons, we chase Health Defaulters. And as the Committee is well aware, under the terms of the Health Enforcement and Defaulter Recovery Act we are unable to release the names of any individual we are seeking until a full fourteen days after they have missed their scheduled Health Check.'

He leaned back and smiled politely.

Carlotta turned pink. 'You do not need to remind us of the law, Mr Paterson, we were instrumental in drafting the legislation. But if the HET has stretched its remit to look for missing German nationals then this is something that should be brought to the attention of my colleagues.'

Mona saw Stuttle look over his shoulder at the Press. A civil servant moved forward discreetly and said something to Carlotta. Mona assumed it was something along the lines of her breaking the law if she divulged any further information. Carlotta turned even pinker.

'I'm informed that this session has run over time. Thank you to everyone for attending.'

Everyone stood up except for Mona, Stuttle and Paterson.

Paterson turned to his boss. 'What was ...?'

Stuttle gestured to him to keep his voice down, but he leaned across Mona. 'Will you tell the Right Honourable

174

Member for Nippy Sweeties that that's not how things are done?' His voice echoed round the Chamber.

Stuttle reached over and pushed Paterson's elbow off the microphone button. 'I think you just told her yourself,' he hissed.

3

Maitland raised his fist and brought it down hard on Kate's door. He repeated the action several times, but the hammering failed to provoke an answer.

Bernard had a hand pressed to his forehead as he tried to process what was going on. 'So these girls are friends of Colette's? Do they know she's pregnant?'

'One of the things I want to find out.' Maitland thump, thump, thumped again, to the same effect. After a second's thought he turned on his heel.

'Where are we going now?'

Maitland didn't answer, and strode off down the corridor, ignoring the heads that had appeared in Kate's neighbours' doorways, summoned by his pounding. Bernard watched him go until he turned the corner, at which point he unwillingly decided to follow him rather than negotiate his way solo back out of the rabbit warren of Milne's Court. 'Are we still looking for Colette's friend? I thought we were focusing on Heidi for the moment?'

Maitland stopped abruptly at another door. 'Louise? Are you in there?'

After a brief pause it opened to reveal a thin girl, with long, straight hair and a tear-stained face. She seemed to recognise Maitland, and held the door open for them both to enter. Another girl – bigger, with curly hair – was sitting in a chair. The room screamed heritage: long red velvet drapes around a bay window, walls feet thick, solid stone everywhere. He'd have loved a room like this at uni. His undergraduate bedroom had been a six by four cell, with walls so thin he could hear his next-door neighbour breathing.

'Where is she?' Maitland walked toward the seated girl. 'Kate?'

'We don't know.' The girl had her hair tied back in some kind of hair-clasp. A few irrepressible curls had fought their way out, and she pulled absent-mindedly on them. 'We already told you that.'

'Yes,' said Maitland. 'But I thought you were lying then, and I think you're lying now.'

Bernard waited to see how she would respond to this accusation. In his experience Defaulters and witnesses never responded well to being accused of deception. Even when evidence of their duplicity was laid out in front of them like a row of playing cards, people tended to continue to protest innocence. *I never missed my Health Check. I was there, the nurse never wrote my name down.* Kate, however, showed no such emotion. She walked to the bay window, and stood in the alcove, staring down into the courtyard. 'I think you should leave now, Mr Stevenson.'

Maitland swivelled round and approached the other girl, who was now sitting at the end of the bed, knotting an edge of the duvet in her hand. 'Louise, tell me where Colette is.'

She glanced over at her friend's back, looking for direction.

Maitland knelt down next to her on one knee. It looked like the unhappiest proposal ever. 'Louise, Colette is pregnant.'

The girl was shaking now, and moved away from Maitland, as if putting physical distance between them could stop his questioning.

Maitland's voice was soft and authoritative. 'She needs proper medical care. It could be fatal for her if she caught the Virus now.'

Bernard guessed if Maitland pushed just a little bit more she might give in. It was a pity Carole wasn't there. She was so good at this stuff; two minutes of her motherly concern and the girls would have been crying everything out on her shoulder.

'Louise, we can help her. The HET will get her all the medical support that she so desperately needs right now. Just tell me where she is.'

The girl buried her face in her hands.

Maitland exhaled, a long angry sound of exasperation. He looked over at Bernard, and then, as if sensing he wouldn't get any inspiration there, got to his feet. Bernard tried not to be offended. After all, his colleague wasn't wrong. He was uncomfortable enough at the fact they weren't looking for Heidi, without having to cross-examine a couple of teenagers.

Maitland had changed his focus. He walked over to Kate and stood beside her staring down at the cobbles and students.

'What did you mean the other day, when you said it was unfair the things that were said about Pastor Mackenzie?'

Kate moved further behind the curtain.

'You meant that people talked about him having inappropriate relationships with women in the congregation, didn't you?'

No response.

'Kate?' Maitland hauled the curtain back. The girl flinched at the sudden movement. She looked exposed, like a tiny animal that they had backed into a corner.

'Maitland,' said Bernard, a warning tone in his voice.

'This is a friend of yours that is missing, isn't it? Not just some random stranger you don't give a shit about?'

'You obviously know it all already.' She went to move away but Maitland shot his arm across to the wall, effectively trapping her in.

'Shall we discuss this all at the nearest Police Station?'

'Fine!' she shouted, and pushed him.

He stumbled and pulled on the curtain to keep himself upright. The crimson velvet came away from its rail and pooled on the ground between them.

'Let's go,' she yelled. 'And I'll tell the Police the same thing. I do not know where Colette is!'

'Really, Kate?' he shouted back. 'You don't seem all that surprised to find out that your friend is pregnant, news which is pretty hot off the press. When did you last speak to Colette?'

She didn't answer.

'Your friend is going to end up dead at this rate! Is that what you want?'

The room was silent, punctuated only by the sound of Louise sniffing. Kate wasn't meeting Maitland's eye, and Bernard wondered if his colleague was actually getting through to them.

'Look,' said Maitland. 'I'm going to think the best of you. I'm going to assume that you two have enough common sense to realise that you have to tell me where Colette is, but you just want to speak to her first. So,' he looked at his watch. 'I'm going to give you until noon today to either get her to call me, or

179

for you to tell me where she is. And if I don't hear from you by then,' he walked over to the door, 'I'm having you both arrested. See how good that looks on your graduate CV.'

He slammed the door.

Bernard apologetically picked up the curtain and placed it on the chair. 'Sorry about that.' He backed out of the room, Kate glaring at him, and Louise still sobbing quietly to herself.

'Maitland – wait up!' His colleague was already weaving his way through the maze of corridors in the direction of the High Street.

'Bernard, just leave me alone.'

He trotted after his colleague. 'What's going on? Shouldn't we be taking them in for a formal interview? They obviously know something they're not telling us.'

'I would if I could.'

'But we can. Under the powers given to the HETs under the Virus legislation ...'

'Yes, Bernard, I know all that. But the Guv doesn't actually know that we're here and not working full-time on the German girl case.'

Bernard's heart leapt into his mouth. 'I assumed you'd cleared this with him. Mr Paterson will be furious.'

'Yeah, well, only if he finds out. But we can't exactly turn up with a couple of interviewees from a different case.'

'But ...'

'Stop being such an old woman.'

'But ...'

'Bernard, go and do something else!'

Spending the rest of the afternoon somewhere Maitland wasn't seemed like a very good idea, the only problem being he didn't know where that somewhere should be. 'What should I do?'

Maitland started walking again, and flung a dismissive arm in his direction. 'Go and check on Carole. Didn't she have some kind of lead at the hospital?'

4

Paterson was sitting with his head in his hands.

Stuttle was being surprisingly supportive. He'd insisted that they go back to his office for a 'debrief'. His assistant had provided them with drinks and a range of chocolate biscuits of such good quality that Mona had had a moment or two's reflection on the size of SHEP's hospitality budget. Stuttle had been happily holding forth on the subject of Ms Carmichael MSP for the best part of ten minutes.

'The thing you have to remember about Carlotta, John, is that she's trying to make a name for herself on the back of this Virus. And she's none too pleased about the German's comments about the Scottish approach. Doesn't reflect well on her, what with her being the political lead on all this.'

Paterson grunted.

'But she's overplayed her hand this time,' said Cameron. 'We'll put in a formal complaint, of course, that she's breached the confidentiality of a Health Defaulter by mentioning her nationality. She did say she was German, didn't she? I didn't imagine it?'

'Yes.'

'This could work out well for us. Probably won't get her sacked but might get her off our backs for a while.' He reclined on his seat, his hands behind his head. 'Yes, this could work out pretty well all round.'

Stuttle's PA reappeared with a tray full of correspondence. Stuttle idly picked up the first letter and glanced at it. Something in it caught his attention and he snapped forward, his earlier relaxed pose disappearing. His head turned in the direction of the Guv. 'Did you pay a visit to Victor Thompson's bar?'

The Guv suddenly seemed to be finding his luxurious leather seating uncomfortable. 'Yes, but . . .'

'Mona, can you leave us, please?'

'Eh . . .' She looked at her boss, who was contemplating his feet.

'Now, Mona.'

Stuttle's tone brooked no argument, so she picked up her bag and headed out. As the door closed behind her, she heard an explosion of curses from the SHEP boss. Stuttle's PA stopped typing at this unexpected noise.

Mona indicated the room she'd just vacated. 'You might want to stick the kettle on again.'

'Mona!'

Marcus's look of surprise quickly turned into an overeager smile, and he cleared a pile of papers, topped by what looked like a number of computer games, off a seat for her. It was a measure of how badly the morning had gone that she felt almost pleased to see him. It was certainly nice to have someone making her feel welcome, after her unceremonious exit from SHEP's offices.

'So, to what do I owe the honour?'

She forced a smile. 'I'm here to see if you've turned up anything new from the German girl's e-mail.'

If anything could stop the Guv being booted out of the HET, it would be a swift resolution to this case.

'Ah, *les enfants de Camus*.'

He was looking at her over the top of his glasses, to see if she was impressed by his grasp of European languages. She wasn't.

'Anyway, I was about to ring you because I have some news that I think will make you very happy.' Marcus sat back in his chair and smiled at her, a Cheshire cat of smugness. 'Care to guess what it is?'

'Quit pissing about, and just tell me,' Mona snapped. She felt a twinge of remorse at his hurt expression.

'Take a look at this.' He swivelled the screen round to face her. 'This is Heidi's G-mail account. This e-mail came in about eight o'clock this morning.'

Mona perused the contents.

'Who's it from?' asked Mona.

'Dr Beeching, apparently.'

Marcus laughed. Mona didn't. Detecting that she was having a sense of humour failure today, he continued at a faster pace.

'In reality, an anonymous G-mail address. Check out the wording.'

She leaned in toward the screen, and read the message out loud. 'Dr Beeching invites you to attend a select gathering of friends at the Railway Tavern this evening. Usual terms. K.'

This was good. This was very, very good. She felt a sense of excitement stealing over her, and grinned at him. 'Fancy a trip to the Railway Tavern, Marcus?'

He looked delighted at the invitation. 'I'll get the first round.'

5

The security turnstile beeped, and Carole waved to him as she entered the hospital.

'How did it go? Are Edinburgh's teenagers now safe from risky Virus behaviour?'

She laughed. 'It went OK, I think. The kids mainly just looked bored.'

'Not sure I entirely blame them.' Bernard took the large cardboard box Carole was carrying out of her arms, catching sight of the red lettering of the leaflets 'Ten things every Young Scot needs to know about the Virus' as he did so. 'Sorry to drag you back here. You must be desperate to get away.'

'I'd have been up here later anyway to visit Michael.' She frowned. 'Can't say I'm ecstatic about bothering that poor woman though.'

'I know, but I think there is something in your suspicions that she's connected to our case.'

'Really?'

'Yup. I checked out with our colleagues at Police Scotland and one of the Church of the Lord Arisen girls who overdosed on the drugs was called Kirsty McLeod. So, all very similar to the situation with Colette and Heidi. Have you any idea why Maitland's so worried about his Defaulter?'

Carole looked surprised. 'You'd probably know that better than me.'

He made a small non-committal noise.

'Did Maitland not say that she is pregnant?' Carole continued. 'I mean that would be a good reason to be worried.'

'True. I just got the impression that it was more personal. Did he ever mention Pastor . . .?'

Carole took his arm. 'This is it.' She pointed to a small sign on the wall which indicated *Sanctuary*. 'This is where I met her.'

Bernard admired a piece of hospital art while Carole disappeared inside. He'd being staring at the pastel hues for a matter of seconds when she reappeared.

'Empty.'

'What about trying the ward?'

'Not the easiest places to get access to. I mean even aside from the Virus, there are all the child protection issues . . .' She tailed off. 'I suppose we could go up to the ward and cause a fuss until they let us in?'

Bernard thought for a minute. Causing a fuss wasn't exactly his strong point. He tended to stand an embarrassed distance behind Mona while she blagged and bullied her way into places. He definitely lacked the throwing-your-weight around skills that their ex-Police colleagues had. 'Shall we check out all the public areas first?'

'Good idea.' She looked relieved. 'Let's have a wander.'

They walked through the central hall of the ERI, eyeing up the people buying magazines and gifts in the shops. Carole grabbed his arm. 'I've spotted her – she's in the café. Far side, in the red coat.'

Bernard looked over. Kirsty's mother was focused on her half-drunk cup of coffee. He wondered, in fact, if she was almost asleep. Her posture radiated exhaustion.

186

Her hair needed washing, and grey roots were showing through the auburn.

'So what do we do now?' he asked.

'I suppose we go over and talk to her. I'd better make the first move, seeing as I spoke to her before.' She took a deep breath. 'I wish I was back working in the NHS, or in my shop. This isn't my area of expertise at all.'

He nodded sympathetically, but had a slightly shameful feeling of relief that again he could fall in behind someone else's lead. He followed Carole as she walked over to the woman, and said hello.

Kirsty's mother stared at her for a second before recognition set in. 'Oh, it's you. I thought it was a doctor with some news.'

'Sorry. I just wondered how you were doing?'

Carole sat down at the table, uninvited. Bernard followed suit.

'I'm Carole, by the way, and this is Bernard.'

'Aileen.'

'How's your daughter?'

'The same as yesterday. And the day before that. As she will be tomorrow. And every day after that.' She looked up. 'Who are you? Are you from the Police?'

'No, no.' Carole raised both hands. 'We don't work for the Police. But we do work for the Health Enforcement Team.' She laid her ID on the table. 'And I wanted to speak to you about the Church of the Lord Arisen.'

The woman closed her eyes. 'Them. The people that ruined my daughter's life.'

'You think they were responsible for her drug overdose?'

'My daughter was not suicidal.' There was fury in the woman's tone. 'She was scared of the Virus, of course she

187

was, but she would never have done something like that. *They* did this to her.' The woman played with her coffee cup, rolling it from side to side against her palms. 'Of course, the Police don't believe me. All I know is that my daughter changed when she got involved with them. That long-haired minister and all his groupies.' She looked up suddenly. 'Who are you looking for?'

'Of course this is all confidential under the terms of the Health Enforcement Act ...' Carole tailed off.

'I understand,' said Aileen.

'But two girls from the Church, Heidi Weber and Colette Greenwood, both missed their last Health Checks. We're obliged by law to try to find them.'

'I know Colette – she visits my daughter regularly. Why did she run off?' Aileen looked panicked. 'She's not involved in drugs, is she?'

'We couldn't rule it out, but it's not the line of enquiry that we're following. It would really help if you could tell us the last time you saw her?'

Aileen thought for a moment. 'It's difficult. You lose all track of time in this place. Monday, perhaps?'

'And how did she seem? Did you speak to her?'

'Not really,' said Aileen. 'I usually go and have a shower when Colette comes in. Glad of the break.' She laughed, without any humour. 'I left them as usual. When I came back she was talking to my daughter, and crying, but to be honest, we all do that.'

'Did you hear what she was saying?'

Aileen thought hard. 'I think she said something along the lines of "this can't be happening", but I assumed she meant Kirsty's situation.'

'Have you any idea at all where Colette might go if she was in trouble?'

She pondered the question. 'Sorry, I don't.'

'Thanks for your time. I won't bother you any longer.'

'It wasn't a bother.' She finally gave up on her coffee, and put it back on the tray. 'If there is anything else I can do . . .I'd hate any other mother to go through what I did.'

Carole stood up to leave but Aileen grabbed her hand.

'Why were you in the Sanctuary? Were you following me?'

'No. My son, Michael, my eldest, is recovering from the Virus. He's upstairs in the Young Adults' Virus ward.'

Aileen stared at her, unsure if she was lying or not.

'For real.' She pulled back her sleeve to show her the wristband that allowed her to enter Michael's ward.

The mother stared at it. 'Will he be all right?'

'They think so.'

'You're lucky. So lucky.' She started to cry.

Carole sat down and put her arms round the weeping woman. Bernard wondered whether he should leave. His colleague looked up, and with a silent movement of her eyes managed to convey the message that he should go. The shameful feeling of relief flooded back, and he stood up, nodding Carole a silent goodbye.

6

Mona looked at her watch, shielding it from the sun so she could read the time. It was twenty minutes since she'd rung Paterson and asked for his help to identify where on the defunct railway system tonight's rave might be taking place. He'd been sceptical on the phone, but she was sure he'd call if he wasn't coming. It was more likely he was lost. She wandered back down the cycle track and out on to Trinity Road and found herself face-to-face with her boss. 'How did you manage to talk me into this, Mona?'

She passed him a leaflet showing the outline of the former railway route. The brochure was designed for the cyclists and runners who now used the pathways, but it would do for her purposes.

'I mean, this idea came from Bernard which means we really should be treating it with extreme caution.'

She started walking back up the track. 'I think he might be right this time, though.'

Paterson grunted, but followed her. 'Remind me what the purpose of this wild goose chase is.'

'Thanks for the positive frame of mind, Guv.' She stifled a smile. 'We're looking for any indication that an illegal meet-up might have taken place, you know, bottles, fag butts, etc.'

'I get the picture. Where are the others?'

'Maitland's at Granton, Marcus from IT is helping us

190

out covering the Portobello end, and the man himself, Bernard, is at Restalrig.'

They quickened their pace, with Paterson covering the left side of the path, and Mona the right.

'Guv?'

'What?'

'Be discreet though; we don't want anyone clocking us and deciding to call tonight off.'

'Thanks for the advice, Mona. I have done this kind of thing before.'

They walked in silence for a minute or two, while Mona summoned the nerve to ask the question they were both waiting for. 'Guv? What did Cameron Stuttle say?'

Her boss stopped. 'I think the best that can be said for it is that I still have a job. For the moment.' He started walking again. 'Let's just find this railway place.'

In the last century Edinburgh had boasted a thriving train system, linking all corners of the city. The Beeching Axe fell heavily on the city, though, and all that remained of its suburban lines were the odd place name, an occasional footbridge, and the network of old lines that were now a car-free route for cyclists and walkers.

A Labrador bounded up to the Guv, and sniffed at his ankles.

'Good boy.' Paterson bent down and gave the animal a pat. The dog's owner nodded to them as he walked past. The Guv gave the mutt a last pat and moved on. 'Off you go now, shoo.'

The dog shot a mournful glance after him, then ran on to catch up with his master.

'Think you've got a fan there, Guv.'

'Well, that's one, anyway.'

A cyclist sped past without a glance, manoeuvring

seamlessly to one side in order to avoid them. Occasionally Mona could hear the sound of children in the gardens that backed onto the path, but mostly it was so silent you could forget that you were in the heart of a city.

The old station from the days when these were active train lines was now a house. It struck Mona as a spooky place to live; she wondered if, when the occupants were lying in bed at night, they heard phantom trains rushing past their windows. Or, more likely, gangs of neds wandering past up to no good.

This reminded her of her mission, and she started to focus on the task in hand. She drifted to the side of the cycle path and began to check the embankments for discarded cans and bottles. Nothing caught her eye, so she sauntered on until they came to the first tunnel. After a quick check to make sure no-one was about, they stopped at the entrance and had a good look at it.

The tunnel was about a hundred feet long and straight, allowing you to see from one end to the other. At its highest point it was about thirty feet high, made out of single bricks stacked one on the other in a gently curving arch. A miracle of Victorian technology.

She took a couple of steps into the tunnel, and felt the temperature immediately drop. It was darker, even allowing for the light from the ends and the electric lighting on the walls. The air smelled damp, and Mona felt the atmosphere cling oppressively to her clothes. There was the usual smattering of graffiti tags, and anti-Virus slogans, although it was hard to tell if the vandalism was new or historic. Mona wandered over and touched one of the walls; as she had suspected it was wet to the touch. She rubbed her hand on her coat. If this was where young people wanted to party, they were welcome to it.

She wandered over to her boss. 'Once we get through this tunnel the road forks – you take the left and I'll take the right.'

'Nope,' said Paterson, shaking his head.

Two older women on bikes came into view. They stepped to one side to let them pass, and the women smiled their thanks.

'No? You've got a better plan?'

'No, I think we've found it. This is it. This is the place.'

She wondered if he was winding her up. 'How can you be so sure?'

'Mona,' he sighed theatrically, 'after all these years of working for the Police, I think I can trust my gut instinct. Oh yeah, and that.' He pointed to the roof of the tunnel.

'Welcome to the Railway Tavern' was written in white paint.

7

'So, tonight...' Paterson eyed his team. 'Tonight we need someone down there checking out what's happening.'

'Got to be me, really, Guv, hasn't it?' said Mona. She felt an energy in her bones she hadn't felt since she joined the HET. This was proper Police work.

Maitland snorted. 'It's a rave. You'd stick out a mile, Grandma.'

'Grandma?' Mona glared at her colleague. 'I've got all of two years on you.'

'Four years, actually, and you are an entire generation older when it comes to dress sense. See these?' Maitland balanced his foot on the desk. 'Two hundred quid's worth of Adidas's finest. State of the art.'

'So?' She wasn't sure what Maitland was getting at.

'So – check out your feet.'

Everyone looked at her shoes. She drew her feet under her chair.

'They're Clarks.' She shrugged. 'They're comfortable.'

'Yeah, well, they might be useful when Bernard pukes on them...'

Bernard's head snapped up from the copy of *The Plague* he was surreptitiously reading under the desk. 'I did not puke!'

' ... but you're not going to pass for twenty dressed like that.'

'Enough!' Paterson slapped his hand on the desk. 'This conversation proves to me that you are actually insane, Maitland. I've never spent more than thirty quid on shoes in my life, including the pair my wife insisted I buy for our wedding.' Paterson cast a scornful glance at Maitland's footwear. 'Anyway, you're both going.' He looked at her. 'Although maybe, Mona, you do need to take a look at your wardrobe for tonight.'

'Eh ...'

Mona turned to see that Bernard had his hand half in the air as always, as if this was a Higher English class rather than a team meeting.

Paterson closed his eyes. 'Bernard, you've done great work so far, but trust me, this isn't where your talents lie.'

'I don't want to go, but I was thinking, shouldn't we turn this over to the Police? I mean we think there's going to be serious drug dealing ...' He tailed off as his three colleagues glared at him. 'I'm just saying.'

Mona thought for a moment Paterson was about to explode.

'Bernard ...'

The Guv's tone was struggling to remain within the boundaries of reasonableness. She wondered how long he could keep it up.

'It is currently ten past five. If the rave begins at, say, twelve midnight, that leaves us less than seven hours to find someone in the higher ranks of the Police Force who is willing to round up a herd of non-immune PCs and send them into a bunch of hot and sweaty young people, containing, we think, at least one Health Check Defaulter.'

'But there may be drugs involved ...'

'Even with forty-eight hours' notice we'd struggle to find a Chief Super who'd OK a raid on a bunch of students who may, and I stress may, be swapping the contents of their granny's pill cupboard.'

'With all due respect, Mr Paterson, it's more serious than that. We're talking the importation of drugs into the country for resale to vulnerable young people.'

'Prescription drugs. Anything short of a boatload of heroin landing at Leith Docks is not going to get the Police Head Honcho risking the health of his men. Back me up here, Mona.'

'Totally.'

Mona winked at Paterson, who smiled. She suspected that, as correct as his arguments were, his main consideration was his desire not to give the case over to Police Scotland. Like herself, he felt the need for a half-decent collar.

Bernard raised his hand again. 'But ...'

'Bernard, shut up.' Paterson walked into his office and picked up his jacket. 'Time for some team building.'

8

Paterson returned from the bar with a tray containing two pints of lager, two lemonades and six packets of crisps.

'Thanks,' said Bernard, staring at his unasked-for pint. He looked nervously around the pub. It was a fairly basic model of hostelry, with no carpet, music, or women (with the notable exception of Mona). He caught the eye of an elderly patron in a checked cap, who glared at him over the top of his pint of stout, and flicked him the finger. He swivelled hurriedly back to his colleagues. Paterson's idea of a 'good place for a quick drink' wasn't the same as his. But then he had a horrible feeling this wasn't going to be a quick drink. He looked discreetly at his watch, wondering if he could at least nip outside and phone Carrie.

'It's amazing this place is still in business,' he said. 'Considering the number of pubs that have closed since the Virus began.'

'It's all down to the devil-may-care attitude of the regulars,' said Paterson, unloading the drinks. 'They were more upset by the smoking ban.'

'Where's mine?' said Maitland, eyeing the lemonades with disgust.

'We're working tonight, remember?' said Mona. 'Have a crisp.'

Paterson took a long drink of his Tennent's. 'So, Bernard, that was a cracking bit of detective work back there.'

Bernard nearly choked on his lager at the unaccustomed praise.

He tried not to flinch when Paterson put a hand on his shoulder.

'No, really, Bern, don't think we'd have got there without you.'

'To Bernard.' Mona raised her glass in a toast.

'So, Bernie, I hear you're really into sport,' said Maitland through a mouthful of Cheese and Onion.

'I played for Scotland, actually.'

Drinks were lowered all round, and his colleagues stared at him. 'Really?' said Paterson. 'What sport?'

'Badminton.'

Maitland and Paterson looked at each other then burst out laughing.

'Badminton?' said Paterson. 'That's not a sport! That's what kids play on the beach, or old ladies play on a Tuesday morning to keep fit.'

Bernard felt a small volcano of irritation erupt somewhere inside him. 'I accept that it's not a game of brutality like football or rugby. It's a game of strategy and intelligence. And you need to be hyper-fit.'

'Let yourself go a bit now have you, Bernard?' asked Maitland.

He placed his pint carefully back on the table. 'I could kick your arse any day in a fitness competition.'

Mona laughed and punched his arm. 'Go, Bernard!'

Much as he would have liked to defend his chosen sport further, Bernard's conscience was getting the better of him, so he decided to risk his boss's wrath and phone home. 'Back in a minute.'

He dialled his landline, and got the answer machine, then his wife's mobile, which went straight to voicemail. A tiny frisson of fear knotted his stomach muscles; he resolved to say his goodbyes and get home.

When he returned to the table Paterson was checking his phone single-handed, still holding on to his pint. 'The missus checking if I'll be back before the kids go to bed.'

Bernard's eyebrows shot up. 'You've got young kids?'

'Why are you surprised?' Paterson gave him a hard stare. 'Are you saying I'm too old?' He grinned as he opened a packet of Salt and Vinegar. 'Second wife. Are you married?'

'Yes.'

'Take my advice. Stick with her. A current wife, an ex-wife and two sets of kids is an expensive business.'

'What does your wife do, Guv?' Mona looked interested.

'She's still a student at the moment. She was halfway through her degree when she got pregnant...'

'Christ,' interrupted Bernard. 'How young is she?' He clasped a hand over his mouth in horror at what he had just said. He pushed his lager away, reflecting that he really couldn't handle alcohol, and waited for Paterson to kill him.

To his surprise, his boss just laughed. 'She was a mature student, you tosser. Anyway, she's in the last year of her degree now so hopefully she'll finally be able to go out and earn some money.'

Bernard picked up his coat to leave, but as he did so his mobile rang. 'Actually I should just get this ...' He wandered to the far side of the pub, inadvertently straying near to the flat-capped old man he had offended earlier. The man grunted at him and he swiftly relocated.

199

'Hello?'

'Where are you?'

There was a strained quality to Carrie's voice. He glanced round his surroundings and made an informed decision to lie. 'Still at work.'

'Really?' There was a pause. 'Because it sounds like you are in a pub.'

Bernard made the kind of sound that didn't quite indicate either yes or no.

'Are you coming home now?' He hated the whine in his wife's tone. 'We need to talk.'

She was right. There were lots of things that would benefit from them sitting down and hammering out. They could revisit their grief, compare where they were on the ladder of recovery. They could discuss his wife's declining fertility, the need for both parties to be in agreement on the issue of conception, admit to the obvious injustice that men could take more time about these things than women. But they'd done nothing else but circle round this argument for the past six months. Bernard thought about going home, then looked over at his colleagues. Amazingly, they seemed the more attractive option. 'The thing is ...'

'Fine,' said Carrie and hung up.

Bernard mooched back to the group. 'I guess it's my round.'

'Not for me.' Mona stood up. 'I need to go home and find some unsuitable footwear, apparently.'

'Try putting your hair in bunches,' smirked Maitland. 'And get one of those wee rucksacks in the shape of a teddy bear.'

Mona ignored him. 'See you back here at eleven.' Bernard bent down to pick up his bag.

'Hoi,' said Paterson. 'Where do you think you're going?'

'But ...' Bernard pointed in the direction of his departing colleagues. 'I thought we were ...'

His boss thrust his empty glass toward him. 'Oh, no. As you so rightly said, it's your round.'

The shoes all looked ridiculous. There was nothing in the shop that would allow her to walk comfortably, never mind dance. Mona looked round the shop in disgust. The music was far too loud, and of a banging and beeping nature that she'd never listen to out of choice. She picked up a shoe at random, checked its price tag, and rapidly replaced it on the shelf. The assistants all appeared to be in their teens, and none of them seemed keen to attend to her, confirming again that she was in the wrong place. She was about to head for the door but a vision of Maitland and his over-priced trainers swam into her mind, and she turned around.

Mona sighed and examined the footwear display again. The one thing all the racks had in common was that they contained items that were nothing like the contents of her shoe tree at home. Much as she hated to admit it, Maitland might be right about her not blending in. Not that she was bothered that she didn't look like a twenty-year-old clubber – Christ! Who'd want that look anyway? But in the interests of professionalism she wanted to look the part.

'Y'all right?' A sales assistant with bright pink hair appeared at her side.

'Yes!' she said. 'I mean, I'd like to try something on.' She surveyed the rack again, and picked the least-worst option. 'These in an eight, please.'

She sat on a seat with one shoe on and watched the other

customers go past. A girl with long dark hair caught her eye. She had on black leggings, and a baggy mesh jumper that had slid off one shoulder. She wouldn't look out of place at a rave, and more importantly, this was a look that Mona was sure she could recreate from her existing wardrobe. Her eyes slid to the girl's feet and she realised with a smile that she was wearing the same boots that Mona was waiting to try on. The girl noticed her looking and smiled back at her. Mona blushed and looked away, and was glad when the assistant reappeared.

'Biggest we've got is a seven, I'm afraid. Would you like to try a different shoe?'

Mona tried to summon the energy to choose something else, and failed.

'No, thanks.' Sensible boots it would have to be.

She ate some pasta in front of EastEnders, then sorted through her wardrobe for potential outfits, which she quite enjoyed. She generally hated the whole 'getting ready to go out' thing, but this was more like dressing up for a play. She chose the outfit that resembled the girl in the store's image most closely, then pulled her trusty Dr. Scholl's on. She hesitated, then went into the bathroom, opened the cabinet and pulled out some make-up. She squinted at the finished result, then stepped back into the bedroom to survey the overall look. She couldn't be sure, but she was about ninety per cent certain she could blend in.

Mona checked her watch. 9.30. Still plenty of time before she was due to meet Maitland. She paced up and down the hall a few times, then she grabbed her car keys and set off in the direction of Amanda's flat.

Over the next few hours in the pub, Bernard learned a great many things. He learned the best way to disarm a violent suspect. He learned how to gauge if a suspect was about to become violent. And he learned that Paterson had thought he was a 'bloody idiot' when he first joined the team, but had reconsidered this and now thought that he was a 'bloody idiot with potential'.

Bernard gave a wan smile. 'Thanks for that.'

'No, really,' Paterson pointed at him with his pint glass. A small amount of lager splashed over the side and landed on Bernard's leg. He thought it best not to complain.

'I thought, "What are they doing sending me this over-educated loon who keeps quoting statistics at me?"'

Bernard tried to smile enthusiastically, but the alcohol had gone to straight to his brain. The world was starting to look fuzzy.

'I thought, "He's exactly the kind of waste of space we're getting in the Police now, no good in a bar brawl but can quote chapter and verse on equalities legislation. Just the sort that gets himself promoted and hugs a desk for the next twenty years."' Paterson stopped for a mouthful of lager. 'But you, Bernard, you're all right.' He belched. 'And it's your round again.'

Bernard stood up and realised he was very drunk. He'd had four pints, which was more than he'd had since …well, more than he'd ever downed in one go. Consumption of alcohol was not compatible with top-class sportsmanship. He wondered if he dared return with a soft drink.

'What'll it be?'

'A pint of lager and a Coke. And another couple of bags of crisps.'

He looked over to see Paterson deep in conversation with the checked cap man. The two of them looked over at him, and Bernard immediately felt paranoid. What was his boss saying about him?

'There you go, pal, pint of Tennent's and a Coca Cola for the lady.'

'There aren't any ladies,' Bernard turned round in confusion, then saw the barman's smirk. 'Oh, very funny.'

He walked very slowly back to the table but still managed to spill a fair amount of Paterson's pint. Paterson pointed in disgust to Bernard's Coke but didn't say anything.

'So,' said his boss, leaning uncomfortably close to him, 'do we now know each other well enough for me to ask you a very personal question?'

'Eh,' Bernard attempted to move discreetly in the opposite direction from his Team Leader, 'what would that be?'

'When did you get the Virus?'

Bernard lowered his drink, and stared at Paterson. 'Is that a very personal question?'

'Well, you know how it is,' he leaned back, then took a long drink, 'if somebody says they got it in the First Wave, it's fine, but if they were in the Second Wave or later, there's a pretty high chance that they lost somebody. I mean, even these days there's a pretty high death rate . . .'

'One in forty chance of death if you catch it now. You were in the First Wave, then?'

'Oh, God, aye. Me, the missus and the kids were all laid up for a week with it. I was cursing at the time, of course, no idea how lucky we were to be immune to this new strain. And you?'

'Second Wave.'

'Oh.' Paterson contemplated his pint. 'Did you . . .?'

The unspoken question floated between them. Bernard chose not to answer.

'So, you were one of the lucky ones.' Bernard took a long sip of his Coke, while he got his emotions back under control. 'Must have been great going through the Second Wave knowing you were safe.'

'It was strange. I remember one day, at the height of the panic, I turned up at the Station to find that only me and one PC – also immune – had turned up for work. Everyone else was either ill, caring for a family member, or so completely bricking it that they weren't leaving the house.'

Bernard spluttered. 'So the entire Leith Police response consisted of two people?'

Paterson shrugged. 'It wasn't like anyone was in danger of being mugged, raped or burgled. Any bastard approached you, all you had to do was cough.'

They looked at each other, then started to laugh, with great aching sobs of mirth overtaking them both. Bernard felt himself tip over into hysteria. He put his hands over his face and tried, unsuccessfully, to stop the tears from flowing.

'So, Bernie,' said Paterson.

Bernard wiped his eyes and looked blearily up at his boss.

'Who do you blame for today's state of affairs?'

Bernard ran the back of his hand across his eyes, and thought for a moment. 'Well, in no particular order, the Government for not listening to the likes of Bircham-Fowler during the First Wave. If they'd taken on board his warnings about the pandemic not tailing off, they might have been better prepared for the Second Wave. I blame the pharmaceutical companies for rushing into vaccine tests that ended up killing their test subjects, thus pandering to every conspiracy theory going that the Health Service was actually trying to kill people ...'

'Making our job ten times harder ...'

'Making our job ten times harder. And I blame the general public for being so stupid as to listen to the conspiracy theorists and, for example, not going to the doctor when they're ill because they think the pills will make them worse. And,' he stopped for a crisp, 'I blame the chickens who started all this.'

'Of course. Let's not forget the good old fowl.' Paterson poked his arm. 'If I'd said to you five years ago, Bernard, that we'd lose a million people to an illness and the country would still manage to keep going, would you have believed me?' He started on his new pint, making an impressive dent in it with just one swallow.

Bernard thought for a minute. 'Yes, actually I would.'

'No!' His boss looked at him in disbelief. He pointed the glass at him again, but this time Bernard managed to swing his leg out of the way before the lager cascaded over the side.

'No, really. In the Spanish flu epidemic of 1918 they estimate three per cent of the world's population died. And that was hot on the heels of the First World War. And life went on.'

Paterson slapped Bernard's leg, and was surprised to find it wet. He wiped his hand on his own leg and carried on. 'So, Bernie, how did they cure Spanish flu?'

'Ah,' said Bernard. 'They didn't. It just ran its course.'

Paterson stared at his half-empty glass. 'Well, that's depressing.'

'I suppose it is. But without the Virus I would never

have had the joy of working for the Health Enforcement Team.'

The two of them looked at each other then burst out laughing.

'How did you end up at the HET, Bernie?'

Bernard thought for a minute how best to explain the disappointing trajectory of his life so far. 'Well, I spent the first fifteen years of my adult life playing professional badminton and studying Sport Science, then realised I'd got as far as I could. Trouble was, I was qualified for nothing else, so I did a Masters in Health Promotion and this is my first job.'

'Another depressing thought. Anyway drink up that Coke. It's my round and I'm not coming back with anything other than two pints.'

Bernard started drinking, and the room began to quiver. Paterson stepped past him to the bar, and he used his time alone to look at the picture of his son that he still carried in his wallet. He felt the tears welling again. He'd messed everything up. He hadn't saved his son, and he couldn't save his marriage. And now, when he should be at home with his wife, he'd somehow got himself trapped in the pub with his boss, too drunk to stand up.

A pint of lager was plonked on the table in front of him, spilling some of its contents as it landed.

'Get that down you.'

As Bernard picked up the glass, he wondered what would happen if he passed out here.

9

Mona pulled up near the Pioneer Arms and checked her watch. Bang on time. She'd sat outside Amanda's flat for the best part of an hour and seen nothing except pulled curtains, no Heidi, no Amanda, and no mysterious male. As she approached the Pioneer she saw a slight figure stagger out of the pub, reel round in a complete circle, and come to rest against a parked car. It was only when Paterson appeared in the doorway that she realised the figure was Bernard. She felt an unaccustomed pang of concern for him, and picked up her pace. By the time she reached them, Bernard had slid down to the ground.

Mona grabbed him by an arm and hauled him upright. 'You will see him into a taxi, Guv, won't you?'

Paterson waved a reassuring hand at her, then fell over, giggling. Maitland appeared at her side.

'What's going on?'

'I'm going to take a wild guess and say that the Guv got Bernard drunk.'

'Nonsense!' Paterson was vertical again. 'Just a bit of team building.'

'I don't feel too good,' said Bernard.

Mona let go of him, concerned that he might be about to throw up on her. She turned to Maitland. 'Maybe we should see them both into taxis?'

Maitland took her by the arm and steered her away.

208

'They're grown-ups. They'll be fine.' He looked at his watch. 'Nearly midnight. I think we can safely join the party.'

Mona cast a last worried look at her colleagues, who were now standing with their arms round each other's shoulders. 'OK. My car's just here.'

Mona slid the Ford Focus into gear and they drove off in silence. The streets were quiet, with only the occasional pub-goer winding his way home. It was, after all, a cold Wednesday night. Mona wondered who would go to a late-night, mid-week rave. Students, she supposed, but didn't students all work these days as well? She felt the slow spread of excitement throughout her body. She remembered this feeling from CID, the hours of waiting before a raid, when every muscle felt pulled taut, aching for the off. She looked over to Maitland expecting to see a similar picture of exhilaration, but instead her colleague was staring, unsmiling, straight ahead.

'Are you OK?'

'Yes, fine.' He fidgeted around on the passenger seat. 'Just trying to get comfortable in this ridiculously small car.'

'You're welcome to the lift, by the way.'

'Thanks.' He peered over at her feet. 'Nice shoes. Glad to see you took my advice.'

She slammed on the brakes, and Maitland bumped his head.

'Ow!'

'Sorry,' she smiled back. 'Just realised we need to park. Don't want to leave the car too close.' She signalled to pull out again, and turned the corner into a residential area at the side of George Heriot's School playing fields.

He peered at her. 'Are you wearing make-up?'Much

to her annoyance she felt a blush stealing across her face.
'Yes.'

He burst out laughing.

'I think the traditional response is,' she put on a Sean Connery accent, 'My, Miss Whyte, but you're beautiful.'

'I wouldn't go that far, but you're certainly looking less of a hound than usual.'

'Cheers, pal. Very chivalrous.' She pulled up next to a Volvo, and reversed backwards into a space. 'Let's take the Ferry Road entrance. That'll give us time to scope out what's going on.'

Maitland got out and slammed his door, which echoed loudly along the empty street. Mona glared at him.

'Sorry.' He looked round. 'Where the hell are we?'

'There's a cut-through along the end of the school grounds.'

'Is there?'

'Yeah, it runs between the playing fields and the railway line.'

Maitland looked doubtful, and she bristled with irritation. He never believed anything she said. She took off confidently toward the short cut, reflecting that Bernard, for all his faults, did tend to give way to her opinions.

'Here it is.'

Maitland made no effort to catch her up, and the two of them walked along the narrow lane in a convoy six feet apart.

The lane led them out on to a main road. During the day, Ferry Road was one of the busiest streets in Edinburgh, the main route for traffic heading north through the town. At this time of night it was deserted. Mona stopped beside the pathway that led down to the cycle track. Maitland ambled up beside her, leaned on the fence and looked down the concrete steps.

'This is it then?'

They walked down the steps and into the old railway line. The track had been concreted over to give a solid surface for walking or cycling, and on either side of the path the trees and bushes had been left to grow wild. In spite of the regular street lamps, it was a spooky place to be after dark.

'So, what's our story if anyone sees us?'

Mona shrugged. 'Same as everyone else. We're going to a party.'

'Yeah, people will think we're boyfriend and girlfriend.' He turned to her with a serious expression. 'Do you think we should hold hands?'

'No, Maitland, I do not think we should hold hands.'

Maitland laughed. After a pause he asked, 'So, have you got a boyfriend then, Mona?'

She walked on for a few steps, uncomfortable at the intrusion into her private life. It wasn't, she supposed, an unreasonable question to ask of a colleague.

'Not that it's any of your business, but no, I'm not seeing anyone at the moment.' She thought for a moment. Was she supposed to show a similar interest in Maitland's life? 'Am I right in thinking that there is a woman currently being stupid enough to waste her time on you?'

'Certainly is. Do you want to see a picture?'

'No, I was just asking to be polite. Anyway, shut up, we're nearly there.'

They walked on in silence.

'You know,' said Maitland, 'if we're nearly there I don't hear too much in the way of party noise.'

At that moment the railway tunnel loomed out of the

darkness, and Mona could make out people moving about in the gloom.

'Here goes.'

As she went to walk toward the tunnel Maitland grabbed her arm and pulled her back.

'Careful, mate!' A man on a bike nearly crashed into Maitland, who muttered an apology.

Still holding Mona's arm Maitland leaned toward her, and for a minute she thought he was going to kiss her. Instead he brought his mouth close to her ear. 'I know what they're doing in there. Have you got earphones on you?'

'Yeah, but ...' She tried to pull away, but he kept a firm grip on her arm.

'It's a silent rave.'

She looked at him in confusion. 'What?'

'A silent rave – they're all dancing around to their own music, probably to a synchronised playlist.' Maitland looked along the track into the tunnel. 'We can't go in there without earphones – they'll mark us as tourists right away.'

'Have you got earphones on you?'

'No.' He looked annoyed. 'I just splashed out a hundred quid on a new set and tonight, you know, I thought they might get nicked or dropped or something.'

'Then I'll have to go in on my own.' She felt slightly nervous at the thought, but also delighted at getting one over on Maitland.

'I don't think that's a good idea – give me yours.'

'This is my call.'

The sound of footsteps interrupted them, and they turned to see two girls walking along the cycle path in their direction.

212

Maitland lowered his voice. 'OK. Well, I can't hang around here – I'm going to walk to the main road. If you don't catch me up in,' he looked at his watch, 'say, forty minutes, I'm coming back to look for you.'

'Fair enough.'

He took a step back and said loudly, 'See you later, sweetie.'

'Shoosh.' The girls looked at him disapprovingly. One of them pressed her finger to her lips as she walked by.

'Sorry,' Maitland murmured.

Mona exchanged a glance with her colleague, then watched as he strode off into the darkness. Then she took out her phone, plugged her earphones in, and walked into the tunnel.

Bernard tried unsuccessfully to unlock his front door. He missed the small circle of metal completely, and his key scraped down the paintwork, scattering flakes of blue paint at his feet. He leaned his head against the wood, giggling. Pushing himself upright he tried again, focusing all his attention on the very small slot. This time he was successful, and he stumbled into his hallway. He closed the door as quietly as he could behind him, then undid this good work by tripping over his own feet and crashing through into the living room.

He waited on all fours for Carrie to appear and shout at him. After a couple of minutes when nothing had happened he got up and hit the light switch. He debated putting the kettle on, but the pull of the sofa was strong. He decided to sit down, just for a minute, but felt his eyes closing. Just before the blackness hit him he saw a letter tucked into the mirror above the mantelpiece. His name was on the envelope.

Strange. Why was Carrie writing to him?

He slumped back on the sofa, and within seconds he was asleep.

The tunnel was lit by a single overhead strip light. Mona felt quite disorientated when she stepped into the throng of bodies, after her solitary walk through the dark. She'd guesstimate there were about a hundred young people taking part, tightly packed together, swaying in time to inaudible music. Judging by the co-ordinated movement of the crowd Maitland was probably right – they all appeared to be listening to the same playlist. And Maitland was definitely right about something else: she did look older than all of them. She was, however, pleased to see a range of sensible footwear; she'd be sure to cast that up to her colleague.

She edged her way along the side of the crowd, moving slowly up the tunnel. She tried to move in unison with the other dancers, which wasn't too difficult, given the limited room. When she reached the far side of the tunnel she stopped, and looked back at the scene. It was a bizarre sight. She'd been to raves before – not many, it was not her thing – and the word conjured up a riot of day-glo colours on a black canvas in her mind. But watching a sea of people dance, without music, under the harsh lighting made her want to burst out laughing at the absurdity of it all.

Someone bumped into Mona, nearly knocking her off her feet. She turned to see a young man, who held up his hands in the universal sign of 'sorry, mate.' She gave him a thumbs up and in return he shot her a cheery grin, and vanished into the crowd.

There were several girls dancing in front of her wearing

only vest tops and jeans. Surely they were cold? She shivered. What was the attraction of dancing in a tunnel in the middle of the night? Even as a teenager she hadn't seen the appeal of nightclubs – all the queuing and jostling, and drunks. You'd have to pay her to do that now, and tonight, someone was. A girl with pigtails danced past her, wearing a brightly coloured mask over her mouth. Otherwise, the dancers seemed to be ignoring any kind of Virus protection. It must be great to be twenty and think you are immortal. She hoped that none of them suffered any consequences from their night out.

There didn't seem to be much in the way of drinking going on here, except for water. She scanned the crowd to see if anyone was dealing, and sure enough, spotted a guy making his way methodically round the throng. He was tall, around the same height as Maitland, maybe even more. Despite the darkness outside the tunnel, he was wearing sunglasses and a jester's hat.

She swayed gently through the dancers in the direction of the dealer. She ended up face-to-face with the man who had bumped into her earlier; he smiled and tried to grab her round the waist. She laughed and politely manoeuvred away from him, and kept going until she was behind the tall guy.

When he turned to face her she grinned, and kept eye contact with his glasses. There was something familiar about him; it wouldn't have surprised her if she'd come across him in her previous life in CID. Enterprising sellers of drugs had moved quickly into the Virus market.

The dealer wasn't returning her smile. She looked encouragingly down at his pocket, but he just shook his head slightly and walked off. Did he recognise her as Police? Or did he just like to know all his customers personally? In a crowd of a hundred people it was likely that he did know most of his customers, or at least recognise their faces. He had disappeared into the crowd.

Mona checked her watch. Time was marching on, so she decided on one last trip around the crowd, then to head back to Maitland. As she turned to leave she caught sight of someone in the crowd who looked familiar. A small, spiky-haired woman was swaying along with a couple of other dancers. One of the ravers she was with leaned over to the woman and pulled out one of her earphones to talk to her. She threw her head back, laughing at her friend's joke. As her head came back up she looked round the crowd, and stopped dead when she caught sight of Mona. Mona slowly mouthed her name, 'Amanda'.

She stood where she was, waiting to see what Amanda's reaction would be. The object of her attention looked distinctly uncomfortable, and made no attempt to make eye contact. She turned and moved off, away from Mona. Mona tried in vain to push through the crowd. One of the dancers objected to being pushed past and shoved her. She toppled backwards, starting a domino effect that resulted in someone sending three people over banging their heads off the tunnel wall. By the time she'd checked they weren't hurt, and had made her apologies, her target had vanished. She grunted with annoyance. Why was Amanda here? She'd made it clear she didn't socialise with Heidi, and yet, here she was at a party that Heidi was invited to. Was it a coincidence? Or was Amanda looking for her flatmate?

Mona quit the tunnel and started walking back along the silent path, trying to see if Amanda had headed in this direction. Within minutes she was aware of a noise behind her. Was it footsteps? It could just as easily be wildlife in the undergrowth. She spun round to face her pursuer, feet apart, poised to defend herself. The path was deserted. Was something, or someone, in the bushes? It was impossible to tell. She stepped up her pace, wishing that she'd brought something to defend herself with. She was fairly sure that the sounds were also speeding up. Mona decided to stop and brazen it out.

She turned back to face the tunnel. In the darkness it was difficult to tell if anyone was there or not. She waited a couple of seconds for someone to show themselves, peering into the gloom. If anyone was there, they weren't rushing to make their presence known. She pivoted slowly round, and continued on her way. After a couple of steps, a figure detached itself from the undergrowth and grabbed her.

'Hello, sweetie.'

She pushed Maitland off, and looked round. There was no-one there.

'Did you know someone was following you?' he asked.

'Yeah.'

'He ducked back into the bushes when I stepped out.' Maitland walked into the middle of the pathway and looked both ways. 'You OK?'

Mona suddenly felt very tired. 'Let's go.'

Ferry Road remained as quiet as when they'd arrived.

'So, what did you find out?'

'Not much.' Mona let out a long sigh of annoyance. 'There were about a hundred kids there, all bobbing about in bloody unison. There was at least one guy selling drugs.'

'Recognise him?'

They turned down the cut-through, this time walking

217

side by side. 'Hard to tell. He was tall, but wearing a hat and glasses.'

'The guy following you was tall.'

'Makes sense. I think I spooked him.'

They walked in silence for a couple of minutes.

'There's one other thing. Heidi's flatmate was there.'

'Guess she'll be getting a visit tomorrow?'

'Yup.' Mona yawned. 'Suppose we'd better head home then.'

'Don't you want to hear what I found out?'

She looked at him in surprise. 'What?'

'Quarter of an hour after you'd gone I bumped into a very nice, very drunk young lady weaving her way toward the party. She asks me for a light, and I oblige, then she asks if I'm going to the Railway Tavern. I say no, 'cause I've just had a big fight with my girlfriend, and she says she's just fallen out with her bloke, so one thing leads to another ...'

'You dirty bastard.'

'Calm down, I just offered her a shoulder to cry on. Anyhow, we started chatting about the good times to be had at the Railway Tavern, and she's saying what a great bloke "Big K" is, and how she would never have heard of Loopy and H if it wasn't for him, and what a godsend it was to know that there was something that actually worked against the Virus, 'cause you know how the Government never tell you anything.' He broke off laughing.

'Big K?'

'Could be a very tall drug dealer?'

'Or a man called Kevin?'

'Or both?'

THURSDAY

THE HEALTH
OF STRANGERS

|

Bernard was bent over the bathroom sink, his head resting against the porcelain, when he heard the metallic sound of his phone's ringtone for the second time in ten minutes. He tried to stand up but was poleaxed by a wave of sickness. By the time he managed to control his stomach, the ringing had stopped. He ran the taps, desperately trying not to look at the contents of his stomach lying in the basin, then walked slowly into the living room. By the time the phone rang for the third time, he was ready.

'Hi, Mona.'

'Where are you?'

Mona's voice rattled with impatience. He went for sympathy. 'I'm not feeling too ...'

'Good. Yes, I can imagine. Some advice, Bernard, don't go drinking with the Guv.'

Bernard's jaw dropped. He'd hardly been a willing participant.

'Anyway, grab a shower and a coffee, and get yourself over here in a taxi.'

She rang off before he could protest, and he implemented her plan. By the time he pulled on his shoes, he was actually beginning to feel human again, and with a degree of caution he got to his feet. As he did so he caught sight of the envelope with his name on it. Immediately the nausea he'd been fighting came back, as did the memory of the previous

221

night. He snatched the letter and his coat. Trying not to breathe, he locked the flat door behind him, the missive tucked in his inside pocket, unread, waiting for him to get the nerve to open it and find out if his marriage was over.

'You're not going to be sick, are you?'

Mona was looking at him as if he was a very bad smell that had invaded the comfort of her Ford Focus.

'Why does everyone think I'm always about to vomit?' Bernard turned and stared out of the window at the flowerbeds of Pollock Halls. He'd have made a more spirited retort if it weren't for the fact that he was still feeling seriously nauseous. Mona turned on the radio, and the sound of Professor Bircham-Fowler filled the car.

'The unpopularity of the health services in general, and most notably the Health Enforcement Team is greatly hindering the fight against the Virus ...'

Mona snorted. 'It's hardly our fault that people are too stupid to know what's good for them.'

'People are dying needlessly from bacterial pneumonia due to the lack of trust in the antibiotics being prescribed.'

The interviewer broke in. *'Though you can't blame people for being concerned, I mean the vaccine trial deaths raised a lot of questions ...'*

Mona swore and turned the knob to off.

'I suppose the vaccine fiasco is our fault as well.'

Bernard watched a row of ferns swaying gently in the breeze, wondering if his day was going to get any better. He burped silently and tried to focus on the case. 'So, do we know what this Kevin guy looks like?'

Mona reached into her pocket and unfolded a printout of Kevin's health record, including an over-pixelated photograph. The two of them stared at the page.

222

'Not the best photo in the world,' said Bernard. 'Did the guy you saw last night look like that?'

Mona looked at the picture. 'Maybe, but under a jester's hat and sunglasses it was hard to say. We'll have to chat to the nurse.' She turned off the car radio. 'Come on, sunshine. Time to go.'

Bernard groaned and opened the car door.

The Health Enforcement Clinic was set up in a common room on the ground floor. The blinds were closed to give some degree of privacy, and Bernard winced at the sharp neon light coming from overhead. The nurse was middle-aged, and sported a short no-nonsense haircut. She regarded Mona's ID card with confusion.

'I'm not sure what you're doing here – I thought you only investigated people that didn't show up for their Health Check?'

'That's usually the case.' Mona snapped her ID shut and put it back into her pocket. 'But we've reason to believe that one of the students due here today is responsible for the non-appearance of another student at her Health Check.'

The nurse was looking more confused by the minute. Bernard couldn't blame her. She scanned her records. 'Who are you looking for?'

'Kevin Calman.' Mona offered her the printout. 'Do you recognise him?'

She squinted at it. 'Yes. But he's such a lovely lad. Very polite.'

'Has he said anything to you about his view of the Virus?' asked Bernard.

The nurse started unpacking the contents of her bag. 'Well, he's got some daft ideas on that, but to be honest

223

all the students here have some silly theory or other.' Her face clouded. 'He's not in any trouble, is he?'

Before he could say anything Mona jumped in. 'No, no. Just give us a shout when he comes in.' She grabbed Bernard's sleeve and pulled him toward a chair. He sat staring at his watch, as the minute hand edged round.

At 8.45am prompt the door flew open, and in rushed a girl with wet hair.

'Sorry, Maggie, I slept in.'

'No worries, love, my 8.45 is running late as well.' The nurse raised her eyebrows at Bernard and Mona. 'Can you wait outside for a minute or two?'

They got reluctantly to their feet and filed back into the hallway. Bernard leaned his head against the cool corridor window.

'He's not going to show.' Mona sounded almost cheerful at the prospect. 'Looks like this Calman guy could be our man. We should . . .'

He didn't get to hear his partner's suggestion as she was interrupted by a ringing sound from her inside pocket. She delved into her jacket and retrieved her phone.

'Hello?'

Bernard stepped back from the window, and wiped the condensation from the glass off his brow. He glanced over at Mona, and was surprised to see how concerned she looked. She noticed his interest, turned her back on him and took a few steps down the corridor.

'I'll be right there.' Mona snapped her phone shut.

'Who was that?'

'Amanda – sounding upset. I'm going to head on over there. Can you hang on here for a while, Bernard, just to make sure Kevin doesn't show?'

'But what if he does turn up?' His stomach lurched,

224

and he felt a bubble of acid at the back of his throat. He wasn't sure he could cope with a face-off with their suspect at the best of times, let alone in his current state.

Mona checked her watch. 'He won't.'

'But if he does?'

She sighed. 'Ask him to come down to the office. I'll meet you there.'

The door to the common room opened and Bernard was nearly knocked over by the damp-haired girl.

'Sorry!'

Bernard looked round for Mona, but she'd gone.

2

'Thanks for coming so quickly.'

Amanda stood in the doorway of the flat. Her left eye was swollen and yellowing. She had a matching set of bruises around her right wrist.

Mona looked her up and down as she stepped into the flat. 'You've been in the wars. What happened?'

Amanda closed the door.

Something felt different about the flat; it took Mona a second or two to realise that the former gloom of the hallway had been replaced by a neon glow. She looked up at the ceiling where the light bulb was burning brightly. Mona wasn't surprised at the sudden upgrading in the illumination. If she'd taken the beating that Amanda had, she'd be scared of dark corners too.

'I saw you last night. I notice you didn't come over to say hello.'

A tear escaped down Amanda's cheek, and she wiped her eyes with the backs of her hands. 'Sorry, things are just getting so ...when I saw you I ...'

She looked so small and scared that Mona relented. 'OK. Why don't you tell me how you came by the bruises?'

Amanda rubbed her wrist. 'I'm so frightened.'

'Who are you frightened of?'

Amanda looked at her as if she was crazy. 'Kevin, of course.'

Mona tried to remember which of the doors led to the living room. She took a guess, and guided the distraught girl through to the sofa, sitting down next to her. 'Kevin did this to you?'

'Yeah. He must have been at the rave last night. He followed me out of there and ...' She tailed off, and wiped her eyes again.

'Amanda, there's no need to be scared. Just tell me what happened.'

'He just won't leave me alone. He thinks I know where Heidi is ...' She pulled a cushion onto her lap, turning it round and round in her hands.

'Is he still staying here?'

She shook her head. 'He picked up his stuff a couple of days ago. I never wanted him here, never. But he was a friend of Heidi's, and he was going to pay a share of the rent.'

There was a long silence. Mona was about to prompt Amanda when she continued.

'It was OK at first. In fact, I really liked him at first because he was dead friendly, you know?' She paused. 'But I think he knew that Heidi was rich. He started talking a load of nonsense to her about drugs that could stop you catching the Virus, and this group that he was involved with ....'

'The Children of Camus?'

'Pretty stupid, huh?'

Mona smiled. 'Except a lot of people did believe him, didn't they?'

They looked at each other.

'Did Heidi believe him?'

Amanda laughed, a little mirthless sound. 'That's the really stupid thing. All that education and she fell for it.'

227

She paused. 'We fought about it, actually. I was worried that someone was going to kill themselves, messing around with all that stuff.'

'But Kevin wasn't worried?'

'No. All he could see was pound signs. He didn't care if someone died – why should he? All the drugs were bought and paid for on Heidi's credit card.'

Mona tried to make sense of all this. 'And The Children of Camus website – is that Kevin?'

'Yes.'

'Amanda, where do you think Heidi is?'

'I don't know.' She started to cry again. 'But you've got to find her before Kevin does. Where *you* think Heidi is?'

'We don't know.'

Amanda looked surprised. 'But what are you doing to find her? Are you talking to her other friends? She has some German friends – maybe they know something?'

Mona walked around the room, thinking. She stopped at the sideboard, in front of a photograph in a solid wooden frame. The photograph showed Heidi and Amanda sitting on a wall, arms round each other. A calculation took place at the back of Mona's mind.

'I don't remember this photograph being here last time I visited.'

Amanda grunted. 'S'been there for ages.'

There was another picture frame lying face down, its supporting arm sticking out like a dagger. Mona turned it over and saw it was a novelty frame, cheap green plastic decorated with red love-hearts. In the centre was a picture of Amanda kissing Heidi's cheek. Heidi was laughing at the camera.

She swivelled round to face Amanda.

'Which room did you say was Kevin's?'

Amanda's eyes were fixed on the silent television set. 'He doesn't have a room, he sleeps on the sofa, or with Heidi.'

'Really?'

Amanda hugged her toes, turning herself into a small ball. 'Heidi's parents are really, really, strict.'

Mona picked up the heart-infested picture frame, and lifted it up to show Amanda. 'And she couldn't tell them that you and Heidi are in a relationship?'

Silence filled the room. Outside Mona could hear cars passing by, and voices calling to each other. Amanda stared back at her.

'Come on, Amanda, these pictures weren't here last time I visited. You've put on a show for me. You promised Heidi you wouldn't tell anyone about your relationship, didn't you? But if you help me guess that you two are together you've not broken your promise, have you?'

The girl pressed her head down into her legs. 'I love her so much.'

Mona sat down next to her. 'You should have told us this straight away – it might be relevant to finding her.'

'I couldn't!' she wailed, her head still buried in her knees. 'It's supposed to be a secret. You understand these things?' Amanda sat upright. 'You understand about these things...' she took Mona's hand in hers, 'don't you?'

Mona snatched her hand away and got to her feet. 'I'll be in touch. In the meantime call me if you hear from Kevin or Heidi.' She walked as quickly as she could back to the front door, but hesitated before opening it. She turned back to see Amanda standing behind her.

'Please.' Amanda caught Mona's hand and raised to her face.

Mona stood for a second or two with her other hand

229

raised in an involuntary surrender. Amanda moved in toward her. Mona held her close for a moment or two, intending to push her away as soon as the girl was in control of her emotions. The warmth of Amanda's body ran through her, and when she reached up and pulled her lips toward her, Mona didn't resist. Her hands crept up to Amanda's face, then her common sense kicked in and she pushed the girl away.

'Sorry.' Amanda held her gaze. 'I shouldn't have done that.'

'No, it was …I mean …' She stopped, uncertain what she wanted to say. The light was hurting her eyes as she tried to make sense of all the things that were wrong with the situation. 'What's going on here, Amanda? Your girlfriend is missing, you tell me how much you love her, yet here you are throwing yourself in my direction?'

Amanda put her hands to her face, and her shoulders shook. It took all Mona's self-control not to hold her again.

'I'm sorry.' The words came out in between sobs. 'I'm so sorry, but I thought if I …I thought if we …I thought you would help us without going to the Police.'

'That's not my decision. I'm sorry.'

'You need to find Kevin. And soon. You will let me know as soon as you hear anything about Heidi, won't you?'

Mona nodded, backing out of the flat. Running down the stairs of the tenement, she made it out into the fresh air, and leaned against the railings while her heartbeat returned to normal. She looked up at the flat's window to see a tiny figure watching her. Amanda waved.

She turned on her heel and left.

3

'Maitland?'

His colleague swore at him.

Bernard hovered at the side of Maitland's desk. His colleagues cursed so much that he often found it difficult to interpret what it meant. Sometimes the swearing was a sign that Maitland or Mr Paterson was stressed, and in need of peace and quiet. And sometimes it was just their way of saying hello.

Without looking up, Maitland motioned a thumb in the direction of Bernard's desk.

The gesture was helpful, and he resigned himself to the fact that Maitland wasn't going to tell him what to do. Mona's mobile had gone straight to voicemail every time he'd called her, and he was left wondering if he'd done the right thing by coming back to the office. Maybe he should have gone to Amanda's flat? He was pretty sure that Mona could handle whatever situation she found herself in, and she could have called him if she wanted his help, but still...He looked over to Paterson's office, and wondered if he should talk to his boss. This was a very unappealing option, so he decided to text his partner, and if she didn't get back he'd go and talk to the other man in the office who would swear at him.

He sent his message then sat staring at the phone, willing it to beep. He heard a voice behind him, and realised that

Maitland was speaking to someone. Without turning round, he began to tune in to what was happening.

'Emma, pick up the phone.' Maitland was talking as quietly as he could into his mobile. 'For Christ's sake, Emma! This is my fourth message.'

Paterson appeared in the door of his office. Bernard looked to see how his colleague would react. Maitland gave his boss a wave and pointed to the phone at his ear, in a signal aimed at convincing Paterson he was hard at work. It seemed to succeed, as their Team Leader nodded and retreated back into his office. Bernard went on staring at Maitland, who gave him a different hand signal, which again helped clarify the situation. Bernard turned his back but continued eavesdropping.

'Can I speak to Emma Francis, please?'

Maitland's girlfriend, he assumed. Or possibly recent ex-girlfriend, if Maitland's mood was anything to go by.

'No, no, thanks. No-one else can help.'

Bernard heard the sound of Maitland's phone being thrown down, then, after a brief pause, picked up again.

'Emma, I know you are not planning to talk to me, but I spoke to your work who said you're off sick, and if I don't hear from you in the next ten minutes I'm going to phone your mother, and ask her if you are suffering from the Virus.'

Bernard was no expert on women, he would be the first to admit. However, despite his lack of expertise he knew that if Maitland wasn't already dumped, he would be soon.

Maitland's phone rang.

'You shit!'

Even from six feet away, Bernard could hear the outrage. In fact, he could hear every word she was screaming.

'You know my mum would freak out.'

'I know, I'm sorry, I was getting desperate.'

He dropped any pretence that he wasn't listening and turned round to watch Maitland, who was too caught up in the conversation to notice.

'Are you OK?'

Emma's voice had returned to normal, depriving Bernard of her side of the conversation. Maitland heaved a sigh of relief, leading Bernard to assume Emma had confirmed that she was, in fact, all right. His colleague's features morphed almost immediately into a look of fury.

'Then what are you playing at, disappearing off without even leaving a note?'

The phone emitted a squawk of annoyance. 'You've moved out?' His surprise showed in his tone. 'What do you mean "the stunt I pulled last night"?'

There was a pause while Maitland listened to his crimes being detailed. 'Oh, that.' He stood up. 'Where are you? I'll come over and we can talk.'

Bernard's phone beeped, and he looked down to see a message from Mona saying she was on her way. He'd been so caught up in enjoying Maitland's distress that he had almost forgotten about her. Maitland was still standing by his desk, and now had one arm into his jacket.

'We need to sort this. I'll get some time off – just tell me where you are?'

Bernard assumed Emma had hung up as Maitland shoved his phone in his pocket and pulled on his coat. He looked over at Bernard, who smiled cheerfully back.

'So, what stunt did you pull last night, then?'

'Mind your own business.'

Maitland looked so furious that Bernard manoeuvred his chair out slightly from the desk, in case he had to leap

233

out of the way of a fist. After a second or two, however, a look came over his colleague's face that, in anyone else, Bernard would have described as sheepish.

'I pretended that I was interested in religion, so that she'd take me along to the next church service. She fell for it for about thirty seconds, then got pretty annoyed.'

'Pretty annoyed?'

'Yeah, in a kind of "moved all her stuff out" sort of way.'

'Strange that.'

'Yeah.' Maitland gave a small laugh, then a huge grin spread across his face. 'And I know where she's gone. Pastor Mackenzie's house.'

'You planning on going somewhere, Maitland?'

Both of them jumped as their superior officer appeared beside them, carrying a stack of files.

Maitland stuttered an explanation, but it was clear that Paterson wasn't really paying attention.

'Because I need you here. It turns out I've made a bit of a – em – misjudgement,' he shifted the files to his other arm, 'regarding your Defaulter.'

'Oh yeah?'

'Yep. I mentioned to Stuttle that you were chasing a girl that was pregnant, and he said he hoped that we were following the High Risk Accelerated Defaulter Procedure, what with expectant mothers being so susceptible.'

'The what?' asked Bernard.

'That's what I thought. What I actually said, though, was of course we were. Then I rushed back here, read Sections 27-34 of the HET manual and found out that we needed to do a Risk Assessment . . .'

He handed Maitland the top file.

'And inform the NHS High Risk and Vulnerable People Virus Team.'

A second file was passed across.

'And ensure that the Defaulter File is updated with all the relevant information about how long she's been up the duff, etc, etc.'

The third file was shoved under Maitland's chin. He dropped the files onto the nearest desk, which happened to be Bernard's. 'But I don't know how to fill in any of this stuff.'

'That's why I've given you all the guidance to read first.'

Maitland kicked Bernard's desk. 'I should be out there looking for Colette not dealing with this crap.'

His boss held up his hands. 'I don't make the rules, I just file the paperwork. Make a start now and you should be done by teatime.' He turned to Bernard. 'And you and Mona, in my office now. I'm expecting a visitor.'

With impeccable timing, Mona had appeared at the door.

'Be right there, Guv.'

'How did you get on with Amanda?' Bernard asked.

'Never mind that, Bernard, guess who I just saw in Reception?'

'Marguerite?'

'No!' Her question was answered by the appearance of Doctor Toller, immaculately dressed as always, and carrying a bundle of papers.

The German nodded to them, before disappearing into Paterson's office. Bernard and Mona exchanged a look, then both got to their feet and followed him. Their boss was installed behind his desk, and Toller fitted himself neatly into the orange plastic chair.

'Good news, chaps,' said Paterson. 'Heidi has made contact.'

'Really?' said Mona, surprise showing in both her look and tone. 'Where is she?'

Doctor Toller took a moment before answering. 'She's in Germany.' He didn't lift his eyes from the file resting on his knees.

'In Germany?'

'Yes.' Toller continued to flick through the file without looking up. 'We received an e-mail from her saying she had returned to Germany and wished to have some peace and quiet. She indicated she would move back here when she felt happier.'

'But she can't be in Germany,' said Mona. 'You have her passport.'

The three of them looked at Toller, who still did not look up from his papers.

'I do not have Heidi's passport.'

'You do!' Mona looked to him and Paterson for backup. 'At our first meeting you said you had it. Herr Weber mentioned it as well.'

Toller's gaze moved from his knees to the roof of the office, without stopping at their faces en route. He continued staring over their heads. 'I said no such thing.'

'But ...'

'Mona.'

Bernard could hear a warning tone in Paterson's voice. 'Doctor Toller has told you he doesn't have Heidi's passport.'

Bernard raised his hand. 'Actually, Mr Paterson, I'm pretty sure that ...'

Toller got to his feet. 'I will remain at The George

236

Hotel until tomorrow, but I do not anticipate that you will need to speak to me again.'

'She's not in Germany.' Despite her boss's warning, Mona was standing her ground. 'You know it and I know it. Christ, even Bernard could work out that much.'

'Thanks,' Bernard muttered.

'Every moment we're wasting here, Heidi is in danger. Guv,' she turned to Paterson, 'we need to get Police Scotland in on this.'

Paterson opened his mouth to speak but closed it again when Toller stood up.

'You think I don't care what happens to Heidi?' The German spat the words out. 'You think she's just some statistic to me? I've known Heidi all her life. Jens Weber and I were at university together. I've spent holidays, Christmases, with her. She grew up playing with my children. You think I would endanger her life by pretending that she is safe when she is not?'

Mona stepped in between Toller and the door. 'Heidi is not in Germany.'

Toller shook his head in disgust. Paterson jerked his head at Mona and reluctantly, she stepped out of the way. The Toller took the opportunity to leave, but as the door closed behind him, Mona renewed her protests.

'He's lying, Guv.'

Bernard nodded his agreement.

'I know,' Paterson said quietly.

Mona slammed her hand down on Paterson's desk. 'So, why did you let him go?'

He looked at Mona's hand, raising an eyebrow. She had the good sense to move it.

'What am I supposed to do? It's a diplomatic matter. If he wants to pretend that Heidi is alive and well and living in Bavaria, and her parents, and all the agencies involved want to play along with that, there is nothing we can do. SHEP have already agreed to German health services taking over. Case closed for us.'

'Until her body turns up somewhere on our patch.'

He pointed a finger at her. 'On Police Scotland's patch, you mean.'

Bernard's phone rang. He left Mona and Paterson arguing and stepped outside to answer it.

'Hi, it's Marcus here.'

He closed the door behind him as quietly as he could. 'How are you doing?'

'Great. How's the hunt for your young German going?'

Bernard grunted into the phone.

'That good, eh?' His phone laughed. 'Well, this might cheer you up. Have you seen today's news? But, what am I saying – you're a Sports Science graduate, of course you haven't read the paper.'

'I read *the Guardian* every day, actually.'

'A complex man of hidden depths. I like that. Anyway, check out the article on page nine – is that Heidi's dad?'

Bernard hung up without waiting to say goodbye. He dug his unread paper out from under his desk and spread it across his desk.

He flicked to page nine, the International News section of the paper. His eye was immediately caught by a small picture of Jens Weber under the headline *'German minister in call girl scandal.'* The article detailed Weber's involvement with a ring of high-class prostitutes, a story which had apparently gripped the whole of Berlin. In light of the scandal Herr Weber was standing down as a member of the Bundestag. As Bernard would have anticipated, his wife was standing by him.

'Poor Heidi,' he said to no-one in particular. He looked up as the door to Paterson's office was slammed.

'Mona?'

'Not now, Bernard.'

'Mona! You really have to see this.'

Impatiently, she glanced at the article he was pointing at. Bernard read the headline aloud. '"German Minister in Call Girl Scandal".'

Mona looked at him. 'No, not Heidi's ...'

'Oh yeah.' Bernard grinned. 'Heidi's dad. Herr Weber.'

'No!'

She read the article silently, then looked at Bernard.

'This does mean that Heidi would have had a good reason to go into hiding,' he said. 'I mean, if she knew this was all about to kick off I can't blame her for heading to the hills. Pretty embarrassing, your dad getting up to all that.'

'You think Herr Weber knew that the Press were about to publish this when we spoke to him? He'd need to have some nerve.'

'It would explain why Toller wanted everything dealt with quickly and quietly.'

Mona laughed, mirthlessly. 'Nothing Doctor Toller does is obvious.' She sat on the edge of his desk. 'Bernard, did anything strike you as odd in there?'

'You mean apart from Herr Doktor Toller lying his arse off?'

'I mean about the *way* he lied.'

'I don't get you.' Whatever test Mona was giving him, he was failing. 'We said "you have her passport" and he said "oh no I don't."'

'But he knows that he already told all three of us that he had it. He knows we know he's lying.' She made a complicated hand movement to emphasise her point. 'He could have made up some story, said she travelled on a fake passport, or something.'

Bernard pondered this for a moment. 'He's too sharp to do that by mistake.'

Mona looked over her shoulder in the direction of Paterson's office. 'I think he wants us to keep looking for her. And I don't think he was lying when he said he was concerned about Heidi.'

Bernard bit his bottom lip. 'He was very keen to let us know he was staying at The George for another night.'

She threw another glance toward their boss. 'I reckon we've got about five minutes before the Guv comes out here with something else for us to do.'

Bernard picked up his coat. 'Just so I know, Mona, does Mr Paterson get very annoyed when you do the exact opposite of what he asks you to do?'

Mona just smiled. 'Let's go. And while we are en route I need to tell you something interesting about Amanda and Heidi.'

4

Toller did not look surprised to see them. He stood in the doorway of his hotel room, neither welcoming them in, nor making any effort to conceal the room behind him. Unlike his boss, Toller did not appear to merit a suite of rooms. Over his shoulder Mona could see a fairly small bedroom, his suitcase lying open on the bed.

'I have told you absolutely everything I know about the situation.' Toller's voice was a calm monotone. 'Heidi is safe and well in Germany. Please leave me to pack in peace.' He reached forward and shook Mona's hand. 'Good day.'

As the door shut in their faces Bernard looked at her in amazement. 'Why did you let him do that?'

Mona smiled, enjoying his confusion. She opened her hand and showed Bernard a folded-up piece of paper. He reached out to take it but she closed her hand, and strode into the lift. As the door closed behind them she unfolded the note.

My apologies for the subterfuge. I would be extremely grateful if you could meet me by the Walter Scott monument in Princes Street Gardens in one half-hour.

As the lift hit the ground floor Mona put a finger to her lips. God knew who would be hanging around the Reception area. The last thing she wanted was Bernard asking lots of questions at the top of his voice. She put on her best look of irritation, and flounced out of the lift and across the lobby.

'Well, that was a waste of time.' She spoke loudly, over her shoulder. 'Come on, Bernard, let's get back to the office.'

She left at such a pace that she could hear her colleague running to keep up.

'Apologies again for the intrigue.' Toller motioned to them to join him on the bench. 'I thought it would be pleasant to meet in the shadow of one of your great writers.' He pointed up at the monument.

'Don't mention it. Is your room bugged?'

Toller laughed. 'Perhaps. Jens and I are not on the best of terms. If I was in his position I would want to know if I remained loyal or not.'

'Do you?' asked Bernard.

There was a silence, which was broken by the sound of Mona's phone ringing. Embarrassed, she muttered an apology.

'Do you need to answer that?' asked Toller.

She reached into her bag and turned her mobile off. If Paterson was looking for them, she'd deal with the trouble later.

Toller reached into his pocket and brought out a packet of Malboro.

'Do you mind? Sorry, I did not offer you one. Would either of you?'

They both made polite noises declining his offer.

'Of course not.' He struck a match with one hand. 'The Policewoman and the Sportsman. I am not so virtuous as you.'

'Not virtuous, just . . .'

'Enough, Bernard.' Mona glared at him. This wasn't the time for a lecture on the evils of smoking from her health-aware colleague. She addressed Toller.

'Heidi isn't in Germany, is she?'

Toller laughed. 'Perhaps she is. Perhaps even now she is sitting in her father's summer house in Wannsee, making lunch and wondering how she can ever show her face in public again after her naughty Papi's disgrace.'

Mona stared at him. 'You don't believe that.'

He looked serious. 'No, I don't. Her father is fooling himself if he thinks that Heidi has run off because of him.'

'Was she aware of the . . .' Bernard struggled to find the right word, 'the situation with her father?'

Toller leaned forward and contemplated his shoes. 'Yes, I had the pleasure of telling her that the Press had been asking questions, and the story was likely to break soon.'

'How did she take it?'

'Pretty well.'

He blew out a ring of smoke. Mona fought the urge to waft it away with her hand.

'But then she hates her father.' Toller sat back.

'Why?' Bernard looked confused.

'Because she loves her mother. This is not Jens's first indiscretion by any means.' He stubbed out his cigarette. 'And now, you tell me what you know about the situation.'

She looked at her partner. 'Where do we start, Bernard?'

He took a deep breath and began. 'Heidi was involved with a fringe group opposed to the Government's handling of the Virus called The Children of Camus. We think they are led by her supposed boyfriend, Kevin.'

'Heidi's boyfriend? I got the impression from her

243

parents that he was a very nice boy. Very studious. What did you mean "supposed" boyfriend?'

Mona looked at Bernard. He raised his eyebrows but didn't offer any help.

'I have some news that may surprise you, Doctor Toller.' Ridiculously, she felt herself blushing. 'Heidi is a lesbian. She's in a relationship with her flatmate, Amanda.'

Toller stared at Mona. His cigarette burned down to the end and singed his fingers. He cursed and dropped it. 'Heidi is a lesbian? How can this be? Are her parents aware of this?'

'No. Amanda seemed to think they would not take it well.'

'But how could Jens and Maria not have known this? Heidi was very close to her mother – surely she would have told her?'

'Young people can be very good at hiding things,' said Mona.

'So, what do The Children of Camus do?' asked the Doctor.

'Lots of pretty stupid things, such as illegal meet-ups,' said Bernard. 'But the thing that worries us most is they have this conviction that consuming drugs called Luprophen and Hyrdosol can prevent the Virus.'

Doctor Toller looked horrified.

'Utter nonsense, of course,' Bernard continued.

The German sat with his eyes closed. 'Actually, it is not nonsense. Please tell me Heidi had nothing to do with these drugs.'

Mona looked at her colleague in confusion. 'I'm afraid Heidi ordered £2,000 worth of them over the Internet shortly before she went missing. We believe she was intending to sell them on to her friends in The Children of Camus.'

Toller pulled out another cigarette and slowly proceeded to light up. 'I need to tell you both something in confidence.'

'I'm not sure that we can give you any promises about confidentiality if it affects our investigation.'

'Of course.' He thought for a minute. 'I have to tell you anyway. It is crucial to Heidi's safety. Our Government has been working with a pharmaceuticals firm on a trial of the two drugs that you mentioned. I cannot stress enough how secret these trials were. Jens was the Minister in charge of these operations — if Heidi has abused knowledge she gained through her father she will be in a great deal of trouble.'

'Oh dear,' said Bernard. 'I'm afraid we'll have to let SHEP know about this.'

Toller laughed.

'Doctor Toller,' said Mona, 'we will have to tell our bosses about this. It's relevant to the case.'

'The trials have been very promising to date.' He stared at her, his blue eyes unblinking. 'How much do you think a patented solution to our viral problem would be worth?'

Mona waited for Bernard to express an opinion, but even he seemed to realise this was rhetorical. You couldn't put a price on something that would lower even slightly the chances of dying from the Virus.

'Heidi leaking this information could cause commercial chaos for the firm concerned. There are many people who would be very dismayed at what she has done. There are many people who would wish her harm. You need to find her, get her to me and I will ensure we keep her safe.'

Mona sighed. 'Do you have any idea where Heidi

could have gone? Is she still in this country?'

'Yes. As you correctly identified we have her passport. One of the many reasons her father is fooling himself.'

'Would she stay locally, do you think, or is there somewhere she is familiar with that she would go to?'

'Her bank card has not been used since she went missing, although I was not aware she had a credit card until you mentioned it. Prior to her disappearance she withdrew the maximum amount she could from her account on three consecutive days. I assumed the £1,500 was money to fund her disappearance, although now I wonder ...'

'£1,500 is a lot for a student to have in their bank account.'

Toller smiled. 'Heidi is not an ordinary student. Unfortunately some of her so-called friends seemed to have realised this.'

'So, with £1,500 cash she could lie low somewhere for a few weeks.' Bernard said.

'Or she could be up to her neck in drug dealing, and in serious danger.'

'Or dead.' Herr Toller said. 'Let us not forget that possibility.' He slumped back on the bench. 'I am sorry. This is very difficult for us all.'

'So, you have no idea at all where she could be?'

'No, I am very sad to say.' He sighed. 'Do you?'

'No. But I know a man who might.' She got to her feet. 'Come on, Bernard. We have your mobile number, Herr Toller. If we find out anything at all, we'll be in touch.'

'It is imperative that you let me know as soon as you find her, so that I can arrange appropriate protection. Please get in touch as soon as you know *anything*.' He raised a hand in farewell.

Bernard looked back over his shoulder. 'He's lighting up again. He's going to die of lung cancer before we've found Heidi.'

'At the rate this investigation is going, quite possibly.' She started walking.

'Mona, you know what has always bugged me about this case?'

'What?'

'You know the girls that committed suicide from the Church of the Lord Arisen?'

'Yeah.'

'When we spoke to the mother of the girl in the coma, Kirsty, she was convinced that it wasn't suicide.'

Mona pulled a face. 'Yeah, but parents often find that difficult to accept.'

'But I was surprised that they committed suicide, even with the Virus, and everything. They were young, had family support, a network of friends, a strong faith – all these are strong protective factors against suicide. Do we know what drugs they overdosed on?'

Mona stopped walking. 'It was an antidepressant. You're thinking it could be Luprophen?'

He nodded. 'How much damage have Heidi and her pals done?'

She started moving again, mulling over what her colleague had suggested.

'Where are we going?' asked Bernard.

'I'm going to pay a visit to Marcus the Geek, and you,' she stopped and showed him her phone. There were seven missed call messages. 'You are going to call Maitland back and see what he wants.'

'Oh God, not Maitland again.' Bernard looked almost comically annoyed.

'Just ring him.'

Before he could protest any further she ran toward Princes Street, elbowing her way through a crowd of people gathered round one of the evangelists who seemed to be permanently stationed at the entrance to the Gardens these days. The preacher's voice drifted over to her as she waited to cross the road.

'Repent, sinners! We have brought this plague upon ourselves. We have gone against the Lord. We have not listened to His Word and in return we will bring the plague sevenfold upon this world.' Mona turned, and saw the evangelist was looking straight at her.

'By our adultery, by our degenerate behaviour, we have turned from the Lord. By our behaviour we have brought death to the innocents.'

Speak for yourself, she thought.

5

'I need a witness when I speak to this guy.' Maitland jabbed his sandwich in the direction of Pastor Mackenzie's house. Through a mouthful of ham-and-mustard he continued, 'He's a slippery customer. Let's hope he hasn't buggered off somewhere while I was sitting filling out forms in triplicate for Cameron bloody Stuttle.'

Bernard shifted uncomfortably in the passenger seat of the pool car. He was desperate to get back to the search for Heidi, but hadn't managed to avoid being dragged here by Maitland. He wondered if he would benefit from some assertiveness training in order to allow him to deal effectively with his colleagues. 'Did you get them all completed?'

There was a brief pause. 'After a fashion. Anyway, we both know this is more important.'

'Is it?' Bernard stared at him. Maitland's vendetta against Pastor Mackenzie was pretty low on his list of priorities. He was aching to get back to the Heidi case, although he had to admit, without Mona's directions he wasn't sure exactly what he should be doing on it. 'I don't think we should be here, Maitland. We can't go interviewing someone just because you think your girl-friend has moved in with him.'

Maitland nearly choked on his Diet Coke.

'She hasn't moved in with him! She's just confused.

Anyway, I already explained to you that it's perfectly acceptable to re-interview leads in a Defaulter case.'

This was true. When he'd returned his call, Maitland had given him a fabulously convoluted explanation why they were legally entitled to speak to Pastor Mackenzie again, which he hadn't entirely followed, but hadn't felt able to refute either. He looked over at the Pastor's neat, semi-detached house and garden, wondering if they were going to be faced with a harassment complaint.

'Bernard!'

'What?'

'Stop daydreaming – it's time to go.' Maitland squashed the cardboard wrapper that had recently contained his sandwich and threw it onto the back seat.

Bernard wondered if he had a stomach for the fight that would start if he voiced further concerns. Maitland glared at him.

'What?' he barked.

Bernard decided that he definitely did not have the nerve for an argument right now. 'Just not sure we should be parking on a yellow line, that's all.'

Maitland nearly took the gate off its hinges as he threw it open. He marched up the path, rang the bell, and when it had not been opened after thirty seconds, started hammering on the door. Bernard placed a restraining hand on his arm, which was immediately thrown off.

'Emma! I know you're in there!'

Through the frosted glass of the door they saw the outline of a figure.

'Emma – I can see you! Let me in – you're not safe here!'

There was a clattering of keys on the other side of the door, which was then flung open. The woman who stood there was tall, slim, with short fair hair, and an expression that implied she wanted to kill Maitland. Bernard warmed to her immediately.

'Not safe here? You're the one causing a disturbance.'

Maitland enveloped her in a hug, which she quickly repelled.

Pastor Mackenzie appeared behind Emma. 'Emma, are you sure you want to talk to Maitland at this point?'

Maitland turned bright red. He pushed his girlfriend to one side and stepped into the porch. 'Right, you,' he pointed at the clergyman, 'you're coming with us. My colleagues in Police Scotland will want to interview you about an allegation of rape made against you.'

'What?' said Emma and Pastor Mackenzie in unison.

Bernard grabbed his arm. 'Maitland, is this official HET business?' he whispered.

Maitland shook him off. 'You heard me. Get your things.'

Over Pastor Mackenzie's shoulder Bernard saw the door behind him move slightly. He was aware of a flash of long blonde hair, framing a delicate, heart-shaped face. Bernard blinked. He'd been wrong about something. When he was fifteen and on holiday with his parents, he'd seen Michelle Pfeiffer in a restaurant. He'd stared, open-mouthed, confident in the knowledge he would never be in the same room as such beauty again. Yet here was *this* woman, proving that theory completely wrong.

'Colette – it is Colette, isn't it?'

She gave the slightest of nods.

Maitland tried to step into the hallway, but neither Pastor Mackenzie nor Emma moved an inch. He balanced uneasily on the tiled front step, and looked back at him for support.

251

Bernard stuck his head round the side of Maitland. 'We're from the Health Enforcement Team – we've been looking for you.'

Colette sighed, leaning her head against the banister. Her long blonde hair fell across her face. Bernard thought she looked like she should have been in a pop video.

'Donny told me. Am I under arrest?'

There was a soft West Country lilt to her voice.

'We need you to accompany me to a Health Check, but...' Maitland caught Pastor Mackenzie off guard, and elbowed his way past him. Without looking back he took Colette's arm, and ushered her gently into the room she had come out of, which turned out to be the kitchen. Bernard followed as quickly, and as apologetically, as he could.

Maitland spoke softly. 'What are you doing here, Colette, after that pathetic excuse for a minister,' he dropped his voice even further, 'took advantage of you?'

'Malcolm?' Colette looked at them in surprise. 'Took advantage of me?' She shook Maitland's hand off her arm. 'Did Donny tell you that?'

Maitland looked at Bernard, his expression echoing the girl's confusion, then back to Colette. 'But you *were* raped?'

The girl collapsed onto one of the kitchen seats, and started to cry. Bernard felt himself being pulled violently backwards, as Emma grabbed both their arms and hauled them out of the kitchen.

'Nice one, Maitland. Even by your usual standards of tact that was superb.'

She motioned them into the front room of the house. Out of the corner of his eye he could see Pastor Mackenzie disappear into the kitchen.

252

'Emma, what's going on?' Maitland asked.

'Keep your voice down. She was raped, but not by Malcolm.'

'By Donny?'

'Jesus, no! Please stop trying to guess. Donny's a good guy. For someone that works in law enforcement you're not too hot on spotting villains, are you?'

Maitland glared at her and threw himself down on to the leather of the burgundy sofa. Bernard placed himself gently on the other corner.

'Just tell me who,' asked Maitland.

Emma perched on the arm of the sofa, and lowered her voice. 'That businessman who owns the pub you were talking about – Vince something?'

'Vic Thompson?'

'Yeah.'

'Christ,' said Maitland, sinking further into the cushions.

'So why . . .?' began Bernard.

'Why did Donny think Malcolm was responsible?' said Emma, asking his question for him.

'Yes.'

'Because Donny would have got himself killed squaring up to Vic Thompson. He got the wrong end of the stick about Malcolm, and it was safer for everyone just to let him think that.' She hit Maitland on the shoulder. 'You owe Malcolm a huge apology, you know.'

'I suppose.' Maitland did not look all that contrite. 'But there's something not right about the set-up at Morley's, Emma. I mean that back room is full of vulnerable young women. Why is it all women? Where are the men?'

'A good question.'

Pastor Mackenzie was standing in the doorway.

253

'My congregations are eighty per cent female. Most church congregations are eighty per cent female these days, if you care to look. Women seem in particular need of comfort in these dark times.' He sat down in an armchair. 'Perhaps all the men are in the pub, Mr Stevenson?'

'You're up to something, Mackenzie.'

The Pastor looked exasperated. 'Is it not even remotely possible that all my church is interested in is providing reassurance to individuals troubled by the Virus? Have you been in the Police so long that you can't believe in anything good?'

'I'm not in the Police; I'm in the Health Enforcement Team.' Maitland got slowly to his feet. 'Colette,' he called, 'I'm sorry but we need to go.'

She appeared, wearing her coat.

'I'll come too,' said the Pastor.

'Over my dead body,' said Maitland. 'Emma, can you come?'

Emma and Pastor Mackenzie looked at each other and he gave a slight nod.

Maitland was turning purple again. 'You don't need his bloody approval!'

Emma addressed herself to Bernard. 'Give me a minute and I'll get my bag.'

He nudged Maitland toward the door. 'We'll be in the car.'

6

Mona peered through the glass pane on the door to the computer suite. The IT guys were both concentrating on their screens, shoulders hunched, their hands tapping away at the keyboards. She wondered if they were researching the Virus or playing computer games.

'Hi.'

The typing stopped. Marcus did a double take when he saw Mona walking through the door. He grinned at Bryce, and leapt up to find her a seat. Mona felt a stab of irritation. She wasn't sure she could bear half an hour of an IT nerd fawning over her, even to get the information that she needed.

'I wasn't expecting the pleasure so soon. What are you two working on now?'

Word travelled fast.

'The same – missing Germans etc.' Mona sat down and avoided looking at either of the IT staff.

Marcus frowned. 'It's just that I saw the e-mail saying that Heidi had been found in Germany, case closed.'

'The e-mail?' The Guv must have been unusually quick off the mark.

'Yeah, Paterson cc'd me into an e-mail round your team saying there would be no further work undertaken on this case. He was quite emphatic on that point.' He looked at her. 'Didn't you get the message?'

255

'No.' Mona pulled her chair up the side of the IT guy's desk. 'Anyhow, we may need a favour. I need an update on Heidi's e-mail traffic.'

'But you're not working on the case now.' One of his eyebrows emerged above the rim of his glasses.

'The case is still open.'

There was no response from Marcus.

'Cases remain open until the Defaulter is found.' She could hear a slight screechy tone to her voice. It wasn't pleasant.

He leaned back on this chair, his hands folded behind his head.

'Please, just check her account to see if there have been any recent e-mails.'

He unfolded his arms and slapped his hands down on his knees.

'That's a sackable offence, Mona, hacking into someone's e-mail account without legitimate reason.'

'There is a legitimate reason – Heidi is in danger!'

'OK,' he nodded enthusiastically. 'Get me authorisation from Paterson and I'll happily do it.'

She glared at him, and he winced under the violence of her stare.

'I'm sorry, I'd dearly love to help you but not at the expense of my job.'

Mona felt a sudden urge to throw something across the room. She settled for standing up and shoving her chair back. She reached down and grabbed her bag.

'Are you going back to your office?'

'No, actually, I'm going to find a café with decent Wi-Fi and put in every password I can think of until I get into Heidi's account.'

A look passed between Marcus and Bryce.

'Yes, I know it could take me a while to guess, not least because it might be something in German ...'

The look passed between them again. Bryce raised his eyebrows and returned to his computer.

Marcus sighed, and signalled to her to sit back down. 'Mona, Heidi could, in theory, choose any combination of words and numbers in the world.'

'Oh God, this is doomed.' She slumped back in her chair.

'But people don't generally do that, do they? Most people go for something really straightforward, and incidentally, easy to hack, like their name and 123.'

A vision of mona123 came into her mind and she wondered how Marcus knew her password. Did IT read their e-mails? It was probably just a lucky guess. She'd change it tomorrow, although she might have to ask Bernard how to do it.

'So you could try heidi123 or weber123, but ...'

'But what?'

'But Heidi's young, she's IT literate, and we're pretty sure she's got stuff in her inbox that she definitely doesn't want anyone to see. So my guess is that she's gone for something really random, like the first letter of each word in a particular sentence out of a book.'

'Probably something in German. So, I'm back to being doomed.'

'Except, most people do write their passwords down somewhere, unless they are doing something really stupid like using the same password for everything.'

mona123. She was definitely changing it tomorrow.

'And Heidi definitely wasn't doing that. She kept an encrypted document with all her passwords on her laptop, which could only be hacked by the smartest of tech geeks,' he pointed to himself, 'which is the only reason we got into her e-mails.'

Something occurred to her. She grabbed her bag, and pulled out her laptop, almost dropping it in excitement.

'What's your Wi-Fi code?'

'Seriously? There's no chance you could do this somewhere else?'

'Please, Marcus?'

He wrestled with his conscience for a second, then passed her a sheet of paper with the Wi-Fi code.

'Have you cracked it then?' He stood next to her, waiting to see what she typed.

She pulled out the fluffy pink book, and gently picked at the cover. As she had recalled, the outer layer was designed to be removed. She eased it off, and stared at the neatly written line of poetry. *So wise so young, they say do never live long.*

Marcus ran his finger over the sentence. 'You reckon this is it, then?'

'Yup.'

'That's you halfway there, then.'

She stopped typing Heidi's e-mail address into G-mail.

'What do you mean, "halfway"?' 'Well, even if this sentence is the right code, you could use a capital letter at the beginning of the password where she hasn't or vice versa. Or it could be all lower case, or all capitals.'

'Oh, God. Oh well, here goes nothing.'

She typed in the e-mail address. At the password prompt she typed 'swsytsdnll.'

A message appeared in the centre of the screen telling her that either the address or password was wrong, and advising her to check that her Caps Lock wasn't on.

She tried again, with capital letters this time. SWSYTSDNLL.

Again, the error message appeared. She slapped the diary in frustration, and swore.

Third time lucky. Swsytsdnll.

Heidi's e-mails appeared.

'Fantastic!'

Marcus looked markedly less delighted than she felt. 'Just remember, if anyone asks, you worked that out all by yourself.'

'Whatever.' She grabbed her phone and called Bernard. 'We're in!'

He cheered, then she heard him say. 'High Five, Maitland?'

A faint voice said, 'Get stuffed, Bernard.'

There were no e-mails in Heidi's inbox. Mona panicked until she noticed the row of folder icons at the side of the screen. 'She files all her e-mails, Bernard,' she said. 'A woman after your own heart, I would have thought.'

There was the sound of laughter from her phone. 'It would be helpful if there was one marked "Illicit Drugs" or "Loopy and H", wouldn't it?'

'There's one marked "Purchases".'

She clicked on the Purchases folder. The first e-mail thanked Heidi for her order, and noted it would be dispatched to the address she had given when she ordered. Mona relayed this to Bernard.

'Not overly specific, is it?'

'There's a file marked "Personal" – I'll try that.'

She clicked over. The first e-mail was from Kevin, and had been sent a few hours earlier.

'Bernard, listen to this.'

'OK.'

'"Heidi, I don't know why you aren't answering my texts but I'm not waiting any longer. I'm going to find you. I know you've gone to Dunblane."'

'"I'm going to find you." Is that a threat?' Bernard sounded pensive.

'It could be. I wonder how he knows she's in Dunblane?'

'Dunblane? That's near Stirling, isn't it? Must be about an hour, maybe hour-and-a-half's drive from here?'

'Fancy a trip, Bernard?'

'Let's just hope he's gone straight there. I'll get the car from Maitland as soon as we've dropped off his Defaulter, then I'll pick you up.'

'Fine.'

'Mona?' The phone sounded anxious.

'What?'

'We need to let Mr Paterson know.'

He was right, but there remained a danger that the Guv would just hand it over to one of the Stirling HETs to deal with.

'Mona?' Bernard's tone was insistent.

'Leave the Guv to me.'

She hung up, placed her phone on the table and sat staring at it, working out what she could say to her Team Leader that would still result in them being allowed to go to Dunblane. Inspiration was in short supply.

Mona's mobile rang, and an unfamiliar number came up on the screen.

'Hello?'

A faint voice said something unintelligible at the other end.

'Who is this?' Then she realised. 'Amanda, is that you?'

The voice whispered again.

'He's here.'

7

'Finished speaking to your boss?' Maitland shot Bernard one of his more annoying smirks.

'I was speaking to Mona, as you well know.'

'Exactly my point.'

Maitland was driving them to the nearest Health Check Centre, which was in a GP's surgery at the West End. The two girls sat in the back, and Maitland had taken the precaution of putting the child locks on, in case they were planning to hop out at a traffic light.

'So, what are the two of you up to?'

Bernard affected a look of innocence, but left it a second or so too long to answer. 'What?'

'You and Mona – you're plotting something that the Guv doesn't know about. Is this to do with that German lassie you were after?'

Before Bernard could answer there was a banging on the internal window of the car. He turned round to see Colette waving to him. He fumbled around until he got the intercom working.

'What's up?'

'Do I have to tell them about …about the rape?'

'No,' said Bernard. 'You are not legally obliged to tell the nurse anything. You don't even have to tell her you are pregnant.'

Colette's face lit up. 'Really?'

261

'Yes, though you're going to have to tell your doctor at some point. If you get the Virus both you and the baby are in serious danger.'

Colette didn't answer.

'The Health Enforcement Team can't make you have an abortion, or haul you into hospital against your will, Colette. All we want to do is make sure you are not infected.'

She still didn't reply. He looked at Emma, who shrugged helplessly. He turned back in his seat, but left the intercom on.

'Do you know about health stuff, Bernard?'

Colette's voice made him jump. He turned back in her direction. 'I know about the Virus, I'm not a doctor.'

She started to cry again, and Emma reached over and took her hand.

'What if I damaged my baby taking that stuff?'

'What stuff – Loopy and H?' he asked.

She looked miserable. 'Everyone was doing it, all my friends. It seemed like the only way to protect ourselves.'

Maitland swivelled his gaze between the road and the reflected image of the back seat. 'That friend of yours in hospital, and the ones that died, were they taking Loopy and H?'

'Yes.' Her voice was a whisper.

'So, your friends die after taking the stuff, and you don't have enough common sense to give it a wide berth?'

'Leave her alone, Maitland.' Emma pulled her friend toward her. 'She's been through enough.'

'Just one more thing that we have to ask.' The car slowed, and Maitland pulled into the side of the road. He turned round to look at his passengers. 'We understand that you've been the victim of a crime, Colette.'

The girl buried her face in her hands. Maitland went on, 'We can support you to make a formal complaint to Police Scotland. There is a specialist Rape Unit ...'

'Leave it, Maitland.' Emma looked furious.

Bernard tried to help. 'The complaint would be dealt with very sensitively.'

'Colette knows she can make a complaint, but she doesn't feel up to it at the moment.'

'So, Vic Thompson gets off scot-free, ready to attack some other pretty girl that ends up in his bar?'

'Stop pressuring her, Maitland, it's her decision to make.' The couple glared at each other through the Perspex wall.

Maitland gave up, and turned back to the wheel. 'OK. Let's get you in for your Health Check.'

The Health Check would take all of five minutes, an anticlimactic end to their three days of activity. Maitland and Emma settled themselves onto the orange plastic chairs in the Waiting Room, and watched as the nurse escorted Colette through a set of swing doors, and into the long white corridors of the medical centre. Bernard stood swaying from foot to foot in his eagerness to get out of there and meet up with Mona. Now that the case was completed, Maitland appeared to be focusing all his attention on his girlfriend, possibly ex. Bernard suspected that any minute now there would be an outbreak of Maitland charm, aimed at seducing the poor woman back into his life. He decided to get in quick.

'Maitland?'

'Yup?' He didn't take his eyes off Emma, who was busy

flicking through a magazine, in what Bernard assumed was a concerted effort not to engage with her boyfriend, possibly ex.

'I need the car.'

Maitland turned his head slowly in Bernard's direction, and he sensed his colleague was not going to make this easy for him.

'I heard you say something to Mona about getting the car.' He smirked and spun the keys round his finger. 'Why?'

Bernard stared at his colleague. He was pretty sure that Maitland didn't figure in Mona's circle of trust on this issue. He wasn't overly confident Mr Paterson was in that particular loop, if he was honest. Either way, he wasn't in a position to spill the beans to Maitland.

'Just give them to me.'

'No.'

Maitland's smirk was getting more punchable by the minute Bernard made a grab for the keys, but his colleague whisked them into his pocket.

'Come on, Bernard, don't be a dick. What's Mona up to?'

'Maitland.' Emma closed her magazine, and sighed. 'Can I have a word with you in private?'

Maitland looked from Bernard to Emma and back. Bernard enjoyed the obvious dilemma his colleague was experiencing between patching things up with his ex-girlfriend or continuing to torment him. Maitland scowled at him, but flung the keys in his direction.

'But I want to know what's going on.'

Bernard fled down the corridor, hoping that the quiet word Emma was seeking with his colleague was to tell him that he was dumped, binned and quite considerably surplus to requirements. And in this case, there would be no need for Emma to reach for the 'It's not you, it's me' speech. It was definitely Maitland. He was smiling as he reached for the door handle. As his hand grasped it, his mobile rang again.

8

The protocol relating to HET/Police interaction was a delicate and ever-changing minefield. Every time the Team thought they were clear on when the HET was required to refer their activities to the Police, and vice versa, a new memo clarifying the situation would appear in the Guv's in tray, setting back their understanding each time. However, Mona was forced to admit, a teenager with a crate of drugs and an irate dealer looking for her, merited a word or two with the local Force. Likewise, she'd gone far enough with Amanda without involving some of her local colleagues. Although on that front, at least, things were about to change. Amanda had whispered to her on the phone that she had already called 999. Mona had told her to stay hidden, and that she was on her way.

She stuck out her hand and hailed a taxi. The black cab driver caught sight of her and did a U-turn. She clambered in, giving Amanda's address, then sat back on the black leather to consider what to do. The questions were, when and how to make the call. It should come from the Guv, which would involve a long conversation, quite a lot of shouting, and a fatal delay in them getting up to Dunblane. Mona held her mobile in her hand, debating who to call first. She opted for Bernard.

'Kevin is at Amanda's.'

She waited while Bernard absorbed this information.

266

'So, should I meet you there?'

She closed her eyes. 'No. You need to go to Dunblane.' Bernard could be halfway there before she phoned. She'd sort Amanda out, phone the Guv, and deal with the flak, hopefully getting over to Dunblane for some of the action herself.

'So I just set off, with no idea why I'm going or where Heidi might be?'

'No, you set off, find the local Police Station and wait there. I'll square things with the Guv and let you know what's happening.'

He didn't sound convinced. Mona had some sympathy with his doubts. She had a moment's reconsideration about setting off for Dunblane herself, but she wanted to check the emergency call had gone through OK. A vision of Amanda's bruised face swam into her mind.

'Phone Toller en route. Ask him to contact Herr Weber – he might know why Heidi would head there.'

'And if I do manage to find where she's staying what do I do then?'

'You phone me. I'll be half an hour behind you on the motorway.'

'Mona?'

'What?'

'You can't just head off to Amanda's on your own – Kevin is dangerous.'

'I won't be on my own. She's called 999.' The taxi pulled up in Amanda's street. She shoved a ten pound note in the direction of the driver, and stepped out into the street. There was no sign of any Police cars. She checked her watch. Surely the emergency call should have been answered by now? She walked swiftly to the corner of the street and had a scout around to see if there was any sign of a response car on one of the streets nearby, but saw nothing. She pulled her sleeve back, checking her watch for a second time, and jogged slowly toward Amanda's flat. As she approached, the door opened, and a middle-aged woman appeared. She kept up her pace, and held the door as the woman exited, giving her a polite smile as she did so. The woman gave her a sideways glance, but didn't challenge her, and she slipped into the lobby.

Mona made her way up the stairs, her back sliding along the polished tiles of the wall, alert and braced for action. The flat's door was slightly ajar; she flicked it open with a finger and peered in. The lights were off, and she stood on the doorstep listening for signs of life. Edging her way into the gloom, she winced at the creak of the floorboards beneath her feet. Her toe caught the edge of the bookcase, jolting one of the ornaments on the top. The tiny china bell spun round in a delicate arch before it plunged off the side, smashing onto the wooden floor. At the sound, a door flew open and a figure ran full tilt at her.

'Thank God,' said Amanda, clinging to her. 'I'm so glad you're here.'

'Kevin?'

'He's gone. I don't think he realised I was here.'

'And you're OK?' Mona could feel Amanda's head nod against her shoulder. Relief flooded over her, and she gently pushed her away.

'Did you come on your own?' Amanda asked.

'Yes – are the Police here yet?'

'Not yet.' She shrugged. 'I didn't really know what to say to them though. I don't think I made it clear what an emergency it was.'

'What did Kevin want, anyway?'

'Just to pick up his stuff.'

'I thought he'd already taken his stuff?'

There was a pause. 'Yeah, he took his bag already, but then he came back looking for something. Look.' Amanda walked back past Mona and pushed the door to her room open. Mona stuck her head round. There were clothes everywhere, and every drawer was opened.

'He searched my room. I don't know what he was after.'

'Is it OK if I take a look?'

'Sure.' She stood watching Mona, moving from foot to foot. Her nerves were showing and Mona rooted around for a task to focus her mind.

'Why don't you make us a coffee?'

She nodded, and disappeared into the kitchen.

Mona picked through the debris of the room, trying to work out what Kevin had been looking for. How much did he know about Heidi's departure? A thought occurred to Mona.

'Amanda?' she reopened the door and shouted through to the kitchen.

'Yes?' She could hear her clattering around.

'Has Heidi ever mentioned a place called Dunblane to you?'

The clattering from the kitchen stopped. 'No – is that where you think Kevin was heading?'

'Possibly.'

At the end of the bed, half-hidden by a duvet, lay a suitcase. Mona looked back toward the door to check that Amanda wasn't there, then opened the lid. A selection of T-shirts and jeans were shoved into the case, weighed down by a pair of green hi-tops. Was Amanda going somewhere? And if so, why hadn't she mentioned it? The cupboard door in the corner of the room remained shut. Mona opened it as quietly as she could. The hangers were empty; she assumed the clothes that had been in there were now in the suitcase. Her eyes drifted to the floor. A blue holdall was lying on the floor, one very much like the bag that Kevin had left in the flat. The bag that Amanda, not five minutes earlier, had said was gone.

'So, why do you think Kevin's gone to Dunblane?' Amanda's voice echoed from the kitchen.

Mona got back to her feet. 'We're not sure that he has,' she lied, and reached into her pocket for her phone. 'It's just one possible lead.'

'Well, thanks for the heads-up,' said a voice emanating from behind Mona's right ear.

A man's voice.

Bernard dialled Toller's number for the third time. On his two previous attempts it had rung without anyone picking it up, then cut out. This time, however, a voice answered.

'Toller here.'

'Doctor Toller, we think Heidi has gone to Dunblane.' There was a brief pause at the other end of the line. 'It's Bernard from the HET by the way.'

'Yes, Bernard, I recognise your voice. Dunblane, you say?'

He swerved to avoid a parked car. He hated speaking on the phone while driving, but it seemed an unavoid-able piece of law-breaking given the situation. 'Yes, it's a small town near Stirling.'

'I know.' There was some static then Toller's voice came through again, loud and clear. 'I am not clear why Heidi would be there.'

Bernard drove over a speed bump and nearly dropped the phone. 'Could you phone Herr Weber and see if he has any ideas?'

'Yes. Absolutely. I know Jens has been to Scotland many times. He may have taken the family there on previous holidays.' There was a brief silence at the other end of the phone. 'I will call his wife and ring you back.'

9

Mona turned around slowly, then tilted her head to look at the very tall, dark-haired man standing there. She would be the first to admit that the attractiveness of the opposite sex wasn't really her specialist subject, but she was pretty sure that this was a guy that could break a thousand teenage hearts. She stared at him, trying to work out what was going on. Had they been wrong about Kevin? Was this actually K? And where was Amanda? Had this man hurt her?

The situation clarified itself when Amanda walked back into the room holding a large kitchen knife. She smiled, and gently tapped its pointy end.

'Ouch, sharp!' She laughed and sucked her finger.

Mona felt a hot prickle of adrenalin. Her eye flicked round the room, checking out the exits, as she tried to figure out what was going on.

Amanda reached under her bed and pulled out something brightly coloured. Mona struggled at first to work out what it was, but as she thrust the bundle toward the man, she saw it was a handful of silk scarves.

'Get her tied up.'

The tall guy looked round the room. 'What to?'

She tutted, then disappeared out the door, reappearing with one of the sturdy kitchen chairs.

'Sit!'

Amanda pointed the knife in the direction of the seat. Mona didn't move. What were they planning? Murder? Torture? Once she was sitting down and tied up she didn't fancy her chances.

'Didn't you hear her?' The man grabbed her by the shoulder and forced her down. 'Sit!'

He worked quickly, securing her wrists and ankles against the wood. Amanda inspected the work.

'Looks good.'

The two of them stood watching her.

'Anyway, you need to get going.' Amanda nudged the man in the ribs.

'Where?'

'According to this nice lady,' she pointed to Mona, 'Heidi is in Dunblane.'

She closed her eyes. What had she done?

'And where is that?'

Someone kicked the chair, and she opened her eyes. Amanda was standing very close to her.

'Mona, where is Dunblane?'

She felt a wave of anger rise from her stomach. 'Get a map.'

Amanda laughed. 'Probably some middle-of-nowhere place up north. Anyway, I've got Heidi's address book – let's see if it's in there.' She pushed him in the direction of the door, followed the man out of the room, then stuck her head back in. 'Don't go anywhere, now.'

Mona spat out a curse at her, then sat trying to get her breath under control. Things could be worse; she wasn't dead, and no-one appeared to be about to torture her. Unfortunately, that was because she had made it all so bloody easy for them. She strained toward the hall, trying in vain to hear if they really did have an address. After a couple of minutes the door slammed, and there was silence.

'Amanda!'

She reappeared. 'Yes, sweetie?'

'Untie me right now, and I may not have to report this to the Police.'

Amanda laughed. 'You really surpassed my expectations, you know that? I got you over here thinking that you might let slip some tiny hint of where my bitch flatmate is hiding out with my stuff. But you've gone well beyond that. You've delivered her up to me on a plate.'

Mona pulled against her bonds, succeeding only in tightening their grip, and increasing her own fury. 'You'll get done for this, you know.'

'Will I?' Amanda snorted. 'After the high-quality investigation there's been so far? I'm home and dry.'

'No, you're not.'

This provoked another laugh. 'You never know when to give up, Mona. I like that. You are also dim. I like that too.' She scooped up a handful of her remaining clothes, threw them into the suitcase, and ceremoniously dropped Heidi's address book on top of them. She bent down and started to zip up the suitcase. 'I mean, all it took was a few hints to you that Heidi and me were an item and you couldn't do enough for me.'

She was struggling to get the overfilled suitcase closed. Mona watched as the girl sat on top of the case and tugged some more at the zip.

'But then people are so gullible, Mona, aren't they? Take students, for instance. All those brains, yet all it takes is a couple of blog posts suggesting a conspiracy and before you know it, you've got a full-blown cult on your hands.'

Mona wriggled her hands in an attempt to establish how loose her bonds were. 'They're not gullible, just scared and vulnerable.'

Amanda smirked. 'Scared, vulnerable, and loaded. K had the perfect business – students putting up the money, taking all the risks, selling the drugs. And still thinking he's a genius for pointing out the truth to them.'

The suitcase finally closed. Amanda got to her feet and pulled it upright. She sauntered toward Mona, and to her horror, sat on her lap, facing toward her with one leg on either side. Mona tugged at her bonds.

'Vic Thompson is an arsehole. A lousy cheating arse-hole who still owes me money. Not a bad shag, although I expect you don't want to hear about that.'

She ran a finger gently down the side of Mona's face. She jerked her face away, but Amanda grabbed her chin and turned her back to face her.

'Poor old Mona. Have you told your colleagues you're a dyke?'

She closed her eyes. 'Fuck you.'

Amanda laughed. 'Thought not.' She wriggled from side to side then continued. 'So this is the deal, right. You are going to sit there for a couple of hours and not try to contact any of your colleagues.'

Mona opened her eyes again. 'Why would I do that?'

'Because I'd like to get my gear, get my money, then bugger off somewhere abroad for a while. I'm thinking somewhere hot, nice beach, you know? And if I don't make it out of the country I'll tell your colleagues in graphic detail about the affair we've been having, ever since you turned up on my doorstep to talk to Heidi.'

275

Amanda leapt to her feet and put on a sad face. 'There's poor little lesbian me, missing my girlfriend, when you come along and take advantage of me.'

'That's all lies!' Mona shouted.

'Well, duh. Anyway, it's not totally untrue is it, sweetie? If I'd given you the slightest opportunity you'd have had your tongue straight down my throat. Thought I was going to have to fight you off me in the hallway, you were so intent on consoling me.'

'I'm not gay.' Mona tugged violently at the bonds round her wrists.

'Ha!' Amanda smirked. 'I believe you. Thousands wouldn't. Not least, all your Police pals. Or Health Office, or whatever your mob call yourself now.' She picked up her suitcase. 'Anyway, lover, got to go. Here's one for the road.'

She held Mona's face in her hands, and planted a kiss firmly on her mouth. Without looking back she closed the bedroom door, and Mona heard the front door being shut.

She stared at her reflection in the dressing room mirror, and let out a yell of rage.

10

Bernard motored along the M90, with one eye on the road and the other watching his phone. He tried to calm his nerves by remembering what he knew of Dunblane. He'd been there years back while on holiday with Carrie. They'd taken their ancient car and tootled around from village to village, lazy and loved-up. He thought about the letter, still unread in his pocket.

A road sign loomed into view, indicating the junction for Linlithgow. Bernard tried to do a mental calculation of how far he had left to drive, and nearly went smashing into the back of a Fiat Punto that was hogging the inside lane.

He took each of his hands off the wheel in turn and dried the palms on his jeans. Why hadn't Toller phoned back? Or why hadn't Mona phoned to say 'Joke's over, Bernard. We weren't really sending you to look for a bad guy'? He could picture her saying it.

As he drew near to Falkirk his phone rang. He reached for it, but in his hurry knocked it off the seat so it landed in the footwell. Cursing, Bernard pulled off the motorway at the next junction. He drew into a lay-by and scrabbled around for it. The ringing had long stopped by the time he reached it. He picked it up and saw it was Toller who'd called. He pressed redial.

'I was right.' Toller sounded triumphant. 'The Weber family had several holidays in Dunblane when Heidi was young. Unfortunately, Jens was not clear on the name of the house they stayed in. He thinks perhaps Mitre House. Or possibly Martyr House?'

'Mitre House? Do you have an address or anything?'

'No. I am sorry. It was twenty years ago. Frau Weber is looking through her old correspondence as we speak.'

'Did they remember anything else? What did it look like?'

'This is a stupid memory, perhaps, but they mentioned a sculpture of a bird at the front gate?' Toller sighed. 'There was a bridge, perhaps? And the house may have been white? I'm afraid I don't know, Bernard. I would very much like to assist. I will telephone them again, and anyone else that I think might be able to assist us.'

'Don't worry about it. You've been very helpful.' Bernard hung up with an oath. He clicked on his phone's browser and called up a search engine, which produced no results for either Mitre or Martyr House. Was there any point in going on? After a moment's thought he decided he'd come this far and might as well keep driving.

He got back onto the main road and put his foot down. He drove through Stirling without his phone ringing again, and saw the directions that pointed to his destination.

He drove slowly through the centre of the town until he saw the familiar blue sign of the Police Station. The feeling of relief this provoked was short-lived, as on his approach to the building he saw a sign stating 'Closed due to Virus Staff Shortages'.

'What now?' he said out loud. He dialled Mona's number, which went straight through to her voicemail. 'Shit.' Why wasn't she picking up? She must have been expecting him to call.

278

He paused beside his car. He could drive back the way he came until he found a Police Station that was actually staffed, but nowhere else was likely to know the location of the house they were looking for, at least not from the limited description he could give. He looked from his car to his phone, seeking inspiration, and decided that the most useful thing he could do was try and locate Mitre House.

There was no-one around so he drove on again and motored slowly until he started to see people. He stopped three teenage girls, all hair and short skirts, who giggled a lot at his enquiry but couldn't shed any light on it. A woman pushing a buggy shrugged off his question impatiently, while her toddler leaned a chocolate-smeared face forward to have a better look at him. At his third attempt he got lucky. Two grey-haired women pulling trolley bags stopped.

'Mitre House?' The pair of them stared at him, then turned to look at each other. They were very alike, sisters probably, distinguished only by one having straight grey hair, and the other permed.

'Yeah, it's a holiday cottage. Possibly painted white? A statue of a bird in the garden?'

'Possibly painted white? I think the landlord should have given you better directions, son.' The pair of them laughed, a similar, sisterly laugh, then took pity on him.

'Do you think he means the house up over the bridge?'

'Yes,' said Bernard excitedly. 'A bridge was definitely mentioned.'

The curly-haired one nudged her sister. 'That'll be John MacDonald's laddie's cottage.'

Her sister nodded solemnly. 'The one that's a doctor in Glasgow.'

'Aye, he rents it out when he's not using it.'

Curly sister rested an elbow on the window ledge of the car and gave him directions. A whiff of perfume reminded him of his mother.

'Straight through the town, son, then carry on for about a mile and you'll see a wee stone bridge off to your left. Turn up there then follow the road round to the right and keep going for ...' She turned to her sister. 'How long would you say?'

There was much shaking of heads. 'Oh, it's a bit of a drive, son. Maybe twenty minutes?'

'It's quite isolated, then?' asked Bernard, surreptitiously wiping the sweat from his palms again.

'I wouldn't live there, son.' She laughed, stepped back from the car and took hold of her trolley bag again. 'Hope you find it.'

Bernard thanked them, and pulled away from the kerb. His palms were now so wet that he was in serious danger of losing control of the wheel. For a second he considered whether a small car crash would be preferable to actually locating Mitre House. He could say to Mona that he had done his best but circumstances had forced his hand.

She'd kill him.

He drove through Dunblane, as instructed, and turned off at a narrow stone bridge. This led on to a lane, lined on either side by hedgerows. The car bounced along an uneven track for half an hour without encountering a single car coming the other way. 5.40pm. The light would be fading soon, even on a beautiful April night like this, and his chances of achieving anything in the dark were remote.

Sorry, Mona, I tried.

He made a half-hearted attempt at a three-point turn,

bumping hedgerows on every manoeuvre, then abandoned it in favour of driving on until a suitable spot to turn round presented itself.

A drive appeared on the right of the road, about fifty metres ahead of him. His spirits rose as he nosed the bonnet back in the direction of Edinburgh. This good mood continued until the car completed its turn, and his passenger window drew level with a stone at the side of the road with 'Myrtle House' painted on it. Just to confirm that this was, in fact, his destination, a rusty sculpture of three little birds stared back at him.

Bernard stopped the car, willing the sign to rearrange itself into something that couldn't possibly be the Mitre/ Martyr House that he was looking for. When the lettering remained stubbornly Myrtle-shaped, he pulled out his mobile, which immediately started to ring.

'Bernard, it is Karl Toller here. I have an address for you ...'

'That's OK, I ...'

'After we spoke I had a good idea. I thought, Heidi must have paid cash for this rental, as it is not on her bank or credit card statement, so I had my people ring all the agencies we could find with properties in Stirlingshire to see if anyone had paid in cash, and an agency based in Edinburgh said that a young woman ...'

'Karl, I've found it.'

'Oh, you have?' He sounded almost disappointed that his brainwave hadn't saved the day. 'Then I must let you go. Please, Bernard, take care of Heidi.'

'I will.'

He was annoyed to notice that his hands were trembling as he dialled Mona's number. The phone rang a dozen times, then was redirected to her answering service.

'Shit.'

He dialled Maitland's number. This time it did not even ring before going straight to the answer service. He left a message about his and Mona's whereabouts, hoping that it wasn't too garbled.

There was nothing else for it. He gathered all the courage he could muster, and dialled Paterson's number. The phone rang out.

'Shit, shit, shit.' Bernard ran his hands over his hair. 'What do I do now?'

He put his mobile on the seat next to him and restarted the engine. He reversed, bounced off another hedgerow, then pulled into the gravelled driveway. He winced at the noise; if anyone was inside they would definitely be well warned that he'd arrived.

It looked as if he wasn't alone. A hire car sat parked at a forty-five degree angle to the house. Whoever was here hadn't taken the time to stop and park neatly. There was a moment's deliberation where to park. Should he block the hire car in, or leave the house's occupant the possibility of a quick getaway? He flipped a mental coin, and drove over to the far side of the house.

Bernard dialled Mona's number again and left a message on her answering service. 'Mona, it's me. I've found the place, it's called Myrtle House. It looks like there is someone staying here. I'm going to knock on the door and see if anyone answers. Give me a ring as soon as you get this.' He got out, throwing the phone in the direction of the passenger seat.

The house wasn't what he'd expected. Bernard had imagined some old, stone-built affair, but instead it was a 1970s creation, heavy on the stone cladding and sporting an asymmetric roof.

Accepting that his phone was not about to ring, he climbed out and walked up to the front door. He rapped on the door, his stomach tightening as he waited for a response.

There was no answer.

He turned the handle, and to his surprise, the door opened.

11

Mona's phone rang. She listened to the twelve rings with mounting frustration. It would be Bernard, she just knew it. Poor, useless, Bernard, who was in far too deep. Whom she'd got in far too deep, and left to drown so that she could check out the woman that she ...

That she what, exactly?

She pulled gingerly at the ties around her hand, worried about making them even tighter. She suspected Amanda and her friend knew what they were doing when it came to tying people up.

She reviewed her options.

She could start shouting; sooner or later she would attract the attention of someone else in the building. She could yell through the door to them the nature of her predicament, and get them to call the Police. But she didn't relish the thought of the local plod finding her in her current state. It would be bound to get back to the CID and she'd been the butt of enough jokes since the whole supposed adultery fiasco. Even worse, the Police might bring the HET with them. The thought of Maitland finding her like this was more than she could bear, especially given the second wave of embarrassment that would arrive if Amanda was found, and made good on her threat.

Alternatively, she could manoeuvre herself until she

found something sharp to cut through her ties. There was a big margin for error with this approach. The potential was there to accidentally slit her wrist and bleed to death. The end result would still involve being found tied to a chair by her former colleagues, the only advantage this time would be that the embarrassment would be posthumous.

And then there was her final option. She could stay where she was and let Amanda make a clean getaway. She'd still have the short-term discomfiture of explaining how she ended up in this position, but in the long run it would save herself a lot of hassle and difficult questions.

Her phone rang again.

It would be Bernard. Poor, desperate, Bernard. She started looking round the room for sharp edges.

Bernard stuck his head in to the hallway, and looked to the left and right. There was an expanse of brown carpet in each direction and a row of closed doors, none of which gave any indication of possible occupancy. At the foot of the stairs a large star-shaped wall clock was ticking noisily, which only served to reinforce the complete and utter silence elsewhere.

He placed a foot tentatively into the house, then quickly withdrew it again.

He didn't know what to do. If Heidi was here alone, he needed to find her. A vision of the survival rates table he'd encountered in his HET training came into his mind. How much did the likelihood of death increase with every hour a sufferer was left untended? The figure wouldn't come to him, but the pictures in the handbook crowded into his head, making the thought of getting Heidi to a nice, clean hospital seem the only possible plan. But, best case scenario, she could be fit and healthy, just scared to death of encountering K, which frankly, made two of them. Either way, he needed to find her and get them both to safety.

He stepped back into the house. 'Hello?'

His voice echoed through the building. The stillness continued for a minute, then a noise, a low sound that could have been a cough, came from behind one of the doors. Bernard took a deep breath, wiped his palms again, and looked round the hallway for anything he could use as a weapon. He picked up a brass cat that was lying at his feet; its weight confirmed its day job as a doorstop. Not ideal, but it would have to do.

He pushed the door open, inch upon inch, until he had a good view of the living room. There was a bundle of blankets on the sofa that turned toward the door as he opened it. A young man's face the colour of snow peered over the top of the blanket. Bernard returned his red-eyed stare. Whoever this was, he was in the latter stages of the Virus.

'Heidi.' The man spoke. 'I can't find Heidi.'

He touched the man's forehead. His face jerked away but not before Bernard had felt the burning skin beneath his fingertips.

The young man was getting agitated. 'Heidi!' He tried to sit up, and failed. He fell back onto the sofa, banging his skull on the arm of the chair.

Bernard picked up a cushion from an armchair and stuck it under his head. 'Keep calm, I'll look for her. Can you tell me who you are?'

The head on the cushion lolled toward him. 'I'm Kevin.'

Bernard stared at him. Was this really the man that Heidi was fleeing from? He didn't look particularly

286

frightening, but then the Virus was a great leveller. No-one looks threatening with a temperature of thirty-nine degrees.

He took a step back from the sofa. 'What are you doing here?'

Kevin closed his eyes. 'Hiding from K.'

'But you're . . .oh.'

So, this was not the bogeyman they'd been hunting. Kevin was just another naïve student who thought he could outsmart the Virus with prescription drugs. K, however, remained a drug dealer of some note who was probably going to arrive any minute.

'Kevin.' His eyes opened for a second, then closed again. 'Kevin!' He gave him a little shake until the sick man focused on him. 'I'm going to get you some help.'

He gave the slightest of nods, then closed his eyes.

Bernard reached into his jacket pocket, where his fingers felt in vain for his phone. He tried his other side, and with increasing desperation, he dug into his jeans. He closed his eyes and tried to recall when he had last used it. A memory of throwing it in the direction of the passenger seat came to him, and he cursed. He looked down at Kevin, and noticed his mobile sticking out of his top pocket, and snatched it. He didn't respond. Bernard dialled 999. A woman's voice answered.

'What service do you require?'

'HET response.'

'Code please.'

'924.'

There was a pause while the operator checked that he had given her a bona fide reference. Obviously he checked out, because she asked him for his location.

'Myrtle House, about half an hour outside Dunblane.'

He could hear the sound of typing.

'Can you be more specific?'

He wasn't sure that he could be. 'I'm on the, eh, I think the north side of Dunblane,' he was aware he sounded insane. 'There was a bridge?'

The clicking of the keyboard stopped.

'We'll need to do a satellite trace to find you.' Click, click, click. 'Right you are, response is on its way.'

An immune paramedic would be on his way, followed by a Police car. One problem solved.

'Keep the line open.'

Bernard agreed, and put the phone down carefully on the table.

Now on to the second challenge. He looked round the room that they were in. It was a large open-plan living/dining room, typically furnished as a holiday let. There was a hatch leading into the kitchen. Bernard stuck his head through and saw a couple of mugs lying next to the sink, and a pot sitting on the cooker. He turned back to ask Kevin if they were his work, but the invalid's eyes were firmly shut, his breathing beginning to sound laboured. Bernard decided to do a quick check of the upper floor.

He trotted up the stairs of the cottage, and found himself in a narrow hallway. He turned the handle of the first door and pushed it. It opened slowly, its progress impeded by the thick carpet. The room held two single beds, separated by a small chest of drawers topped with a lamp. The room smelled faintly damp, with a staleness to the air that made Bernard think it was unlikely that anyone had slept there recently. He opened the door on the other side of the hall, and found a double-bedded room, with a similar unloved feel to it.

He walked to the third door and found it slightly ajar.

The curtains were drawn, so Bernard flicked the light switch, which illuminated a rucksack, a pink T-shirt, and a pair of jeans laid out on the bed. Someone, probably Heidi, had arrived here and not taken the time to unpack properly. He looked through the backpack. She'd brought quite a lot of clothes, which suggested she'd been intending to stay for a while. So, where was she?

Bernard walked over to the window and pulled back the curtains. The room overlooked a large, neatly kept garden. He stared into the dusk and tried to make sense of what had happened. Heidi had arrived here, got some of her things out – maybe intending to change into them before Kevin arrived? Then something had happened, although the lack of evidence of a struggle made him think that K hadn't appeared on the scene.

Perhaps Heidi had just gone out for a walk? Bernard's eye was caught by a summer house in the garden, a wooden building that looked like an oversized Wendy house. A thought occurred to him. Maybe she hadn't gone far at all.

He dived down the stairs, and poked his head round the living room door. The patient was sleeping on the sofa.

'Kevin?'

There was no response, so he left him to his dreams and went in search of a door to the garden. He guessed, correctly as it turned out, that the garden was accessed from the kitchen. There didn't appear to be a key hanging up nearby. He raked around in the cutlery drawer without any success, then stuck his fingers into a row of pots resting on the dresser, where he was rewarded only by a dead spider. He shook his hand vigorously and it fell to the floor. In desperation he rattled the door handle. It opened.

The grass was damp, and he bounced as he walked. Someone was keeping the lawn in good condition. He slowed down as he approached the summer house.

'Heidi?'

The door was open, but nobody answered him.

'I'm here from the Health Enforcement Team.'

Please be asleep in here, thought Bernard. Please don't be . . .

There was something black sticking out of the bottom of the doorway. As he drew closer he could see it was a boot, with a solid gripped sole, and a small heel. A woman's boot. He took two steps forward and stopped. A denimed leg was attached to the boot.

'Shit.'

Heidi was lying on the bare wooden floor of the summer house. Bernard bent down to feel for a pulse, but recoiled when he realised her skin was cold. Reaching out again he found that her body was rigid.

Balanced on the edge of a wooden bench were the remains of a cup of tea, and two small tubes of pills. Bernard picked up the tablets and examined them. *Luphrophen*. They looked completely innocuous. Like aspirin, perhaps, or some other painkiller. Not something that would do this to you. Not something that would kill you.

He looked down at the figure lying at his feet, and felt a lump rising in his throat. 'Stupid girl.'

Where was the ambulance? Not that it would be much use to Heidi, but at least they could save Kevin. And, even aside from the possible arrival of K, Bernard wasn't enjoying being here alone. He checked his watch, and found it was fifteen minutes since he'd called for help. It had taken him twice that just to drive up the road from Dunblane. Maybe Mona would answer her phone this time. He walked slowly down the steps of the summer house, across the garden and round the side of the house. He let himself into the car and shut the door.

For a minute he sat with his head in his hands, then realised that the state Kevin was in, there wasn't really time to feel sorry for himself. He looked across to the passenger seat for his phone, but didn't see it. He felt a wave of panic. Could K have been in the car and taken it? Rationality fought back and he realised it was much more likely it had slipped onto the floor.

He lay down on the passenger seat, and started rooting around underneath it. Eventually his hand closed round the phone, and he let out a sigh of relief. This was OK, he could do this. He would be able to hold his head up high at the HET; he'd completed the task he'd been sent to do without messing up. With that happy thought, he closed his eyes, leaning back. A distant buzz irritated the countryside silence. What was it? His eyes snapped open as he realised it was the noise of a rapidly approaching motorbike. He froze. Two minutes later he heard the sound of the tyres turning on to the gravel drive.

12

Mona had spent quarter of an hour reviewing all the opportunities in Amanda's bedroom, and come to the conclusion there was only one viable option. She manoeuvred herself over to the dressing table, and using her head, she knocked a framed picture of Amanda and Heidi onto the floor. To her disgust it bounced slightly out of reach. She slowly manipulated her chair next to it, then raised it up, and dropped it onto the glass with all her weight.

Carefully, she tilted the chair forward until her head was on the bed, then she slowly slid down, until her knees were on the floor. Keeping her hand as far back as she could, she then tipped on to one side, so she was lying on the floor. She edged over to the broken photograph, and reached behind her. Her hand clasped around a shard, which pricked her finger. She resisted the instinct to drop it, leant it against the silk restraint and moved its sharp edge up and down. To her relief, she felt the material give way. A couple of minutes later she was free.

She stood up and looked round for her phone, glass crunching beneath her feet. She was standing on the photograph frame. Impatiently she kicked it away, and it shot across the room, scattering not one, but two pictures as it went. Mona picked them both up. One picture, the one which had been shown to the world, was of Amanda and Heidi. The other showed Amanda with another girl, a blonde. The two girls had their arms round each other's shoulders, and their heads were leaning against each other, a perfect portrait of intimacy.

Her mobile rang again. Following the sound of ringing, she sprinted through to the other room and answered it, the photograph still in her hand.

'Mona?' whispered Bernard.

Whispering was never good. 'What's happened?'

'I'm in Dunblane,' the mumbling continued. 'The Police Station was shut, so I found the cottage where Heidi was staying but I got here and she's dead . . .'

'Shit.'

'Yeah, and Kevin's here but he's not K . . .'

'I know.'

'You do?' Bernard sounded surprised. 'Anyway, Kevin's got the Virus, now some guy on a motorbike has just pulled up and gone into the house. Do you think that's K?'

Mona put her hand against her forehead and closed her eyes. 'Probably. Has he seen you?'

'No, I don't think so. I'm hiding in my car and waiting for the HET emergency response team.'

Mona leaned on the sideboard. 'Here's what you do. You start your engine, drive for five minutes then dial 999 again, OK? Then phone me and tell me you're still alive.'

There was a silence at the other end of the line.

'Bernard?'

There was some static, then her partner's voice came through loud and clear. 'What if the motorbike guy kills Kevin?'

Mona felt more than her usual sense of irritation with Bernard. Could he not just get out of there and leave it to the local Police? 'There's nothing you can do. Get your arse moving. OK?'

There was another pause before he answered. 'OK. I'm leaving now.'

Mona shoved her mobile into her bag. She turned to go, then stopped short when she heard a very faint movement. Dropping her bag, she crept over and peered out into the flat. A figure was gently pushing open the door to Amanda's room. As it opened, the hallway was illuminated, and she could see a long, thin, shadow on the floor. Had K returned? She stepped back and looked round for a weapon. Before she could find anything of use, the door to the living room opened. She slammed it with all her might and was rewarded with a scream of pain from the intruder. She yanked the door back open, and the man fell forward into the room.

'Maitland!'

'Jesus!' Her colleague rubbed his injured nose. 'Last time I act as your backup.'

'Sorry. Thought you were someone else. How did you know I was here?'

'Bernard left me a phone message.'

She grabbed her bag. 'We need to get back to the office.'

'OK. You dropped something.' Maitland picked up the photograph. He went to pass it to Mona then hesitated. 'I know her.'

'You know her? From where? Is she another Christian?'

'No, no, nothing like that.' He turned the photo round to face Mona. 'I met that girl the night we went to the rave. She was going on about how wonderful K was.'

They stared at each other, then back at the picture.

'The two of them look pretty cosy. Reckon she's a dyke?'

'I don't know. I really don't.' Mona took the photograph back. 'We need to get back to the office sharpish.'

She opened up her bag and was delighted to find that both her purse and her car keys were still there. She'd pictured Amanda making off in the pool car, probably the only thing that could make her current explanation to Paterson even worse. She headed out of the flat and ran down the tenement stairs, leaving Maitland to pull the door shut and follow her.

'So, what's going on?' asked Maitland, as they climbed in.

Mona gave him as quick an overview as possible. Maitland listened in silence, shaking his head from time to time to indicate his opinion of his colleagues' stupidity.

'And now you're going to have to phone Paterson and tell him all this?' he asked.

'No, Maitland,' she said, putting the car into gear. 'I'm driving. You'll have to do it for me.'

Maitland rolled his eyes and dialled the number. After a few seconds he said, 'There's no answer, and his voicemail's full.'

Mona silently cursed Paterson's mobile phone skills. 'Phone Bernard and check he's still alive.'

Silence filled the car while Maitland attempted to make contact.

'Bern? You OK?'

Mona listened to Maitland's side of the conversation, which consisted of him saying 'yup' at regular intervals.

'OK, pal, stay where you are. Let the big boys deal with this now.' He hung up. 'He's sitting in a lay-by a few miles down the road, waiting for the Police and ambulance service.' He laughed. 'Poor Bernard. I bet he wet himself when he realised that bloke had turned up.'

'Don't be mean, Maitland.' She tried to work out what to do. 'Bernard did his best.'

'Red light!'

'Shit!' She slammed on the brakes. 'Oh, God. There's nothing else for it – you'll have to phone CID.'

Maitland looked at her, incredulity wiping the smirk from his face. 'And say what?'

'We need a search put on Amanda Harris and her boyfriend.'

Maitland pulled out his phone. Mona attempted to tune out as he explained to someone from CID exactly what had been going on, but even from the driver's seat she could hear yelling at the other end.

'Yes, Sir, we're heading back to the office now.' Maitland hung up, put his mobile in his pocket, and looked over at her. 'And that was the phone call that puts an end to your and Bernard's careers. Well, your career, anyway. It wasn't like Bernard had one to begin with.'

'Thanks for the support.' Mona kept her eyes on the road. 'What did CID say?'

'They're on it. Circulating Amanda's Green Card info to all airports and ferry terminals. Sending additional backup to Bernard. What you'd expect really. And we are under strict instructions to head back to the office and not move until they contact us. But you know the best bit?'

'What?'

'You've still got to tell the Guv.'

'Oh, God.'

'Shall I try his number again?'

'Thanks, you really are too kind, but I think we'll wait until we get to the office now.'

'You know, I've heard he literally breathes fire if you annoy him enough.'

'Shut up.' She pulled the car round and into the HET car park. 'Maitland, how do we know about the existence of K?'

'E-mail signatures. Drunken blonde going on about him at the rave. And didn't you say Amanda sent some bloke up to Dunblane?'

'Yeah exactly – she was definitely giving the orders. It didn't sound like she was in thrall to some cult leader.'

There was a pause as Maitland processed the information.

'And some blonde woman throws herself at you, very eager to tell you all about him.' She brought the car to a stop and climbed out. 'We've been played. Amanda and her female friend are behind all of this Camus stuff, but all the drugs are bought on Heidi's credit card, and the e-mails are signed by K. She's keeping herself well out of it. If the dark-haired guy I met is K, I got the impression he wasn't the sharpest tool in the pack. Whatever he was, he wasn't a cult leader.'

Mona abandoned the car across two parking spaces, and they hurried into the building.

'Where's the Guv?' Mona burst into the office. The only person there was Carole Brooks. 'And what are you doing here?'

'Michael's back home now, and my husband's looking after him so I thought I'd come in,' she said. 'I don't know where Mr Paterson is though. I've not seen him since I got here. Have you tried him on his mobile?'

'Of course,' said Mona, dialling the number again. There was a faint but distinctive ringing sound from within Paterson's office.

Maitland peered in the window. 'The Guv's not a fan of modern technology,' he chuckled.

Mona thought she might just snap and hit him.

'Are you OK?' Carole asked.

'She's looking a bit peaky because she's just committed career suicide.'

'Shut up, Maitland.'

He ambled out, still smirking.

Carole sat down next to Mona. 'What's wrong?'

Before Mona could unburden herself, Marcus appeared in the doorway.

'Can I have a word?'

Mona put her head in her hands. From under her hair she said, 'Is there any chance at all this could wait until later, Marcus?'

There was a brief silence from the world outside her bob, then Marcus said, 'It's just that I was thinking about the Toller guy that you mentioned, and it's really been bugging me because I was sure I'd heard the name before, I mean it's quite distinctive, isn't it? Anyway, I realised why it was familiar.'

Mona stayed still.

'The name Karl Jürgen Toller has been popping up on a couple of websites we monitor.'

Mona raised her head. He smiled back at her.

'And if I can use one of these, I can show you what they say.'

'Use mine,' said Carole. 'Google is still open if you want to look for him.'

'Google?' The IT guy laughed. 'The sites we look at don't come up in a search engine. We're talking the hidden web here.' He reached into his pocket and pulled out a small notebook, which Mona tried to look at. He smiled politely and manoeuvred it out of her gaze. Using the information in it he typed in a web address which seemed to consist of mostly numbers.

'*Et voilà*,' said Marcus. 'Conspiracy theories relating to Karl Jürgen Toller.'

She peered at the screen. The site he had uploaded had nothing on it except row after row of densely written white text set on a black background.

'I don't understand,' she said. 'What is it?'

'It's all kinds of crazy.' Marcus made a sound that was half snort, half laugh. 'Think The Children of Camus only with twice the paranoia, and, in fairness to these guys, a lot more research.' He pointed to the screen. 'If you click on Toller's name there,' he pressed the mouse, 'it brings up a whole page of why he's on their hit list.'

Mona sat down on Carole's chair, and read the screen with interest.

'So, let's get this straight. Toller has interests in …'

'Is a Director of,' corrected Marcus.

'Is a Director of a pharmaceutical company manufacturing Luprophen and Hyrdosol.'

A patented solution to the Viral problem. There are many people who would wish Heidi harm. Mona felt dizzy. 'I need to speak to Bernard.'

She dialled his number. It rang twelve times, then his voicemail picked up.

'So, who *is* Doctor Toller?' asked Carole.

'He's not who we thought he was,' said Mona. 'We really need to find the Guv.'

A large and familiar figure appeared in the doorway.

'Why?'

13

Bernard put his phone back in his pocket. As usual, his colleague had used the fewest possible words to convey to him that he was an idiot. *Let the big boys deal with it.* That was how Maitland saw him: some kind of errand boy, or trainee perhaps, good for taking the piss out of and not much else.

He dug into his pocket and pulled out the letter from his wife. It was pretty crumpled now, so he smoothed it out and carefully tore open the envelope. The letter was three lines long. *Three lines.* Carrie had managed, in as few words as possible, to let him know that their marriage had failed, due mainly to his many shortcomings. The people in his life weren't even bothering to waste words on him now. Still, not to worry. When the Guv finally caught up with him he was sure no expletive would be left unused in the dressing-down that was sure to follow their doomed mission.

Once, for a brief few months, he had been the top badminton player in Scotland. There had been talk that he could be an Olympic hopeful, and a couple of sports magazines had interviewed him. It had been a strange and unnatural feeling, the interviewers probing him for his background, his thoughts on badminton, his view of the world. He didn't make the team, and the world went back to ignoring him. Did he prefer it this way? He really wasn't sure.

Bernard checked his watch. Where was the ambulance? Where were the Police? K could be doing anything to Kevin. A thought crept forward from the back of his brain. He could ... His hand lingered on the ignition key for a second, then he removed it. He couldn't.

Let the big boys deal with it.

His phone rang. He looked at it for a moment or two, then fired the ignition, and turned the car around.

The front door was wide open but there was no sign of anyone.

From inside the house he heard a voice, a strident, angry yell. He couldn't hear what was being said, but there was no mistaking the tone.

He stepped silently through the door for the second time, and paused. The house was quiet, but as he listened he could hear the faint groan of the floorboards overhead. Bernard looked up at the hall ceiling and listened as the creaks moved from room to room. He wondered where he'd left the doorstop he had picked up earlier. He scanned the hall, but it wasn't anywhere to be seen. The door to the living room was ajar; with some trepidation he pushed it open, but Kevin was still lying there, sleeping his restless sleep.

Bernard placed one foot on the bottom tread of the stair and quickly withdrew after it creaked noisily. Giving up on stealth he walked as swiftly and calmly as he could up the rest of the flight. At the top of the stairs he could see the door to Heidi's room was open, and a man was bent over searching through her stuff, scrabbling about like a rat on a rubbish heap. Bernard opened his mouth to speak, but his throat was so dry he couldn't make a sound. He swallowed a couple of times and tried again.

301

'It's not there.'

The stranger swivelled round. He was tall, easily Maitland's height if not more, with thick, dark hair that fell forward in a long fringe, and a couple of days' growth of stubble gracing his cheeks. His first thought on seeing him, was that he matched very closely Mona's description of K from the rave. His second thought was that the guy looked both very tired, and extremely annoyed to see him.

'Who are you?'

Bernard held onto the door jamb for support and tried to stop his voice from trembling. 'I'm from the Health Enforcement Team.'

The man who was probably K stared at him for a second, then burst out laughing. Bernard realised that for a criminal, being caught red-handed by the HET was not the problem that being busted by say, the Police, or even Neighbourhood Watch, presented.

K knelt down and went back to raking through Heidi's possessions.

'Really – the Loopy and H aren't there.'

K turned round, looking interested for the first time in their conversation. 'What?'

'Did you know that people have died after taking this stuff?'

With a speed that took Bernard by surprise, K leapt to his feet and grabbed him by the lapels. 'Are you calling me a murderer, mate?'

Bernard struggled to get free. 'Technically, I think it's culpable homicide.'

Just as quickly his assailant dropped him, sprinted along the hall and down the stairs. Bernard followed him at a safe distance. In the living room K made straight for

302

the sofa, and grabbed hold of Kevin by his shirt front.

'Wake up! Where's my gear?'

Kevin moaned but didn't open his eyes. K pulled him closer and Kevin's head fell back, as floppy as a marionette. Raising a hand K slapped him hard across the face. Bernard jumped down the last few steps.

'I really wouldn't do that.'

The man stared at him.

Bernard dived forward and clutched K's arm. 'He's got the Virus.'

The man dropped Kevin back onto the arm of the sofa. This failed to rouse the sleeper, and a ribbon of blood dripped from his nostril.

'I'm immune,' said Bernard. 'Are you?'

14

'Congratulations, Mona.' Paterson said. 'This could really be what it takes to get the HET closed down.'

Carole was looking at her. Mona could sense that every fibre of her colleague's body wanted to help her, and that she was trying desperately to think of something to say that would calm the Guv down.

'Is it really that bad, Mr Paterson?' she asked.

Mona closed her eyes. Trying to play down the significance of what they'd done was only going to enrage her boss further. It was that bad. It was very, very bad indeed, but Carole was unstoppable.

'I mean, Mona and Bernard were trying to help a Health Defaulter who was in danger.'

'Yes, and while doing that they failed to involve the Police at the appropriate moment, broke numerous rules and protocols, and,' Paterson threw a pen at Mona, 'let's not forget, did exactly the opposite of what I told them to do.'

His pen bounced off the side of the desk and landed at the feet of Maitland, who stood in the doorway. The Guv ignored his arrival and kept talking.

'So, Mona, if I've understood the situation correctly, this drug dealer, as well as the massed ranks of the Stirlingshire constabulary, is descending on Bernard in Dunblane, but what about Amanda? Where's she gone?'

Mona thought for a second. 'Well, if she's got enough cash she's probably already getting out of the country. She knows we're on to her. But the fact that she's sending her messenger boy after Heidi suggests that she's determined not to leave without the money she's made, or ...'

'She's not made enough to leave.' Paterson looked up at her. 'Which makes her ...'

'Dangerous. Guv ...' Before she could continue, her mobile rang. She looked at her boss, unsure if she should take the call.

'Well, answer it.' Paterson gestured in the direction of her ringing pocket. 'It could be CID.'

'Hello?'

'Mona Whyte?' The voice sounded familiar, but she couldn't place it. 'It's Vic Thompson here.'

'Mr Thompson.' She motioned to her colleagues to be quiet, and pressed the button for speakerphone. 'This is Mona, how can I help you?'

'That girl you were looking for – I've been thinking about it. She *was* here.' Vic's voice echoed around the room.

'Really?' Mona looked at Paterson, who raised an eyebrow. 'What jogged your memory?'

Vic ignored her question. 'She's a friend of a woman called Amanda Harris, who, I'm afraid to say, it has come to my attention, has been dealing drugs in my bar.'

She glanced at Paterson who rolled his eyes.

'You'll be informing the Police of that fact, Sir?'

There was a pause. 'Absolutely. But,' he laughed, a high-pitched, strangulated sound, 'as you are aware I've had my run-ins with the Police in the past. That's why I've contacted you first. Amanda's a public health risk. You need to get a team over to her flat at ...shit, I can't remember her address. It's Marchmont somewhere.'

She looked round at her colleagues; their faces reflected her own confusion.

'Absolutely, consider it done. We have her details.'

'And there's one other thing . . .'

'Yes, Sir?'

There was a silence, then a sigh at the other end of the line.

'I have a number of guns that I use when hunting, Miss Whyte, all fully licensed of course . . .'

'Of course, Sir.'

'One of them is missing.'

She looked at her boss, who was already reaching for his coat. 'Are you at Morley's, Mr Thompson?'

The nervous, high-pitched laugh came through again. 'I am. Perhaps I shouldn't be.'

'Stay there and lock the doors. We're on our way over.' She clicked her mobile shut. 'Carole – phone CID again.'

Paterson made for the door. 'Update them about Mr Thompson's concerns and tell them to get a response round there sharpish.'

'Yes, Mr Paterson.'

'Come on, you two,' he pointed at Mona and Maitland.

'But, Guv,' protested Maitland. 'CID told us not to move.'

'We're meeting them there; they can hardly complain we're out of contact. C'mon now. I've a bad feeling about this.'

The three of them stood at the top of the stairs to Morley's, looking down at the long-haired man who was trying unsuccessfully to pull the door open.

'Afternoon, Donny, where's your boss?'

The ponytailed figure turned round. 'You lot again?'

His face rippled with exasperation. 'I thought you'd found Colette?'

Maitland started walking down the steps. 'We have. This is a different matter ...'

Paterson pushed past his colleague. 'Where's Vic?'

'I don't know.' Donny peered in through the window, holding his hand up to his face to block out the light. 'The door shouldn't be bolted.'

'We told him to lock it.' Mona stood next to him, peering in.

'Why?'

Mona ignored Donny's question. 'Can you give your boss a ring on his mobile and tell him Mona Whyte is here and he needs to let us in?'

Donny opened his mouth as if to ask another question, then thought better of it and dialled his boss's number. They heard a faint sound of ringing from inside the building.

'It's gone to his messaging service.' The barman held the phone up to Mona. 'Is Vic all right?'

Paterson continued the policy of ignoring Donny's questions, and rattled the door handle. 'Is there another way in, son?'

'Yeah.' Donny began walking up the stairs. 'The back alley.'

They retraced their steps up to the pavement. Mona tripped, banging her knee. She cursed. Why wasn't Vic answering his phone?

'This way.' Donny pointed them down a small lane which ran between Morley's block and the neighbouring tenement. They picked their way in between the bags of rubbish, until they had travelled the full length of the building.

307

'This is the back entrance.' Donny pointed at a solid metal door. 'Leads straight into the ground floor.'

Paterson looked at the reinforced steel in disgust. 'Not the most accessible way in, is it, son?'

Donny pointed at a small window. 'A good shove on that and we can get in. I've done it before.'

To prove his point, he walked over to the window and gave the frame a good thump. As predicted, it opened slightly. He slid his hand inside and undid the catch.

'I'll climb in and unlock it.'

Paterson put a restraining hand on his shoulder. 'Not so fast, sunshine, we don't know who's in there. We'll wait for CID.'

'Guv!' protested Mona and Maitland in unison.

'We could pop in there, get the door open, have a recce, no problem.' Maitland moved toward the window.

'No chance.' There was a firm shake of the head. 'As I said, we don't know who's in there. Maitland, get round the front and keep an eye out for CID.'

While Paterson was focused on her colleague's retreating back, Mona took the opportunity to pull the window open and have a look inside. There was a sound, something that could have been a very faint cry of anguish.

'Guv!'

Paterson turned round, and strode back toward her. 'Get away from there.' He pulled her away from the frame, and stood guard as if expecting her to try to push past him. She pointed over his shoulder.

'There's someone shouting for help in there.'

Paterson's look radiated suspicion.

'Honestly, I heard something.'

He pushed open the window, and again, a soft sound of pain drifted out.

308

'Guv?'

He looked back down the alleyway. There was a continued absence of cavalry. 'Oh, God. OK. But be careful in there.' He knitted his hands together. 'Need a leg up?'

She stuck her foot on her boss's palms, and manoeuvred herself sideways through the space, and onto a desk at the other side. She'd barely landed on the wood when Donny's head appeared beside her.

'Hoi!' The Guv's voice could be heard outside. 'Where do you think you're going, son?'

Donny grinned at her, and rolled off the desk onto the floor in a manner that suggested he'd used this method of entry several times before. She pointed at the back door.

'Get that open, and do not leave this room.'

He indicated an open box on the wall. 'Keys are gone.'

'Is there another set?'

'Should be one in the desk somewhere.'

'Find it and get out.'

She left him opening the desk drawers while she investigated further. The office door opened onto a windowless corridor. She stuck her head out and looked up and down the hall. There were several doors, all of them firmly shut, revealing nothing about who or what was waiting for her behind them. Amanda wouldn't think twice about shooting her, if she stood in the way of her escape.

'Help!'

The voice was weak, but unmistakeably male: Vic in all probability. She stood where she was, straining to hear if there was anyone else in the building. There was a faint shuffling sound. Slowly, making as little noise as she could, she edged along the wall, and stopped opposite the room the noise seemed to come from. On the balls of her feet, she approached the door, turned the knob and threw it open, before flattening herself against the wall. She tensed, awaiting gunfire, or someone appearing from the room, but the silence continued.

'Help me!'

Still cautious, she stepped into the room and stopped abruptly. Vic was lying on the floor, rivulets of blood ebbing away from his body. On the wall above his head there was a large wooden cross. A vision of the preacher from earlier came into her head. *Repent, sinner.*

'Shit.'

She grabbed her mobile and dialled 999, but before she could get through, the room was full of people. Maitland and Paterson appeared at her side, and a couple of guys she vaguely recognised from CID were on their radios ordering an ambulance.

'Donny,' she turned and spoke to the bartender, who was leaning, ashen-faced, against the wall, 'do you have any towels?'

He fled, reappearing a minute later with some bar cloths. She bent down next to Vic, wrapping the towels firmly round his wound.

'Ambulance is on its way.'

He gave a slight movement of his head to show he understood, and closed his eyes.

'No, Vic, stay awake.'

His eyes opened again.

'Talk to me, who did this?'

There was silence, and Vic struggled to get his breath. Eventually he spat out a word.

'Amanda.'

Behind her she heard one of the CID men say to Paterson, 'Who is Amanda?'

Twenty minutes later Vic Thompson had been safely stretchered out of Morley's and into the back of an ambulance, with Maitland and a CID man sent to ride shotgun. The other CID guy was deep in conversation with Paterson, in a low enough tone that Mona couldn't quite make out what was being said. It didn't take a genius to work out that the tone of the conversation was along the lines of what-was-the-HET-playing-at? She tried in vain to remember the detective's name; Josephs? Jacobs? Something like that, anyway.

She turned her attention back to Donny, who was sprawled on one of the bar's leather couches. The colour had begun to return to his cheeks, and Mona noticed him nervously checking his watch.

'Are you late for something?'

'We should be opening up by now.'

There was a chorus of snorts from Paterson and the remaining CID man.

'Forget about opening up, son,' the detective said, walking over to them. 'This is a crime scene. Give it five minutes and my colleagues will be swarming all over this place.'

'But ...' He leaned back in his seat, then after a moment's contemplation got purposefully to his feet. 'I can probably go then, if I'm not opening up.'

Paterson motioned him back down. ''Fraid not, son. We've got a few questions for you about what's going on here.'

The CID man coughed. Paterson acknowledged the intervention.

'I mean, of course, that my colleague from CID here has a few questions, what with this now being an attempted murder enquiry.' He winked at the detective. 'But, son, I

311

know you've had a shock, and I think the best thing for everyone concerned would be a cup of tea. Care to show me where the kitchen is?'

Donny looked at Mona, seeking a second opinion on whether refreshments were the way to go. She smiled encouragingly. 'A cup of tea would be great.'

'OK.' He slowly got to his feet. Paterson ushered him through the door. As soon as it closed behind him, the detective started speaking.

'You're ex-CID, aren't you? Mona, isn't it?'

'Yep,' she said, without turning round. 'Mona Whyte.'

The detective didn't offer any clues as to his own name. 'Quite a story your boss was telling me about your involvement in all this.'

She felt suddenly weary. There would have to be a lot of explanations to CID, SHEP and probably a lot of other people too, but right now she really did want that cup of tea.

'I know he's your witness, but can I ask him a couple of questions?'

The CID man scowled at her.

'We'll share all our knowledge of the case, of course, but just right now it would be great to ask Donny some questions while he's ...' She struggled for the right word.

'Unsettled?' The detective helped her out. He thought for a moment. 'OK, have a crack at him, but we want everything you know.'

The Guv appeared, holding the door wide so Donny and his tray of mugs could fit through. He placed four mugs of tea in front of them. Mona picked up hers, and sat down next to him.

'Are you OK to answer a couple of questions?'

'I suppose so.' He sighed. 'Still a bit shocked, to be honest.'

'Totally understandable.' Mona pulled the photograph of Amanda and the blonde girl out of her bag. 'Do you know this woman?'

Donny looked at it for a second, his brow knotted. 'Yeah – that's Mandy Harris, isn't it? What's she got to do with this?'

'And do you recognise the woman with her? It could be her girlfriend?'

'Girlfriend?' Donny gave a confused laugh, looking from Mona to Paterson, and back. 'Hardly. It's her sister, Angie.'

Of course. The relaxed intimacy of the photograph. It was a family picture.

Paterson leaned forward. 'How do you know them?'

'Angie's boyfriend worked here, and she was in here all the time.' Donny took a slow drink of his tea. 'When Mandy moved to Edinburgh a year or so ago, she started hanging out here too.'

The puzzle was rearranging itself in Mona's head. 'And Angie's boyfriend's name?'

'Kieran Shaw. He doesn't work here anymore, though.'

'Why did he leave?'

Donny shrugged. 'Don't know. I wondered if it was because he wasn't happy about Mandy and Vic getting together.'

'Amanda and Vic were in a relationship?'

'For a while. I think he found her a bit, you know.'

'A bit what?' asked Paterson.

'Bossy. A pain in the arse,' Donny said. 'I think he binned her, because he told all the staff she was barred. Haven't seen her since.' He turned to Mona. 'Why are you asking all these questions about Mandy? It wasn't her that shot him, was it?'

'We're still trying to establish what has happened.' Mona ducked the question. 'How long ago did Vic bar her?'

'A month, maybe? Or even six weeks. I'm not totally sure.'

'And Colette,' said Mona, 'and all the other religious girls. How long have they been coming here to church?'

Something approaching a blush spread across Donny's cheeks. He shifted around in his seat. 'Colette had nothing to do with any of this . . .'

'Absolutely.' She raised both her hands in a placatory gesture. 'We're just curious how Mr Thompson came to be running a weekly service here – it seems a little out of character?' She caught the eye of the CID man, who raised an eyebrow at her. Explaining all this was going to take a while.

'That was Mandy's idea.' Donny shook his head, almost smiling, as if he still found the religious proposition ridiculous. 'She was living with some German lassie who went to church, and she got to know the vicar guy . . .'

'Pastor Mackenzie?'

'Yeah.' There was a brief silence while they waited for him to continue, but instead Donny looked at his watch. 'Can I go now?'

'Five more minutes.' Mona was sure that he knew more. 'So, why did Amanda want Vic to have a church here?'

The barman shifted in his seat, keeping his eyes firmly fixed on the floor. He gave a shrug of his shoulders and sat contemplating his fingernails.

The Guv leaned forward. 'If there's been something

314

going on here, better to mention it now, son, otherwise your next conversation on the subject might be down at the Station.'

'Or,' said the CID man, 'we might have to invite some of the churchgoing young ladies in for a chat.'

He was good; five minutes listening to the conversation and he'd already identified Donny's weak spot. What was his name? Johnstone? Jacobs? Jacobson! Ian Jacobson, she was sure of it.

Ignoring the detective Donny addressed his comments to Mona. 'I just pour drinks here, I don't get involved.'

'But you see things.'

He sat back in the chair and folded his arms. 'Less than you'd think.'

'OK, OK, I get the picture. You don't want to talk to us.' Mona stood up. 'Off you go then.'

Donny didn't move.

'Seriously, off you go.' She pointed to the door. 'Of course, we'll have to get our information elsewhere, starting, of course, with . . .' She left the sentence hanging. Donny glared up at her.

'If I talk to you, you'll leave Colette out of this?'

'As far as I can, yes.'

For a moment he said nothing, obviously weighing up whether this was a good enough offer. He must have decided it was the best he could hope for, because he started to talk. 'Mandy had it in her head that she could sell all kinds of shite to the students that were coming here – pills and stuff, making out it would stop them getting the Virus. She set up a website all about it, with all this student-friendly shite about French writers and stuff.'

'So, she was dealing drugs.' Mona exchanged a look with her boss. 'Where was the money coming from?'

'First off, the German lassie. She was so into it she just about handed over her credit card. Mandy used it to start putting on raves. Made a lot of money out of those, selling drugs and that.'

Mona noticed that Jacobson had started discreetly taking notes. 'And where does Vic fit into all this?'

'He wasn't happy about drugs being dealt in the bar.'

'Really?' said Mona and Paterson in unison.

Donny grinned. 'I mean, he wasn't happy about Mandy selling shit and not cutting him in.'

'I can imagine.' Paterson's tone was dry.

'So, they came to some kind of arrangement, then she started on about Vic owing her money. She was round here yesterday shouting the odds. I overheard Vic talking to one of the bouncers about her, about giving her . . .' He punched the air.

The black eye. Not Kevin's doing at all.

'Then Kieran was round here looking for Vic, moaning about the German lassie and her boyfriend backing out on them, saying they didn't want to do it anymore.'

'So, what did he do?'

'I think he had a word with them.'

And then they both quit town.

'So, Heidi and Kevin didn't tell anyone what was going on?'

'Not as far as I know.' He thought for a minute, his lower lip hanging out. 'Though they did tell the vicar guy.'

'Why didn't he go to the Police?'

'Because Mandy's smart.' Donny looked at them. 'Pastor guy turns up on her doorstep, threatening to get the Police involved, and she shows him a little video she's got, that means he's going to keep his mouth shut.'

'A video of him?'

'I dunno.' He shrugged. 'But I know Mandy films everything on her phone. Everything.'

The memory of Amanda's hallway came back to Mona, brightly lit as a film set.

The sound of hammering echoed through the bar.

'Sounds like the rest of the team's here,' the CID man got to his feet. 'Got a key, pal?'

'I'll just get it.' Donny stood up and headed toward the bar.

Detective Jacobson waved his notebook at Mona. 'Care to fill in a few blanks for me?'

She sighed, and nodded.

15

'Immune?'

In a second K was beside him, his long legs propelling him across the room. Bernard took a half-step back, and stared up at the face that was now far too close to him. He nodded, trying hard not to bump heads with his aggressor.

'He's got the Virus?'

'Yes.' His voice was hoarse. 'Look.' He cautiously pointed at the sofa. Without losing eye contact, K reached out and closed his fingers round Bernard's neck. He tightened his grip, and Bernard felt panic rising up in him, rushing from his toes up toward his brain. Every muscle was urging him to move, but the part of his mind that was remaining rational told him this was a very bad idea.

K's hold on his neck tightened slightly; breathing was beginning to get difficult, and against the silence of the room he could hear the frantic sound of the air going in and out of his nostrils. Without warning, his captor released him. He leaned forward, hands on his thighs, and took several deep breaths.

A gurgling sound came from the direction of the sofa. K's eyes flicked repeatedly between the sofa and the door. Bernard decided to jolt him out of his indecision.

'You need to get out of here. Statistically, four out of ten people in close contact with a Virus victim ...' The words were barely out of his mouth, when he felt the full weight of K's fist connect with his face. He staggered back. 'Ow!'

Blood was spurting from his nose. As he put his hand up to try to stem the flow, K grabbed him by both shoulders, and threw him against the wall. He fell, awkwardly thrashing around for something to right himself with, his head cracking against the grate of the fireplace. 'Please,' he held a hand up in front of his face. Ignoring this, K aimed a couple of kicks at his ribs.

'Where's Heidi?' Another kick.

Pain surged through Bernard's body. He closed his eyes, and let out a sob. Would K leave him alone if he told him the truth? He might just turn tail and head back to Amanda, leaving him and Kevin alone, where, please God, the Police would find them soon enough. But if he left he might get away; the Police wouldn't know to stop him, and all this would have been for nothing.

Without moving, he spoke. 'She went out on her bike to get food and stuff. She's been gone a couple of hours.' He opened his eyes. K was staring down at him, the expression on his face radiating confusion.

'So, she'll be back pretty soon, right?'

'Yeah.' Bernard sat up slightly, waiting to see if he was kicked again. K didn't move, and he got, painfully, to his feet. 'We should get away from Kevin.'

'All right.' K grabbed his arm, causing all kinds of pain to shoot through his body, and propelled him back into the corridor. K looked round for a minute then kicked open the door to the kitchen and shoved him in. Bernard stumbled into a seat.

'And you keep your mouth shut. I don't want you shouting out and letting her know I'm here.' K wandered

319

in after him. 'I'm starving.' He began opening cupboard doors, searching for food. Bernard's heart somersaulted at the possibility that the shelves would be stocked with a range of fresh goods that had been recently purchased. His luck held, as each cupboard turned out to be empty.

'I told you, Heidi's gone to get food. Anyway, won't she see your bike?'

'Nope.' K sauntered over to the kitchen table, holding a packet of fairly unappetising biscuits he'd located. 'I hid it well out of sight.' He sat opposite Bernard and pointed at his head. 'You're bleeding.'

Bernard touched his head, bringing his fingers away bright red. He pulled several sheets from a roll of paper towels, which he folded up and held against his head. K watched, a strange, lopsided grin on his face. Bernard wondered how much longer the Police would take. They'd have the satellite directions to get them here, even in spite of the poor quality directions he'd been able to give. But staffing levels were short everywhere these days. Calls that should have been answered in minutes had been known to take hours.

K was going to start getting angry when Heidi didn't show. He needed to keep him distracted. What would Mona do in his situation? He suspected she'd make good use of the time by digging for information.

'So, you're a friend of Amanda?'

K stared at Bernard for a second or two. 'She's my bird's sister.'

'Oh, OK.' He reached for a clean piece of kitchen roll and racked his brains for what to ask next. He wasn't that good on small talk at the best of times. The thought of dinner parties with his wife's friends used to give him sleepless nights, all the polite chitter-chatter, and Carrie raising her eyebrows if he strayed onto topics that actually interested him, like politics, or the history of linguistics, or Virus statistics across the world. These were not the ideal circumstances to be undertaking his first professional interrogation.

'Have you been together long?' Bernard waited for K to shout at him, or worse, for asking questions, but he seemed willing to talk.

'A year maybe?' He considered the question. 'I met her at a club in the Grassmarket, and we moved in together a couple of weeks later.'

'A whirlwind romance.'

'What?' K's mouth was hanging slightly open, and Bernard wondered again if the supposed drug-dealing mastermind wasn't the brightest star in the Heavens. He decided to risk another question.

'Did you meet Amanda at the same time?'

'Yeah. Ange said her sister was moving to Edinburgh, and would it be OK if she dossed with us until she found a place.'

'Oh, that must have been nice.' Even to his own ears, this sounded ridiculous. A look of annoyance came onto K's face, and Bernard braced himself. However, the irritation didn't seem to be with the question.

'She started hanging around the bar where I worked...'
Morley's.

'Yeah, she was always coming in, and making eyes at Vic.' He paused. 'Tosser.'

'Right.'

There was a silence, and the kitchen clock could be heard tick-tocking.

'Where's the German bint got to?'

Bernard could feel the slow drip of blood beginning to

321

pool in the collar of his polo shirt. 'I'm sure she'll be here any minute.'

K reached across the table and grabbed his jumper, slowly pulling him closer. 'You lying to me?'

Bernard dropped the kitchen roll, and gave a small yelp of pain as his ribs made contact with the side of the table. 'No, she'll be here, I swear . . .'

K's grip loosened slightly. 'What's that noise?'

Bernard listened. A whirring sound appeared to be getting louder. It sounded like the rotating of blades. It sounded, improbably, like the noise a rapidly approaching helicopter would make. Getting to his feet, K reached inside his denim jacket and produced a knife. He flicked it open and pointed it in Bernard's direction.

'Not a word.'

Bernard nodded. He was finding it difficult to breathe at the moment, never mind speak. K opened the door a crack and peered out. The whirring sound was deafening, indicating that the helicopter was overhead. Every shelf in the kitchen was vibrating. A large volume of Mrs Beeton fell off its perch onto the table, shattering Bernard's nerves even further. From the way that K had jumped, it looked like it didn't do him any good either.

There was a thump from outside. Bernard guessed the aircraft had landed. It had to be Doctor Toller's doing; the HET couldn't have mobilised those resources in a month of Sundays. He strained to hear what was going on; even though the chopper had landed it was still making a fair bit of noise. Suddenly the whirring sound stopped, to be replaced by a brief silence. Was that the sound of the front door opening? K's back was giving nothing away. Suddenly K stepped away from the door, flattening himself against the wall, knife poised.

They both listened to the sounds of whispered conversations in the hall. It was hard to estimate how many people there were out there. He heard a door open very slowly. Whoever was outside must be searching room by room. Bernard had a vision of the searcher having a knife sunk into him, and began to slowly pull the cookbook toward him, until he was holding it in both hands. 'He's in here!' Bernard shouted.

K lunged at him. With his last bit of strength he flung Mrs Beeton in K's direction, distracting him enough to allow the large man in military uniform who had appeared in the doorway to hook an arm around his neck. K let out a squawk of pain, a very satisfying sound to Bernard's ears. The soldier held his prisoner tightly.

'Who are you pair?'

Bernard stood up, a bolt of pain shooting up his ribs.

'I'm Bernard,' he croaked.

The soldier looked at him doubtfully.

'From the Health Enforcement Team.'

'Ah.' The military man smiled. 'We've been looking for you, sunshine.'

'And this man is wanted for ...' Bernard stopped, wondering how best to explain the situation. Fortunately, the soldier didn't appear to need an update.

'Deal with this one, will you?'

A colleague relieved him of K, who left throwing a string of curses over his shoulder.

The soldier stepped back into the hall. 'Anyone else on the premises?'

'Don't go in the living room!' He raised a hand to stop the soldier, and winced as the whole of his left side screamed out in pain. 'There's a man in there suffering from the Virus.'

'I'm one of those lucky immune bastards.' The soldier winked at him, kicked open the living room door and walked in. Bernard followed as quickly as his aching bones would let him, eager to check for himself that Kevin was still breathing.

The soldier exhaled heavily and tutted. 'He's not looking too clever.'

Kevin's skin had darkened, with a mottled shade of purple replacing its earlier pallor. Bernard swallowed. The state the boy was in, even if the ambulance arrived now it would take nothing short of a miracle to save him. He stumbled over to an armchair and lowered himself into it. What a waste. What a ridiculous waste of two young lives. A tapping sound at the patio window disturbed his thoughts; another soldier stood there.

'Is that him?' He shouted through the glass, gesturing at Bernard.

'Yeah, and he's fine, but we've got a Virus case. Get Wooky, will you?'

Wooky, when he appeared, seemed to be some kind of medic. He certainly knew what he was doing when it came to dealing with the Virus. Bernard watched him take Kevin's temperature, and give him an injection. He tried to stand, and further jolts of pain went through him.

'You all right, mate?' said the soldier. 'Want a hand up?'

'No!' said Bernard, with visions of being hauled to his feet. 'I mean, no thanks, I'll get up by myself.'

'What happened to you anyway?' The soldier was joined by his mate, last seen framed by the French doors. They both looked at him curiously. 'Did laughing boy out there give you a kicking?'

Bernard put his hands on his knees and decided to

pause there for a moment before progressing to his feet. 'Yes. In a nutshell.'

The faint sound of sirens could be heard.

'Police.' The soldier laughed. 'Better late than never.'

Bernard grabbed hold of a bookcase to help him complete the task of getting vertical. As he did so he noticed a trail of blood down his left sleeve. When he touched the back of his head he felt an open flap of skin. His head began to swim and he had a horrible feeling he was about to faint.

Wooky appeared at his side and took his arm. 'All right, pal, let's have a look at you now.'

'He's had a doing,' said one of Bernard's new military friends.

'So I heard. Does this hurt?' He pressed on Bernard's ribs. Bernard screamed and his new pals fell about laughing.

'Right, outside you two.'

Having got rid of the soldiers, Wooky helped Bernard to the sofa, and gave him a couple of painkillers, with a warning that they might make him feel sleepy. 'We need to get you to a hospital, mate. Strict instructions to get you back to Edinburgh if at all possible.'

Bernard leaned back and closed his eyes. As he drifted off into unconsciousness he heard the soldiers speaking.

'Time to get the place cleaned up, boys.'

16

'So, he's basically OK?'

'Yup. The dozy prick's had a kicking, but he's going to be all right,' Maitland said. 'The guy on the phone seemed to think Bernard had been a bit of a hero, which personally I find very difficult to imagine.'

'A hero?' Mona felt a strange sensation, one that was not entirely unlike jealousy. 'What the hell was he doing going in there, anyway? He told us he'd left.'

'Where is he now?' asked Carole. 'Are they taking him to hospital in Stirling?'

'Naw, here's the weird thing. The guy said the military are flying him back to the Edinburgh Royal Infirmary, and someone will let us know when he's arrived.'

'The military?' said Mona. 'Why are they involved?'

He shrugged.

She let out a cry of exasperation. 'Why did it have to be you that took the call, Maitland? Anyone else would have asked a few questions.'

Marguerite stuck her head round the office door. 'There's someone here to see you.' She pointed at Mona.

'Me?'

'Well . . .'

Mona recognised the tone. Marguerite obviously had an interesting story to tell, and was planning to take her time about it.

'...I say you, but actually they asked for Bernard, and when I said he wasn't here at the moment their exact words were they'd like to speak to someone in the HET team who isn't Maitland.'

'What?' Maitland appeared at her shoulder. 'Why not me?'

Despite her mood, Mona smiled. 'Who is it?'

Marguerite bustled into the room, obviously enjoying the intrigue. 'He wouldn't give me his name.' She leaned toward Mona, lowering her voice slightly, 'but he's wearing – oh, you know?' She pointed at her neck with both hands.

'A tie?'

'No, the black and white thing –a dog collar, that's it. And the minister's got a blonde girl with him.'

'I'll handle this one.' Maitland headed to the door.

'Guess again.' Mona got to her feet. 'Tell him I'm coming. Carole, give me a shout if we hear anything else about Bernard.'

Maitland blocked her way.

She glared up at him. 'You can't go and see someone who has specifically asked not to see you. Let me past.'

'I've got to come with you.'

'Why?'

Maitland opened his mouth, then realised that Marguerite was still in the room. He made a little wave motion in the direction of the exit. 'Maybe you could keep our guests company, Marguerite?'

She looked reluctant to leave without having the mystery of the clergyman in Reception sorted out to her satisfaction.

'Seriously, Marguerite, I'll be down in a minute. See if they want coffee or anything.'

Grudgingly, she left the room. Mona closed the door

behind her, and turned her attention to Maitland. 'Well?'

'I think it's probably Pastor Mackenzie from the Church of the Lord Arisen downstairs.' He was avoiding her eye. 'And I think that's my girlfriend that's with him.'

'Girlfriend?'

'OK, possibly ex-girlfriend.'

'Then it's even more inappropriate for you to come with me.'

'I'll just say hi,' he said, 'and then if she tells me to get lost, I promise I will.'

'No way.' She slid out of the door. 'The HET's in enough trouble without a harassment charge.'

'Trouble you and Bernard brought our way,' Maitland shouted after her, but didn't attempt to follow.

Marguerite had shown the visitors to a small meeting room on the ground floor. Mona knocked gently on the door. 'Pastor Mackenzie, I assume?' She stuck out her hand.

'Yes.' He gave her a weak handshake.

'Mona Whyte, from the HET. My colleagues at CID are wanting a word with you.'

'We're on our way there.' The blonde girl spoke. 'I'm Emma.'

The girlfriend. Definitely too good for Maitland.

'So,' she drew the word out. 'How can I help you?'

'I, I mean, we,' the Pastor gestured from himself to the girl and back, 'have been talking and we thought that there are some things that we needed to bring to your attention, with regard to the investigations the HET have been making into Heidi's disappearance. Unfortunately it may also relate to the deaths of two of my parishioners.'

'That is very helpful of you, Sir, but really at this point

328

we need you to give that kind of information to Police Scotland.'

They looked at each other, and Emma spoke. 'We will speak to the Police, we just thought that the information would help you in finding Heidi.'

'Are you saying that you withheld information from my colleague when he came to speak to you, Pastor Mackenzie?'

'No!' The Pastor leaned forward with his head in his hands. 'Well, yes. I did, but we weren't worried about Heidi then.'

'And you are worried now?'

'We haven't heard from her, and ...' He tailed off.

Emma spoke, quietly. 'He couldn't say anything. There's some video footage ...'

Amanda. 'And the Pastor here was more worried about being compromised than actually protecting his parishioners?'

'Compromised?' The minister looked up. 'The video wasn't of me. Oh, God,' he looked to Emma, 'where to begin with all this?'

'Start with *that woman*,' she spat out the words.

'Heidi brought a friend, well we thought she was a friend, to meet us. A girl called Amanda Harris. She was really enthusiastic about us getting out of our "middle-class box" as she put it, and spreading the Word in the most difficult places. She said she had a contact at this pub called Morley's, who would let us use their back room. I jumped at the chance. But I was stupid. I was taking young people into an environment that I didn't understand and making them vulnerable.'

He paused, as if waiting for her to comment. When she didn't speak, he continued.

329

'Amanda turned out to be the worst kind of person, a drug dealer. As soon as I realised that her church idea was more about giving her a forum to deal drugs I told her I was going to the Police. Then she produced her little trump card, and said she wouldn't be the one doing time.'

'Meaning?' asked Mona.

'Amanda had a video of Heidi and Kevin selling some drugs, I think antidepressants. I think Amanda had taken it surreptitiously on her phone. You have to understand that Kevin and Heidi thought these had some kind of impact on the Virus, they're not criminals. But, as soon as I saw it I knew that we had to go to the Police. So, I spoke to Heidi and Kevin and gave them an ultimatum. If they didn't go to the Police Station and confess themselves, I would do it for them. But then ...' He stopped.

'But then they ran off?'

He nodded.

'I'm afraid I have some bad news for you. We've traced both Heidi and Kevin, and I'm sorry to say,' she took a breath, 'Heidi is dead, and we're waiting for news about Kevin.'

Emma let out a small cry, and the Pastor put his arm round her shoulder and pulled her toward him.

'We're seeking Amanda to help with our enquiries about Heidi's death, and with another incident.'

The two of them stared back at her, hollow-eyed.

'Please stay where you are. I'll ask CID to send a car over to pick you up.'

'Thank you.' The Pastor's voice was barely a whisper.

Mona returned to her desk to find the office deserted, and a scribbled note alerting her to Bernard's safe arrival. Apparently, he would be available for visiting in the morning.

She rubbed her eyes, exhausted. She'd turn the machine off, and have an early night.

She closed down the programmes, then did a last check of her e-mails. She hovered over an e-mail 'FAO Mona Whyte, HET Officer.' It came from a G-mail account, the address a jumble of letters and numbers. Was it spam? There was an attachment with the e-mail, and ignoring every memo she'd ever received from Marcus, she clicked on it.

A small video file sprang up in the centre of her screen. Two women kissing, in the unmistakeable surroundings of Amanda's hallway.

There was no sound with the file. Mona played it over again and stared at the tiny vision of herself on screen, holding Amanda close. No message, no soundtrack, no threat. What was this? A warning?

17

Bernard watched his reflection on the window of the ward. If he tilted his head forward and to the side, he could just about see the large dressing attached to his skull. He made a slightly incautious move to the left, in order to get a better look and felt a jolt of pain shoot up his ribs. He was manoeuvring himself back against the pillows when he realised there was someone on the other side of his reflection. His wife was watching him.

'Here he is.' A nurse ushered her into his room. 'The hero of the hour.'

'Not a hero, honestly.'

The nurse beamed at them both. 'I know, just doing your job. That's what you Policemen always say, isn't it?'

'I'm not . . .' he began, but the nurse had vanished.

Carrie perched on the end of the bed.

'So, how does it feel to be a hero?'

He laughed, then winced. 'That's overstating it a bit.'

They gazed at each other in silence. Bernard, as always, cracked first. 'How are you?'

She answered the question by bursting into tears. 'I'm sorry, I should be asking you how you are.'

He leaned over as far as his ribs would let him, and touched her arm. 'Please, sit down.'

She reached into her bag for a tissue, and still sobbing, pulled a chair up to the bedside.

'How did you know I was here?'

'Your colleague, Carole, I think she said her name was, phoned the flat to speak to me.'

'You were at the flat?' At the thought that his wife had moved back home, he experienced a range of emotions, not all of them positive.

'I was picking up some things.' The thought of this provoked another burst of crying. 'I am so sorry. I should never have left.'

'I got your letter, thank you.' He couldn't help himself. 'Very concise.'

Carrie's shoulders heaved. She took a deep breath. 'I mean, seeing you lying there, if I hadn't gone, maybe you wouldn't have done something so dangerous.'

He reached for her hand. 'Even if you'd been sitting at home waiting for me, I would still have had a job to do.'

She laid her head against his arm. They sat in silence for a couple of minutes, then she slowly sat up. 'How did we get here, Bernard?'

'We lost a child, Carrie.' He took her hand. 'Fifty per cent of couples in that situation split up. We're just in the unlucky half.'

She gently pulled away. 'So, this is it then. We are splitting up?'

The pain in his side throbbed. 'I absolutely will not bring another life into the world while the Virus is here.' He shifted around on the bed, trying to get the pain under control. 'But I know what that means for you. And with every passing month we're putting more pressure on our relationship, so . . .'

'Stop!' She held up a hand, and sat perfectly still, her eyes closed.

Bernard eyed her anxiously, unsure whether this was a

prelude to either tears or shouting, but to his surprise she picked up her bag and got to her feet.

'I understand.'

'You do?'

'We're not doing each other any good, Bernard.' She slipped her bag onto her shoulder. 'I'm going to go. I'll get the rest of my things from the flat, and I'll be in touch.' She smiled. 'Promise me you won't do anything else dangerous.'

'Carrie.'

She stopped at the door.

'I do still love you.'

She turned back, and he could see that she was crying again. She walked over to him, and kissed him gently on the forehead.

'Goodbye, Bernard.'

18

Mona got into her car and sat for a minute with her head resting on the wheel. The evening stretched ahead of her. Should she head home, stopping only at an off-licence on Leith Walk that knew her far too well, and possibly also the Shapla Bangladeshi takeaway? Then she could sit alone in her flat, brooding and worrying. She put the key into the ignition and turned the wheel in the direction of her mother's house.

One home-cooked meal, and several hours of quiet but not unpleasant television viewing later, she let herself be persuaded to stay the night. But alone in her childhood bedroom the thoughts that she'd been avoiding all evening came crowding in. Every time she closed her eyes her mind went over the day's events, and, whichever way she looked at it, Mona did not come out well. What had she been thinking? Bernard, God bless him, hadn't noticed how she'd messed up but Paterson and Maitland certainly had. She wouldn't put it past Maitland to realise why her judgement had been off, either.

And, oh God, Amanda was out there, plotting, planning, about to infect her life with her lies.

Mona got up and put on the light. She lay flat on the floor and reached under the bed for her suitcase. She flicked it open and, ignoring her diaries this time, she pulled out an envelope. She held it upside down and photographs cascaded out. One by one she picked them up and sorted them out until she'd mapped out most of the floor with her old school friends.

'What are you looking at?'

Mona looked up to see her mother standing in the doorway to her room. Her mother looked frailer than ever, a desiccated husk of a woman in a furry, tartan dressing gown.

'Just some old stuff.'

Her mother came in. She surveyed the gallery of faces. 'What a lot of pictures of Susanne.' She circled her hand over them. 'But then you did have a bit of a crush on her.'

'A crush?' Mona's head snapped up.

Her mother looked embarrassed. 'Oh, you know what I mean. You were good friends with her.'

Mona stared at her mother, at the taut skin and jutting bones that were all that remained of her. How long did she have left? The hospital could have given her six months to live, and Mona would be the last person to be told. This thought made her feel nauseous, so she focused instead on the photographs of Susanne.

'Maybe "crush" would be the right word.'

Her mother sighed, and picked up the clothes Mona had left on the bedroom chair. She folded them neatly one by one and placed them on top of the bedside cabinet. Having cleared herself a space she sat down.

Mona toyed with one of the pictures. 'Well, say something, Mum?'

Her mother looked down at the floor, then up at the ceiling, then finally directly at her. 'You like girls, Mona, I know that. Not that you would talk to me about it. You could have a live-in girlfriend for all I know ...'

336

'I don't.' Mona started to collect in the pictures, slotting them into the envelope one by one.

'Oh, well, there's some news for me.'

They sat in silence. Mona watched as her mother smoothed down the pile of clothes. Just as the absence of words was starting to feel uncomfortable, her mother spoke again.

'You could have spoken to me about it, you know.'

Mona wondered if this was true. 'I spoke to Dad once, when I'd just joined the Police.'

'What did he say?' Her mother's face was a study of surprise.

'He said that any girl that came out as a lesbian in the Police Force would be mad, because she'd never be accepted. So, I thought it best not to say anything.'

Mona's mother pursed her lips. 'That was your father all over. It didn't matter how hurtful something was, if he didn't talk about it, it wasn't really happening.' She picked up a picture of Mona from her desk and looked at it. 'Do your colleagues know?'

'No. At least they *didn't* know, but something may have happened at work to change that.' Mona sensed her mother trying to find the right words to say. She ran her finger along the top of the picture she was holding, as if looking for invisible dust, then replaced it on the desk.

'Will you be OK?'

Mona shrugged. Maybe she would be OK. Maybe tomorrow Paterson and Maitland wouldn't give her a hard time about today's disasters. Maybe Amanda wouldn't make good on her threat, or if she did maybe Bernard and Carole would be so supportive that going to work every day wouldn't be hell. Or, maybe everything would go completely and utterly tits-up, and this time next week she'd been standing on Princes Street with a sign saying 'Unemployed and Immune. No job too infectious.'

'Well, this is always your home, remember that.' Her mother got to her feet, and patted Mona on the shoulder as she went past.

'Mum?'

Her mother stopped in the doorway. 'Yes?'

'Your next hospital appointment, I could get time off, you know, and come with you?'

Her mother nodded, smiling, and disappeared into the darkness of the hallway.

Mona picked up the envelope of photographs. She'd done it. After years of imagining the moment, she'd actually had an honest conversation with her mother, and the world hadn't ended. If she could just make it through the next couple of days, maybe everything would work out.

FRIDAY

RAT-CATCHING

I

Bernard woke up and yawned. He rolled over, and a searing pain in his side dragged him painfully into full consciousness. The events of the previous day crept slowly back into his mind.

'I was just coming to wake you.' A nurse appeared. She reached across him, picked up his unresisting wrist, and took his pulse.

'Am I free to go?'

She gave a short, high-pitched laugh. 'It's not a prison! But you need to wait until the doctor's done his rounds, in about an hour.'

With help, Bernard got out of bed, and into the room's *en suite*. He wondered what he'd done to get a single room. These days it was practically unheard of for anyone not suffering from the Virus to be given a private space; it was just about the only downside to being immune. He suspected Toller's involvement, again. Bernard showered, dressed, and was halfway through a hearty hospital breakfast when the doctor arrived.

'So, the tests came back clear. There doesn't appear to be any damage to any organs, or anything like that. And I'm afraid there's not much we can do for broken ribs, except issue you with painkillers, and strict instructions not to undertake any further heroics.'

'Ah, you heard about...'

341

'The plucky HET officer? Yes, you're the talk of the nurses' station.'

Bernard blushed, and the doctor laughed.

'I mean it, though.' She lingered in the doorway. 'You need to give yourself time to recover. If you hang on here for a few minutes I'll get you sorted out with a prescription to see you through the next few days, and I'll write to your doctor updating him on your situation.'

'OK.' He had no intention of ever undertaking anything heroic, or even foolhardy, ever again. When the doctor had gone, he got cautiously to his feet.

'You look surprisingly well. I was expecting to find you flat out and hooked up to a machine.'

Paterson was standing in the doorway.

Dizzy at the sight of his boss, Bernard sat down on the bed again.

'I'm free to go, apparently, as soon as they've given me some painkillers.'

'Mona's just parking the car.' Paterson stepped into the room. 'We can drop you home on our way to the office.'

'Have Mona and I still got jobs?'

Paterson snorted. 'Well, that remains to be seen.'

'And . . .' He cleared his throat. 'Have you still got your job?'

'Yes, despite my inability to control either my staff, or my temper, I still have. I've just come out of a very awkward meeting with Cameron Stuttle on that subject.'

'You sound relieved,' said Bernard.

It was Paterson's turn to look surprised. 'Of course I'm relieved! Didn't you realise how close we all came to getting our jotters?'

342

'Yeah, but . . .' he tailed off, as his boss stared at him.

'"Yeah, but" what?'

'It's just that you obviously hate your job, and,' he shifted on his pillow, 'and I thought you might not be that bothered about getting sacked.'

There was a brief silence. 'That may or may not be true, but the main issue is I've got two young kids to support, to say nothing of my two older ones who're still pretty quick to tap their old man for cash, and a student wife who would kill me if I got the boot.'

'Oh. Not looking for a career change then?'

'A career change?' Paterson snorted. 'The only place people in my position end up is standing next to the door in a supermarket, looking out for young mothers with a couple of cans of soup up their jumper. Mark my words, Bern, every time you see a security guard, you're looking at an ex-law enforcement professional who's had his dreams shattered.'

Bernard wondered if this was true. It was certainly plausible.

'So, all in all, I'm glad we're still here. Now we're going to draw a line under this case, forget about it, let it go, and get back to doing whatever it is we do.'

'I have a question.'

'Oh, good.' Paterson raised an eyebrow. 'Well, hit me with it.'

'This "whatever-it-is-we-do", is it the right thing?'

His boss laughed. 'Where to begin with that one?' He rested his face on his hands for a second, and wearily rubbed his eyes. 'Remember when we were in the pub the other day, and you were telling me about Spanish flu?'

'Yes.'

'Well, I think you got the wrong pandemic. What's

happening now is more like the Black Death. And you know how they dealt with that?'

Bernard opened his mouth to respond, then realised that the question was rhetorical.

'People thought that the plague was being spread by cats and dogs, so they rounded up all the strays and killed them. Guess what happened then?'

'The rats multiplied?'

'Exactly!' Paterson slapped the bedside table, nearly knocking Bernard's grapes to the ground. 'We concentrate on rounding up the junkies, and the people with mental health issues, and dragging them in for their Health Check, because that's who the *Daily Mail* likes to think is responsible for all our Virus problems. And all the while the real villains, the rodents like Vic bloody Thompson, are out there making the situation ten times worse.'

'So, is anyone out there rat-catching?'

Paterson shrugged. 'I don't know, Bernard. I really don't.'

Mona locked the car, and wondered what she would say to Bernard. The inexplicable feelings of jealousy that she'd felt earlier had returned. She should have been the one doing the heroics. She was the Police Officer, trained to deal with life-and-death situations like that. Bernard was a health promotion officer, trained to take blood samples from old ladies.

She pressed her Green Card against the machine, and was admitted to the foyer. As she stuffed it back in her bag, she caught sight of a familiar figure disappearing into the WRVS shop.

Oh shit. She had to get to her colleagues. She ran round to the lifts and jabbed the button. After thirty seconds she

344

decided it was taking too long and pushed open the door to the stairwell, and took the stairs two at a time. Arriving at the ward, she flashed her HET card at the nurse and, after a cursory look at the name board, ran down the corridor in search of Bernard's room. She caught sight of her colleague and boss deep in conversation.

'Guv.' Her boss glanced over at her. 'I need to …'

'Mr Paterson, just before we go,' said Bernard, 'I want to say thank you for advocating for us with Mr Stuttle.'

'Guv!'

They both ignored her, and she struggled to get her breath.

Paterson offered Bernard a hand out of the bed. 'I didn't. After the way you two behaved I'd let them sack you. But a certain German appears to have intervened and …'

'Guv! Doctor Toller's here to see Bernard.'

There was a gentle cough behind her, and she realised the German was standing there.

'Thanks, Mona, I think we've grasped that now.' Paterson turned to Toller. 'What can we do for you?'

'Nothing, nothing.' Toller said. 'I am merely here to check that Bernard is making a good recovery. I hope the helicopter flight was comfortable?'

'Eh, yes, under the circumstances.' Bernard edged round to look at Doctor Toller. 'Do you know how Kevin is?'

'I'm sorry to say he didn't survive the journey to hospital. Despite your best efforts we found him too late.' Toller studied a piece of hospital art on the wall of the room. 'I am here to say that there will be no further action against either Mona or Bernard. I guarantee this.'

345

The three of them exchanged glances.

'With all due respect, Doctor Toller, you are not in a position to make that kind of guarantee,' said Mona.

Toller smiled. 'No, but the Chair of the Parliamentary Virus Committee is, and I am happy to say she has given me that undertaking.'

Paterson leaned over to Bernard. 'He probably caught Carlotta Carmichael's man speeding on the Autobahn.'

'Actually, Mr Paterson, there's no speed limit ...'

Paterson rolled his eyes and stepped away.

Toller continued to stare at what was obviously a fascinating watercolour. 'And in return, there will be no public statement from either of you on the matter.'

'No public statement?' Paterson sounded amazed. 'Mona and Bernard will have to go to court as part of the assault charges.'

'What he means, Guv, is that we'll not mention publicly his role in all this.'

Toller smiled at her. 'A very astute deduction, as always. The German Government would prefer to be as little involved in this as possible.'

'I didn't mean the German Government, Doctor Toller, I meant you personally.' She walked over and stood between him and the artwork. 'I wanted to thank you for your honesty the other day.'

He stared at her.

'You know, when you told us what people would do to protect their interests in Luprophen and Hyrdosol? You told us everything except the fact that the interest was yours. This will be news to you, Bernard, but Doctor Toller is a company director of the firm that manufactures Loopy and H.'

'I told you almost everything.' He smiled again,

346

and stepped away. 'I did not mention your own Government's interest in my company's research. It would be very foolish of you to incur the wrath of your own Government, as well as any other ...' He paused, looking for a word. 'Any other parties. And neither you, nor your colleagues are stupid. In any proceedings related to a certain Amanda Harris, you do not mention me, you do not mention Heidi and you do not mention drugs.' He nodded a goodbye to them, and pulled the door shut behind him.

'The only positive thing that I can say about that man is that he pulled out all the stops to get Bernard out alive, with the helicopter and everything,' said Mona.

'Actually, I don't think the helicopter was for my benefit. I heard the army guys talking about clearing up. I don't think you'll find any trace that Heidi and Kevin were ever in Dunblane.' Bernard looked mournful. 'I believed every word he said.'

'I didn't.' The Guv snorted. 'I knew the first meeting I had with him that he was dodgy.'

Bernard was frowning. 'But he works for the German Government.'

The Guv laughed. 'People like Toller don't work for the Government, they work *through* the Government. All that shit he was giving about being so upset about Heidi, because he'd known Weber since they were at university together? First thing I did was check that out online. They were never at uni together.'

The Guv's IT skills were better than Mona had given him credit for. Come to that, his detection skills were better than she'd thought. A suspicion was developing in her mind that her boss was a lot smarter at the politics of all this than he ever let on.

'So, why didn't you say anything to us, Guv?'

'Because, Mona, all I wanted was Toller off my patch before any of my staff ended up dead.'

'Dead?' Mona shook her head in disbelief.

'Yes!' He looked from one to the other of them. 'For God's sake, Heidi ended up dead, Kevin ended up dead, Weber's disgraced. Bad things happen around that one.' He jerked his thumb in the direction of the door.

'But, we should tell someone,' said Bernard.

'Who?' said Paterson, throwing himself back in his chair. 'Should we just drop a letter to the German Government? Dear Chancellor, your advisor Doctor Toller is a bit of a lively one, watch your back. Yours sincerely, A Wellwisher?'

'Stuttle,' said Mona, eagerly. 'He's mad at Toller. So is Carlotta Carmichael – she could raise it at a Governmental level.'

'And the fact that people who annoy the dear Doctor end up deceased isn't a problem?' Paterson's finger wagged between them. 'You still think we should get involved?'

'Yes!' they said, in emphatic unison.

Paterson sighed. 'You know, it has never occurred to me before, but you too are very much alike.'

Bernard and Mona looked at each other.

'Really?' She didn't see the similarity.

'Oh, yes, Mona. Both naïve, both idealistic, both going to get yourselves killed rather than give an inch to pragmatism.' He looked at them again. 'He wouldn't need to kill you, Mona. All he needs to do is destroy your credibility. Anything in your past that he could rake up?'

She stared at Paterson. He knew perfectly well about her past. He had the good taste to look away, but he added, 'Or, Mona, anything in your present?' He turned his attention to her colleague. 'And, what about you, Bernard?'

Bernard shifted nervously on the bed.

'Anything in your private life you don't want to see public? How is your wife taking your son's death?'

Mona stared. Bernard had lost a child? He swallowed several times, then slowly and, it appeared, painfully got to his feet. 'I'm not discussing that with you, Mr Paterson.'

'If you want to keep your family life private, don't annoy Toller.'

Without looking at either of them, Bernard walked out and closed the door behind him. In the silence, they listened to Bernard's footsteps disappearing down the corridor. For a man with broken ribs, he was moving pretty fast.

Mona stared at her boss. 'So, Toller gets away with it then?'

'Toller gets away with it. If she's lucky, and Toller doesn't track her down, Amanda gets away with it. Capitalism survives to fight another day, the multi-nationals go from strength to strength...the Government isn't in charge anymore, Mona.' The Guv stood up. 'Whoever comes up with the cure for the Virus is going to have every Government in the world by the short and curlies. And people like Toller aren't going to let anyone get in their way.'

He got up.

'Drive Bernard home, Mona, and take the rest of the day off. Come in tomorrow ready to find some other poor sod that's out there with a high temperature and a lack of friends.'

Mona drove a silent Bernard back to his flat. He refused any offer of assistance, so she left him there and turned the car in the direction of the office. Back at her desk she slid into her seat. In next to no time she could be out of here: five minutes tops while she logged off, and watched the screen fade to black. Then she could pick up her bag and head straight home.

Reaching for the mouse, her eye was caught by another e-mail from an unfamiliar address, a G-mail address with what appeared to be a random selection of numbers and letters in it. Her stomach turned over, and for a second the room span away from her. *Amanda*. What now? The threat, the blackmail, relating to her previous e-mail?

Her hand hovered over the mouse, then she gave in and viewed it in the preview panel. The message was only three words long.

'Help us.
Amanda.'

The e-mail had an attachment. More blackmail? But who? She turned the volume control to its lowest audible level, double-clicked, and pressed play. The picture was shot at an odd angle (from a bag? a pocket?), and the film quality wasn't good. Despite this, the figure in the picture was recognisably Heidi. She leaned her ear toward the computer's speaker.

'And this guy's a friend of your dad's?'

A woman's voice, northern, probably Amanda, although possibly her sister.

'A friend?'

A German voice, with the funny American-accented English she shared with her father. Heidi. She laughed.

'Not really a friend, but more a work colleague of many years.'

'So, he's manufacturing the stuff?'

'Yeah. The tests have all been very positive, but it's all very quiet, hush-hush ...'

'Because ...'

'Because they want to make the big money from it, yeah.'

'And if we had the money we could buy it over the Internet, simple as that, and save lives?'

There was a silence. Heidi stared, unknowingly, at the camera.

'I have money. I can buy it.'

There was a rattling sound. She looked up to see Carole and Maitland come in. She muted the sound.

'Oh, hello.' Carole took her coat off. 'How's Bernard?'

'Fine. Just dropped him home in fact.'

'Coffee?' Maitland pointed a thumb in the direction of the door.

'Not for me. I'm about to head out. You two go.'

Maitland headed out the door. Carole lingered for a minute.

'Sure you're OK?'

'Totally, yeah.'

Her colleague looked unconvinced, but headed off in search of caffeine. Mona watched her leave. As soon as she was out of sight, she reached for her bag, and raked through it until she found a business card. She paused for a second staring at it. Heidi's story couldn't end here, not with Toller walking away from the mess, or, worse pursuing Amanda.

Oh, God, Amanda. She closed her eyes and she could see her as she had been the first time they had met, when they'd got her out of bed. The tiny, naked figure had seemed so vulnerable. Her eyes snapped back open. She knew now that Amanda was anything but weak. But, still, she'd need more than her wits to keep ahead of Toller. Whatever she felt toward Amanda, she didn't want her dead.

She picked up her phone. And if it all ended here, Bernard would get all the glory. Which was fine, he deserved it, but she'd spend the past few months as his bloody nursemaid, making sure he didn't get hurt or cock things up. Wasn't she entitled to a bit of credit? She dialled. 'Cameron? It's Mona Whyte.'

The voice on the other end of the phone, though surprised, was welcoming.

'I'm sending you something electronically. Can I come and see you?' Her mouse hovered over the 'send' icon, misgivings suddenly entering her mind. She doubted that Paterson would take kindly to her involving Stuttle in the affair. Continuing to work for him after going over his head would probably be impossible.

Her finger remained static above the mouse. Would she miss the HET? The Guv, definitely. She'd miss the compassion of Bernard and Carole, although not their lack of understanding of how the world really worked. And Maitland, well, she could live without the arrogance and sexism, but he was sharp, and not afraid to get his hands dirty. But if she did nothing, if she let Toller cover all this up, then what was the point of the HET, or the

Police, or any of the other agencies that worked to stop the Virus? They might as well all go home, and accept that the Government wasn't in charge any more.

Her finger finally found the mouse. She turned off her computer and picked up her car keys, then spent a minute or two emptying her few personal possessions out of her desk drawer and into her bag. Taking a last look around the office, she picked up her coat.

She wouldn't be back here.

ACKNOWLEDGEMENTS

Huge thanks are due to everyone at Sandstone Press for all their support in producing this book, particularly Moira Forsyth.

I was very grateful for the beta reading of the manuscript by Sophie Milne. Her fine eye for detail sorted out many an inconsistency.

A number of very scary books were consumed while mulling over the plot lines of *The Health of Strangers*. If you want to know more about influenza, I recommend the definitive work on the subject *Flu: A Social History of Influenza* by Tom Quinn. If you are want to give yourself the screaming heebie-jeebies about all the different ways animal infections are going to end up killing us all, *Spillover* by David Quammen is the book for you. And if you want to know what it feels like to live through the birth of a new disease check out *And the Band Played On: Politics, People and the Aids Epidemic* by Randy Shilts.

Thanks to friends, both old and new, who have been hugely supportive of my writing.

And finally, thanks to my husband and sons, whose ability to occasionally leave me in peace meant that the damn book actually got written.

Turn the page for an exclusive first look at *Songs by Dead Girls*, the second book in the *Health of Strangers* series.

MONDAY

NAUSEA

1

It was a horrible noise, the kind of unnatural high-pitched squeal that Bernard often found punctuating his nightmares. The fact that he was currently wide awake didn't make the noise any less excruciating. It took all his self-control not to stick his fingers in his ears. Mona, the creator of the ungodly noise, pulled the remaining bits of shrink-wrap off the stab-proof vest provoking yet more shrill squeaks.

Bernard shivered. *'Beware of all enterprises that require new clothes.'*

'What?' Despite her question, Mona's profile radiated a certain degree of indifference which made it difficult for him to work out if she did actually want to know more. He decided to venture further down the path.

'It's a quote from Henry David Thoreau. You know – the nature writer? Advocated simple living? Spent years in a forest?' The look of annoyance on his partner's face clarified that she wasn't interested in updating her knowledge of woods-based philosophers at this point in time. 'Never mind. Can I have a look at it?'

She passed the vest over to him. It was a solid

torso-shaped affair, rigid, although lighter than he was expecting, with a strange rubbery feel to it.

'I don't know what you are complaining about.' Mona's blonde bob covered her face as she set about unwrapping the second vest. 'This is about keeping us safe. Remember that HET officer in Aberdeen who tried to retrieve a health defaulter from a crack den and got a knife in the balls for his troubles?'

'Not exactly the body parts that will be covered by these.'

She tutted. 'Oh, well, put in a special request for a reinforced rubber codpiece.'

A fug of depression settled around his shoulders. He'd been in the car with his partner for all of ten minutes and already she was annoyed with him. It wasn't unusual for them to spend the best part of a working day trapped in a car together. As members of the North Edinburgh Health Enforcement Team it was their job to find people who'd missed their monthly health check, a front-line attempt to stop the spread of the Virus. This involved a lot of driving, knocking on doors, being lied to, sitting in wait, and eventually catching up with the defaulter. On the days when he had inadvertently irritated Mona, eight hours of close contact with her could feel considerably longer.

He tried to avert this looming disaster with some humour. 'Not sure it's really an area worth protecting. It's not like it's in use.'

'Spare me, please.' She continued with her peeling, then suddenly looked up, with a slightly more conciliatory expression on her face. 'No chance of getting back with your wife then?'

Glad as he was that Mona was no longer scowling at

him, he didn't feel inclined to enter into that particular area of discussion. 'Not looking for one. Anyway, shall we suit up?' He slipped his jacket off, then tried to fit his arm into the appropriate opening. The rigidity of the vests, and the limited dimensions of the car made this no easy task, and he accidentally elbowed Mona.

'Sorry. It would be easier to put them on if we got out of the car.'

'No. I don't want them to notice us and do a runner.'

They were parked on a quiet side-street in Morningside, one of the most affluent areas of Edinburgh. The property currently attracting their attention was a terraced, sandstone building, with a large sloping garden leading up to it. The grass had not been cut for some time.

'Not a bad residence for someone without a job,' said Bernard.

'I suspect the wages of sin are paying for it.'

'What makes you say that?'

'Number One,' Mona held up a finger. 'This is a nice bit of town, and that's, what, a three, maybe, four-bed house. You're looking at the best part of half-a-million. Who is paying the mortgage on that?'

'Our defaulter could have a very rich daddy? Or she could just be renting?'

'Even the rents in this bit of town are eye-watering. And I have another point. Number Two.' She was now holding two fingers up. 'This is a fabulously expensive house, and look at the state of the garden. Every other lawn in the street looks like the grass was trimmed into place with nail scissors, yet this place looks like waste ground. And have they washed the windows any time in the last few years?'

'You sound like my grandmother.'

'Grandma could probably do a very good job of knowing a wrong 'un when she sees one. And my third and most important point is, we're here, so there must be something dodgy going on.'

'Not necessarily.'

'Ha! In all the months we've been doing this, how many people have defaulted on their Health Check for reasons that were not to do with over-consumption of drink or drugs, or who were not in some way participating in illegal activity?'

He thought for a second. 'Occasionally they turn out to be dead?'

'Usually due to the over-consumption of drinks or drugs. Anyway, turn round, Bernard, and I'll get the straps.'

He obediently presented his back to her. 'What do we know about today's defaulter?'

'Alessandra Barr, twenty-five, missed her Health Check three days ago. And I don't want to be judgemental or anything, but take a look at her picture.'

She held up their Chaser List, and Bernard stared at a photograph of a gaunt young woman. She had badly-dyed blonde hair, which sat awkwardly with her dark colouring.

'Has she got two black eyes?' Bernard ran his finger across the photograph.

'Yep. The day she turned up to get her Green Card photo taken, she had a face full of bruises. I'm going to go out on a limb and say she's not a soccer mom.' She opened her door. 'Shall we?'

Bernard tried to ignore the knot of fear in his stomach.

Unlike Mona, he didn't have the confidence that Police College and years of law enforcement experience instilled. He'd previously worked in health promotion, where the day-to-day work of encouraging breastfeeding and smoking cessation had left him woefully underprepared for the realities of working at the HET. Most of the defaulters they chased were less than delighted to see them, and he had spent many work hours being sworn at, spat at, and occasionally punched. He wondered if he'd ever get through the day without this ever-present feeling of doom.

'Mona!'

She stopped with her hand on the garden gate. 'What?'

'What's our plan here?'

'We knock on the door, ask whoever answers if we can see Alessandra. If they say no we insist that we come in, using the powers bestowed on us by the Health Defaulters Act blah, blah, blah. The usual.'

'But what if she makes a run for it?'

'Then you stop her.'

'What with?'

Mona raised her hands in the air and wiggled them. 'These.' She started walking again. 'Because rightly or wrongly, they're the only weapons that the HET have seen fit to supply us with.'

She pressed the bell, which made no sound.

'Try knocking.'

'Thanks, I wouldn't have thought of that.' Mona hammered on the wood. The sound echoed through the house, but didn't appear to rouse any occupants.

Bernard left the path and peered through the crack in the curtains. 'I don't see anyone, though it's not that easy without the lights on.'

Mona knocked for a second time, and again was met with silence. She turned the handle, and the door opened. 'Result! Come on.'

Bernard stepped over the threshold, both aware and annoyed that his heart was beating ridiculously fast. Amongst his many secret fears was that on one of these jaunts he was actually going to have a cardiac arrest. His only hope was that the heart failure would be instantly fatal, and wouldn't involve him having to face the ridicule of the HET team from a hospital bed. He tried to calm his nerves by focussing on the surroundings. The hallway was dark, with the only light coming from the open door behind them. It was uncarpeted, but not in a trendy stripped back wood kind of way, more in the mode of 'we haven't been living here long enough to cover the floor'. Or maybe, as in Mona's theory, the over-consumption of illegal substances had made investing in carpeting a low priority. There were a number of doorways leading off the hall, and, from what he could see in the gloom, a rather magnificent staircase straight ahead of them.

Mona turned to her right and shoved open a door. He made to follow her.

'What are you doing?' she hissed.

'Coming with you?' he whispered.

She pointed at him, then at the door opposite, indicating he should check that room. He mouthed an irritable 'OK', and turned his back on her before she could see the look of fear on his face. He much preferred being two steps behind her. Bernard would have taken a blow to the head or a knife in the vest quite happily just so long as Mona was making all the decisions. Back up he could do. Pole position was a different matter.

He reached for the handle and tried to remember what he'd been taught in his month-long induction to the HET. He seemed to remember that there had been a whole day about 'Encountering Hostility and How to Respond'. He paused with the door slightly open, and tried to remember the key phrases.

Be confident. Breathe. Show respect. Moderate Your Tone. Keep Your Distance. Know Your Exits.

He wiped the sweat from his hand, and threw the door wide. There was no response, so he flicked the light switch. To his relief the room was empty, although there was a lingering smell of cannabis in the air suggesting that it had been in use not so very long ago. In common with the hallway, the room did not benefit from any floor covering. Furniture was sparse, with the large and gracious room hosting only a dilapidated sofa, a coffee table, and a TV of a size and depth that predated the birth of the flatscreen. The absence of furnishing meant a limit to places where someone could hide, although there was a door in the corner of the room, potentially a cupboard. He walked swiftly across the room and pulled it open to find it led on to another room. He caught his breath as he saw a figure coming toward him.

'Hey.'

Mona.

She reached past him and turned on the light, illuminating the kitchen. Once upon a time, the fittings were probably state of the art, but it was difficult to tell from the layer of grime which covered the work surfaces. Unwashed dishes were stacked on every unit.

'If your grandmother didn't like dirty windows, Bernard, she'd have a fit looking at this place.'

He pulled a face. 'How can anyone live like this?'

'Beats me. Puts the state of the Guv's office into perspective, though. Anyway, there's no-one here; let's try the upper floor.'

At the top of the stairs they separated again, Bernard to the left and Mona to the right. He opened the first door he came to, which as he expected was a bedroom. The curtains were drawn, but enough sunshine was sneaking through the cracks to allow him to see that the room was actually somewhat better furnished than downstairs. There was a rug on the floor, for starters, two ancient double-wardrobes, and an incongruously ornate dressing table. There was also a double bed, upon which, he realised with a start, there was a large, person-shaped lump. A lump that was lying extremely still. Whether he was looking at a live body or a dead one was not clear, and a sudden hope it was a corpse flitted through his mind, to be followed immediately by a chaser of remorse. However unpleasant some of the defaulters were, they were still his fellow human beings, and he didn't wish any of them dead.

He did, however, wish that he wasn't on his own. He looked round but Mona had vanished into another room. He could go after her, explain what he'd found, and confirm to her – if it was ever in doubt – that he really couldn't hack it. Or he could stay here and try to pretend that he wasn't in imminent need of a defibrillator. He took a deep breath and turned back toward the divan.

'Hello.'

His voice was high-pitched and squeaky, rather like shrink-wrap peeled off plastic. *Be confident. Breathe.*

368

With a conscious effort he lowered his voice. 'Excuse me.' *Show respect.*

The lump in the bed didn't move. He took a step toward it, and could see a mass of long brown hair spread across the pillow. He felt a certain amount of relief that this was a woman. In his experience, women weren't any less likely to throw a punch at you, but for the most part they tended to do less damage. It didn't appear to be Alessandra, however, unless she'd radically changed her look since her photograph was taken.

'Excuse me.' His voice was getting louder, and snippier. He caught himself. *Moderate Your Tone.*

His tone of voice, inappropriate or otherwise, wasn't provoking a response. After a careful consideration of the duvet he was pretty sure that it was going up and down, blowing his corpse theory out of the water. This was a warm body, who might not take well to being awoken by a strange man in her house. He shot a glance over his shoulder. Perhaps under the circumstances Mona would be less threatening than him? Tempting as this was, it was a cop-out. With a sigh and a quick check how many steps it was back to the door – *Know Your Exits* - he walked over to the bed and shook the woman gently by the shoulder.

The body rolled toward him, revealing broad shoulders, a hairy chest and three days of stubble. 'Who the fuck are you?' The man sat up, and grabbed his arm.

He tried to wriggle free. 'We're from the Health Enforcement Team. If you let go of me I can show you some ID. We're looking for Alessandra Barr...'

The man was looking at him with a strange expression on his face. His grip on Bernard's arm slackened.

369

'Are you OK?'

The man responded by opening his mouth and vomiting profusely down Bernard's front.

He snatched his arm back. 'For Goodness' sake!'

Mona appeared in the doorway, and surveyed the scene.

'Oh, Bernard.' She stared at his ruined vest. 'This is the reason we keep our distance.'

*

Songs by Dead Girls will be available from Sandstone Press in 2018.

www.sandstonepress.com

[f] facebook.com/SandstonePress/

[t] @SandstonePress